Praise for

Dragon Lovers

"Romance lovers with a fondness for fire-breathers will be delighted."
— *Publishers Weekly*

"In this enchanting anthology, four award-winning romance authors work their usual literary magic to create a quartet of entertaining novellas." — *Booklist*

"A magical volume." — *Fresh Fiction*

"Lighthearted, fun tales that take readers and the female lead characters soaring with dragons." — *The Best Reviews*

"Enchanting. . . . From knights and lords to a modern-day handyman, from exotic Japan to Regency England, these stories soar with imagination, adventure, and magic to delight those who long for a bit of a fairy tale and a lot of romance." — *Romantic Times*

. . . and for the Authors

Jo Beverley

"Arguably today's most skillful writer of intelligent historical romance." — *Publishers Weekly*

continued . . .

Chalice
of Roses

JO BEVERLEY
MARY JO PUTNEY
KAREN HARBAUGH
BARBARA SAMUEL

A SIGNET ECLIPSE BOOK

SIGNET ECLIPSE
Published by New American Library, a division of
Penguin Group (USA) Inc., 375 Hudson Street,
New York, New York 10014, USA
Penguin Group (Canada), 90 Eglinton Avenue East, Suite 700, Toronto,
Ontario M4P 2Y3, Canada (a division of Pearson Penguin Canada Inc.)
Penguin Books Ltd., 80 Strand, London WC2R 0RL, England
Penguin Ireland, 25 St. Stephen's Green, Dublin 2,
Ireland (a division of Penguin Books Ltd.)
Penguin Group (Australia), 250 Camberwell Road, Camberwell, Victoria 3124,
Australia (a division of Pearson Australia Group Pty. Ltd.)
Penguin Books India Pvt. Ltd., 11 Community Centre, Panchsheel Park,
New Delhi - 110 017, India
Penguin Group (NZ), 67 Apollo Drive, Rosedale, North Shore 0632,
New Zealand (a division of Pearson New Zealand Ltd.)
Penguin Books (South Africa) (Pty.) Ltd., 24 Sturdee Avenue,
Rosebank, Johannesburg 2196, South Africa

Penguin Books Ltd., Registered Offices:
80 Strand, London WC2R 0RL, England

First published by Signet Eclipse, an imprint of New American Library,
a division of Penguin Group (USA) Inc.

First Printing, January 2010
10 9 8 7 6 5 4 3 2 1

Library of Congress Cataloging-in-Publication Data
Chalice of roses/Jo Beverley . . . [et al.].
    p.   cm.
"A Signet Eclipse book."
ISBN 978-0-451-22902-1
1. Love stories, American.   2. Grail—Fiction.   3. Historical fiction, American.   I. Beverley, Jo.
PS648.L6C46   2010
813'.08508—dc22   2009031038

Set in Adobe Garamond
Designed by Alissa Amell

Printed in the United States of America

Contents

❦

Dear Reader,

This collection of stories grows out of the complex and mysterious legends surrounding the Holy Grail. Most people see this as beginning with the chalice used by Christ at the Last Supper. One of those legends says that Joseph of Arimathea, a merchant and follower of Jesus, brought the sacred cup to Britain. Because of that tradition, all the stories in Chalice of Roses are set in Britain, but in different times and circumstances.

The Christian Grail myth might have blended with even older Celtic legends of a vessel of abundance that blessed those who found it. The pot of gold at the end of the rainbow is one of those mythic forms, though we haven't gone to Ireland in this anthology.

Each of us has taken our own view of the ancient chalice, of the symbolism of roses and the power of love to heal wounds and bring peace, and we hope you'll enjoy the result.

Best,
Jo Beverley, Mary Jo Putney,
Karen Harbaugh and
Barbara Samuel

The Raven and the Rose

BY
JO BEVERLEY

Chapter 1

S ister Gledys of Rosewell was sinning again.

She was dreaming of her knight and knew she should wake herself up, but she didn't. Alas for her immortal soul, she didn't want to lose a precious moment of these visions, and her heart already raced with wicked excitement.

As always, he was fighting, clad in a long chain-mail robe and conical helmet. He wielded a sword and protected himself with a long shield on his left arm. Sometimes she saw him afoot, but he was generally on a great fighting horse in battle or a skirmish.

That didn't surprise Gledys. Strife, punctuated by outright war, had ruled England for all the eighteen years of her life, but that life had been spent in Rosewell Nunnery, so how could she create such scenes? By day she prayed earnestly for peace, so how could she dream of war so vividly by night?

Every clash of weapons rang in her ears, every squeal of angry horses, every thud of blows. Leather squeaked, metal jangled and the stink of men and horses buffeted her. Hooves cut clods from the ground, and horses breathed like bellows. When these dreams had begun the horses had spewed steam into frosty air and the men had also clouded the air as they howled with pain or roared in triumph. It was summer now, however, and the air swirled with dust and fury.

Then a chunk of earth whipped past her face and she realized she was much closer to the fighting than ever before.

Too close!

She tried to raise her arms to shield her face, tried to stumble back out of danger. It didn't work. It never did. In these dreams she was powerless to move, as if paralyzed.

A horse's massive backside swung in her direction. She flinched from its flailing tail and the shod hooves that could kill if it chose to kick. She heard screams nearby. She'd scream, too, but she could no more make a sound than she could move.

Now she was willing to escape.

Wake up! Wake up!

She remained frozen in place, her eyes unalterably fixed on one warrior, and could only pray.

Lord, have mercy.

Christ, have mercy. . . .

It was a dream. It had to be. No one could be killed in a dream.

Holy Mary, pray for me.

Saint Michael the archangel, pray for me.

But then she wondered whether this was punishment. Punish-

ment for her sinful attraction to her knight, and for her secret longing to escape, to explore the world beyond Rosewell.

Saint Gabriel, pray for me.

Saint—

A great rattling thump jolted the litany out of her mind.

A man bellowed.

Someone had come off his horse. Had that been a death cry?

Not her knight, at least. Not her knight. He fought on, but now
against a huge grunting man.

All angels and archangels, pray for him!

Saint Joseph, pray for him. . . .

He was being driven closer to where she stood. Despite the danger, Gledys's frightened breathing changed to a pant of excitement.
Would she finally see something of his face? *Closer, closer, come
closer. . . .*

This longing was surely the worst sin of all, but she surrendered
to it now, murmuring unholy prayers.

But even when he was almost on top of her she could tell little.
Beneath his helmet, a hood came down on his forehead, the front
part rising up past his chin, and the helmet had a piece that extended
down over his nose. She could see only lean cheeks and bared teeth.
Was she imagining a pleasing countenance? He wheeled his horse so
that his back was to her, and she glimpsed missing teeth in the snarl-
ing red mouth of his opponent. The bigger man landed a hard blow
on her knight's arm, causing him to stagger to one side.

Gledys screamed and tried to run to him, but she was still frozen.
Her knight fought on, turning his shield into a weapon, slamming
his opponent's sword hand with it and kicking him with a mailed

boot. His horse joined in with hooves and teeth, and the din made Gledys want to cover her ears.

How had that blow to his arm not maimed him?

How was it that he could fight on so fiercely?

She realized that she'd closed her eyes, and forced them open, dreading what she'd see. Somehow, her knight's opponent had been unhorsed, but the big man scrambled to his feet and unhooked a mighty ax from his saddle. An ax! Her knight leapt off his horse to face him, laughing.

Laughing?

Yes, laughing!

Was he mad?

Mad or not, he was beautiful, even sheathed in gray metal. So tall and broad shouldered, and moving as if burdened by nothing but a shirt, leaping away from another attack on strong, agile legs. It must be a mortal sin to think of a man's legs, but she'd pay the price in hell.

Be Saint Michael, she prayed. *Or Saint George.*

It wouldn't be so terrible a sin to be fascinated by the warrior angel who defeated Lucifer, or the saintly dragon slayer. She might even be receiving blessed visions symbolizing the defeat of heathens in the Holy Land by Christian crusaders.

But in her heart she knew better, and now, watching her knight breathing hard but still smiling with a burning delight in violence, she knew it yet again. These dreams came from Satan, and the swirling chaos of men and horses was a vision of hell. . . .

Gledys blinked, realizing that her view had expanded. Now she could see many fighters, but also others behind them. People in ordinary dress, some of them screaming and yelling, but with excitement.

Spectators!

This wasn't a battle. This must be what they called a tournament, where knights played at war. Heaven only knew why. People watched for amusement, including women, some of high rank. Gledys glimpsed richly colored gowns and cloaks. Flimsy veils fluttered in a breeze and the sun glinted off precious metals and jewels. Beyond the watchers stood a stone castle on a grassy mound, where colorful pennants danced against blue sky. There were people up there, too, watching.

Why was she forced to endure this from down here?

Another man came off his horse and she remembered her knight. Was he safe? Yes! He stood his ground, although still hard-pressed by his bigger opponent, both of them breathing heavily, even staggering as if they might collapse together in a metal heap.

Gledys fixed her eyes on him by her own intent now, praying that he be safe. As if summoned, he looked past his opponent, straight at her. His lips parted in astonishment.

He *saw* her?

Gledys tried to reach out, to speak to him, but she was still mute, still frozen in place. She saw the battle-ax swing and tried to scream a warning.

Perhaps he understood, for he turned, ducking. The weapon still caught his helmet, knocking it askew, and he stumbled to one side, down to one knee.

Gledys screamed again. Knew again it couldn't be heard in her dreamworld.

He was already up, his attention glued onto his opponent as he forced the other man backward. He was younger, stronger, magnificent. He would win! But then his eyes flicked to her once again. . . .

"*Don't*," she tried to cry. "*Don't be distracted!*"

The burly man could have killed him then, but exhaustion won and he collapsed to his knees, dropping the ax, wheezing for breath. Her knight sucked in air, too, hands braced on his knees, heaving with it. But then he straightened and turned, seeking her, seeing her. A smile lit his face and he took a step toward her.

Gledys smiled back in pure joy.

At last she would meet him.

At last!

❧

"No!"

Gledys was so used to being mute, she almost shouted the word, but choked it to a mere grunt, fist stuffed into her mouth. She was back in Rosewell Nunnery in the dark dormitory.

No, not back.

She'd been nowhere else.

Though so powerfully real, it had been another dream.

She blinked up into the darkness, teeth in her knuckles to suppress a wail at being snatched out of sleep at just that moment. He'd *seen* her. He'd been coming to her. They might—oh, heaven, oh, hell—they might have touched.

Gledys clutched her nightcap. It had been a *dream*, just like all the other ones. Her knight wasn't real. His opponents weren't real, nor were the watching people or the castle. Still she grieved, as she always did when snatched out of that unreal land.

Grieved. That was the word for it. Grief as she was wrenched away, then aching grief as precious details melted from her mind like caught snowflakes melting in the palm of her hand.

Her knight. Fighting, as usual . . .

No, not as usual.

People watching. Women, even. A tournament.

A castle . . .

But even as she tried to pin such things in her mind, they slipped away, slipped away.

And were gone.

Her memory was blank, except for knowing she'd dreamed of her knight again, and one precious image. Her knight looking at her, seeing her, moving toward her. She held on to that so it would etch deep in her mind, even though it carried with it the sinful way her heart had thundered and her mouth had dried.

Did other nuns have wicked dreams? No one ever described such things at the weekly open confession, but Gledys wasn't surprised. The punishment would surely be terrible.

There was another reason to stay silent, however.

Confessing might make the dreams stop.

Despite awareness of sin, despite the horrors she saw, Gledys needed the dreams as a person needed food and drink.

She flung an arm over her eyes, blinking against the sting of tears. They should be tears of repentance, but they were of simple unhappiness. A holy heart was a tranquil heart, but since the dreams had begun, she'd lost all tranquillity. She'd ceased being happy in the only home she'd ever known and in the satisfying routine of busy days.

Instead she cherished the fragments of dreams and restlessly gleaned any detail of the world outside the nunnery. She ached for the wider world, and often wasted time looking at the only bit of it visible from Rosewell—the top of the great hill that lay a few leagues away.

Glastonbury Tor.

The conical hill rose out of flat, marshy ground and was crowned by a small monastery dedicated to Saint Michael. In itself it was a place of ancient pilgrimage, but on lower ground at the base of the tor stood a holier place—the magnificent abbey famed throughout England for its connection to Christ, and to the sacred cup used at the Last Supper. Legend said that Joseph of Arimathea, he who in the gospels had given his tomb for Christ's body, had brought the cup there.

Another legend was even more wondrous. It claimed that he was uncle to Jesus of Nazareth, and had brought the youthful Christ to England on trading voyages. They had come to Glastonbury and there Christ, son of a carpenter, had helped build a church. Without doubt a small, ancient church stood in the abbey and was said to be a place of miracles.

So holy a place and she so powerfully drawn to it, but she would never see it, never pray in that church. She was at Rosewell for life and would never travel beyond its boundaries. She hadn't taken her eternal vows yet, for at Rosewell they were taken only at twenty-five, but she would, because the vows of poverty, chastity and obedience she had said at fifteen could be put aside only with permission from the family and the abbot of Glastonbury.

Sometimes a family discovered an unexpected need for a marriageable daughter, but she'd have no such reprieve. She'd been given to Holy Church when she was weaned so that she could pray for them and their causes, following a family tradition. Nothing would change.

And why think of reprieve? Rosewell was the only home she'd ever known, and it was a tranquil place of beauty and honest work.

She would allow herself no more restlessness, no more longings for the outside world, and especially no more longings for a misty dream of a man. She forced her mind to a meditation on the blessings of a simple life, silently reciting familiar prayers. Gradually those prayers helped her return to slumber.

A cock's crow woke her to the first light of the day and the glorious dawn chorus of birds. Moments later the bell rang for morning prayer and she got out of bed. Her mind flickered to dreams, but she sternly governed it into gratitude for the new day.

She and the other sisters in the dormitory rose and dressed. She donned her robe of undyed wool over the linen chemise she slept in, knotted her belt, then tied her sandals. She took off her sleeping cap, ran her comb through her short hair and then draped her linen headrail on her head. She tugged the front to be sure it was level with her eyebrows, crossed the long ends at her throat and tossed them behind, crossed them there and brought them to the front again.

She and the others looked one another over to be sure all was in order. Once any adjustments had been made, they formed a short procession and went outside to join the other sisters for morning prayer. Facing the rising sun, they sang lauds for God's blessing of a new day. In winter this was hardship, but in summer it was Gledys's favorite office of the day.

After prayers the small community went to cleaning work, for they shared these tasks. Next they sat to break their fast, listening to a reflection on summer bounty, and then they dispersed to their separate employments.

Rosewell had been set up four hundred years ago to give women a place to live completely apart from the world, so they provided almost everything for themselves. They raised their own food, made their own drink and even repaired their own buildings.

Rosewell was especially designed to free them from the world of men. If anything was needed from elsewhere, it was brought here by women. Priests were necessary, but the ones who traveled here from Glastonbury Abbey were always elderly.

So how, Gledys wondered, did she construct dreams about men? About warriors? How? She realized she'd halted in crossing the compound and was looking at the tor as if it might give her an answer.

No! She turned and hurried toward the brewery.

Rosewell was like a village of wooden buildings surrounded by a palisade. The wall was not for defense, being only a little taller than the tallest sister, but to keep animals out of the gardens. Some sisters were leaving now through the open gates to work in the fields, fish ponds and orchards outside.

The true boundary of Rosewell was the circle of woodland that surrounded its lands. That was the limit beyond which no sister of Rosewell ever ventured. Those trees also blocked any sight of that outside world—except for the tip of Glastonbury Tor.

Gledys shook these thoughts away and hurried toward the open brewery door. She was blessed to have this particular work. The Lord Jesus had turned water into wine in a truly miraculous way, but the ordinary process was no less so to her. A sour mash of barley became a clear drink that nourished the body and lightened the mind. A mush of fruits became a rich, heartening wine.

She went in, greeting her superior, Sister Elizabeth, a vigorous, thin woman with a big nose. She was old enough to be Gledys's mother, and both cheerful and kind.

"Are there any particular tasks today?" Gledys asked as she put on a large apron.

"Nothing special, dear. Get started on the new ale while I finish the yeast." She dipped another twig in the tub of yeast and drew it out slowly so it became coated with the grayish matter and then hung it to dry. The yeast would sleep and keep its powers until it was needed. When a batch of barley mash was ready, a twig would be stirred in it, and it would come to life again.

Another miracle.

Sister Elizabeth had started the fire beneath the boiler. Gledys fed it more wood and then adjusted the trap by the hole in the roof so the smoke would escape cleanly.

"There's a tricky breeze today," she said.

"Tricky times," said Sister Elizabeth. "New fighting to the east. King Stephen lays siege to Ipswich, and in retaliation, Duke Henry attacks Stamford."

It was fortunate that Rosewell didn't have a rule of silence, for Sister Elizabeth liked to hear news from the women who brought them supplies, and pass it on. She had reason to be particularly interested, however. She had come to the nunnery at age twelve and had clear memories of her worldly family, who were directly troubled by the present strife.

Gledys had come here as an infant and had no memories of any other home. These days, however, she was as interested as Sister Elizabeth in news of the war. Because of her knight. She hated to hear of fighting. She wanted him to be safe.

"News travels slowly," she said. "Perhaps the fighting is over by now."

"If it's over there, it'll be starting somewhere else."

Gledys rolled out the big vat. "Duke Henry could have decided to go home. He has so many lands—Anjou, Normandy, and now with his marriage to Eleanor of Aquitaine he has her lands as well."

Sister Elizabeth snorted. "Men like him never have enough." She smiled sadly at Gledys. "Such a longing for peace you have, dear, and always have had, but I doubt England will see it soon. Eighteen years of strife have sown enough enmity that for many the original problems don't matter anymore."

Gledys grabbed a stiff brush and a bucket of water and wished the world were as easily scrubbed clean of its muck as this vessel.

Eighteen years ago, when Gledys had been in her cradle, King Henry had died, leaving his crown to his only legitimate child, his daughter, Matilda. She was the wife of the Count of Anjou, however. Despite having sworn to support her, most of the barons of England had disliked the thought of a woman ruling them, especially one married to a foreigner, and they'd backed her cousin, Stephen of Blois. War had been fierce for a while, but then it had simmered down to strife and local feuds, but King Stephen was weak. Many barons ruled their lands like princes, and the only law was the mailed fist.

Now Countess Matilda's son was of an age to take up the claim, and she had given her right of succession to him. In November, Henry, Count of Anjou, Duke of Normandy and of Aquitaine, had landed in England to lead his family's supporters in the struggle. Ever since, England had suffered under skirmish, siege, battle and destruction. A peace had been broken; a truce had come and gone. Mercenaries roamed the countryside, pillaging when not paid. Towns burned and people died, many of them innocent ordinary folk.

Perhaps it was no wonder she dreamed of battle.

"Who brought this latest news?" she asked as she rinsed the vat.

"Marjorie Cooper, when she brought the new cask yesterday. When you were out cutting twigs."

The cooper's wife was generally a reliable informant. Gledys scrubbed and rinsed. "The king and the duke made peace in the winter. Why couldn't they hold to it?"

"Because it suited neither, as you well know."

"Yes," Gledys admitted.

That agreement had been forced on both parties. Henry of Anjou would get the throne when the king died, but that could be years, for Stephen was only fifty-seven. King Henry had lived a decade longer than that. King Stephen would keep his throne, but deprive his own son of the succession.

"If the king was willing to hold to the arrangement," Sister Elizabeth said, "his son, Prince Eustace, never will."

"Eustace of Boulogne." Gledys almost spat it. Twenty-three and steeped in evil.

"Aye, Marjorie says many of the barons who've supported King Stephen are going to Duke Henry's side for that reason alone. They don't want that young man on the throne."

Gledys looked up sharply. "Perhaps that gives hope of peace. And Duke Henry seems to be a godly man. Remember when his troops pillaged around Oxford? He commanded that all the booty be returned."

"Godly or clever," said Sister Elizabeth dryly, "but either would be better than Eustace. The water's boiling."

Gledys set the heavy vat beneath the boiler, then went to the stores for malt.

War, active or merely simmering, had thrown England into chaos all her life, and it was hard for her to believe peace possible or even imagine what it would be like. She'd lived protected from war's evils, but she'd heard of them: villages razed and towns burned, crops destroyed or stolen when they came to harvest. The strong oppressing the weak with no effective law to stop them, and endless feuding violence.

Peace seemed as mythical as the holy cup Joseph of Arimathea had buried on Glastonbury Tor, and as impossible to find. She'd heard that people crept to the tor by night to dig, seeking the sacred chalice and the miraculous bounty it was said to provide.

But in this day and age, miracles didn't exist.

Chapter 2

"What happened to you out there?" Rannulf demanded gruffly as he and the squire, Alain, helped Michael de Loury out of his battered armor. Michael winced as he bent his bruised arm. He also had a headache from that last blow.

"Distracted."

"In a battle, that'll get you killed." Rannulf was a rawboned, bow-legged man of fifty-six who served as Michael's man-at-arms, but he'd been one of Michael's trainers and never forgot it.

"I know, I know. I thought . . ." Michael stopped himself from mentioning what he'd seen. Bad enough to let his mind wander during a fight. If he mentioned visions . . . !

"It's my first tournament," he said as he flexed his body, newly freed from the weight of the mail and the heavy padded gambeson, assessing the many aches and pains that he hadn't noticed in the getting. "I'm not used to women around."

Alain said, "Speaking of women . . ."

But Rannulf spoke over him. "Should have thought of that. Good work on Willie Sea, though. Not many defeat him, and his ransom'll be a pretty penny."

Michael was pleased himself. Sir William of Seaham was ten years older and a formidable, experienced fighter. His age had counted against him in the end.

"Speaking of women," persisted Alain, hopping with excitement, "they'll all be hunting you after a victory like that."

Alain was fifteen, stocky and with a snub-nosed, rough-molded face only a mother could call handsome, but he had more experience with women than Michael, who was twenty-two and handsome enough to find it a curse. Especially when his brothers teasingly called him "angelic Michael."

But Alain's words strangely echoed warnings given by Michael's mother.

"Stop talking with your cock," Rannulf growled to Alain, and to Michael: "Lie down."

Michael obeyed and Rannulf poured oil on his hands and began to massage kinks out of Michael's body with hard, strong fingers. It hurt, but felt wonderful at the same time. Some knights had women to do this for him. He didn't dare.

It was all his mother's fault. Her condition for allowing him to leave the monastery had been two vows—that he not leave England until he was twenty-five years old, and that he remain chaste until he married. At twelve, the first had bothered him more than the second, for he'd dreamed of going on crusade, but now, at twenty-two, the second gnawed at him like a wolf.

She'd sweetened it by talking about a noble purpose here in England and a lovely bride whom he would love as soon as he met her. His destined bride for whom he remained pure. The one with whom he would finally—God be praised—cease to be pure.

But she was a long time in coming.

Unless she was the demoiselle he'd sometimes glimpsed at the edge of fighting, dressed in a green gown, white veil fluttering. He'd told himself that couldn't be so. That she was an illusion. No gentle lady would be in such a place.

But today he'd imagined her only yards away, right in the middle of the tourney.

Which proved her impossible. Chastity was driving him mad.

He'd seen no sign of his great purpose, either. Only the rough living and boredom of army camps and a murky war where no one claimed to know which side was right. He followed his father's allegiance. That was all.

Heaven be praised for this hasty tourney. It had been the most fun he'd had in years, and would be more so if not for those vows.

On her deathbed his mother had burdened him with something else. Advice only, not a vow, but she'd been intense when she'd said, "You are a skilled fighter, Michael, but mask it. I've done what I could, but your skill could mark you for what you are. It could—"

She'd broken off then, perhaps to catch her breath, but perhaps for other reasons. He'd given her a drink of sweetened, watered wine and asked her to complete her words.

She'd said, "Such prowess will attract the attention of tempting women, and make your vows difficult. Not that your looks won't do that anyway," she'd added with a sigh. She'd taken his hand then, hers frail and hot with fever. "I could wish this hadn't fallen on you, my dearest son, but we live in dreadful times, and as I approach heaven I begin to hope that you will be the salvation of us all."

Michael hadn't known what to make of that, and his heart had twisted anyway at the truth of her words. She was dying, and it would be soon. When she'd asked that he renew his vows, of course he'd obeyed. He'd kept them, too, with teeth-gritted resolution and difficulty. His chaste behavior couldn't go unnoticed in army camps, though no one believed the full extent of it. He was thought discriminating and probably with a secret mistress, but at times men amused themselves by pushing tempting wenches at him.

Damn them, and damn . . .

No, he couldn't even form the thought of damning his mother, but she'd left him a hard road and the nagging puzzle of her words: "I've done what I could. . . ." His father knew nothing of the vows or their purpose, but once, Michael had asked whether there'd been anything special about his younger years.

"Apart from your mother's obsession with sending you to a monastery?" William de Loury had asked. "Some family tradition. Nonsense, when it was clear in the cradle that you were made to fight." But then he'd frowned in thought. "There was the matter of your twin."

Michael knew he'd been a twin, the other babe dead at birth. "What was special about that?"

"The other lad was born first, but died." His father shrugged. "Nothing to that, but the midwife said something years later about your being the first. I suppose it's easy to get twins mixed up, but it didn't matter. One was dead, and with older brothers, neither of you was my heir."

Michael, too, hadn't been able to see that such a detail mattered, and yet he often remembered his mother's reaction to his leaving the monastery at Saint Edmundsbury when he was twelve. . . .

"Turn over," Rannulf said.

Michael rolled onto his back.

He'd expected wailing and recrimination, but when she'd wept it had seemed to be because he'd been so unhappy there. She'd said, "I truly believe this might be for the best." He'd managed not to berate her for sending him to the cloister, and had put her gibberish down to emotion. Women allowed emotion to overturn their wits. Everyone knew that.

He let Rannulf's ministrations clear his mind, but that opened the door to memories. Memories from only hours ago.

Wavy brown hair beneath a filmy veil, and a sweet, round face with full, soft lips, blue eyes fixed on him with concern. Her hair was strangely short, but no matter. Hair grew. Shame that her green gown hadn't been laced to her curves, as the fashion went at the moment, but he'd still seen how lovely those curves were. The trimming at hem and sleeve spoke of wealth. But he didn't care whether she was rich or poor.

His father would cuff him if he said that. Marriage was for lands and power.

But what had she been doing in the field of contest? He hadn't understood it then, and didn't now, but there she'd been, in danger of her life. Then, in a blink, she'd disappeared. He'd rushed to search, thinking she might have been knocked into the dirt, but there'd been no trace of her, and there was Willie Sea to deal with, to arrange ransom, even though Michael's mind was a tangle.

To love an illusion made no sense, but he didn't know what else to call the obsession that had ridden him for months now. Having seen her so close, he could think of nothing else. He felt almost drunk with it, and he needed to see her again as a man in a desert needed water.

He longed to kneel before her, to take her small hand, to lay his victories, his prowess and everything he possessed at her feet, just as the troubadours sang of love. In accord with their stories, life without her held no savor. He had to find her.

When he found her, he didn't want the stink of battle to linger on him.

He surged up from the bed and swept his cloak around his naked body. "Attend me," he said to Alain, and headed off to the communal bathing tent. The squire hurried along with a pile of clean clothing.

Rannulf had found quarters in the village, which had proved wise in recent rains, when the camp had run with streams and tents had let in water. It meant Michael was walking past people's homes and shops, but after a month they were used to seeing fighting men on the way to the bathhouse. He attracted little attention other than the usual saucy comments from the women. That reminded him that there were only children, matrons and crones left in Allacorn village. Any nubile young women of respectable families had been sent away to safety. Good thing the army traveled with its own whores.

In the camp men called out congratulations on his defeat of Willie Sea. It all sounded good-humored, but Michael knew he'd made

himself a target. Tomorrow, some would strive to defeat him for the
reflected glory. He was going to have to keep winning or pay ransoms
until his purse was empty.

That didn't seem to matter.

Only his bride. His beloved.

"Sir?" Alain prompted, and Michael realized he was standing in
the street like an idiot. He moved on, but he couldn't stop his eyes
from searching for her. Insanity.

But when he found her, he'd marry her, even if he had to carry
her off in the teeth of opposition from her family. He was only a
younger son, without land or fortune, but . . .

Alain nudged him. "To your left. The duke!"

Michael jerked back into the moment and turned to see Henry
of Anjou. The duke was supposed to be in Nottingham besieging
the castle, ten leagues away, not here with the force set to guard the
road from the south. Lack of action near Allacorn had led to boredom and the informal tournament, but Michael wondered if the
duke had come to put a stop to it. He was known to think tourney
fighting a waste of time, and for his temper.

He seemed in good humor, however, joking with his entourage of
barons and knights. Perhaps the siege had become tedious. The duke
was well-known for his boundless energy, so it would be like him to
dash over here to see the situation for himself.

He was sandy haired, with nothing extraordinary about his looks,
two years younger than Michael and a head shorter, but the vibrant
energy and power that infused him could take the breath away. If
energy and power could win a crown, Henry of Anjou would have
England, and soon.

Michael gathered his wits and bowed.

"Michael de Loury," Duke Henry said in his gruff voice. "Your father holds Moreborn Castle in Herefordshire."

"Yes, my lord," said Michael, impressed by the man's ability to remember such details. He didn't know whether Henry of Anjou had the right to the throne or not, but he'd support him anyway for his brains and fighting prowess.

"You're the talk of the camp, de Loury. I don't normally approve of tourney fighting, but bored men are troublesome, and skills must be practiced. De Bohun and I will field parties in tomorrow's melee." He shot a sharp glance at one of the lords around him, and Michael wondered if there was more than friendly rivalry there. "I've wagered money, and I intend to win. Will you be in my party?"

Michael had no choice but to bow again. "I'm honored, my lord."

"Good; my side must win. Make sure it does." The duke moved on and Michael did, too, but so much for his mother's advice to mask his abilities.

"An honor!" Alain declared excitedly. "You'll really show them tomorrow. You'll leave the rest in the dust."

"If God wills," Michael said, beginning to see the bright side.

He had the attention of the future king of England, but to make anything of it he must fight his best and ensure that the duke's party won. Success could put his feet on the path to greatness, and perhaps his bride's family wouldn't be so reluctant to approve the wedding. It went against his mother's warning, however, and he'd always suspected that she'd seen problems other than the attention of tempting wenches.

Why was his life so complicated? Other men could embrace the chance for glory and progress without doubt. Lucky Henry of Anjou had been born to a great destiny and encouraged to it from a young age. *His* mother hadn't tried to lock him away in a monastery. The Countess Matilda hadn't demanded vows before letting him loose into the world. She hadn't died before telling him the full meaning of it all.

Michael wiped off a scowl before entering the crowded tent, which was thick with noise and steam—and temptation. Women in light, damp clothing moved amid the communal tubs bearing ewers of hot water, drying cloths and oils to massage knotted shoulders.

He shed his cloak and climbed into a tub, congratulations on his victory over Willie Sea swirling around him like the steam. Should he cover himself with glory tomorrow or not?

He might not get the chance. He saw Sir William of Seaham, furred like a bear, glaring at him from another tub across the room, silently threatening retribution.

⚜

After the simple midday meal, Gledys returned to the brewery with Sister Elizabeth, easily following the rule of appreciation. Summer was in full richness and the gardens inside the wooden palisade billowed with blossoms worked over by insects, and ripe seedpods ready to burst and provide flowers for the future. The air was full of perfume and green growth. Summer was so lovely that she wondered why God had created winter. She'd heard there were lands to the south where winter didn't exist.

There she went again, questioning God's wisdom. It was surprising that He didn't strike her dead, especially when her other sins were added to her tally.

"Stop staring at the tor," Sister Elizabeth said. "You'll never get to go there, and that's that."

Gledys looked forward again, bowing her head. "I know, but it's so close, and we're attached to the abbey there. And both abbey and tor are holy. People make pilgrimages there, so why are we barred from it?"

"Because we live a holy life here. Come along."

Gledys followed, but said, "What if it's true that Christ himself was once at Glastonbury? That makes it as good as the Holy Land itself."

"Just stories. It's not in the Bible."

"The Glastonbury priests sometimes talk about it."

"Good for business," said Sister Elizabeth cynically.

Gledys knew that was true. In these troubled times, religious foundations competed for pilgrims and the gifts they brought.

"Work, Gledys. There's all that fruit to be crushed."

Gledys obeyed, applying a big pestle to a tub of blackberries, but she didn't think Saint Joseph was so easily dismissed. She couldn't remember whether his being a tin merchant was in the Bible, but if so, he could have sailed to this part of England. If he knew Jesus of Nazareth well enough to give over his tomb, it was possible he'd taken him on journeys, wasn't it?

The old church definitely existed—the one said to have been built by Christ himself. Some of the sisters who'd come here at an age to remember had seen it: a small, very old building where miracles occurred.

The famous thorn tree existed, too.

It bloomed every Christmastide, which was a wonder in itself, and a flowering sprig was brought to Rosewell every Christmas Eve. It was said no other such tree grew in England, so it had to be a miracle, and what other explanation was there than the one legend provided—that it had grown from Joseph of Arimathea's staff when he thrust it into the ground while resting?

But none of this explained her own fascination with the tor. When she looked at it, her heart ached with longing and she felt as if she might fly there if she only allowed herself. Her feelings were so similar to her longings for her knight that she wondered whether there was some connection. But he was fighting near a castle.

Then she realized something odd: She saw him in dreams when she was asleep in the dark, but he was always in daylight. Moreover, in her dreams, she wasn't wearing her habit or her sleeping shift. She wasn't sure what she was wearing, but knew it wasn't that. When she tried to pry open her memories to discover more, of course she failed.

So frustrating! But did these oddities prove her experiences were merely dreams?

Or did they prove that she had holy visions?

"Work, Gledys!" Sister Elizabeth said sharply.

"Your pardon," Gledys said, and returned to her task.

⁂

Michael tried to resist the insanity, but he spent the evening searching for his bride, even though it meant running a gauntlet of envious congratulations, snide comments and eager whores. Eventually he gave up and accepted an invitation to drink with Robert de Waringod. He needed refreshment, and Robert was a friendly knight who was part of the castle garrison. That was one place Michael hadn't searched as yet.

Michael turned the talk to what ladies were in residence there.

"Lady Ella and her attendants," Robert said. "And a couple of young daughters."

"Her ladies?"

"She sent her younger attendants off with her older daughters, wise lady that she is. No need to court trouble." He eyed Michael. "We all know you're particular, de Loury, but stick to whores. Safer in the end for landless men like us."

He left and Michael considered his words.

Landless men. That was what he was, and such men could not marry, but land could be won through a great man's favor.

He drained his pot. Tomorrow he'd leave every opponent in the dust, and then he'd fight with heart and soul to put Henry of Anjou on the throne.

He would win his bride.

Chapter 3

In late afternoon, Sister Elizabeth was summoned to a meeting with the abbess and cellarer to go over inventory. Gledys was set to record supplies on tally sticks. As she notched the sticks, she gave thanks for a job that took concentration and stopped her mind's busy whirling. She was tallying the supply of bungs of various sizes when she felt someone behind her. She turned quickly, wondering at the same time why she should feel alarmed. There was no one in Rosewell to fear.

But this was a stranger. She was a nun, but dressed in black rather than the unbleached wool of the Rosewell habit. The hunchbacked old woman obviously needed the staff in her right hand, and her neck curved painfully as she looked up at Gledys. What had brought her on a journey to Rosewell?

"Sister, may I serve you?"

"My name is Sister Wenna, and I come from Torholme."

Gledys felt a tingle of excitement. That was the nunnery close by Glastonbury Abbey, situated at the base of the tor. "It must be a special honor to be so close to the abbey, Sister. It is such a sacred place."

"It was sacred before the time of Christ."

Shocked, Gledys protested, "Nothing was sacred before Christ."

The woman clicked her tongue impatiently. "Why, then, do people revere it?"

"Because of Joseph of Arimathea. Because our Lord might have visited there."

Another impatient click of the tongue. "*Why* did Saint Joseph and our blessed Lord visit there?"

Gledys stared at such an extraordinary question but she grasped one thing. "They did? It is known?"

"Yes, they did," Sister Wenna said, but as if that were irrelevant. "The question is, why? Because it was a sacred place even then. It and the tor. As you know."

"I?" Gledys took a guilty step backward. "I know nothing of such pagan matters. It's unholy." Was Sister Wenna an apparition of Satan, come to tempt her even more?

As if reading her mind, the old woman crossed herself. "Sixty years I've been a nun at Glastonbury, so don't think me a tool of the devil. Many places in England were worshiped before Christ by our ancestors."

"Not by mine," Gledys said firmly. "My family is Norman."

"Half Norman. Your Gascon grandfather was given the lands and widow of a man who died at Hastings. Don't you know that?"

Gledys was startled into stammering, "N-no. I have never been told any details of my ancestry, and a sister of Rosewell is not curious about such things."

Sister Wenna's straggly gray brows rose, as if she knew of Gledys's sinful curiosity. "Know now: His wife, your grandmother, came from a special family."

"Special?" Gledys asked. "In what way?" This conversation was disturbing. She wished Sister Elizabeth would return. She wished evening weren't creeping in, turning sunlight into fire.

Instead of answering, the old nun demanded, "What do you think of Glastonbury?"

"Nothing!" Gledys exclaimed in instant denial, but then she tried to cover guilt with babble. "I came here as an infant, so if I was taken there then, I don't remember it. It's my family's tradition: All seventh children are given to the Church. . . ."

"Yes, yes, I know. The blessed seventh of the garalarl line." When Gledys gaped, she shook her head. "You don't even know that? Well, there's no time to explain. You are summoned—"

"By Mother Abbess?" Gledys asked in alarm, moving toward the door. "Why did you not say so?"

"No!" The old woman grabbed Gledys's sleeve.

"Then by whom?" Gledys pulled back, but was afraid of hurting the ancient, knobby fingers. "What do you want, Sister Wenna?"

"Peace," the old woman said fiercely. "And you can bring it."

"What?"

Sister Wenna let Gledys go and leaned heavily on her staff again. "Listen to me. You are of a sacred line, with roots thousands of years old. Thousands! Long before the time of Christ. All through history, new growth has grafted to the mighty trunk as earthly powers and beliefs come and go, but the ancient sap rules. Every land has these mysteries, but not all have kept the knowledge alive, and they pay the dreadful price."

The old nun sagged, her back a painful arch.

"Sister Wenna, would you not like to sit? There's a bench outside in the sun."

The woman ignored her. "The sap, the sacred power, flows through the females, so when Joseph of Arimathea married a woman of our ancient line he blended one mystery with another. Deliberately, I'm sure. Thus we often now call it the Arimathean line. To acknowledge your descent from a saint is no sin."

Gledys considered the implication with alarm. "But to claim descent from . . . what did you call it? The grarl line?" Perhaps it was in the harsh English tongue, now used only by peasants.

"Garalarl." It came out like a guttural snarl.

"Garalarl?"

"The garalarl is a sacred vessel that blesses with abundance. The name is also given to the bloodline that serves it. The powers flow through all of the line to some extent, but only a seventh child of a garalarl woman can respond when the cup summons. If male, he will know how to protect the chalice and its maiden. If female, she will know how to bring the chalice into this world. She will be a garalarl maiden, like you."

"Me?"

"You are a garalarl maiden, and you are summoned—"

"*Where?*" Gledys broke free of the old woman's claw.

"Wherever the raven leads."

Gledys rolled her eyes, wondering why she'd let this wit-addled old woman upset her. "Sister Wenna, let me take you to the infirmary. Sister Clarise has soothing drafts. . . ."

"It will soothe me only if you leave immediately."

"Leave Rosewell?"

"As if the thought has never crossed your mind. It calls you. Don't deny it!"

"What calls me?"

"The holy chalice."

"Nonsense."

"Very well, the *tor* calls you. Deny that, if you dare."

Gledys longed to, but instead she turned as if pulled by ropes to the window that gave sight of the hilltop, where the Monastery of Saint Michael was gilded by the setting sun.

"That's not peculiar," she said from a dry throat. "It's all I can see of Glastonbury, where Christ once walked."

"Where legend says Joseph of Arimathea buried the holy chalice."

Gledys refused to respond.

"Legend, as usual, is wrong."

"Wrong?" Gledys turned, bitterly disappointed.

"It wasn't buried; it was moved."

"Moved?" Gledys's head was beginning to pound, but now she hoped Sister Elizabeth wouldn't return yet. She had to know more. "Moved where?"

"Somewhere beyond our earthly realm. All that questing and digging when no one will ever find it that way, and certainly no man. It can be summoned back to us only by a rare and blessed woman like you."

Gledys saw that tossed like bait, but she still snatched it. She couldn't help herself. To be rare and blessed . . .

Sister Wenna smirked.

"A rare and blessed woman joined with her protector," Sister Wenna said.

"And if it does come?" Gledys asked, almost in a whisper. "What then?"

"Evil is defeated, and peace reigns. For a while, at least, mankind being weak."

"Peace," Gledys echoed, but then reality dropped back over her. "This is truly to be desired, but I am no such miracle worker, Sister. I'm a good and steady worker, but even there my mind wanders."

"Of course your mind wanders! You must have been feeling the summoning for years."

For years? Yes, perhaps that was true, and it had all become more urgent and disturbing recently.

"If I can help bring peace, why have you not come to me before? War has scourged England all my life."

"Garalarl lore has been lost or twisted since the Normans came, and those chosen to guide us have grown weak and indecisive. Families of the line no longer follow the ways, and pure sevenths are rare. It's mere chance that you have been protected. Your family is sunk in ignorance. Which is an unlikely blessing, as it turns out. If they'd remembered the truth, they might have strangled you at birth."

Gledys gasped in disbelief, but Sister Wenna said, "The de Brescars are the type to see war as opportunity, not curse, but fortunately they saw advantage in the tradition of sending a seventh child into the Church. You were born just as war erupted, and they had no worldly need of another daughter, so why not? Perhaps your prayers would put them on the winning side."

Gledys wanted to deny that description of her family, but couldn't. "They never ask me to pray for peace," she admitted. "Only for victory against this enemy or that, along with requests for prayers for their own dead and maimed."

"But you prayed for peace anyway."

"Always."

Sister Wenna nodded. "As I said, sevenths have not been preserved, so there are few who are suitable, and it was necessary to wait for you to achieve womanhood."

"I became a woman three years ago," Gledys pointed out. "Why wasn't I called upon then?"

Sister Wenna's sunken eyes shifted. "Reasons," she mumbled.

Before Gledys could demand them, the nun said, "But now I have decided that the time for dithering is over." She straightened more than Gledys would have thought possible and raised her free hand in a strangely clawlike gesture. "I have come here, Gledys de Brescar, to summon you. Succeed, and peace will reign. Fail, and you condemn this land, and perhaps the whole world, to bitter sorrow."

Gledys shivered. "Fail in what?"

"In finding the holy chalice."

"But I don't know where it is!"

"You have only to leave, to follow the raven and the golden path."

Gledys put a hand to her pounding head. Perhaps this was all another dream. "I can't leave. You know that. It wouldn't be allowed."

"You'll have no difficulty," Sister Wenna said, hunched and prosaic again. "Rosewell has served its purpose well, but that time is over."

"What purpose?"

"It's kept you virginal. That's not certain at all nunneries, alas, but you'd have to be a miracle worker to become spoiled at Rosewell. That's why it was set up this way," she added. "For garalarl maidens. Are you ready?"

"Ready for what?"

"To leave, seek, act!"

"*I cannot leave!*" Gledys shouted.

"*You must!*" the crone croaked back. It would have been a yell if she were capable of it. "We have struggled to bring peace alone—"

"Who's 'we'?"

"—but it has been broken in our hands again and again. And now true peril looms."

The old nun fell silent, perhaps debating whether to say more.

Gledys couldn't bear it. "What peril?" What could be worse than what they had?

"There is another ancient line, as old and powerful, that gains its power from blood, pain, death and grief. That power has gorged on eighteen years of strife, and those of the line have become strong enough to steal the holy lance from the Templars."

Gledys felt light-headed. "The lance that pierced our Lord's flesh at the crucifixion? It still exists?"

"It does, and it isn't sanctified as the chalice is. The lance exists entirely in this earthly realm and retains its warlike nature. In the wrong hands, it inflames anger and violence, and drives people to war. It is now in the hands of King Stephen's vile son, Eustace of Boulogne, and, unchecked, he will use it to keep the war raging."

Gledys put a hand to her dazed head, trying to make sense of it all. "Who is 'we'?" she asked. "Who has struggled to bring peace alone?"

"We of the garalarl line who have preserved the lore. But even among us too many hesitated."

"Why? If peace is within our grasp, why?"

The old woman sighed. "The cup brings peace how it wills, not as mere mortals wish, and the garalarl adepts are mortal souls with mortal frailties. They seek to control the outcome. The arguments among us have been as divisive as those among the barons. For eighteen years the choice has been between Countess Matilda and Stephen of Blois. Matilda is a haughty woman who brings destruction in her train—and a woman! Even among us, many of us women, that appalled. Stephen is weak and easily led. His weakness has created anarchy, but at the beginning he seemed to many a safer choice.

"But now the countess has given her right of succession to her son. He's male, able and seems good. Still, some worry that he will be too strong, while others bleat that at twenty-one, he's too young. 'Wait a while, wait a while,'" she muttered, clearly echoing endless debates. "But the time for waiting is over. Armed with the lance, Prince Eustace has inspired his father to break the truce. Unhindered, he will set fire to England, and the only power able to overcome the lance is you. You and the sacred cup."

Gledys stepped back from that appalling idea. "Me? I'm nothing. A woman. A nun."

"A garalarl maiden," snarled Sister Wenna. "Not nothing. Everything!"

Gledys hugged herself and turned to pace the room. If ever she'd wished to be important, she took all such wishes back. She didn't want such a calling, but the truth of Sister Wenna's warnings ached in her bones, fed by her dreams and her longing for the tor. She even felt it now, like the heavy air before a storm, or a shaking of the earth beneath her feet.

But this summons felt like a call to martyrdom.

She turned back to the old nun. "If I do this, will I die?"

Sister Wenna shrugged, as if that, too, were irrelevant. And perhaps it was.

"It's not normally the way of it. Your predecessor lived to a good age."

"My *predecessor*?"

"I told you. Thousands of years. There have been many. Enough of this. You must set out to find your protector, and then together you will summon the holy chalice."

"How do I find him?" But then a wondrous idea crept in through fear and confusion. "He will be a knight?"

"I spoke of holy sevenths," the old nun scoffed. "No, he'll be a monk."

Gledys's chest ached as she surrendered that sweet hope. "At what monastery?" she asked.

Sister Wenna's eyes shifted again, but then she sighed. "We don't know."

"What? You knew about me, but you don't know where my protector is?"

"No, which is another reason for the delay in summoning you. But you will be led to him."

Gledys rubbed at her temples through her head cloth. "None of this makes sense. How can a nun and a monk oppose Prince Eustace, especially if he possesses the holy lance, and it has the powers you describe?"

"With the power of the garalarl. Have faith."

"So I'm supposed to find my monk and then together we'll summon the chalice. That is all that is required to bring peace? What of Prince Eustace and the lance?"

"There will be a struggle to regain the lance and return it to its proper place, but that is for the Templars. Your duty will be done. There is only one more thing that you must know."

"What?" Gledys asked warily.

"Eustace may have a more dangerous plan yet, and it is another reason some have hesitated to summon you. The secrets tell us that if the chalice and the lance are ever brought together, they will create unimaginable power. Power that should never exist, in good hands or bad. Once that happens, destruction will sweep not just England but the whole world. Do you understand me? The whole world."

Gledys flinched from the intensity and the very idea, but it was hard to reject Sister Wenna's words. Her eyes glowed with an unearthly truth that Gledys felt resonating in her own bones.

"Unlike the lance," Sister Wenna said, "the chalice is vulnerable only when summoned into this earthly plane."

"Then perhaps those who hesitate are right. Perhaps I shouldn't summon the chalice."

"The lance is already in evil hands, and only the chalice can oppose it. We must take the risk, and a true pure protector will keep both you and it safe."

"Pure?" Sister Wenna had stressed that before.

"A virgin," Sister Wenna said bluntly.

"Oh," Gledys said. That certainly ended any hope that her protector was her knight. She couldn't imagine that laughing warrior refraining from bodily pleasures. "That is why he'll be a monk."

"Yes, but not all monasteries are strict. We can only trust in God and the garalarl."

That combination seemed sacrilegious, but Gledys accepted that somehow she now embraced the unbelievable. Even so, she said, "It seems wrong that we leave our service to God. We have both taken vows."

Sister Wenna made an impatient sound. "It has happened before. Your predecessor was Sybilla de Fontmarie. She left here in 1101 at the age of twenty to marry a young man who had been a monk at Saint Edmundsbury Abbey."

"What happened in 1101?"

"You don't know recent history, either? King Henry seized the throne on the death of his older brother, King William Rufus. The next-oldest—and likely successor—was Robert, Duke of Normandy, but Henry was in England and had himself crowned. It could have led to something like the evil we endure now. Robert invaded, but then he abandoned his efforts. Under King Henry, England was blessed with thirty-five years of peace, because Sybilla de Fontmarie and Richard de Grotte knew their duty."

Names made this all more real. Had Sister Sybilla of Rosewell been restless before she was summoned? Had she stared in bewildered longing at the tor?

"Then my family will summon me to marry my protector?"

Gledys said. "Why did you upset me with talk of leaving here immediately, with needing to find him?"

"There's no time for all that. You must leave now, find him and lie with him in a sacred site. That will summon the garalarl."

Gledys stared. "*Lie* with him?"

"Mate, then. You know what I mean."

"With a *stranger*?" Gledys protested, her voice climbing. *"Without marriage?"*

"The garalarl won't mind your lack of vows."

Gledys remembered the back door beyond the storage rooms and backed toward it, crossing herself. "No, no. I'm sorry, but this is all wrong. You must have come from Satan. I'll listen to no more."

Sister Wenna was unimpressed. "You're summoned, Gledys of Buckford. Listen or not; you no longer have any choice."

Those words pursued Gledys as she fled through the storage rooms and out into the bloody sunset light.

Chapter 4

She expected to be pursued, but she could easily outrun such an old woman—unless Sister Wenna turned into a raven and took flight. A glance back showed no one, and she couldn't run around Rosewell without raising questions, so she made herself walk as if on an errand.

Where should she go to think, to decide?

It couldn't be right to sin like that, but Prince Eustace was truly a vile man. Hadn't Sister Elizabeth told her that barons were deserting the king because they couldn't bear the thought of a man like Eustace on the throne? Against her will, she looked toward the tor, which now glowed as if afire. Just sunset, but there had been such power in Sister Wenna's words.

What if she, Sister Gledys, did have a special calling? What if the tor had dominated her thoughts for so long for a reason? What if she could bring peace, precious peace, to her land? What if the price of her failure was Eustace of Boulogne on the throne of England, inflicting evil here and even farther afield? Over the whole world?

Another thought crept in: Would she have fled in horror if her protector were her knight?

That would be a vile state of mind, and yet it might be true.

She felt as if she were already married to him and being asked to lie with another. When she thought of such intimacy with him, however, no amount of willpower could stop her heart from beating faster, from yearning so strongly that she might not need a holy calling to sin, only opportunity.

Wicked, wicked, wicked!

Gledys fled to the chapel.

The Rosewell chapel was small but lovely, built of stone four hundred years ago. The inside walls were whitewashed and decorated with painted pink roses, and small windows in the side walls let in light and birdsong. A simple wooden cross stood on the plain altar cloth, dark against the precious glass window that glowed in shades from cream to amber. It faced west so that the setting sun added fire to the squares of glass, and the light gilded the pale walls and the bleached whiteness of the altar cloth. Even the smells were soothing here—wood, wool and candle wax alongside traces of the incense used by the priests during some services.

Gledys turned to her favorite meditation—walking the labyrinth painted on the stone floor. The coiling paths, turning back on themselves again and again, allowing no choice but to follow, always soothed her mind and allowed her prayers to flow. She entered at the single opening and immediately felt solace. The chapel was God's tranquil place, and the labyrinth a path to Him. Here, He would guide her.

"Bring peace to this land," she murmured. "But peace without my having to act."

Everything about Sister Wenna's summoning terrified her, but it was the loss of her knight . . . "Deliver me from temptation. Give me a sign, Lord. Show me the holy way."

Nothing happened. Of course. Had she believed for a moment that she was some special instrument of God? Too soon she came back to the entrance, the labyrinth walk completed, but her prayers unanswered. She turned toward the cross and said the dutiful words: "Thy will be done."

A golden flash startled her. She blinked. It must have been the sun glinting off something on the altar. But what?

Ah. Nothing miraculous. Simply the chalice, but the precious silver goblet, as old as the chapel, shouldn't be out except in preparation for a Mass. Of course, no one in Rosewell would steal it, but between Masses, it was locked in the sacristy chest.

Had it been there all along?

Wouldn't she have noticed it?

Perhaps Sister Thomasine, the sacristan, had come in while she was praying. Had a priest arrived unexpectedly? Were they to have a Mass? That would be a blessed opportunity to drive any devils away.

She was alone, however.

She turned toward the small side door, intending to find the sacristan, but it felt wrong to leave the chalice unprotected. She tried a soft call: "Sister Thomasine?"

No answer. Very well, she'd take the chalice with her into the sacristy. If Sister Thomasine was there, she'd be irritated, but it felt wrong to abandon it. Gledys climbed the three shallow steps to the altar and reached out—but then swiftly drew back her hand.

There was blood inside the cup! A small pool of blood.

After a heart-stopped moment, she leaned forward again and saw it wasn't blood—of course it wasn't—but a deep red rose petal.

A deep red rose petal?

"What are you doing!"

The shrill voice made Gledys jump back. She turned to face Sister Thomasine. "Nothing, Sister! I was simply wondering why the chalice was out. Whether I should—"

"You should do nothing!" snapped the woman, grabbing the vessel and clutching it to her ample chest. She was round in body, but sharp in nature. "Return to your brew house, Sister Gledys."

Gledys resented the tone of that dismissal, but she bowed and escaped, shaking.

She hated anger, and it was rare in Rosewell. Gledys had realized almost immediately that the sacristan had left the chalice out and was afraid Gledys would reveal her sin of carelessness.

She herself was shaken by other things.

When Sister Thomasine had clutched the chalice to her chest, the bowl had been tilted forward, and it had been empty. There'd been no rose petal inside or on the floor, where it might have tumbled. Of course, it might have fluttered away, being so light, but wouldn't she have seen that?

The main fact, however, the thing that had disturbed her before Sister Thomasine's arrival, was that such a rose petal was impossible.

Few roses bloomed as late as August, but more than that, she'd never seen a bloodred rose. Rosewell's rose gardens were famous, but the blooms were nearly all white, cream and pink. Two that bloomed a deep pink were considered almost miraculous.

She halted, breath caught.

She'd asked for a sign. Had she been sent one? During Mass, the wine in the chalice became the blood of Christ.

No, no, she didn't want to be part of any miracles. They usually ended with a martyr's death.

There was one rose that held some blooms into summer and even into autumn. It had been sent to Rosewell by a crusader, and might come from the Holy Land itself. She remembered it as deep pink, but she hurried to the rose garden, hoping she was wrong. Hoping that it bloomed at this time of year, and that the petals were bloodred.

When she arrived, she saw the Autumn Damask rose and sighed. It did still have some blooms, but their color was nothing close to that deep crimson. She went closer to be sure. The flowers were a beautiful color, the deepest pink of a sunset, but not bloodred.

She straightened and turned, searching the garden for some new rose, some undiscovered wonder, but of course there was no such thing.

So where had that rose petal come from?

And just as puzzling, where had it gone?

It had appeared in a chalice that was used in a Mass, which was a reenactment of the Last Supper. That led her mind to the cup that Joseph of Arimathea was said to have brought to Glastonbury—the holy chalice, which, according to Sister Wenna, was also in some way an ancient vessel called the garalarl.

She shook her head, trying to deny it all as nonsense, but it was lodged there like a spike. Too many strange things were coming together.

Then something huge whirred just over her head. Gledys ducked and cried out, stumbling backward. But when she looked, there by the Autumn Damask rosebush was a big black bird, head cocked.

A raven.

A *raven*!

She'd never seen one before, for they were woodland birds of the north, but that was what it must be. It was much bigger than a crow, its body almost as big as a goose's, though sleeker and glossier in its black plumage. One golden eye was fixed on her.

Ravens were birds of ill omen, and this one looked it.

Gledys took a careful step backward. "Sweet Lord, I do not wish to go where such a bird might lead."

Craak! it said, making a sound like a scornful laugh.

It rose with a mighty flap of wings, but it did not fly away. It went only to perch on the rose arbor.

Craak! Craak!

Gledys crossed herself.

The bird changed its perch to a nearby upright pole.

No, a lance. Plain wood, but pointed.

A *lance*?

Gledys blinked, and it was a rough pole again. Of course it was. That had been only a trick of the fading light and her overset emotions. The vespers bell must ring at any moment. Pray God it drive this evil bird away. She slid another step toward the exit, afraid to turn her back on the fearsome bird.

It flew to another perch—a sword thrust into the ground.

A *sword*?

No, no, a spade!

Then Gledys saw her knight in his long chain-mail armor, looking at her.

No! Only a dead tree trunk wound around by the stems of a rambling rose. She turned to flee, but saw a golden banner. No, a patch of marigolds. The lance again. A golden cup set with rich jewels whose glow rivaled the sunset, which spilled roses. Bloodred roses.

She made herself stop turning and covered her eyes with her hands. When she slowly lowered them, no strange images danced at the corner of her eye, and the bird was gone. Just another strange dream, but by daylight?

Then she saw another dark shape. It was Sister Wenna, watching her, ravenlike.

"Are you ready to leave yet?" the old woman croaked.

Gledys's throat was too tight for speech, but she managed to shake her head, and blessedly, the vespers bell began to toll. She hurried to the chapel the long way, avoiding the old nun. Sister Wenna and all the rest were only a dream. It had to be so. Gledys wanted no part of ravens, blood, spears and swords.

As she joined the procession, Sister Elizabeth slipped beside her, brows raised in question, and gave her clothing a pointed look. Gledys looked down and realized she still wore her apron. She untied it and carried the awkward bundle until she could put it in a corner. Once in the chapel, she plunged into the familiar prayers as she might plunge into a bath after having fallen in a filthy pond.

But the maddening ideas were not to be washed away. Sister

Thomasine shot her a baleful look—so the incident with the chalice had not been a dream. For the first time she glanced around to see if Sister Wenna was here, praying she was not.

There she was, however, in the chairs provided for the older nuns, standing out in her black robes. Gledys noticed another black-robed nun among the other sisters, a younger one who must be Sister Wenna's traveling companion.

So she was real, and something had driven an old, half-crippled woman on a journey. If she told the truth, she'd been compelled by the fact that an evil man had acquired dreadful power, and Gledys could do something about that.

The prayers came to an end without Gledys finding any answers, and the community formed the procession to go to the refectory for bread and soup, but as the end of the line left the chapel, a great black bird circled, less than two hands above their heads, squawking raucously. Everyone covered and ducked, some exclaiming, some screaming and running back into the chapel.

So the raven had not been a dream, either.

Gledys accepted that she was summoned, and until she obeyed, she and everyone else would be pestered like this. Perhaps, like the trials visited upon Egypt in the Bible, each one would be worse, leading even to the death of innocents, until she surrendered.

The bird had taken a perch on the cross on the chapel roof, but it still gave its ugly *craak!* sound. Those who'd stayed outside looked up at it, pointing and chattering.

Gledys went to Sister Wenna, who stood nearby, unalarmed and unsurprised. "What must I do?"

"Follow the raven."

"It's a bird of ill omen."

"Only to some. Others think them messengers from a holy realm."

"Like the realm to which Joseph of Arimathea sent the holy chalice?" Gledys wanted to sound scathing, but it didn't come out that way.

Sister Wenna nodded.

"Heaven? That means death."

"That should fill any good Christian's heart with joy, but Sybilla de Fontmarie lived to be sixty-two and bore five children. Not seven, alas, but she served in other ways. The garalarl is kind to those who do its will." She held out something. "This is yours."

It was a silver ring with a coiling, complex design. "Mine?"

"As the garalarl maiden. Put it on."

After a moment, Gledys slid it onto the third finger of her right hand. It fit perfectly.

As if at a signal, the bird suddenly swooped from cross to gate. It was a clear command. The gates were normally closed directly after vespers, but the sisters whose job it was to do so hesitated, looking up at the black bird.

With a clap of her hands, the abbess called order. "Enough, sisters. It is only a bird, and supper will be getting cold."

The milling about ceased and the nuns hurried with their superior toward the refectory. The only ones left were Gledys, Sister Wenna and the two nuns hovering near the gates. When they went nervously forward to close them, the raven leaned down. *Craak! Craak!*

They scuttled back.

"I can't just walk out," Gledys said.

"No one will stop you."

That seemed so unlikely that Gledys decided it was a test. When she was forced back and questioned, she would know this was all nonsense. She walked forward a few steps, but then turned back.

"I need supplies."

"No, you don't."

"I need to know—"

"You need nothing. Go! Trust in God. And the raven."

Gledys looked from nun to raven, but she knew she had to do this, and from more than duty. She was compelled.

Her feet moved on their own, carrying her forward, toward the open gates. Expecting at any moment to be stopped, Gledys walked past the gatekeepers, who didn't seem to see her, and then followed the rough road that led through fields that were rapidly disappearing in the fading light.

She didn't even have a lantern. As soon as she reached the dark surrounding trees, she'd lose the road and be lost.

But no one had prevented her from leaving.

By that test, she was on a holy journey.

As if to confirm it, the bird rose into the sky and flapped off ahead of her, drawing her onward. Onward toward the trees, and beyond them, dark against the evening sky, the monastery that crowned the tor.

Sick with fear, pulsing with excitement, Gledys followed the raven into the deepening dark of night.

Chapter 5

"Ho, de Loury! Hero of the day!" The powerful voice conquered even the din of the ale tent.

Michael turned on his stool from the table, where he was drinking with a group of other young knights, discussing the tourney fighting and Henry of Anjou, the chances of action and Henry of Anjou, and the fighting tomorrow in which Michael and some of the others here would fight in Henry of Anjou's party.

The voice belonged to Willie Sea, drunk and troublesome, in a stained, sleeveless jerkin that exposed massive arms furred with the same wiry thatch that covered the rest of him. He had a buxom redhead on his left arm and a huge tankard in his right hand, and a way was opening for him through the crowded space as he headed straight for Michael. He was grinning his gap-toothed smile, but was very drunk.

Trouble. None of Michael's companions was a close friend, so he was on his own. Another of his mother's promises was that he couldn't be killed before he found his bride, but she hadn't promised no broken bones. He remembered remarking that immortality was the best argument he'd ever heard against marriage, but she'd just smiled and reminded him of the vow of chastity.

True enough. What man would choose immortality if he had to die a virgin?

"Brought you a gift!" Willie Sea bellowed. He had an astonishing voice—useful on a battlefield, painful in an enclosed space—and the whole tavern had little choice but to attend to the show.

Michael mirrored the other man's jovial tone. "How generous, when you've already given me your ransom."

"Vagaries of battle," said Willie Sea, without apparent offense. He waved his ale pot. "If you feel guilty, fill this."

Perhaps this wouldn't be too bad. Michael called for the pot boy. When the other man's tankard was full to the brim he raised his own. "In honor of a worthy opponent."

"Amen!" Willie Sea gulped down his ale in one long series of glugs, belched, and bellowed, "Fill her up! And his, too."

Once his pot was brimming over again, he sauntered closer, wench still attached, clearly searching his sodden mind for his original purpose. "Gift!" he declared. "Here you are." He pushed the buxom wench against Michael. "Name's Liza."

Liza was clearly a whore and very willing. She pressed close between Michael's legs and wound her arms around his neck, but he knew she was a test of his manliness.

"Aren't I the lucky one?" she cooed. "First the strongest knight, then the handsomest."

"Strongest, too," Willie Sea growled. "He bested me."

A flicker of worry marred the girl's face, and even in the uncertain candlelight, Michael saw an old bruise on her cheek.

"The vagaries of battle." Michael repeated Willie Sea's words to him over the girl's head as he sought a way out of this. "But we could test it again." He flexed his right arm to indicate what he meant.

After a moment of surprise, Willie Sea cried, "A man after my own heart! Clear a table."

The men at three nearby tables scrambled to offer one. Willie Sea cleared some lingering pots from the nearest with a sweep of his mighty arm. Michael put down his own pot, but the girl stayed stuck to him as he walked over to the table.

She was not to his taste, but by the angel Gabriel's nonexistent balls, she was a sweet armful. His cock was hard and he wanted nothing more in the world at that moment than to throw her down and use her.

Sitting opposite his opponent and putting his elbow on the table to take the grip gave him an excuse to separate from twining Liza. She instantly draped herself over his shoulder, her long, loose hair tormenting his cheek as she nibbled at his ear.

God's teeth. He needed to concentrate. He needed to lose this contest, but not too quickly. In comparison to Willie Sea's dark-haired arm, even Michael's strong one looked weak, but he knew he was strong enough. He always was. Again, because of his mysterious purpose.

As they wriggled their hands together, adjusting their grips for best purchase, Michael said, "Is this a simple contest of skill, or is something at stake?"

Willie Sea showed his missing teeth again. "You lose, you return my ransom."

"But if you lose?"

"By the tomb, you've drained me dry today!"

"Then why don't we fight for the wench? If I win, she's mine for sure. If you win, I return your gift." He turned his head toward the girl. "You'll be a sore loss, sweeting."

The girl pouted at him, but was clever enough to know that showing any displeasure at ending up with Willie Sea would be bad for business and her skin.

"I'll have a kiss from you first," she said saucily. "He's already had more than one, so it's only fair."

There was no way to escape, so when she slid onto his lap, cradled his head in her hands and put skillful lips to his, Michael could only fight to hold on to sanity—difficult when she opened her mouth and tormented him with her tongue. Especially when he imagined it was his bride kissing him so boldly, her moisture blending with his, her tongue . . .

He opened his eyes to break the spell, but saw dark hair, not red. He clutched that hair close to the skull and found it strangely short. She even smelled different. Cleaner, and without any perfume. Except for something that threatened his wits entirely . . .

She drew back slowly, those full lips parted, eyes wide with surprise and a kind of innocence the red-haired whore had lost long ago.

Was he dreaming?

No. Beyond her was the tavern, the circle of grinning men, and Willie Sea opposite. Their right hands were still gripped together.

Mind jangling at this insanity, Michael took the risk of speaking, afraid she'd turn into mist. "Step away now, sweetheart. I wouldn't want to see you hurt."

She slid off his lap and did step back, eyes still fixed on him, huge with questions. He had plenty of his own.

"Be careful," she said in a soft, sweet voice.

He grinned with sheer delight. He didn't understand where the whore had gone and why his bride was here, but she was, speaking to him, concerned for him. He'd held her; he'd kissed her, his true lady in all her perfection.

Willie Sea chuckled. "If there was any question, I'd say I'd won already. The lad's strength's all in his pecker!"

The room rocked with laughter.

Michael dragged his eyes away to lock his gaze with his opponent's, tightening his grip. "We'll see about that."

No more thought of losing. He was fighting for his bride.

A man stepped forward to count the start, and then they were at it, bracing and straining, moving an inch or two one way, then an inch or two the other.

Willie Sea shot Michael a narrow-eyed look, clearly surprised to find this a true contest. Michael grinned and forced the other man's hand a bit lower. But he had to steal a glance, to be sure she was still there.

Willie Sea surged in the other direction and Michael only just stopped the loss. Sweating, grimacing, he forced the other man's hand back, inch by inch by inch.

He heard a soft cry.

He had to look.

She was still there, eyes wide. Who had ever looked at him with such deep, tender concern?

The back of his hand slammed into the table and Willie Sea leapt to his feet, bellowing victory, fists raised. He grabbed his prize for a long, deep kiss.

Michael hurled the table aside and roared in to rescue her. . . .

But she was red-haired and plump, and giving back all that she got.

His bride, his elusive, impossible bride, had gone.

He staggered back to collapse onto a bench. He was going mad.

Gledys flinched away from the horrible man.

And was somewhere else entirely.

She wasn't in that hot, stinking tavern, but alone in the chilly dark. Alone in the woods.

She'd had another dream—a dream while walking!—but what a dream! She'd seen him, touched him, kissed him!

And what a kiss!

She revisited it in her mind—the heat and taste of him, the feel of his big, strong body that seemed to have an energy all its own, almost tingling under her hands. His wonderful smell, distinct even amid stinks of ale, new and old, roasting food, sweat. . . .

She caught her breath.

She was remembering!

The details weren't melting away.

She returned to them again, afraid they'd fade away, but no. They were there, as clear as her memory of meeting Sister Wenna.

He'd stopped kissing her and told her to step back. She hadn't wanted to, but she'd obeyed and she'd seen he was engaged in a strange contest of strength. His opponent had been older and bigger and wearing a tunic that left his huge, hairy arms bare. He looked half animal, and when he'd smiled, showing missing teeth, she'd recognized him as the man her knight had fought in the tournament.

Her knight's forearm looked strong, but it was smaller than the other man's. She'd worried, but she'd reveled in her first clear view of him.

The drinking place had been poorly lit, but even scant tallow light had caught gold from his wavy hair and thrown up the detail of strong cheekbones and a square jaw. She remembered kissing him, his beautiful face between her hands, his lips hot on hers.

Surely he was her protector to come to her like that in a vision while on her quest.

And yet, when she'd first seen him he'd been dallying with a wanton, whose plump breasts almost spilled out of a tight bodice. The woman had leaned on his shoulder and nibbled his ear! Then she'd slithered around and onto his lap to kiss and be kissed. He hadn't been at all reluctant.

But then it had been she, Sister Gledys of Rosewell, whose hands had cradled his head, whose lips had pressed to his, parted, so they shared breath. How?

Well, it was a dream. It seemed anything could happen in a dream, even an unimaginable kiss.

How had she known how to kiss like that? How could she have enjoyed it so much? Enjoyed the heat and taste, and the feel of his silky hair around her fingers, his strong skull beneath her hands. The closeness of their entire bodies.

Gledys forced her eyes open to try to break the spell. Bad enough to dream such things, but to eagerly return to them, wallow in them! Yet Sister Wenna had implied that this was her destiny, her duty, and now it seemed her knight would be the one.

Gledys crossed herself, muttering, "Lead me not into temptation, Lord." But when she added, "Thy will be done," she knew she meant, "Yes, please!"

She'd achieve neither destiny nor desire if she died here, however, and she was lost in a dark, dank wood. She hugged herself and shivered, wondering how far she might have walked, and where she might be. The last thing she remembered was following the road into the woods, wishing she had a lantern.

Through black branches above she could see dark gray sky, but any dim light didn't reach here below. She explored with her hands, finding a tree trunk. It was the trunk of a very large tree, far greater in girth than her arms could begin to encircle. Probably an oak, and very old. It was possible that such ancient oaks lived in the woods around Rosewell, but she'd never encountered one.

"Raven? *Raven!*" she repeated more loudly, for clearly she had no need to fear anyone would overhear her. There was no one around. Not even, it seemed, the raven itself.

She began to pray in a direct and rather desperate way, but then other words trickled into her mind. She found herself saying, "Garalarl, guide me."

Suddenly, a path of light glimmered before her feet.

Gledys blinked, then looked up through dark leaves again, seeking the moon. She knew, however, that there was only a sickle moon at the moment, and indeed, it wasn't even visible. Nor was this cool moonlight. The path shone warmly, as if thousands of tiny candles burned. Sister Wenna had spoken of a golden path. She stepped forward, knowing this was God's work, guiding her to safety. And, please God, to her knight.

But where was she being taken? The ground was so rough, she wasn't sure she was on any kind of road or footpath. She halted, uncertain again, but then at last heard the commanding croak of a raven. It seemed to say, *Come on, come on, you lazy thing!*

"Very well, very well," she muttered, adding an ungracious, "Thy will be done."

After walking only a few more minutes, Gledys found herself suddenly in a glade, in front of a small building, where light escaped around shuttered windows. She knew she should be giving unconditional thanks to God, but she couldn't help wondering who lived in the small house and whether they would help her or harm her. She'd never entered any building other than those in Rosewell, and certainly not a stranger's home.

This seemed to be an isolated shelter, too. She knew charcoal burners lived in the woods, and perhaps foresters. There were others, though. Outlaws hid in the woods, and thieves lurked to attack passing travelers.

What if there were men inside?

She was a nun, but would that keep her safe?

Her body ached for warmth and rest, however, and the miraculous path led right to the door. She stumbled forward and knocked. There was no response.

She called, "God bless you all. May I come in?"

Still no response, but then, it was long after dark and whoever lived here would be asleep. She crossed herself, sent up a prayer and opened the door.

The house seemed to be one room lit by a small fire that burned in the center, ringed around with stones. The smoke rose peacefully to escape through a hole in the roof above. The fire didn't give a lot of light, but enough for her to see that the place was someone's home, but no one was here.

A low platform ran the length of the wall to her right, taking up a third of the width of the room. There was a bed on it—a mattress and some blankets—but no one was sleeping there. It called to her, but she couldn't simply lie down on someone else's bed, especially if it belonged to a man. What would he think when he returned?

Surely he wouldn't mind her warming herself at the fire, so she went forward and crouched down, holding out her hands. As she rubbed them, she continued to inspect the place.

Two wooden chests stood against the left wall, with shelves above holding a few wooden dishes and cups. The space between chests and bed was less than she could span with her arms and held only the fire. There were no other doors, and only two windows, one behind her by the door and one facing her.

She sent a prayer of thanks for the fire and whoever had made it. Her lids drifted down. . . . She pulled herself out of sleep. She was in danger of falling into the flames!

She looked longingly at the bed. That miraculous path had brought her here. She had been guided by a raven, as Sister Wenna had foretold.

So be it.

She pulled back the covers, astonished to find blankets of softest wool. She pressed the mattress and found it seemed to be stuffed with feathers. Who was the owner of such luxury?

Exhaustion silenced questions. She took off her sandals, head cloth and robe and settled into the wondrous bed. It was almost too soft for one used to the hard mattress of the nunnery, but it embraced her, and the thick blanket made her instantly warm. Gledys had no time to say her nighttime prayers before she was fast asleep.

She dreamed again of her knight.

He was in a small, musty room that seemed like the dormitory at the nunnery except that the mattresses lay on the floor, set close together. Someone was snoring. The only illumination was faint moonlight through a small window. Her knight sat on his mattress, back to the wall, staring into nowhere, dressed loosely in white. He'd probably stripped down to his shirt.

Because she'd seen him earlier, she could piece together his features in the dim light. He was still as handsome and noble in appearance—perhaps more so in stillness. Gledys would have been content to simply watch him, but a soft glow appeared in front of her feet—another glowing path that wound from where she stood to him. She allowed it to lead her through mattresses, scattered bags, and satchels safely to where she longed to be.

He turned his head, startled, perhaps reaching for a weapon, but then froze. "You," he breathed.

Gledys could manage only an inadequate, "Yes."

He slowly reached out a hand and she slowly put hers into it, swallowing a sob of joy when they finally, deliberately touched, when his fingers curled around hers. His hand was large and ridged with calluses. Hers was smaller, but not soft and delicate. Perhaps he wouldn't mind.

His fingers tightened, but gently. She knew he could crush her bones if he chose. She squeezed back, overwhelmed by a deep-rooted tenderness. It was as if she'd known him for many years and they were reunited after being apart.

"What's your name?" he breathed.

They certainly didn't want anyone to wake.

"Gledys," she murmured. "And yours?"

"Michael. Michael de Loury."

She spoke it silently, savoring, then asked, "My protector?"

"That would be my honor, sweet Gledys." She heard a warm smile, but no awareness of any deeper meaning to her words.

She'd been transported here, guided to his side. He *had* to be the man she was supposed to find.

"My protector," she said. "And protector of the garalarl. The sacred cup."

He drew her closer, raising their joined hands to his lips so he could kiss her fingers. She shivered right down to her toes. "My lady, I will be whatever you wish me to be, for I know that you are mine. My life, my heart." He pressed her hand against his chest. "Feel how it beats for you."

Indeed, she could feel it, strong and fast, and her heart raced in the same way.

"May I kiss you?"

Did he not remember their previous kiss? Perhaps a godly man always asked permission.

"Please," she said.

He drew her closer still, down onto his lap, against his broad chest. She almost wept with the sweetness of it, for she'd known no such tender embraces from a man. When he put his lips to hers, she had no knowledge of what to do, but she did it anyway.

And then they were kissing as they had before, sliding down onto his mattress, pressing close. Gledys couldn't forget that there were others around, but she couldn't stop, either. His hand explored her body, sliding and gripping, creating sensations she'd never imagined possible. She, too, explored, marveling at hard muscles and heat. And they kissed and kissed until her head swam and her body burned as with a fever.

When he pushed them apart, she knew he was wise, but when he brought her back to him, tucked against his chest, she sighed with pleasure and snuggled there.

Craak!

She started, and he whispered, "What's the matter?"

"Didn't you hear that?" she whispered back.

"What?"

"It doesn't matter." She knew, however, that she'd been recalled to duty. She was not here to embrace, but to summon him to *his* task. "I spoke of the garalarl," she murmured. "Do you know what that is?"

"Grarl?" he queried, mispronouncing it as she had at first. Clearly it meant nothing to him.

"The Arimathean line?" she tried.

He chuckled into her hair. "My heart, I can think of better things to do than play riddles."

So could Gledys, but she held him off. "This is no game. Have you heard the legends about Glastonbury? That the cup Christ used at the Last Supper might be hidden there?"

He relaxed against the wall again, but his arm kept her close. "Yes, that I've heard. By Joseph of Arimathea. Is that what you meant by the Arimathean line?" His hand stroked her hip. "You will marry me?" he asked.

"Willingly," she replied, sealing it with a kiss. "But it can't be yet."

"Alas, I fear not. I must speak to my father and yours. I'm a land-less knight, Gledys. Your family will be hard to persuade, but I will do it."

Gledys put her fingers to his lips to silence him, to tell him such things didn't matter, and anyway, they couldn't wait for marriage. The words stuck in her throat, especially here with others nearby, even asleep.

"We will speak of all that in the morning," she said, then kissed him again. "I'm so happy to have finally found you."

He kissed her back. "No happier than I am to have finally found my true-love bride."

His true-love bride.

They were together now, and tomorrow she would find the words to explain their duty. They would set off to summon the holy chalice, and England would finally know peace. But above all, she would be his and he hers, for all eternity.

Chapter 6

Craak!
Gledys grimaced at that ugly noise, but everything else was perfect. She was warm and cozy and with her knight. She opened her eyes to see bare rafters. Ah, the room where he lodged.

But when she turned her head, she realized she was alone in the bed, alone in the room, alone in the house in the woods! She sat up, trying to see something else, but it was unquestionably the isolated hut.

"No," she moaned, covering her face with her hands. That had seemed so completely real. Every moment of it. She remembered every touch, every word. How could it have been a dream? It had been, though. She'd gone to sleep in this bed and woken in it.

But, oh, it had been sweet, and now she knew her protector's name.

She breathed it aloud. "Michael de Loury."

Her knight, her protector, and she was his true-love bride.

According to Sister Wenna, this mission was urgent, so surely the raven and the path would take her quickly to him. She hurried out of bed and put on her sandals, only then realizing that there was no chill in the air.

Because the fire still burned.

In her weariness last night she'd not noticed that there was no extra wood in this place, but there wasn't. And yet it still burned. She crossed herself, murmuring thanks for the miracle.

She opened the shutters by the door and cautiously peered out. Dew sparkled on grass and branches, but there was no sign of any other person. She turned to inspect the hut by daylight, but there was nothing new to see, and no sign that anyone might have entered in the night to build up the fire. She was swept up in mysteries and miracles, but she had no complaint.

Craak!

She hurried back to the window and saw her raven on a nearby branch.

"You woke me at a bad time," she said, though there couldn't have been a good one.

Craak! Craak!

Somehow she understood that meant, *Hurry up. Time to go.*

She was hungry, but there was no help for that, and she, too, wanted to hurry.

She was about to put on her habit when the raven hopped in through the window to stand on one of the chests. When she approached, it hopped onto the other. Inside the first one, she found a loaf of bread, some hard cheese and a stoppered pottery jug. She tore off a bit of the bread and found it fresh and delicious. She took down a wooden beaker from the shelf, then pulled out the wooden stopper and poured the liquid into her small jug. She took a small sip and found it to be excellent ale.

"What else do you expect from God's brewing?" Gledys said.

She pretended that she was speaking to the raven, but she was talking to hear her own voice. She'd never been alone before and the world felt empty, as if some great plague had swept God's people away. She shook herself. Soon she'd be where Michael was and among many people.

She paused, bread and drink in hand, to revisit that blissful encounter, to wonder if he, too, had experienced it. Surely it must be so. They truly had come together in a dreamworld, as they had in the tavern earlier. Which meant he would awaken as disappointed as she.

All the more reason to hurry. She found her knife and hacked off some cheese, eating quickly, anxious to be on her way. But as she turned to leave, the raven said, *Craak!*

She knew she was supposed to open the other chest.

She flung the lid up impatiently, but then gasped. It contained fine clothing such as she'd never seen before, in rich shades of green, russet and yellow. On top lay a gilded leather belt with a pouch and a sheath that proved to exactly fit her knife. This clearly was also God's gift, yet she hesitated.

"I'm to change out of my habit?"

She didn't know why this shocked her more than anything else, but it did. As long as she wore her habit she was still Sister Gledys of Rosewell. Once she took it off, she would become someone else and belong in a world she neither knew nor understood.

"Do I really have to do this?"

Neither God nor the raven answered. What need, when her direction was clear? All the same, Gledys closed the lid on the clothes and sat on it.

This was the moment of no return. She'd left the only home she'd ever known and broken many of the rules she'd lived with all her life. True, any sister of Rosewell could leave the nunnery if she hadn't taken her eternal vows, but there was a process. Documents were signed to return her to her family. She would formally renounce her vows.

Instead she was following a bird and some lights to heaven knew where.

But—she shot to her feet—she remembered how in her dreams she was never wearing her habit. She'd not seen her clothing, but it felt and moved differently.

She opened the chest eagerly now and lifted out a green robe. Such soft, fine wool, almost too delicate for her work-roughened hands, and skillfully decorated around neck and sleeves with embroidered braid. Telling herself the shape wasn't much different from her habit, she put it on. The sleeves were only elbow-length, but those of her chemise reached to her wrists, so her arms were decently covered.

She buckled the fine new belt around her waist and adjusted the knife and pouch. She checked inside the pouch and found a few small coins. She'd never handled coins and looked curiously at the design. One side showed a man, perhaps the king. The other was stamped with a four-petaled flower.

What were they worth? What would they buy? The idea of approaching someone to make a purchase turned her stomach. She'd rarely met a stranger and never been in a town or market. She'd never purchased anything. She could only trust, and she needed to be on her way.

She took out a cloak of fine russet wool and found some other items beneath—stockings, garters, green leather shoes, a delicate white cloth and a plaited circlet of red and yellow cloth.

Suppressing her qualms, she quickly put on stockings and shoes. The stockings were of a fine weave and would be easily damaged. It would be a shame to walk through rough woodland in the new shoes, but God must know best.

The cloth must be a veil, but it was square, so it wouldn't easily cover her head as her usual one did. She remembered seeing the ladies at the tournament with their loose veils stirred by the breeze. Folly, but so be it.

Those ladies had had long hair to show off, however, either in plaits or hanging free. With her short-cropped hair, she was going to be an oddity. She shrugged and draped the cloth over her head and then pulled the woven circlet down on top to hold it in place.

She wished she knew what she looked like, but there was no one to tell her, or to adjust her garment or hair if they were awry. She could see only from her chest down. She spread her skirt. The green was very pretty, like the green of spring grass, and the russet and yellow made a lovely trim. It felt sinful to take pleasure in such ornament, but if this was God's will, would it not be ungracious to object? What was more, she wanted to look well when she finally met Michael de Loury in reality.

She folded her habit and placed it in the chest with her nunnery belt, then closed the lid. She glanced around the hut to be sure she'd not overlooked anything, then went back out into the warming sunshine, ready to carry on. When she looked around, however, the woodland seemed unbroken, with no sign of a path.

"Now what?" she demanded of the universe.

The raven swept down and around, and then flew into the woods. "There's no path," Gledys protested. "That undergrowth will ruin these lovely clothes!"

Craak! Craak!

Muttering grimly, Gledys marched forward, skirts raised.

But how little faith she had. As she approached the tangled bushes, a path opened, one just wide enough for her to travel safely. There were not even branches low enough to trouble her.

Gledys laughed for joy, all doubt blown away. This was right and good, and soon she'd find her knight with no dreams or visions between them.

Perhaps even at Glastonbury Tor.

❦

Gledys had not walked far when she realized that her magical path had blended with a well-worn one, and she glimpsed open fields ahead. She hurried forward, but when she emerged from the trees she halted, a new panic fluttering in her.

What noise was that? Clashes and bangs, yells and cries. Lord save her. Men were fighting nearby!

The raven swept ahead, however, and she was compelled to follow, but as the noises grew louder, her steps slowed and her heart thumped with fear. Such anger and violence in every sound. Murderous hatred.

But then she glimpsed a stone keep with pennants flying. A keep she remembered. Her heart pounded with a new beat now, and her steps speeded. This was the tournament. This was where she'd seen Michael fight!

She picked up her skirts and ran, but halted again at the sight of a mass of tents and people covering the land on this side of the castle. She tried to take it in, but she'd never seen so many people in her life, or heard such a jumble of noises, from screams to singing, clangs to music. Then she made out roofs near the castle and she realized there must be a small town of some sort there. And also a large open area to the right of the town, roped off all around, in which the men were fighting.

That must be where she'd seen Michael defeat the big man, so he might be there now, but the war camp lay like a barrier between. To get to Michael, however, she'd pass through a fiery battlefield, and so she walked on, head held high.

To her right, she saw rough-looking men caring for many horses. To her left, some jongleurs were building a tower of people for a small crowd. She was following a makeshift road between tents, the grass mostly trodden away. It passed between stalls selling food and drink, and others offering everything from ribbons to blades, and scantily dressed women offering something else entirely. Some of the stall keepers called out to her to buy, but most of the men and women just stared at her. She realized there was no one else like her here, no other finely dressed women walking by themselves. Everywhere she saw just men, hard-bitten women and whores.

Where was the raven?

Was this truly the way she should go?

A rag-swathed child ran forward to clutch her gown, whining for alms. Others appeared out of nowhere, begging, whining, plucking at her skirts. Gledys pitied them, but shrank from them, too. It was as if they'd pull the clothing off her. A woman came out of a tent that was only rags over sticks and yelled at the children to stop, but her eyes were hard. She, too, would probably tear Gledys's clothes off if she thought she could get away with it.

Gledys hurried onward, but her resolve was even stronger now. Those poor wretches must be here for what work and scraps they could scavenge, and yes, probably for what they could steal. But some of them would have been honest folk before the endless strife ruined their crops, killed their menfolk and drove them from their homes.

This was why she had been brought here—not for her personal desires, but to bring peace. To stop Eustace of Boulogne from inflicting war on another generation. She stood taller and walked firmly—but she wished she didn't have to walk this gauntlet of men.

They were drinking at ale stalls, polishing metal, or working with leather or cloth. Innocent enough, but the mass of them almost choked her, as she had hardly ever before been in the presence of men at all. The air stank of smoke, old sweat and roasting meat, but of something else as well, as if the men's cruel mouths and lustful eyes gave off a stink of their own. They didn't move to bother her, but their eyes were hungry as wolves.

Gledys quickened her pace, anxious to be free of the camp, to at least reach the thatched roofs of the village.

"My lady?"

She ignored the voice.

"My lady Gledys?"

She slid only her eyes to the left first, afraid to hope, but then relief and joy flooded through her. Michael de Loury stood staring at her, as if not sure that he could trust his eyes. Laughing, crying, Gledys ran into her knight's arms, and finally, at long last, he was completely real.

In clear daylight she saw that his eyes were very blue, his thick hair a deep honey color and everything about his face perfectly formed, even if he did have a bruise on his cheek. She wanted to soothe it with her fingers. Or her lips.

She'd have to stretch on tiptoe. . . .

Before she could, he moved her gently away from him, and there might even have been a blush on his face as his gaze flicked around. Gledys looked, too, and her cheeks heated at the grins, sly smiles and occasional frowns of disapproval. She couldn't stop smiling, however. She remembered last night, thinking it was as if they came together after being too long apart. That feeling was stronger now, for she was certain this was real.

From the look in his eyes, he felt the same.

"Let me take you somewhere safe," he said. "Though where . . ."

Gledys smiled even more at his confusion. "With you, I'm safe anywhere."

His smile mirrored hers. He began to draw her back into his arms, but then shook himself. "No. Not here. I share a room in a house. It's rough, but so is everything." He frowned. "You shouldn't be here."

Their fingers were twined now and she tightened hers. "Yes, I should. But we do need a place where we can talk. A private place."

He grimaced. "Privacy! But my lodging is probably quiet now. Come." He led her on toward the village, but his brow was furrowed. "Have you been here all along? Do you lodge at the castle?"

"No. I'll explain soon. But . . ." She couldn't keep silent about one thing. "Last night . . . Did you have the same dream as I?"

His eyes searched hers. "It was a dream?"

"I've only just arrived."

He shook his head in confusion. "That can't be. I . . . We . . ."

"It was a dream," she repeated.

"But what about the ale tent? I was most certainly awake there." They'd reached the first houses.

"I'm not lying," Gledys protested. "On my soul, I'm not. I was traveling then. I went into a trance. Later, I was asleep in a house in the woods. I don't understand how it happens, but it is so."

He looked at her intently. "How long has this been happening to you?"

"I've had strange dreams for years, but the ones of you, since winter." They were in the village center now, where shops stood open on the ground floor of every house. "I had the first not long before we heard that Henry of Anjou had arrived in England and taken Malmesbury. Were you fighting there?"

"Yes. You had a vision of me there?"

Aware of people so close on either side, Gledys answered quietly. "I don't remember. Until recently I have seen you only in my sleep. As is usual with dreams, when I awoke, I remembered only fragments. But recently, I've been able to remember." She looked up into his eyes. "Like last night. A precious gift."

"Yes," he said, but his eyes were full of troubled questions. "Here we are," he said, turning to the open door of a narrow house. "It's a simple place," he warned again.

"I've lived a very simple life."

He raised a brow, glancing over her fine clothes.

"Truly, Michael de Loury. I speak nothing but the truth, odd though some of it sounds."

He raised her hand and kissed it. "You are my true-love bride; thus it must be so."

He had to duck beneath the lintel of the door and, once he was inside, his head was only just safe from the raftered ceiling. They entered one long room with a loom at the far end in front of a window. A man worked there, assisted by two young children, the loom clacking with a steady beat. Nearer to Gledys, a thin woman chopped vegetables for a pot.

The weaver's wife exchanged a greeting with Michael, but her eyes narrowed at Gledys.

"My betrothed, Dame Agnes, come with news. We'll do nothing wrong."

"See you don't," the woman said, "and take care of her. Folly to come to such a place, and she so young and pretty."

Gledys couldn't help but smile with pleasure at that description as Michael directed her up narrow stairs into the room she remembered. She saw the same rough mattresses and the same scattering of bags and bundles along with bits of leather and metal she hadn't noticed last night.

Last night.

The ceiling sloped, and he could stand only in the middle, so she went directly to his bed and sat down. He stood for a moment, considering her, but then he smiled with wide delight. "My true-love bride, and as lovely as I've always thought."

Gledys blushed. "Am I?"

"You must know it."

"No."

"Men haven't constantly told you?"

"No."

He laughed. "Where have you been? In a nunnery?"

Gledys's cheeks went from warm to hot, but she couldn't lie. "Yes."

He came to sit beside her, but left space between them. "You're a nun?"

"I've been in a nunnery all my life."

"But then we cannot wed," he said in dismay.

She grasped his hand. "Yes, we can. The vows I've taken thus far are not irrevocable. Those, I would take at twenty-five."

For some reason, he breathed, "Twenty-five."

Gledys asked a question that had been puzzling her. "You aren't a warrior monk, are you? Like a Templar?"

He laughed. "Why think that?"

"I was told that you'd be a monk."

"Ah. I was in a monastery for a while, but when I was a mere lad."

"Did you run away?" she asked.

"No. I was allowed to leave. My father had never approved of it. It had been my mother's desire."

She nodded. "Because you're a seventh child."

"No." But he frowned. "I thought I was the eighth. I had a twin. But now I wonder. What does that mean—the seventh child?"

Gledys took his hand. "That you, like me, are summoned to a great purpose."

"Ah," he said, as if things suddenly made sense. "Explain."

This was the moment, but Gledys didn't know how to put it. "I'll start with Sister Wenna, though that feels like the last chapter of a saga. . . ."

He listened intently, sometimes frowning or raising a brow in disbelief, but unreadable.

"We're supposed to find the holy chalice of the Last Supper?" he said at last. "And Eustace of Boulogne has the holy lance?" Gledys feared he was doubting her entirely, but he added, "If it was stolen from the Templars, that would explain why they've been prowling around like angry lions. Your story would also explain other things, including my mother's strange demands when I left the monastery."

"What demands?"

"That I not leave England before the age of twenty-five. And that I not . . . enjoy a woman until I find my destined bride. As compensation, she promised I would not die before I consummated my love."

Their eyes had locked. "With me." Against all likelihood, he was still pure. They could summon the sacred chalice. But then she gasped. "Once we do, you lose your invulnerability? But then—"

He put his fingers over her lips. "Death would not be too high a price, but I doubt it will come to that. At least, not right away," he added with a smile. Then he leaned down to put a gentle kiss on her lips, but he quickly drew back. "No more than that, yet. You tempt me too much. So we are honor-bound to marry quickly? I have no complaint about that."

Gledys felt her cheeks heat. "The other matter is urgent. We must go immediately to a sacred place."

"What place?"

"I think Glastonbury, but I'm not sure. We will follow a raven."

"A raven?" he repeated, brows shooting up.

"I think so. It's disappeared." At his expression, she grimaced. She couldn't make this sound reasonable. "It's real. It guided me here, but then disappeared."

"Not surprising. They're seen as birds of ill omen, predicting a man's death in battle. One would be killed on sight here, especially with a full battle more likely by the day."

"Why? There hasn't been one for a long time, has there?"

"Because Prince Eustace wants one, and from what you say of the lance, he'll be able to make it happen, even though no one wants such carnage. We almost came to battle in the winter. Duke Henry held Wallingford and King Stephen marched there in full force. Henry drew up his defenses. But then a wild storm blew up, lashing the king's forces with ice and making it impossible to see a spear's throw away.

"That gave the Earl of Arundel and the Templars the opportunity to argue for peace. They swayed the barons as much as the king, and soon King Stephen realized that his supporters were tired of this pointless struggle. It seemed done with at last, but here we are again."

"Because of the lance," Gledys said. "I wonder about that storm. Sister Wenna said that people of our bloodline have been working for peace without summoning the chalice. Perhaps the Earl of Arundel is one."

"And the Templars. They're said to have special knowledge from their protection of Christ's tomb in Jerusalem."

"But none of them can do what we can do." She tugged his hand. "Come, we should start out now."

But he resisted. "Now? This needs thinking on. It is all hard to believe."

"Didn't you hear me? I saw blood in a chalice, and then it became a rose petal. An impossible rose petal. I was led out of my nunnery and no one stopped me. I didn't try to hide. They simply didn't see me. I was guided to a place of rest, warmed by a miraculous fire, and provided with these clothes. And then I found you. These are all miracles." When he still looked dubious, she demanded, "Where are we?"

"Nottinghamshire."

"Wherever that is, I'm sure it's a long way from Glastonbury, and yet here I am, after one short night."

He opened his mouth and shut it again.

"Or do you think I'm lying?"

"Not lying, no. But . . . confused?"

"Insane?" Gledys had great sympathy for Sister Wenna. Suddenly, she saw something hanging on a chain around his neck. "What is that you wear?"

He reached up to pull it free. "This? A ring my mother gave me. I wear it sometimes on my little finger, but not when fighting."

Gledys extended her right hand, showing a similar ring.

He stared at it. "She said it was for my bride," he whispered, freeing the ring from the chain. "But why, if you already have one?"

Gledys slid hers from her finger and put them both in the palm of her hand. She had no doubt. She put them together, and with a click they became one, the coiling silver now making a perfect pattern, the join invisible.

"See?" she said, looking at him. "Michael de Loury, you must join me to summon the garalarl. Now."

He seemed dazed, but she thought he would do it. Then, somewhere in the distance, trumpets sounded.

"Jesu, the time!" He stood and cracked his head on the sloping ceiling. Muttering, he stepped into the middle, rubbing his head.

Gledys scrambled to her feet and grabbed his sleeve. "We have to go now."

"Gledys, sweetheart, that's impossible. I can't just leave."

"I wasn't supposed to leave Rosewell Nunnery."

"But you didn't want to be there. This is my life."

"You are *summoned*."

"Yes, to the tourney. Gledys, to leave without permission could be seen as treason."

She released his sleeve, grimacing in frustration. "Why is there no guidance anymore? Sister Wenna seemed sure that this was urgent. That if Eustace wasn't stopped now, England would be at war for another generation. But she implied this wouldn't require our deaths."

"And it won't." Harried, he said, "I don't want to leave you alone here, love, but I have to go."

She took his hands and smiled. "Go, then. I've been led this far in safety. Fight in your tourney, and we'll leave tonight."

He shook his head. "Impossible. I will still need permission. And supplies . . . I have to go. We'll talk later, but it'll be much later. There'll be a victory to celebrate." He kissed her quickly. "Stay here. It's not safe to wander."

She heard him run down the stairs—or perhaps he jumped down most of them—and then speak to the people below. A little later, the weaver's wife called up, "Do you need anything, Lady Gledys?"

"No, thank you," Gledys called back, and collapsed on his bed. She touched the rumpled covers, remembering the night, but perplexed. She didn't have Sister Wenna's confidence to command, "Go, go." No raven called. No path glimmered.

She'd found her protector, but how was she to persuade him to their task?

Chapter 7

Michael hurried to the shed where Rannulf and Alain lived with the horses and weapons. He was still stunned by the appearance of his bride, the lovely maiden of his dreams, but perplexed by her story. It made no sense, especially now that he was out in the rough and raucous real world. But her story seemed to explain his mother's strange demands, and perhaps his mother had concealed that he was her seventh child.

Then there was the fact that she'd insisted he go into the church. She'd been a practical woman with all her other children—ten born, six growing to adulthood. A good woman, but not excessively pious. Not the sort to insist on at least one son and daughter giving their lives to God, and yet that was what she had done.

"What's the matter with you? Not drunk, are you?"

Michael blinked and realized he was in the shed and both

Rannulf and Alain were staring at him. Perhaps they'd been talking to him.

"No," he said quickly. "Just thinking."

"Well, think about the fighting," said Rannulf, and began to spew information about the men in the duke's party and de Bohun's, and anything else he'd learned that might affect the fighting. Michael paid attention. It seemed the time of concealing his abilities was over, for he needed to make sure the duke's side won.

The favor of Henry of Anjou, future monarch, might persuade Gledys's family to overlook his lack of land. More urgent, if she persuaded him to leave the camp without permission, he might need the goodwill of Henry of Anjou to save his neck.

⁂

The afternoon crept by for Gledys, even though she tried to occupy it with prayer. She wasn't used to an idle life. She smelled cooking from below and then heard voices as people gathered, presumably to eat. Chatter and laughter followed. And then suddenly, a man burst into the room. He was young, tall, gnawing on a crust of bread, and he stopped to gape at her.

Gledys had to say something. "I'm Michael de Loury's betrothed."

The man grinned. "Lucky de Loury! If he gets killed in the tourney, I'm at your service, lovely lady."

He was gone before Gledys could shout her affront at that, but then she had to smile. It was still a new delight to be found pretty. Lovely, even. She wanted to be lovely for Michael.

The weaver's wife came up bearing a bowl of stew, some bread and some fruit. Gledys took the tray and thanked her, but she only picked at the food. Her appetite had gone.

She was aware of the street getting quieter, and she went to the small window to look out. Yes, there were fewer people. She supposed all who could had gone to watch the duke fight. *Just a tournament*, she told herself. *No one's supposed to get killed.*

She remembered the prophecy and found more reassurance there. Michael could not die as long as he remained a virgin.

Then she heard it: the awful sounds of battle, howling from men and beasts, clangs and bangs of blows and damage. She covered her ears, but couldn't leave the window, as if her being there might keep him safe.

Craak!

Gledys jerked and searched. There, on the opposite roof, perched the raven. "You'd best be careful," she hissed. "If anyone sees you, they'll kill you."

It stepped from side to side as if anxious and didn't call again.

"What?" she asked. "What am I supposed to do now?"

The bird moved away, stepping along the roof, but still looking at her.

"Follow? I'm not supposed to leave here."

It opened its beak, but didn't make a noise. All the same, she knew it was a silent command.

"Where am I supposed to go? I've found my protector."

It came into her mind, a clear and dreadful message. She moaned. She'd obeyed and obeyed, but this was the most terrifying task of all.

"I can't *do* this," she protested, but she turned, knees shaking, to put on her veil and go down the difficult stairs.

At the bottom, the weaver's wife frowned at her. "Are you going out, lady? It's not safe out there for the likes of you."

"It seems quieter."

"Aye, many are watching the fighting, but there's still enough around to make trouble."

"I'll be safe," Gledys assured her, certain that the garalarl could ensure that, at least. In any case, idle men around the town were no threat at all compared to what she faced.

She went out into the street, looking around for her guide.

Gone again.

Exhaling with relief, she turned back toward the house, but a flutter of black wings caught her eye. The raven was on a roof down the street, hopping from foot to foot nervously, but clearly indicating the way she must go.

She obeyed, surprised not to be taken to the castle. Instead, the raven led her toward the camp, fluttering sneakily from place to place, trying to avoid being seen. She supposed the bird risked as much as or more than she did. Then the raven took to the air, swooping around and around a large tent gay with pennants before flying away.

How could it abandon her? And yet already men were pointing at it and exclaiming. An arrow streaked upward, seeking to kill. It missed, thank heavens, but Gledys saw the risk the raven had taken. Could she do less than a bird?

She turned toward the tent, seeing a man on guard, eyeing her curiously.

"Whose tent is this?" she asked.

"Why are you here if you don't know?" he asked, playing with her.

"Is it a secret?"

After a moment, he shrugged. "Duke Henry's."

That was what she'd feared. That was what she'd known. She made herself stroll closer. "He's still at the fighting, I assume."

"Probably in the baths by now. Can't you hear that it's over?"

Gledys realized the din had stopped. The sun was setting, too. It was later than she'd thought.

"My lord duke will have won, of course," the guard said proudly.

Gledys swallowed to moisten her throat and forced out the words she knew she must say. "Then he will want to speak to me. May I wait inside?"

The man stared, but then he slapped his thigh and laughed. "You're a bold one, and no mistake. But why not? You're pretty enough to interest him."

He pulled back the flap of a door and called a name. An older man appeared.

"This one wants to wait for him. No harm in it, but make sure she gets up to no mischief."

The older man looked at her sourly, but he gestured, and Gledys had no choice but to enter the gloom of the tent, feeling as if she entered a lion's den. Silently she wailed, *I really don't want to do this.*

"Sit there," the man said, moving a bench into an open space. "Stay there, and don't touch anything."

Gledys sat, her empty stomach churning, but she was curious enough to look around. This part of the tent held a table with benches and one chair. There were other benches and stools and some chests. The man began putting out goblets and platters, and somewhere nearby she smelled roasting meat. A flap in one side was open to let in air and some light, but still it was dim and stuffy here, and she felt as if she struggled for air.

The man suddenly spoke. "What are you doing here, girl? He'll only use you for the night and leave you with a trinket, and you don't look the type."

"I'm not," Gledys said thinly. "I simply need to speak to him."

He shook his head. "There's still time to go home, wherever that is."

Gledys sighed. "No, I don't think there is."

As if predicted by her words, a small party burst in, a group of men surrounding a stocky, laughing man—who sobered at sight of her, his eyes narrowing dangerously.

Into the silence, someone said, "Gledys?"

Her eyes went to the taller figure. She rose to her feet.

Michael stepped forward. "Lord, I don't know why she's here, but—"

A raised hand stopped him. "Let her speak for herself."

Henry of Anjou was not a handsome man, but his energy and power filled the tent, making her shiver.

She fell to her knees. "Forgive me, lord, but I must speak with you."

"And who are you?"

Gledys wanted to say, *Gledys of Rosewell,* but that didn't seem wise.

"Lady Gledys of Buckford, my lord," she whispered.

"Buckford? The de Brescars?" He almost spat it. "They hold fast to Stephen." With that, Henry turned angrily to Michael. "You know her?"

Gledys looked up to see Michael frowning at her. She realized that she'd never given him that name.

But he said, "She's my promised bride, my lord."

"And your family is loyal." The duke looked between them, and then he shrugged. "A mystery, and a pretty one. Eat, drink and we'll explore it."

He threw himself into the chair and the other men took the benches. Servants hurried to serve them. Michael, however, came to stand by Gledys's side. She supposed he was supporting her, but she could feel exasperation coming off him like steam.

Why was she forced to these things? Was this how it went with martyrs? Did they not go to their fate with resolute intent, but instead were carried to fire or gallows with no power to resist, quaking all the way?

The duke washed down some meat with wine. "I spoke with your father not a week ago, de Loury, and he didn't mention this. So she's your leman. No shame in that."

Gledys could hear Michael breathing, but he answered steadily. "No, lord. She is a virtuous maid who will soon be my bride. My father doesn't yet know."

The duke laughed. "Then I'm glad I'm not you. But what's she doing here? In the camp? In my tent?"

Gledys was feeling truly sick. The power of the duke was a physical thing, like a dreadful storm, making her want to melt away into nothingness to escape. She couldn't imagine how the men around him bore it, how Michael could speak so firmly. Her mouth was dry, her heart pounding so hard she felt it should be audible, and she wasn't sure she had breath, but she knew what she had to say.

"I came to the camp, my lord, to find Michael. I came to your tent because I have a message for you."

"For me?" the duke asked sharply. "From your family?"

"No, my lord." She swallowed. "May I be private with you, my lord?"

After a moment of dead silence, Henry of Anjou burst out laughing. "De Loury, you should beat her!"

"No, no!" Gledys gasped, horrified. "I mean with you and Michael, my lord."

"Even worse," said the duke, and the men around him guffawed.

"Gledys, be quiet," Michael said from his throat. "You're making a scandal of yourself." He put a hand under her arm to raise her. "Come away."

"No," said the duke sharply. "I want to know what this is about. Come."

He rose and swept through a curtain into another section of the tent. Gledys was hauled to her feet and pushed after him as gleeful speculation started up behind them. The small chamber contained a bed, some chests and a chair in which the duke sat.

"Well?" he asked quietly, eyes cold on her. "Whose messenger are you, Gledys of Buckford?"

Gledys swayed on her feet, but the words came anyway, thinly but audibly. "I am sent to offer peace."

"Gledys—"

Again a hand silenced Michael. "From Stephen of Blois?" Duke Henry asked in a flat voice.

"No, my lord." Without hope, she said, "From a sacred vessel called the garalarl."

The duke grimaced and drank from his cup. "De Loury, what's she talking about?"

Gledys expected Michael to apologize, even to claim she was mad, but after a moment he said, "Lord, she believes she has a mission to find the holy chalice, the one used at the Last Supper, which will then bring peace to England."

Gledys looked up at him, astonished. Did he believe?

She flicked a glance at the duke. Instead of anger or incredulity, he looked thoughtful. "Why you?" he asked.

A strange question.

"I . . . I don't know," she said, voice trembling. "I am a seventh child, and that is important. . . . Truly, my lord duke, I don't want to be here doing this."

"No, I don't suppose you do. And you, de Loury. What part have you in this?"

"I am also a seventh, and apparently her protector. My lord, this is new to me, too, but"—he paused in thought—"if there's any truth in it, I cannot turn away. England does need peace."

"This struggle is not of my making," Henry said fiercely. "The barons of England swore my mother would reign, and I will hold them to it. There will be peace only when she has her rights, through me."

"You have the right of it, my lord," Michael agreed in a level voice.

"And I don't need miracles to achieve it. Stephen's always been weak, and now he's old and tired. This spurt of activity will fade and he'll capitulate."

Michael spoke again. "She says that Eustace has the holy lance, and that has caused the new resolve."

Gledys expected that to mystify, but Henry's face set in grim lines, too grim for a young man. His eyes turned on her. "How?" he demanded.

Gledys blinked. He believed?

"I don't know, my lord. There is an evil force. . . ."

"Eustace!" he spat, surging out of his chair to pace the small area. "I had word of this from the Templars in the spring, that the lance had been stolen, that it could reinflame the war. I thought it nonsense, but then Stephen almost became a new man, and Eustace burst beyond all restraint. He is ravaging the lands of the abbey of Saint Edmundsbury."

Gledys heard Michael suck in a breath. She knew that name. It was a place, like Rosewell, designed for sevenths. Was that where he'd been sent? And did Prince Eustace have some reason for harrying it other than greed? Was he seeking possible protectors to destroy?

They had to summon the chalice immediately.

The duke turned to her again. "The Templars said that if they couldn't retrieve the lance, the only defense is the holy chalice." He glared into her face. *"So where is it?"*

She leaned away, close to fainting. "I don't know, my lord!" She gasped. "But if Michael and I go in search of it, we will—"

"Go in search?" he raged. "People have been searching for that cup for centuries, and none have found it yet. I don't have centuries!"

"That's not true!" Gledys was surprised by the strength of her own voice. She gulped. "Your pardon, my lord. But I'm told it has been found at least once. When King Henry came to the throne and his brother gave up the struggle to take it from him."

She expected that to please him, but his eyes sparked with new fury. "*What?* Do you know what happened then? Henry Beauclerc seized the throne. His brother, the Duke of Normandy, invaded, but failed. The holder of the crown kept it, and the Duke of Normandy came to grief. Stephen of Blois holds the throne," he snarled at her, "and *I am the Duke of Normandy!* I'll allow no meddling that leads to the same conclusion."

In the face of his fury, Gledys's throat had tightened so much she couldn't have said anything, even if words had come to her. It was Michael who spoke, in that same calm way. She didn't know how he managed it.

"By your grace, my lord, at that time the right king was chosen. King Henry was a strong monarch who brought order to this land. Surely the holy cup would favor the same again. Not Stephen. And never Eustace of Boulogne."

After a seething moment, Henry relaxed a little and sipped from his cup. It was as if cool air suddenly flowed into the small room and Gledys could breathe again.

"True, true." But Gledys could tell he was still calculating. He was not a man who trusted his fate to others. Not even to sacred mysteries.

He paced again.

"I know something of this," he said suddenly. "From my mother.

She had it from her father, that same King Henry. He was born in England and proud of it. He studied some of the ancient traditions. The holy chalice is hidden in Glastonbury, yes?"

Gledys found a thread of a voice. "I am told the cup dwells in no one place, my lord. That there are many places where it can appear. But Glastonbury Tor is the most important. Joseph of Arimathea—"

"Yes, yes," he said, waving a hand impatiently. "But if there are other places, how do you know where to look?"

Gledys thought of mentioning ravens and lights but her courage failed her. "I will just know, my lord. Once we set out."

The duke seemed almost to growl, but then he said, "You have leave to go, de Loury. To go on this mission. Find this holy cup and bring it back to me."

Gledys's jaw dropped and thoughts of King Herod flashed through her mind. He'd commanded the magi to bring back news of the king they sought. They had wisely returned to their homelands by a route that avoided Herod, but what could she and Michael do? She was sure the chalice was not to be possessed.

"If we are allowed, my lord," Michael said smoothly. "I believe none of us is entirely free in this."

"I am," said the duke flatly, dangerous again. "Very well. Bring me peace. But peace in my favor, or you and yours will suffer for it. Go, go, get on with it!"

Michael put his arm around Gledys and escorted her through the outer chamber of the tent, past curious eyes, and into the fresh air. She sagged against him then, her legs losing all strength.

He gathered her into his arms and carried her back toward the village, saying, "Lord, save us all."

"Amen," said Gledys, sucking in breaths. "I do not like any of this. It's too hard."

"Not even being in my arms?"

She stared up at him. "How can you tease?"

He smiled at her. "Why not? We have leave to attempt this mission, which may bring peace. But if I understand the matter right, whatever the end result, we will soon lie together, my lovely Gledys. And that is cause for smiling."

Heat swept through Gledys in a wave, but she said, "I wish we could marry first."

"Love, I would marry you if we could, but we are commanded to be urgent, and indeed, I feel the need. It beats in the very ground beneath my feet like the drums of war themselves. And Eustace threatens Saint Edmundsbury. It wasn't the place for me, but I will not see it harmed."

He lowered her to her feet outside the weaver's house. "We can at least say our vows before witnesses."

He took her hand and led her into the house, where the weaver and his wife were sitting on a bench near the window, relaxing after a long day, sharing a cake. When Dame Agnes moved to stand, Michael waved her to stay seated. "Of your kindness, my friends, we would like you to witness our wedding vows."

"Nay," said the weaver. "You need grander folk than us, and a priest as well."

"We leave on a journey, and need to say them now. It can be done again later with more pomp." He turned to Gledys. "This need only be simple. I, Michael de Loury, take you as my wife, Gledys of Buckford, and will cleave to you all my days. I will love and honor you, and share all I have with you. This I vow."

Gledys swallowed tears and tried to repeat the same. "I, Gledys of Buckford, take you, Michael de Loury, as my husband. I will cleave to you all my days. I will love you and honor you, and share all I have with you. This I vow."

He took the ring she wore on her right hand and moved it to her left, kissing it when it was in place. "Thus it is done," he said, his eyes bright with pleasure, which gave Gledys a sudden qualm. She remembered Henry of Anjou's words, implying Michael's father's wrath.

"You may regret this," she whispered. "I have no money, no dowry or lands. . . ."

He kissed her into silence. "Nor have I. We are destined, Gledys of Buckford, and the rest doesn't matter. But we must go. Wait here while I fetch my horse."

He thanked the bemused couple and left. Gledys gave the weaver and his wife a faint smile and stood by the door, dazed by all that had happened, but feeling the urgency he'd mentioned. It did seem to thrum beneath her feet, as if monstrous armies marched to the tempo of evil drums.

Michael soon returned, riding and wearing a sword, but without chain mail or shield.

"Shouldn't you go armed?" she asked.

"My armor needs repair and I've decided to trust God. And perhaps even this grarl." He rode to a raised stone, which enabled her to mount behind him, a feat as alarming as anything she'd done this day. She wasn't at all comfortable, but with her arms around Michael, she felt completely safe.

"So," he said as they rode out through the camp, "I see no raven. Which way should we go?"

"All will soon become clear," she replied, praying it would be so.

"All will soon become very dark," he pointed out.

"You had such faith a little while ago. Why doubt now?"

"Before the duke, I made the decision to support you despite some doubts. Now, once again, I suspect we're both mad. But then, perhaps the duke is, too."

"It is extraordinary that he knows something of this."

"It's worrying. He wants the chalice, and he'd match it with the lance if he could."

Gledys knew he was right. "He won't get it, but when we summon it, we must be alert for the others."

"At least Eustace is far away in Suffolk."

Gledys thought of pointing out that distance didn't seem to obey the same laws in the garalarl's world, but it was something she didn't understand herself. He'd see.

They were soon free of even the outermost shelters, and following the track into the woods. As they approached, Gledys felt him rein the horse to a sudden stop. "What's that?" he asked.

Gledys leaned to look ahead, and smiled to see the warm glow. "Our path." A dark shape swooped overhead, making the horse toss its head. "And there's our guide. Follow the raven and the golden path, husband, and we will soon find peace."

He made a sound that was half snort, half groan, but he set the horse in the direction of the path. Gledys glanced back and noted how the glow faded as they passed. Would they be led to a resting place? She hoped not. It would be too hard now to lie together without consummating their vows, and they must not do that yet. She hoped they were being led to Glastonbury, especially to the tor. That old longing still ached in her, a deep, pulsing need.

They were in the woodland now but, as before, following a path that seemed to avoid low branches and anything that might snag their clothing in passing. Gledys rested against Michael's back, lulled by the swaying rhythm of the walking horse.

And dreamed . . .

She saw fighting again, and again from a distance. Thank God for that, for this time it was hellish, filled with blood and fire. And the scene was a monastery. Monks ran from armed men. Soldiers grabbed food, wine and coffers. Some threw books onto fires. And in the center, a demonic figure howled with glee, shaking aloft an ancient wooden lance in his mailed fist.

He must be Eustace of Boulogne, despoiling the abbey of Saint Edmundsbury, perhaps seeking to kill Michael and all like him. If he wasn't stopped, Rosewell would be next. Gledys wanted to reach out, to snatch the lance from his grip and use it to kill him.

The scene faded and she saw a woman's hands holding an ancient vessel, more cooking pot than chalice, full of wondrous foods. Then it changed to a taller cup with handles, which brimmed over with golden wine. Then a horn cup of ale, and then a chalice, much like the one at Rosewell, but set with gleaming stones of red and green and blue and full of bloodred roses.

Again a woman cradled it, and on her left hand she wore a ring, the one Gledys now wore. Peace filled Gledys's mind, a peace of rose perfume and sweet music, of sunlight and flowing water.

"Where are we?" he asked.

Gledys opened her eyes and leaned to peer ahead of him. Her joy increased. They were emerging from the woods, and ahead, dark against the gray sky, she saw the great hill.

"That's the tor," she said. "Glastonbury Tor, where the chalice lies. Follow the path and the raven, husband. They will take us to where we need to be."

Chapter 8

The land wasn't flat on this approach, and they rode up and down, but always without hindrance or hazard. As the grade grew steeper, he halted his horse. "Time to walk," he said, swinging his leg over the front to dismount and then lifting her down.

Gledys was stiff and needed to cling for a moment. "How long have we traveled?" she asked.

"Some hours. I gather you slept."

"And dreamed. I saw Prince Eustace with the lance, despoiling the monastery."

"May he rot in hell."

"He will. And then I dreamed of the holy cup, of it washing all hatred and violence away. It is very beautiful."

He took her hand. "Then let us follow our path to it."

"Wait a moment." Gledys freed her hand in order to hitch her skirt higher into her belt, and then took off the silly veil and tucked that over the belt. "That's better."

He laughed and then they followed the glimmering path.

The climb wasn't as steep as she feared, for the glowing path seemed to lead around the hill rather than straight up it. Then it turned back, not to go downward again, but to circle upward in a different direction.

"Strange," he said, halting. "Better to go straight up."

"No," Gledys said, smiling. "I think it's a labyrinth."

"A labyrinth? We have no time for that."

She took his hand. "Follow the golden path, husband."

Now she recognized the pattern, and the spiraling walk raised Gledys's thoughts to God. She was so lost in the physical prayer that she was startled when he stopped her.

"The path's gone," he said.

"Here? We're not at the top."

"You said we should go where we are led." He turned to the right and she saw what he saw—a glow in the very hillside.

Gledys blinked, but it didn't disappear. It looked almost like a window covered by a cloth that allowed a little light to escape. They walked hand in hand toward the light. As they were about to walk through it, however, Gledys stopped to look back.

"What's the matter?"

"I'm trying to see if anyone is following us."

He stared into the darkness, too, but said, "Impossible without the lighted path. Come."

They walked through the rectangle of light and into a sort of cave. It was large, the roof arching high above their heads, and filled with light that seemed to come from the walls themselves. She trembled in awareness of something powerful and old, transcendent, and at the same time dangerous.

There was nothing in the cave except a stone plinth—a rectangular pillar of stone that stood as high as Gledys's chest and looked as if it should hold a statue. She went to it and found it warm, as stone could never be unless it sat by a fire. She traced strange designs intertwined like endless, complex labyrinths, and then saw leaves in the design, and even faces.

She turned to Michael. "Do you hear something?"

"No. Or . . . yes. What is it?"

"I don't know." She cocked her head. "It's as if the hill is singing."

The harmony vibrated in her bones, but in the sweetest way. "Yes," she said, "this is the antithesis of war." She turned and held her hands out to him. "I believe this is where we're supposed to finally come together, my husband."

He took her hands, but said, "I hoped for something softer than rock."

Gledys glanced behind him and smiled. "Will a bed do?"

He turned. "That wasn't there before."

"Or not quite." This looked like the bed she'd used last night. She went to confirm it, and yes, the mattress was stuffed with feathers and the blanket was of the same thick, soft wool. "In this realm distance and even time are different. People and things move in mysterious ways."

Michael touched the wool, too, but said, "Why am I troubled?"

"Because we're used to distance and time behaving as usual." She reached up to touch his hair, to stroke it. "And because we want this so much, so it could be the work of the devil. But it isn't. Satan is the agent of war, not peace." She pressed forward and leaned on his chest. "Lie with me, my husband, and we shall bring peace."

His arms came around her. "Willingly, but I doubt it will be entirely peaceful."

She looked up at him, already tingling with need. "I doubt that, too."

He unfastened her belt so it fell to the ground. She cradled his face and stretched up to kiss him. He stepped back to unbuckle his own belt, with its burden of pouch, knife and sword, but all the time he looked at her, cherishing her with his gaze. Gathering her courage, she raised her gown and took it off, so she stood in only her chemise. He was unfastening his low boots, so she did the same. Then she took off her stockings.

Even the rough ground seemed to have smoothed beneath her feet, and she felt no stone or grit as she walked to the bed, pulled back the covers, and sat on it.

He'd undressed except for his shirt, and he came to kneel before her. "I'd see you naked," he said huskily, with a depth of longing that made her laugh softly with delight as she shed her last covering, amazed to feel no trace of shame.

"I'd see you naked, too," she murmured, embarrassed a little by that bold request.

"Gladly, lady," he said, and took off his shirt before sitting beside her.

She hesitated for a moment, but then couldn't resist reaching out to hold his strong shoulders, catching her breath at the heat of him. It felt as if he alone could be responsible for the perfect warmth of this mysterious place.

He moved down onto the bed, bringing her with him, pulling the covers over them both, and it was as it had been in that dream encounter except that this was completely real and wonderful.

He stroked hair off her face. "I have no practiced skill to offer you in this, my bride."

"Nor have I, and I suspect you've a great deal more knowledge."

"It's a simple enough matter, I believe, and our bodies are made for it."

His calloused hand was running over her, down flank to thigh, up belly to—ah—breast. He cradled it in his hand as if weighing it, and stroked it as if learning every curve. He kissed her there, then gently sucked the peak, tonguing it.

She gasped, and her hands were on him, wherever she could reach, gripping and kneading hard-muscled flesh. Her womb ached for him deep inside.

He moved her thighs apart, edging over her, between her legs, supporting himself on one arm as he touched her below, exploring her, his features still and fascinated. What he was doing made her gasp at each new intense sensation. She raised her hips to him. He muttered something deep in his throat and settled against her. His hardness pushed at her. So strange, so alarming! So right. But still she tensed as he pushed forward, as pain jabbed her.

She knew of this. Even in the convent they knew a woman had a maidenhead that must be broken before a man could enter her and get her with child. A terrible pain, they were told, and nuns were fortunate never to suffer it.

The pain built. She would not scream; she would not scream.

Then, with a sharp burning, it was over and he was in her, filling her in a way that made her cry, "Yes!" She looked into his darkened eyes, smiling, she knew, with lips and eyes, with her whole body, if a whole body could smile. "My husband."

"My precious, beautiful wife."

He began to slide in and out of her, watching her with careful concern, but then his eyes closed and he lost himself in her, and she in him as they pounded together, heat building more heat as if to forge them, fuse them. Heart racing, breath gasping, Gledys gripped his hot flesh and sank teeth into his salty skin as they burst into flame, it seemed, and were consumed by pleasure surely beyond the ordinary mating of a man with a maid.

Spiraling down, they clung together, touching, kissing, laughing a little, exhausted but exhilarated until she came to rest, sprawled, tingling and sweaty, on his chest.

She could have stayed there like that for eternity, but he said softly, "Gledys . . ."

She looked up at him, and then turned.

On the plinth sat a glowing goblet—the one Gledys had seen in her vision, the one made of gold and set with precious stones, full of impossible, bloodred roses. She scrambled up off the bed, grabbing her chemise and putting it on, instinctively covering herself in the presence of the sacred. Then she reverently approached the holy chalice, the ancient garalarl.

He came up beside her, wearing his shirt and braies, and put a hand on her back. "That must have been the most pleasant holy duty ever devised, but what do we do now?"

"Perhaps that's enough," Gledys said.

"Oh, I don't think so."

She elbowed him. "To summon it. Now there will be peace."

"I think not."

The words came from behind and they both spun toward the entrance, where an intruder stood: a man in armor, sword in hand, evil in his pale eyes. Gledys would never have thought the devil could show so clearly in a person, but here surely stood an agent of Satan.

"Eustace." Michael spoke deep in his throat, like a growl.

This was King Stephen's son, whom she'd seen in a dream in an ecstasy of destruction? Her mind went blank with shock, but then she remembered: He was here for the chalice!

She stepped between the cup and evil, willing the chalice to disappear, to go back to its other dimension. But it stayed in view.

"Don't you know?" the prince said, smiling. "Once in this realm, it must stay until the wheel turns toward peace. And while here, it can be captured. I have waited for this moment, and now all is mine. I will unite the cup with the lance and the world will grovel at my feet."

Michael moved, and the man sneered. "No monk will stop me. I won't flinch from cross or holy water."

He took a step forward, confident that he faced impotent opposition, but Michael threw himself to the floor, rolling to avoid the suddenly swooping sword. He thrust back onto his feet at the man's back, a whine sounding as he freed his own sword of its scabbard just in time to block another deadly blow.

Gledys covered her mouth with her hand. Michael wore only light clothing against a fully armored man. He had no shield. And—had he forgotten?—he was no longer pure. He could be killed.

Blades clashed, striking sparks and nearly deafening her as the men twisted and turned. She felt a flicker of hope, for Michael was more agile without metal all over him. But then he landed a mighty blow on his opponent's leg, and the prince only staggered and grunted. A similar blow in return would take Michael's leg off.

"God on high, protect him," she began to pray. "Christ, guard him. Holy Spirit, inspire him. . . ."

The next sweep of Prince Eustace's sword whistled an inch above Michael's ducked head, and Michael's counterstrike was again foiled by armor. Both men were breathing hard, and Gledys remembered the fight she'd seen in her dream, which had been settled in the end by sheer exhaustion.

Seeking extra power for her prayers, Gledys grasped the chalice, feeling the potent song of it down through her bones. *Save him, save him, save him. . . .*

Light burst from the vessel, filling the cave.

A man cried out.

Half-blind, Gledys stared at tangled shapes, one bright, one dark, trying to make sense of them.

When her vision began to clear, the dark one was on the ground, and the warrior of light stood over him, sword raised to kill. He hesitated, however, and Prince Eustace taunted him.

"You can't kill the king's son. That's treason of the highest degree. They'll hunt you down and take you apart piece by piece. You and your whore, too."

Gledys saw Michael inhale and raise the sword higher, ready to drive it down.

Enraged at the foul man, she grasped the cup to her chest and cried, "Curse you, curse you, Eustace of Boulogne!"

The dark figure rolled his head back to stare at her, eyes wide with terror. He howled in a way she'd never imagined a human being could howl, writhing in unearthly agony. She watched in horror as a bloody glow revealed the fires of hell, and they swallowed him.

The cave floor became whole again, shutting off the fiery light, but a ruddy luminescence lingered in the garalarl cup Gledys still clutched. She stared at Michael, who stared back at her. Her heart was thundering in her chest, and she was shaking as if with a fever. Horrified sickness bit at the back of her throat.

Michael put his sword aside and came to her, taking the chalice out of her clutch and replacing it on its plinth. Then he gathered her into his strong arms and she shuddered against his chest. Slowly, eventually, they moved apart, looking into each other's wide eyes, then both turning to the place where Prince Eustace had lain. Gledys expected to see a stain, or even scorch marks, but the ground was unchanged.

"What happened?" she whispered.

In a flat voice, Michael said, "I hope he was sent straight to hell."

"But . . . what will happen if he's disappeared? What if anyone found out that we . . . that I did it?"

His lips quirked with a touch of wry humor. "According to Duke Henry, Eustace is in Suffolk. Whether we're known to be in Nottinghamshire or Somerset, we could not possibly harm him there."

Gledys shook her head at his light tone, but it was helping her settle down. She turned to look at the chalice again, to thank it, but she was only just in time to see the last ghostly shape of it fade, then disappear. The only sign that it had ever existed here was a solitary bloodred rose.

"But he said it couldn't leave until . . ."

". . . the wheel turned toward peace. Praise be to God, that must have happened."

"Because he is dead? Truly dead?"

Michael inhaled. "God is good." He looked around the cave. "Our bed has gone," he said regretfully, "but it's time for us to leave in any case."

He picked up his sword and examined it, grimacing as he rubbed his thumb over a chip in the blade. That mundane action made Gledys laugh. It was shaky, but it was a laugh.

"He thought you were a monk," she said.

"Stupid as well as vile."

"Perhaps the chalice guided you to leave your armor behind. It gave you the advantage of surprise."

He considered that. "Indeed, but I think the darker work this night belongs not to a chalice, but to the ancient garalarl. It may be the agent of peace, but it's also a bloody cup. Come. It's time to leave."

Gledys felt it, too: an urgency as the cave cooled and dimmed, as if they might be trapped here if they lingered. They dressed quickly and hurried to the exit, but there she paused.

The rose had been left for a reason, so she ran back and took it before fleeing into the normality of night.

They rode into the camp when the sun was high, and headed to Duke Henry's tent.

From Glastonbury, they'd been guided to the hut in the woods again, and the familiar bed. There they had found new pleasures in each other. After their breakfast of bread, cheese and ale, they'd left, but Gledys now had a bundle. She'd brought back her habit, for it held good memories. She also had the rose, tucked carefully in her pouch.

Henry of Anjou was outside among a group of men, their horses ready. He was clearly about to leave. When he saw them he halted and abruptly returned inside. They dismounted and followed.

The duke turned to face them. "Well?"

"We think it is so, my lord," said Michael, his manner calm, as he had been with Henry before. "The holy chalice appeared to us, and then it disappeared. It seems this means that the wheel has turned toward peace."

"Does it . . . does it? But you couldn't bring it back."

"We didn't try, my lord."

Henry of Anjou frowned.

Gledys opened her pouch and took out the rose. "But we brought you this, my lord. Evidence, perhaps, of miracles."

He took the flower. "Lovely, and I've never seen so deep a red, not even in Aquitaine, where roses grow particularly well. But I don't need evidence of this sort. I just received good news."

"An offer of a new truce, my lord?" Gledys asked.

He smiled, a wolfish grin. "Better than that. The certainty of peace and victory. Eustace of Boulogne is dead."

Gledys heard Michael gasp, too, and she prayed guilt didn't show on either of their faces.

"He died of an apoplexy in the night. God's judgment, people are saying, for his pillaging the abbey at Saint Edmundsbury." He raised the rose and inhaled. "What's more, I hear good news about his father's health. Stephen is failing. The holy chalice has made its wise choice." He gave the rose back to Gledys. "You have my thanks and my favor. When I am king, you will both get your just reward." He swept out and they heard his horse's hooves pounding away.

Gledys looked down at the rose, which showed no sign of wilting. "I feel sorry for the king, who has lost his son."

Michael drew her into his arms. "A better king, a better man, might not have bred such a son. Rejoice, my love, for now our children will have peace."

She looked up at him. "But we must make sure to have seven, just in case."

He grinned back at her. "A pleasant sort of holy duty." Sobering, he cradled her face. "The holy chalice brings not just peace but a deeply precious love. If the troubadours knew of this kind of love, they'd know their songs were shallow."

Gledys turned her head to kiss his thumb. "My love, my love . . . And we will have a good life. The cup rewards those who serve it well."

"It already has," he murmured, kissing her.

Neither noticed when the rose fell to the floor, nor when it faded and disappeared. But for a while, the sweet perfume lingered as the land of England began a new, harmonious song.

Author's Note

The sudden death of Prince Eustace did indeed signal the end of what is now known as the Anarchy. The death was a final blow to his father, who lost all will to fight, and he reaffirmed the peace treaty that named Henry of Anjou his successor. As he predicted in the story, Henry didn't have long to wait. Stephen died the next year and Henry added King of England to his many titles.

Henry II wasn't an easy man—he ended up warring with his wife and sons, and was responsible for the murder of Thomas à Becket—but he was a strong and efficient ruler. He swiftly restored the rule of law to his ravaged kingdom, and during his thirty-five-year reign he reformed the law, finances and administration of England.

You may have noticed that in this story, no one talks about the Holy Grail. At the time *grail* and *graal* were common terms for a cup, and they gained their mystical meaning only in the next century, as the stories were developed by poets and troubadours. However, the legends about the holy chalice, King Arthur, and Joseph of Arimathea were already old, especially around Glastonbury. There were also stories about even older mysteries connected to the tor, and those I have incorporated here.

There was an ancient church incorporated into Glastonbury Abbey, said by some to have been built by Christ, and the thorn tree still blooms there at Christmastide.

The term *garalarl* is my invention. I wanted a pre-Christian concept, and I also wondered why the legends eventually adopted the terms *grail* and *graal* for the sacred chalice. It would make sense if they were adaptations from an already existing ancient term, and I play with that a little by having Michael mispronounce what Gledys says as *grarl*.

As Sister Wenna implies, each age will wrap its own beliefs around the true heart of the mystery. As you'll see in the following stories.

The White Rose of Scotland

BY

MARY JO PUTNEY

Chapter 1

J ane Macrae's heart was in the Highlands. Unfortunately, her weary body was on a crowded wartime train crawling its way north from Edinburgh. She woke from a restless, unsatisfying doze to find that the young soldier snoring next to her had a hand resting on her thigh. It was the most fun she'd had in months.

She removed his hand, grateful that she had chosen to look "fast" by wearing trousers. These last horrible months in London during the Blitz had made her a dedicated trouser wearer. So much more convenient when running to an air raid shelter or pulling survivors from collapsed buildings, as she'd done twice.

Jane was good at finding people in the rubble. If she tired of working for military intelligence, perhaps she'd join one of the rescue services.

She glanced at the window, wishing she could see the Scottish hills beyond. Railway blackout regulations required blinds over windows and painting all the lightbulbs blue. The effect was eerie, to say the least. But soon she'd be home.

Closing her eyes again, she tried to find a more comfortable spot on a deeply uncomfortable seat. She was one of the few civilians on the poky train. Most of the passengers were soldiers, sailors and airmen heading north to serve at some of Scotland's many military installations. The young, earnest and doomed. Damn Hitler!

Jane's work had kept her in London for these last crazy months. On the whole, she'd coped reasonably well with the constant threat of German bombing. But two days before, she'd been hit by a fierce need to head home to Scotland. The pure, calm energy of her family estate at Dunrath would clear her mind.

Macraes had lived at Dunrath since before the family was called Macrae. The glen had been a grand place to grow up, and not only because it had the best weather in Scotland. As the youngest of a large family, she'd been teased and indulged and taught. Those had been golden days between the wars, though she'd been too young to fully appreciate them. Such times were gone forever. But the peace of Dunrath endured, and it was calling her home.

Though the distance between Edinburgh and Dunrath wasn't that great, the train was a slow one that halted at every tiny station in the empty hills. She kept track of them, since name signboards had been removed from most stations. It would be easy to get off in the wrong place.

Her compartment cleared out two stops before hers, since that station was a transfer point. Already the peace was getting into her bones and unwinding her tension and grief. She yawned. Only an hour or so more . . .

Jane woke when the train lurched to a halt at the next station. This was remote moorland, with only a sprinkling of crofts and villages. She was settling down again when the door to her compartment opened and a wild-eyed lunatic surged onto the train.

Not a lunatic—a pilot. She would have known that even if the stranger weren't wearing a leather flying jacket like hers. Near thirty, she guessed. He was tall and tawny and fit, with a pilot's quickness and the confidence that could seem arrogant.

But what caught Jane's attention and brought her sharply awake was his aura. Magic blazed around him like a city in flames.

The pilot's fevered gaze swept the compartment and locked onto Jane. Two steps brought him to her seat. "You must come with me *now!*" he said in a North American accent as he loomed over her. "It's . . . it's life and death."

She stiffened. A wise woman didn't go off with a complete stranger, particularly one who rose half-crazed. Though her Guardian powers meant she had little to fear from the average man, this man wasn't average.

But Guardians were sworn to serve, and the pilot was in need. As Jane hesitated, a flash of intuition told her that this madman was the reason she'd felt such a compulsion to return to Scotland.

"*Please!*" he said tautly. "Before the train leaves!"

Making a swift decision, Jane said, "Lead on." She rose, swept her rucksack onto her shoulder and followed the pilot into the night.

This late, no one was on duty at the tiny station. Nor were there lights or identification signs. But the familiar shapes of the hills told her she was at Glenberrie, the station before Dunrath. She knew the place well.

Jane almost fell as she stepped onto the platform in the dark. A hard male hand caught her arm. Power flared between her and the pilot with lightning ferocity. She felt seared . . . and, in some strange, unfathomable way, bound to him.

As the train rumbled into motion, rattling the platform, Jane jerked her arm away, breaking the unwelcome connection. "What *are* you? And what the devil do you want?"

The fitful moonlight revealed the pilot's face. He was as stunned as she. "I . . . I don't know." He rubbed his temple, his expression baffled. "I just knew that I had to find someone, and that someone turned out to be you."

Frowning, Jane studied him with mage vision. The hot reds of his aura had turned spiky and uncontrolled. She guessed he was unused to being a focus of magic, and didn't know how to handle it. So where had the power come from? As it dimmed, she guessed that the pilot had exhausted his strength searching for her and was now near collapse.

Wondering what she'd gotten herself into, she said more calmly, "Tell me who you are and what has brought you here."

He swayed on his feet. "You'll think I'm barking mad."

"It takes a lot to surprise me." Even in the fitful moonlight, she could see that he was a handsome devil. She guessed that a naturally buoyant disposition had been tempered by war. "It's obvious you're a pilot. What is your name?"

"David Sinclair." The words dragged, as if saying his name was an effort.

"My name is Jane Macrae," she offered in return. "Your accent isn't British. American?"

"Canadian. From near Halifax." His voice eased a little as he mentioned his home. "You guessed right—I'm a fighter pilot with the RAF."

"So is one of my brothers," she said, feeling the familiar tightness around her heart at the knowledge of how dangerous a pilot's life was. "Squadron Leader Jamie Macrae. Do you know him?"

"You're Jamie Macrae's sister?" His eyes narrowed, as if he was looking for a resemblance in the dark. "I've met him a few times. His reputation is well-known."

"Jamie has been lucky so far." She prayed that would continue. Not like Philip.

"It isn't just luck. As pilots get more experience, we get a lot harder to shoot down," Sinclair said. "Did he give you the flying jacket?"

"No," she said shortly. "You look ready to crash and burn. Do you have a car?"

He produced a key from his pocket. "Morris Minor. Car park."

She took the key. "We need to find someplace quiet where we can talk and find out what is so urgent. And I need to feed you up, too."

"How did you know I'm *starving*?" he said with some surprise.

Because high-intensity magic burned energy like tinder in a bonfire. Going for a simpler explanation, she said only, "An educated guess."

"But there's no time to waste! We need to . . ." His voice faded into bafflement.

"Nothing will be accomplished until you're in better shape." She took his arm, forcing herself to control her vivid response to him. He leaned on her heavily as she led him to the steps at the end of the platform. At this hour, there was no one on duty in this isolated station. Rural Scotland closed down early, and there were no towns nearby.

The steps that led from the platform to the ground had a railing, so she was able to get Sinclair down without either of them falling. The Morris Minor sat in the car park in lonely, lumpy splendor, slewed at an angle that suggested Sinclair had been driving fast and probably recklessly.

He hadn't locked the doors, not that he needed to here. Jane opened the passenger door and handed him in. "Wait," he protested. "This isn't the driver's side. Not like at home."

"You're in no fit condition to drive." She closed the door and circled to the driver's seat. The fact that Sinclair didn't argue proved he was near collapse. In Jane's experience, only a half-dead pilot would allow anyone else behind the wheel of his car.

The Morris Minor was old and worn, but well maintained. As she pulled the choke, then turned the key in the ignition, she asked, "What is your rank? I'm guessing at least squadron leader, and perhaps wing commander."

"You're good," he muttered. "Wing commander. Where are we going?"

She considered taking him home to Dunrath, but it was too far. On the narrow, winding roads and driving at blackout speeds, they wouldn't get there until the next morning. Luckily, there was a good alternative. "My family owns a small croft near here. Macraes go there when in dire need of peace and quiet."

"Sounds good." He slumped into the seat—no small feat, given his height and the confined quarters of the Morris—and went to sleep. Finding her seemed to have relieved him of his frantic urgency, at least for now.

Jane pulled away from the station, driving cautiously. Blackout regulations required headlights to be covered except for three small slits, which gave barely enough light to travel. At the beginning of the blackout, only sidelights could be used, and there were masses of traffic accidents. Since British drivers had been inflicting more harm on Britons than the Nazis were, the regulations had been loosened a little.

She hadn't driven this route since before the war, and the narrow road required serious concentration even then. By the time she reached the small stone croft halfway up a mountain, she was almost as drained as her mad wing commander.

She parked and climbed out, then lifted the key from under a stone and unlocked the door. Inside, she checked that the blackout curtains were closed before lighting two lamps. She enhanced the flames with mage light, since she liked a bright room, then returned to the car.

Opening the passenger door, she said firmly, "Come along, Wing Commander. I'm not strong enough to carry you inside."

"Yes, ma'am." Sinclair swung his long legs out of the Morris and managed to stand, but he might not have made it farther without her help. The blasted man was heavy, and the next thing to unconscious.

The croft house consisted of a long sitting room with a kitchen at one end and a bedroom at the other. Jane had always loved the simplicity of the ancient building and the welcoming warmth of the old furniture and carpets. She hoped the house helped the pilot.

Jane guided Sinclair into a Windsor chair by the kitchen table.

He sat down and promptly crossed his arms on the table so he could rest his head on them.

She found herself tempted to brush her fingers through his fair, tangled hair. Turning away, she wondered where that impulse had come from.

After lighting the peat stove, she surveyed the small pantry. Macrae family policy was to keep the croft well supplied, and whoever had visited last hadn't failed her. What would restore the pilot's energy best? Ah, tins of beef stew.

She opened all three tins and poured the contents into a saucepan, then pumped water to fill the kettle and set it to heat. This was definitely an occasion that called for a bracing cup of tea.

While the stew and kettle heated on the stove, she foraged further and found crackers and a box of McVitie's chocolate digestive biscuits. A feast, under the circumstances.

When the stew was warm, she poured half of it into a shallow bowl and set it in front of the Canadian, along with crackers. "Eat," she ordered. "I'll make tea."

He fell on the stew as if he hadn't eaten in weeks. By the time she'd finished her own more modest portion, his bowl was empty, so she gave him the rest of the stew. As he finished it off, she poured two mugs of tea and set them out with honey and a plate of chocolate digestives. "Is your brain working yet?" she asked.

"Yes, thank you." His voice was much stronger now. "My mother would sneer at canned stew, but tonight, it's ambrosia."

"Sorry there's no sugar. Rationing. But honey is good." Jane had learned to like her tea unsweetened, so she took a deep, gratifying swallow before reaching for a digestive biscuit. "Tell me everything."

He stirred honey into his mug. "You'll think I'm nuts, Miss Macrae."

"My name is Jane, and you did not find me by accident," she said quietly. "Some great power compelled you to seek me out. Neither of us knows why yet, but we will. Describe what happened, and don't censor yourself because you think I won't believe you. The world is far more complicated than most people realize."

"So I'm finding out." He pondered, as if unsure where to start. "I don't suppose you read science fiction?"

Jane chuckled. "Actually, I do. Jamie loves it, and I was always borrowing his magazines with those wonderfully vulgar covers." She sighed wistfully. "He wanted to fly to the moon. Instead he's flying after Messerschmitts."

"Then maybe you'll understand when I say this day has been like science fiction." Sinclair frowned. "I guess it started when I got two weeks' leave. First time off I've had since before the fighting got bad last summer. I hadn't seen much of Britain, so I decided to visit Scotland to see what my ancestors left behind."

"Since you're a Sinclair, are you related to the Earls of Caithness?"

"Maybe, though it would be a long way back. My branch of the Sinclairs sailed to Canada a couple of hundred years ago." He took a biscuit and demolished it in two bites. "I knew most of the clan territory is way north, but there's a Sinclair castle near Edinburgh, and this morning I decided on impulse to take a day trip there to see it."

"Roslin Castle?"

He nodded. "I couldn't go in the inhabited section, of course, but I poked around the old ruins, which were pretty interesting. Then I decided to look at the chapel. As I was going inside . . ." He hesitated.

"This is where the science-fictiony stuff starts. I felt something like a . . . a cloud engulf the chapel. Not a real black cloud, but a sort of . . . of darkness of the soul." He laughed with embarrassment. "Sorry to be so melodramatic."

"This was Rosslyn Chapel?" Jane asked, beginning to get a terrifying idea of what might have happened.

"Yes," he said with surprise. "You know it? I guess you would, Scotland being so small and all. Anyway, I felt as if there were an invisible flood of tar drowning the place. I could barely move. In fact, I wanted to howl like a hunting hound. Then I heard a scream, like someone being murdered. Which is exactly what was happening." His fingers whitened on his tea mug.

"Carry on," she said briskly. "What happened next?"

"I ran toward the scream, which came from a side chapel. A man lay crumpled on the floor and a tall, dark guy stood over him. The attacker saw me and ran off before I could get a real look at him." Sinclair frowned. "I didn't really see the guy run. It's more like he just . . . disappeared. It was very strange."

"What about the man who was struck down?"

"He was pretty old and dressed like maybe a gardener, but he had a face like a saint," the wing commander replied. "There was blood all around him. Somebody had stabbed the poor old guy. But he looked up at me with this amazing smile and said something like, 'God be praised, you're here.' As if he recognized me."

"Perhaps in a way, he did," Jane murmured.

"I knelt beside him to see if I could help, but he just shook his head and said, 'No matter about me, lad; my time has come. But you must save it.'" Sinclair took a deep breath. "I've seen plenty of death in the war, but never murder. This was . . . *wrong*. Evil."

"Very wrong," Jane agreed. "Did you ask what you were supposed to save?"

"Yes, but he was almost gone by then. He whispered, 'You'll need help,' and caught my hand. And this is where things got *really* weird. I felt as if lightning were burning through me. It didn't precisely hurt, but I felt . . . rearranged inside."

"Rather like the sizzle of energy when you took my arm at the railway station?"

The pilot looked startled. "Sort of, but different. Stronger. With you, I thought it was just because you're so beautiful."

To her disgust, Jane found herself blushing. "It was not merely attraction when you touched me. Did the old man say anything more?"

"While I was trying to gather my wits, he gasped, 'You must move quickly. Take my car, behind the chapel.' And then he was gone."

"Did you call for help?"

"This is more of the weirdness. Ordinarily I would have called the police, but this time, I just stood and went outside and found his car. It was the only one there. The key was in the ignition, so I started driving. Or . . . or maybe I was being driven."

He shook his head. "It was the strangest feeling. I knew who I was, but I felt compelled to head north into the wilderness. I drove and drove, never hesitating, always knowing which turn to take. I ended up at that railway station just as your train was pulling in." His gaze was penetrating. "If you don't think I'm crazy, can you tell me what this is about?"

Unfortunately, Jane could. It was disaster. "Brace yourself, Wing Commander. You have just been given the responsibility of recovering the Holy Grail."

Chapter 2

David's jaw dropped as he stared at the cool, impossibly lovely young woman who sat opposite him. With her tailored trousers, auburn hair tied at her nape and well-worn leather flying jacket, she looked like a sleekly sexy Hollywood pinup girl. Not someone who spoke of the Grail as if it were real. He stammered, "Th-the Holy Grail?"

"I'm not nuts, as you so quaintly put it. Nor am I reading your mind."

"You sure seem to be," he muttered. "You are a very scary woman, Jane Macrae."

"I'm rather harmless," she said in her lovely crisp British accent, as if she hadn't just said something outrageous. "The scariness lies in whoever stole the Grail from Rosslyn Chapel."

"The Holy Grail is a myth," David scoffed. "Where I grew up, there are legends about the Templars fleeing to Nova Scotia, but I always figured that was only because Canadians wanted a piece of the story. What does a medieval legend have to do with an old guy being murdered in a chapel?"

"Was the power that sent you roaring north to a railway station a myth, or did it seem real?" she asked mildly.

He hesitated, remembering the intensity of that power, and how compelling it had been. "It seemed real, but I'm not ruling out the 'nuts' hypothesis."

She smiled, her grave face transformed. "If you remember the White Queen from *Alice in Wonderland*, she regularly practiced believing impossible things. It was good advice."

"She worked her way up to six impossible things before breakfast, as I recall." David's mother read Lewis Carroll to the Sinclair children. Maybe that was where his taste for science fiction began. "Is the Grail one of the impossible things I need to believe?"

"Yes, but it's not the first. Better to begin with a simpler impossibility." She frowned, as if wondering where to start. "All people have at least some power that seems a little magical by the standards of daily life. It might be called intuition or the Sight or a hundred other names. This ability might show itself by a person knowing when a loved one is in danger, or by giving someone a vision of the future. My brother Jamie says the best fighter pilots have a sixth sense that enables them to stay a half step ahead of the enemy. Am I making sense so far?"

"Yes," he said slowly. "It's an uncanny knack, other pilots say. I have it; your brother has it. Any pilot who survived the Battle of Britain probably has it. Though it may not be enough if you get into a dogfight with a German who has the same talent."

"I come from a family where such gifts are very strong. There are many such families, and we call ourselves Guardians." She caught his gaze, willing him to believe. Her eyes were a soft, perceptive gray. "Centuries of 'magical' practice and marrying other Guardians have made our powers much stronger than average."

"Surely magic isn't just British?" he asked, skeptical.

"No, there are Guardian families all over the Continent. Other parts of the world have similar magical families, but the flavor and style of magic varies. The British Guardians are what I know."

"What kinds of powers do Guardians have?" he asked, intrigued despite his doubt.

"Healing. Clairvoyance. Hunting. Illusions. The ability to pass unnoticed. Most Guardians can do a range of things, but will have one particular skill that is much stronger. The Macraes are known for producing the best weather mages in Britain." She smiled wryly. "My father and oldest brother both work for the royal weather service. They would be better able to control the weather for us if the Nazis didn't have weather mages of their own fighting for control of the skies."

"No wonder the weather around this little island of yours is so changeable," he said, hoping to see her smile again.

"It's said that the best weather mages come from Scotland because it's so easy to practice here. No one ever notices when the weather changes." There was a glint in her eyes, but not a proper smile.

"Are you a weather mage?"

Jane shook her head. "I have only a touch of talent. It's generally a male ability. All my brothers are better at weather magic than I am."

"So what do you do?" Something impressive, he was sure.

Her gaze moved away from him. "My work is so secret that it's hard to talk about, but . . . these are extraordinary circumstances. Officially, I'm a secretary in Whitehall. A useful but anonymous shuffler of papers."

"What is your real work?"

"I'm very good at seeing patterns in bits of data. I'm also talented at filling in blanks when information is sketchy. So I spend my days putting pieces together." She made a wry face. "I'm accused of being clairvoyant, telepathic or a snoop, but really, it's just that I'm good at seeing the whole picture. This makes me . . . very useful in Whitehall."

"Military intelligence," he said flatly.

She nodded. "Yes, and I believe that is why you and I were brought together. My particular talent might help you fulfill your mission."

"So we're back to the Holy Grail." He sighed and ran a hand through his hair, thinking of how peacefully he'd started this morning at his Edinburgh bed-and-breakfast. It seemed a very long time ago. "You're convincing, but I still have trouble believing in your Guardians. They're too much like a story in a pulp magazine. If you folks have all this power, how come you aren't ruling the world?"

"Any Guardian who tried would be stopped by Guardian enforcers. When we come into our powers in adolescence, we take an oath to serve our fellows." Her mouth twisted. "On the whole, we would rather not be noticed than make attempts to rule the world. Think of all those witches who've been burned over the centuries."

"I'm not sure I believe in these powers, but if they're real, are you even human?" Maybe her not being human would explain why she was so impossibly beautiful.

Jane laughed, which made her even lovelier. "Guardians are entirely human, and we all make the mistakes to prove it. Since you don't yet believe in this particular impossibility, I'll give you a demonstration." She snapped her fingers. The lamps dimmed dramatically. "I enhanced the lamps when I lit them. Now I've removed that extra power. See the difference?"

David gave a soft whistle. He hadn't realized how unnaturally bright the lamps were until they dimmed to the level usual with kerosene lamps.

"I like strong lighting, so I used mage light to make the lamps burn brighter. I'll restore it now." She snapped her fingers again, and the room became twice as bright.

"Isn't this the sort of trick Victorian mediums used to do to impress the customers?" he asked warily.

"Yes, but this is no trick." Another finger snap, and a sphere of light glowed on Jane's palm. "Is a separate mage light more convincing? Here, take it."

If he didn't believe in magic, why was he so reluctant to take the sphere? Reminding himself that he was a swaggering, fearless fighter pilot, David extended his hand. Jane poured the light onto his palm. It buzzed against his skin, a faint but not unpleasant sensation.

Delighted, he tossed the bright sphere in the air and caught it with his other hand. "I still don't know if this is real, but it's sure fun. Do you do white elephants?"

"I could try," she said thoughtfully. She drew her brows together and concentrated. Light appeared on her hand again, this time shaped like an elephant.

"Good Lord, it's Babar!" he exclaimed.

She handed him the glowing shape. "The fact that mage light doesn't fade when you hold it suggests that you have a fair amount of Guardian magic yourself."

"I am not the least bit magical." Nor did he want to be. Yet his gaze remained on the mage lights in his hands.

"Your encounter at Rosslyn probably enhanced your native abilities," she mused. "Or perhaps magical power goes with becoming a Grail warden?"

"But why me?" he asked, baffled. "Surely if the Grail wants a keeper, it can do better than drafting the first guy to come by."

"There was nothing random about your choice. I'd swear an oath on it." Jane frowned. "I wish I knew more about the Grail. My mother is a professor at the University of Edinburgh—a historian specializing in folklore. She says that the Grail is a myth masked in magical mystery—and that can be a form of reality."

"Since my knowledge of the Grail is based on reading Arthurian stories when I was a kid, anything she told you is probably better than my knowledge," he pointed out as he reached for another biscuit. "What's your best guess about what's going on?"

"My mother believes that the Grail exists in a sacred space that lies next to the world we can see. Certain places are gateways to that space. Glastonbury is one such gateway. Rosslyn Chapel is another," Jane explained. "The Grail can be called forth into our world by powerful magic, so portals are guarded by Grail wardens."

"The old guy who was murdered was a Grail warden?"

Jane nodded. "He was probably employed as something like a gardener at the chapel, but his real task was guarding the portal. He surely had significant power, so greater power would be required to overcome him."

"I'm no expert on matters spiritual," David said, "but if that's what Grail power looks like, the thief who murdered him and took the chalice must be a monster."

"Unfortunately, you're right. They say Hitler employs black sorcerers and has looked for other holy artifacts." She bit her lip. "It's quite possible, even likely, that he sent a sorcerer to Britain to steal the chalice."

"Wouldn't theft be more likely from a spy who was already here?"

"Perhaps, but a very powerful mage would be required to overcome the Grail warden and draw the chalice into our world." Jane rose and moved to the window, pulling back the heavy curtains to look out over the wild, uncanny landscape. "As you deduced, I work in military intelligence. Two days ago, Rudolf Hess flew to Scotland. He parachuted from his Messerschmitt near Glasgow, broke his ankle on landing, and was captured and imprisoned."

"Rudolf Hess?" David said incredulously. "The deputy führer?"

"None other."

"Why the devil did he fly to Scotland?"

"He claims he hoped to make a secret peace treaty with the Duke of Hamilton, whom he thought to be a Nazi sympathizer." Jane turned from the window to regard David. "At least, that's his story."

"Hamilton is a famous aviator and RAF officer!" David said, even more stunned. "Isn't he in charge of Scotland's air defenses? Surely he's no Nazi!"

"No, the duke and all three of his brothers are in the RAF. There is absolutely no reason to suspect any of them of secret Nazi sympathies. Hamilton is the one who called the authorities after he met Hess and identified him. My colleagues in London have been speculating that Hess is mad, but now that you've told me what happened at Rosslyn, I think there's another explanation."

Jane pulled the draperies shut, then leaned back against the wall, her arms folded across her chest. "The real purpose of Hess's trip might have been to fly a black sorcerer to Scotland to steal the chalice and take it back to Germany. Hess was losing favor with Hitler. Perhaps he thought that volunteering for a mission like this would redeem him. Hitler has already seized the Holy Spear in Vienna. If the spear and the chalice are united . . ." She shook her head, her expression worried.

David was beginning to wish he'd studied history instead of engineering when he went to university. "The Holy Spear is the one that was allegedly used by a Roman centurion to stab Jesus in the side during the crucifixion?"

"Yes. If the two sacred objects are brought together, their power will be multiplied. Perhaps enough for Germany to win this cursed war."

"The Nazis are doing too damned well even without the Grail," David said bluntly. "We're barely holding them at bay now."

"Then we'd better see what we can do to stop the chalice from leaving Britain." Jane's lips tightened. "If it's not too late already. But since the theft took place today, it's probably still in Scotland."

If the fighting got any worse, Britain might go down in defeat. Any chance of the Nazis being strengthened had to be stopped. "You said you didn't think it was random that I showed up at the chapel when I did. If not chance, then what was it?"

"My mother says that an object that has been venerated for so many centuries becomes almost sentient. My guess is that that the Grail—divine power, magic, whatever you wish to call it—sent out a call to anyone in the vicinity who was qualified to help preserve it. You were closest."

"What would make a person qualified?" David asked, incredulous.

Jane shrugged ruefully. "There's the so-called sacred blood. One legend says that Joseph of Arimathea brought the chalice to Britain, where he and a group of followers established Glastonbury Abbey. Some tales say he married into an ancient pagan line of priests and priestesses. Their descendants could include anyone in Britain or of British descent, like you. The idea fits nicely with my mother's theory that the Christian Grail absorbed the even more ancient power of the Celts. The chalice is said to have qualities similar to the sacred Celtic cauldron—healing and fertility, for example."

"Sacred blood. Right." He shook his head. "What are the other qualifications?"

"The Celts attributed mythic power to being a seventh child, or better yet, the seventh child of a seventh child." Her brows arched. "Are you by any chance . . . ?"

"Actually, I am," David said, taken aback. "The youngest of a family of seven, and my mother is a seventh child, too."

"That puts you in a very small group," Jane said thoughtfully. "The last qualification is to be a good person."

Thinking of Galahad and Percival, he said, "If being a Grail warden means celibacy, I'm resigning right now!"

She laughed. "My mother says that such purity is a medieval Christian addition to the legend. I think a good heart is required, but you seem to have that. It appears that the Grail called out for a seventh child who is an honorable warrior who carries the sacred blood and has the essential quality of being nearby. That call brought you to the chapel, then led you to me to provide the knowledge you would need to rescue the Grail."

He thought again about how very long the day had been. "A farm boy from Canada is supposed to rescue the Holy Grail from an unknown sorcerer. Maybe we all need to start studying German."

"A fighter pilot who admits defeat?" she asked coolly. "You surprise me, Wing Commander."

"Show me a Messerschmitt, or a whole squadron of them, and I'll have a go. But searching for the Grail? I don't know where to start." He gestured at her. "Why not you? You understand all this, and you have magical powers."

"But you're the one who has the connection to the Grail. Though you're untrained, that power that passed to you from the dying warden is very strong. Let's see what you can do with it." She moved to a battered oak sideboard and removed a folded map from the top drawer, then spread it on the table between the lamps. "Calm your mind. Close your eyes if that will help. Then see if you can sense the chalice."

He obeyed, though calming his mind was difficult when his thoughts churned with all Jane Macrae had told him. But as his mind stilled, he found that the world had changed. "I sense a . . . a point

of light somewhere out there. Very bright. Pulsing. It's . . . glorious."
The effusiveness of that embarrassed him, but no lesser description
suited.

"It has to be the Grail." She sounded excited. "Can you tell
where?"

He opened his eyes and studied the map. "We're about here?" He
touched a spot in the Highlands.

"Very good. Now, where is the chalice?"

The knowledge was instant. "There." He pointed to a spot north
of the croft's location.

"Do you know how he's traveling? For that matter, is the thief
even male?"

That was harder. David frowned. "I think by car. And male. I'm
sure of that."

"He seems to be on the main road to Inverness, but there's a
branch to the east coming up. There aren't many roads through the
Highlands." Jane's face was lovely and intent in the enhanced lamplight. "Do you know where he's heading?"

Again the answer was clear in David's mind. "Here." He tapped
the great bay that chopped into the northeast coast of Scotland.

"Moray Firth. That makes sense," she said thoughtfully. "He's
probably going to meet a submarine. Nazi U-boats are common in
the North Sea. Easier for one to sneak into the firth than to bring in
an airplane or a surface boat." She glanced up at David. "Can you
pick up anything else about the chalice or the thief?"

He did his best to clear his mind and learn more, but with no
luck. "Sorry. Though I have a strong sense of the Grail, that's it.
There's nothing else."

"But you do have that connection. I wonder if I can use it? I'm pretty good at reading people, and if I link through you, I might find out more about the black sorcerer." She extended her hands. "Shall we try?"

"You're the expert." Even if he wasn't cut out to be a Grail warden, he didn't object to holding the hands of a beautiful woman. Particularly a woman who had knocked him endwise the first moment he saw her.

He clasped her hands and again felt a jolt of energy. "That zapping between us, like static electricity on a January night. Is that Grail energy?"

"Some of it." There was an odd note in her voice. "Not all. Relax now and close your eyes. This won't hurt, but you might feel me touching your mind."

To his wonderment, he could. Her presence in his head was like a gossamer brush of silk, or the fragrance of June lilac blossoms. Impossible to define, but unquestionably Jane.

"Yes," she breathed. "I've linked through you to the chalice. Dear God, but the energy is splendid! Like nothing I've ever experienced. We can't allow the chalice to be corrupted into evil uses!"

"The Grail is doing its best to resist the sorcerer," he said slowly, not sure how he knew, but utterly convinced. "It's fighting to stay in Britain."

"Good, because we need all the help we can get. Now let's look at the thief," Jane murmured. There was silence for a dozen heartbeats. "He's an SS colonel, and his name is . . . Krieger. He . . ."

She screamed and her hands clutched his convulsively before she collapsed to the floor. David was almost dragged down with her as black lightning seared through him with vicious malice. Dizzily he realized that he was the conduit, and Jane was the target. He caught the edge of the table and drew shuddering breaths until his mind cleared.

He dropped to his knees beside Jane. She couldn't be dead—she *couldn't* be!

He checked the pulse in her throat, sighing with relief to find it strong. Bending, he scooped her in his arms and carried her to the double bed at the far end of the room. She was unexpectedly light. He realized that she was barely average height. He'd thought her taller because of her presence.

He laid her on the mattress and pulled off her shoes, then undid the top button of her blouse. As he perched on the mattress beside her, her eyes flickered open.

"The black sorcerer is no longer a theory," she whispered. "His power is immense. Fortunately he struck us from a distance, or we might both be dead. He was aiming at me, but you must have been scorched as the energy passed through you."

"Some, but I wasn't hit as hard as you." He braced one arm on the mattress as he bent over her. "My skepticism about magic has just vanished. You're okay?"

"I've been better, but no permanent damage was done." She rubbed her temple with tense fingers. "We are going to have to find a way to summon more power when we confront Krieger, or we'll never recover the Grail."

"Can you call on other Guardians? You grew up here and you seem to have a large family."

"Finding other Guardians would take time we don't have." Jane sighed. "The only one I could reach quickly is my mother, who is running the family estate at Dunrath, and she doesn't have the right kind of magic. Everyone else is doing war work, mostly dangerous, and all of it distant." Her fingers tightened on the coverlet. "I . . . I have nightmares about which of them will die first."

He caught her hand, knowing how he would feel if his older brothers and sisters were endangered. "Don't assume the worst prematurely. I suspect you Guardians are hard to kill. Jamie has survived some of the most vicious and dangerous fighting of the war." He frowned, thinking about what she'd said. "Do you have enough brothers and sisters to be a seventh child?"

"Not really, though there are seven of us altogether. Both my parents had children from earlier marriages. Jamie is my only full sibling. He's just a year older, and we were almost like twins growing up. The others are half brothers and sisters. Not that it matters," she added fiercely. "We're all family."

"Maybe the Grail thinks half siblings are good enough, so you're a seventh child, too." He smiled, repressing the impulse to brush back her silky dark red hair. "I say we take any extra power we can get."

She became very still, her gaze searching. "There is another source of increased power. But it's the most outrageous of all."

His smile turned wry. "I think I'm beyond shock. What would that be?"

"That you and I become lovers."

Chapter 3

H er handsome Canadian stared at her, his jaw dropping. "So much for being beyond shock," David said faintly. "I've officially fallen through the rabbit hole. The Mad Hatter will be along any moment now."

Despite his amazed disbelief, Jane could see hot, swift desire flare around him. She was glad for confirmation that the crackling sexual energy when they touched wasn't only on her side. Mutual desire made it somewhat less embarrassing to proposition a man who was, in worldly terms, a stranger.

But he wasn't a stranger, not really. Every fiber of her being responded to him, and the desire was more than physical. Since Philip's death, she had been lonely to the bone, and now she craved David's warmth and kindness. Not as a substitute for Philip, but because she wanted David himself, even if it was for only a single night.

It was easier to speak of the magical situation. "The spear and the chalice are ancient fertility symbols," she said. "Male and female balance each other. Together they have the power to create new life. It's no accident a man and a woman were drawn together for this mission."

She raised a hand and cupped his cheek, feeling the rasp of whiskers. Masculine, and unutterably appealing. "My intuition says that if we're to have any chance of recovering the chalice, we must join to forge a power greater than the sum of us as individuals."

"But I can't do that," he said wretchedly. "It would be wrong."

"I'm sorry; I didn't think. Do you have a wife or sweetheart?" Chilled, she dropped her hand, concealing her painful disappointment. That was merely personal, but the deeper issue remained. They needed this joining to stop Krieger.

"My girlfriend in Halifax broke it off when I decided to join the RAF." He brushed her hair tenderly. "But . . . I'm a pilot from the provinces, and you're a lady. The next thing to a goddess, actually. And we hardly know each other."

"I feel that I know you well, David," she said softly, skimming her hand down his arm. He shivered under her touch. "We've been called together for a great mission, and our minds and spirits have met. I think our bodies need to join, too. Time is short, and nothing will strengthen us more quickly than making love together."

He caught her hand and kissed the knuckles. "Is this love? So soon?"

"I have no intention of falling in love until the war is over," she said, unable to mask the bleak edge in her voice. "But that doesn't mean that what happens between us won't be honest and true."

"You lost someone?" he asked quietly.

"My fiancé." She closed her eyes against the sting of tears. "Jamie's best friend. Another fighter pilot, but not so lucky as you and Jamie have been. He died two days before we were to be married."

"I'm so sorry." He bent and kissed her with the profound understanding of a man who had seen too many friends go down in flames. "If you want honesty—well, it's God's own truth that you are the most amazing woman I've ever met."

He kissed her again, this time more deeply as her mouth opened under his. "And the most desirable, my Lady Jane," he breathed. "If you wish me to worship you with my body, I shall do so with awe and thanks."

Weeping, she drew him down into an embrace. The ice within her thawed, then melted in a rush as the white heat of desire removed all doubts and awkwardness. Dimly she sensed that this was the Grail's gift to them: a passionate interlude that gave joy as surely as it forged them into a powerful weapon.

As their kisses became more heated, they began removing each other's clothes with swift urgency. As his flying jacket and shirt came off, she ran her hands down his back. He had a beautiful body, lean and muscular. She murmured, "Are all Canadian men so lovely?"

He chuckled. "I have no idea, but I guarantee all of us would blush at that description." He nibbled his way down her throat. "Are all Guardian women so beautiful?"

"Those who aren't become good at illusions," she said teasingly. "I may look nothing like what you think. Maybe I'm really scrawny, with buckteeth and bad skin."

"It wouldn't matter," he said as they laughed together.

She was glad they could share laughter as well as lust.

"You may fool my sight, but not my touch," he retorted as he bent to her breast. "This is no illusion."

She gasped, loving his lips on her breast, the press of his skin against hers. She reveled in his scent, his kisses, his joyful exploration of her body. Her energy field opened like a flower, admitting him so their spirits could blend together.

He had an instinctive understanding of what would please her. She used her own instincts to return that understanding. They came together with an intensity that burned away the worries of the war that had turned their world upside down. For this brief hour, nothing mattered but joy and intimacy deeper than any she'd ever known.

They climaxed together, and power whirled around and through them, forging two individuals into a single weapon of light. Then they slowly descended from the heights, panting for breath as they lay in each other's arms in exhausted silence.

The lamplight from the kitchen illuminated the quiet strength of David's face and body as he turned onto his side and drew the covers over them. The Grail had chosen well when it called this man to its service.

Jane's arm was draped over his waist, her knee tucked between his. She knew this intimacy would be brief, and that made it all the more precious. "This night is too short," she murmured.

His arm tightened across her bare back. "I know. But I'll never forget it, no matter how long I live, my Lady Jane."

"Why do you call me Lady Jane?" she asked curiously.

"Because it suits you." He smiled wryly. "Plus, if we're going on a quest to find the Grail, knights and ladies seem appropriate."

Smiling inwardly, she said, "We'd best try for sleep in what time is left," she said. "We must leave at dawn. My guess is that we have at most twenty-four hours before the chalice is beyond reach. Probably less."

"Shouldn't we leave now?"

She shook her head. "He can't travel quickly through the blackout. Using regular lights would attract too much attention. We'd be just as limited, so better to spend the time resting. We'll need it."

"Being with you gives me more strength than sleeping the clock around." His arm curved around her so that he could cup her breast. "But I'll enjoy more time sleeping with you."

"As long as we sleep," she murmured as she covered a yawn.

His expression became grave. "I hate to admit that I never even thought about the potential consequences of making love. That was very wrong of me."

"No need to worry. Guardian women seldom conceive unless they want to, so you're safe enough." Even as she spoke the reassurance, she knew without words that he was more concerned about her safety than his own.

"I can feel the change in our energies," he said thoughtfully. "It's almost like you're a candle glowing inside me. I feel . . . stronger and better focused. More prepared for whatever might come."

"I also feel stronger," she said. "Through you, I'm joined to the power of the Grail itself. It's like stepping into a fountain of light."

"All that and pleasure, too," he murmured as he turned his head and kissed her ear. "Do you think that more passion will create even more power?"

"I don't know." She smiled at him, recklessly deciding that she didn't need more sleep. "But I'd like to find out."

⁂

As dawn lightened the sky, they drank tea and finished the digestive biscuits while consulting the map. "He's taken the road east, away from Inverness, and he's moving pretty quickly," David said, pointing. "As you thought, he hasn't covered much ground since we looked last night."

"It's hard to travel fast on these roads even in full daylight. Maybe he spent some time napping, since he has no reason to think he's being pursued." Jane studied the map. "The farther east he travels from Inverness, the easier it will be for a U-boat to collect him. If the area is remote enough, they might not even have to wait until dark."

David frowned. "Will we be able to catch up with him? As you say, these are slow roads."

"We'll catch him," she said confidently. "Assuming that you can fly a biplane? A Fairey Fox. It's a fifteen-year-old RAF surplus, but well kept."

"I can fly anything," David said with a touch of fighter-pilot arrogance. "Where is the biplane?"

"Not far. The Fox belongs to Jamie and our sister Gwynne, the flying Macraes. They saved up until they could buy their own plane. It's at the family estate at Dunrath."

"Lucky devils," he murmured. "Will they mind if we borrow it?"

"Not for a reason like this." When Jane retrieved her jacket,

David took it away and helped her in. It was a totally unnecessary gesture, and she loved it. This relationship might last only a day, but as she'd foreseen, it was honest and real.

Once again, she took the wheel of the Morris Minor. David looked rested enough to drive, but she knew the way.

The sky was light enough to allow Jane to travel at top speed. As the old Morris whipped around a corner, David said mildly, "The way you drive, I would have thought you'd go in for flying, too."

She laughed. "Jamie gave me some lessons. I enjoyed them, but I haven't the passion for flying that he and Gwynne share." They turned into a rare straight stretch of road, so she pressed down hard on the accelerator. "I do like to drive, though."

"Lay on, Macrae, and cursed be him who first cries, 'Hold, away!'" he murmured.

"A man who likes to torture Shakespeare!" she said with delight. "You have hidden charms, Wing Commander." She glanced at him mischievously. "Almost as fine as the ones that weren't hidden."

He slouched lower in the seat and pulled his RAF hat down. "I see that you're determined to embarrass me back to Halifax, Lady Jane," he said with resigned amusement. "My father warned me about the wicked, worldly women I might meet in the old country." He slanted her a glance in return. "I'm so glad he was right."

She laughed again with more pure happiness than she'd known in . . . a very long time. But the seriousness of their mission settled over her again when she turned onto the rough track that led to the Dunrath airstrip. As they bumped along the track, David gazed at the hill looming above them. "Is that a real castle up there?"

"Yes," she said tersely.

"The family home, I suspect, or you'd say more about it." After a pause, he continued. "Now that I think about it, doesn't your brother have an 'Honorable' in front of his name? Squadron Leader the Honorable James Macrae?"

"He does." Frowning, she pulled up beside the old barn that was used as a hangar. A democratic Canadian might not have much use for the aristocracy.

"So you're the Honorable Jane Macrae?"

She turned off the engine and set the hand brake. "Lady Jane Macrae, actually."

"I knew it suited you!" he said with a mixture of amusement and alarm.

"My father is the Earl of Ballister," Jane explained. "Daughters of earls get to call themselves 'Lady,' while sons are merely 'Honorables' unless they're the heir. My oldest brother, Duncan, has the courtesy title of viscount." She slid from the Morris and retrieved the key to the barn's padlock from under a rock. "He says it's useful for getting good tables in restaurants."

David chuckled as he followed her to the door. "How practical of him. Was your fiancé another sprig from a noble tree?"

"Not at all. Philip's father is a solicitor in Birmingham. Philip was a bright lad who went to Oxford, where he and Jamie shared rooms." She smiled wistfully. "I joined them at Oxford a year later. We had such good times."

The engagement to Philip had been a natural outgrowth of those happy days. They had been friends, then lovers. If they'd had time for a real marriage, they would have dealt well together. She had never doubted that, and she didn't now.

Jane would never love another man as she'd loved Philip. But David Sinclair was a reminder that there were other men, and other ways to love.

She opened the padlock and they swung the doors open together.

"Splendid!" David beamed at the Fairey Fox, which was painted a very unmilitary shade of sky blue. He began prowling around the aircraft, studying every bolt and surface. "It looks to be in first-class shape."

"Angus Macrae, who was a flight mechanic in the First World War, looks after the Fox." Jane rested a hand on a strut. "Keeping the plane ready to fly is sort of a superstition, really. A way of saying that Jamie or Gwynne might come home and take her up at any time. That . . . that they'll be safe."

"There's no shortage of superstitions in cockpits," David said. "Let's get her out into the sunshine. Do you need to leave a note explaining why the plane is gone?"

"Good idea." After helping David pull the plane out, Jane returned to the hangar and found a tablet and a pencil on a desk in the corner. She pondered what to say. *Borrowed the Fox to hunt the Holy Grail* was a little too provocative. She settled for, *Fox needed for urgent mission. Will return as soon as possible. Lady Jane.*

She sealed the note in an envelope and wrote, *Lady Ballister or Angus Macrae,* on the outside and left it lying in the middle of the barn where the airplane usually sat. After collecting two leather flying helmets, she followed David outside. He was checking the movement of the rudder. She wasn't surprised. A good pilot never took anyone else's word about an airplane's readiness.

"Can you fly her?"

"No problem. I learned on a biplane." He knelt to check the wheels, feeling under the cowlings in case mice had made nests.

Guessing what he was too polite to ask, Jane said, "We're nowhere near as rich as you might think. The Ballister title is old, but it's English. In Scotland, the title that really matters is that my father is Macrae of Dunrath—the chief of the clan. Very feudal, and it means he's responsible for all the Macraes in this area. There were never any enclosures in this valley, and there has never been a Macrae of Dunrath chief who slouched off to live on the French Riviera and wasted the family fortune. So the valley is a happy place to live, but no one here is filthy rich."

"That's a good record," David said as he took off the fuel tank cap to visually check the level. "It's easy to be virtuous when one is poor and hasn't many choices. Harder when there is enough money to make decadence an option."

"How is she fixed for fuel?" she asked. With rationing, petrol could be a problem.

"A full tank. I should think it would be more than enough to fly to Moray Firth and back, this being just a little bit of a country," he said teasingly.

"Scotland may be small, but we have plenty of history in every square inch," she said, imperturbable.

"Which is both interesting and burdensome." He paused in his inspection to look at her seriously. "Do you ever yearn to see a land where the horizons go on forever? Where there are still places where no man has ever walked?"

The link between them was so strong that his words conjured vivid images straight from his mind. Vast prairies, endless forest of dark evergreens, fields of eternal snow . . . "It sounds lovely," she said, knowing he hadn't been asking just about scenery.

But she couldn't—wouldn't—think beyond the war. As she tied her hair at her nape with a ribbon, she reminded herself that she might not live to see another dawn. She should be in a panic. Since she wasn't, likely she just didn't have the imagination to believe in her own end.

David turned his attention to the grassy airstrip. "This looks long enough, though there isn't much room to spare. Anything I should know?"

Jane gestured at the rugged hills. "Finding enough level land wasn't easy. This was the only possible spot and it's barely adequate."

"If your brother and sister can manage, so can I." David's gaze lifted to the sky. "It's fairly clear now. Do you have enough weather magic to guess if that will last?"

She extended her weather senses. "No major storms anywhere near, though there might be light showers from a cloud or two." She probed the skies further. "My weather perception is stronger than usual. A result of our energy joining, maybe."

He grinned wickedly as he drained a little fuel from the tank to check that it was clean. "A pity there isn't time to see if we could strengthen it further."

She laughed, but she was very aware of the passing minutes. She tossed him one of the leather helmets and donned the other herself. "Are we ready?"

"Checked and all clear." He swung into the cockpit and moved the throttle back and forth. As he put on the helmet, he asked, "Can you pull the prop for me?"

Jane nodded, having done that many times for Jamie and Gwynne. David engaged the engine, she yanked the prop, and the Fox leapt into roaring life.

She scrambled up into the observer's seat, again glad she'd worn trousers and sensible shoes. As she settled into her seat and put on her headphones, David's voice sounded in her ears. "Pilot to observer. All secure?"

"All secure. Do you need me to navigate?"

"No need. I'll follow the Grail. It burns in my brain like a bonfire at midnight." He pulled the Fox into a turn and taxied to the head of the runway.

"Are we going to succeed, David?" she asked, needing reassurance.

"We will." He laughed. "And now, a-hunting we shall go!"

Chapter 4

D avid pulled back on the stick and roared into the sky, laughing with the exhilaration of flight. Life didn't get any better than this. He had a sweet, responsive airplane under his hands and the most beautiful girl in the world sitting behind him. He didn't even have to worry about Messerschmitts. Yes, they were heading into black peril, but if he died today, it would be for a good reason and in the best of company.

He frowned, his mood darkening. Though he'd long since accepted that he wasn't likely to see his thirtieth birthday, the thought of Jane dying made his blood run cold.

Equally grim was the thought of the Grail's purity being tainted by the Nazis. The safety of Lady Jane and the chalice meant more than his own unremarkable life.

They reached cruising altitude and he made a quiet pilot's

bargain with God. *My life for hers and for the Grail.* Asking for his own survival as well seemed greedy.

He swung north and east, climbing just enough to skim over the rugged hills, since he'd rather not show up on local radar screens. The Moray Firth wasn't much more than an hour away by air, and the Grail was calling him like a siren.

Once he had a good feel for his aircraft, he began to wonder what would happen when they caught up with their quarry. An SS colonel was bad enough. One who could wield black magic was beyond David's imagination.

But his partner was a white magician of great power. Speaking into the intercom, he asked, "Jane, do you have any idea what we'll find when we catch up to Krieger?"

"I've been thinking about that," she replied, her voice calm through the crackles of the intercom. "From my one brief contact with his mind, I know that he's very strong, very focused and jubilant about the fact that he has the chalice in his possession. He was positively gloating. He's supremely confident that he'll be successful. Perhaps he will prove to be careless."

"Do you think he noticed when you studied him earlier, or were you knocked over just from getting close?"

"He noticed," she said dryly. "That's why he slammed back with so much force. Perhaps he was expecting some kind of magical attack, since the Grail is too valuable not to be protected. I thought I could get a reading on him without being noticed. It was not my finest hour."

"Might help us if he thinks he shot down his only pursuers."

"I hope that's what he thinks. The longer he believes he's safe, the better our chances."

David checked his mental map of Scotland to see how far the chalice was from the coast. "We should catch up with him just before he reaches the firth. Then what?"

Jane's sigh came over the intercom. "Your guess is as good as mine."

"He'll probably have some kind of firearm," David said. "Probably a pistol."

"Yes, and that's dangerous. But his magical abilities are much more so. I'm working on a shield that should deflect some of his power." After a pause, she said with determined cheer, "We have one great advantage. You can draw directly on the power of the Grail, and I can reach it through you. That should even the odds magically. As to the physical confrontation—how are you at hand-to-hand combat?"

He thought back to fights with his big brothers. Being the youngest meant having to fight well and smart if he didn't want to be thumped regularly. "Not bad. If I can disarm him and you can shield us from the worst of his black magic, I can handle a fistfight." His eyes narrowed as he gazed at the horizon. "Is that Moray Firth ahead?"

"Indeed it is. Has Krieger reached the shore . . . ?" She caught her breath. "Look out; deadly winds coming!"

Even before she finished speaking, a gale blasted from the northwest and slammed into the biplane with the force of an avalanche. The Fox spun out of control, tumbling sickeningly toward the mountains below.

David fought the bucking aircraft, feeling like a sparrow struck by the hand of God. Or like when he'd been shot down and had to bail out over the Channel. He gritted his teeth. No parachutes on this flight, so it was regain control or die.

And he was damned well not going to die before retrieving the sacred chalice.

☙

If Jane had had the breath, she would have screamed as they plunged toward the ground with terrifying speed. She regained a modicum of control along with her breath and stayed silent. David didn't need distractions.

He managed to pull the Fox out of its dive, but they were treacherously low and the plane was still being knocked about like a shuttlecock. "We can't stay aloft in this," he said, his voice calm. "Look for a landing place."

She scanned the rough green hills. Too steep, too many boulders, too many trees . . . "There! Ahead, two o'clock. I think that will do."

He turned the biplane and headed in that direction. The wind shook the Fox like a bird in a terrier's mouth as he aimed for the short stretch of flat land between two hills. She heard David murmuring to himself, "Steady, steady, come on, Foxie girl, we can do it. We can do it. . . ."

The biplane's wheels touched down on the rough green turf. The craft bounced like a tennis ball, but David managed to keep it from flipping or crunching over on the right wings.

White-knuckled, Jane held her breath. They were approaching a straggly clump of trees at the end of the level stretch with terrifying swiftness.

The Fox shuddered to a stop just before the propeller gouged bark. David exhaled roughly. "Jane, are you all right?"

"That was entirely too exciting," she said unsteadily. "You certainly can fly. But, of course, I knew that."

The wind wasn't quite as bad on the ground, but it was rocking the biplane, and the sky had darkened to near dusk toward the north. "Where the devil did this storm come from?" David said as he climbed to the ground, then offered a hand to help her down from the observer's seat. "Was it beyond the range you can sense when you looked at the weather earlier?"

As Jane stepped onto the ground, she muttered a few words under her breath that would ruin David's belief that she was a lady if he heard. "Krieger's a weather mage," she said grimly. "I didn't realize that from my brief touch of his mind last night. He's pulled together several minor weather systems to create a storm fierce enough to send everyone inside."

"The skies are getting dark enough to let him rendezvous with his U-boat without having to wait until tonight." David glanced up at the black clouds whipping across the sky. "He's within a few miles of the firth. If we can't fly, we'll never get there in time to stop him. Do you have enough weather-working ability to send this storm away?"

"Not even close." Rain began pounding down, and Jane ducked back into the limited shelter of the wings. "My father or Duncan might be able to dissipate it, but they're in London. I wonder. . . ."

She closed her eyes and took his hand as she tried to cobble together a solution. David caught his breath as she drew Grail power through him.

Link this to that, add energy. Yes. The rain and wind faded away around them and the Fox. Yet when she opened her eyes, nearby trees still lashed and rain still fell.

David stared at the water pounding down a yard away. "What are you doing?"

"I'm combining my modest weather ability with my rather stronger talent for shielding, and I'm fueling it with Grail power drawn through you," Jane explained. "The result is a bubble of calm air around the Fox. Wind and rain go around rather than striking us."

He whistled softly. "Can you maintain this while we're flying?"

"I hope so. Visualize white Grail energy flowing from me to you." As energy poured in from him, she imagined stability around them and the biplane. When it felt secure, she cautiously released his hand. The clear space remained. She sighed with relief. "It's working. Do you have enough room to take off again?"

"If I landed, I can take off." He frowned at their emergency airstrip. "But we'd better do it now, before the ground gets too soft from the rain."

Turning the muddy biplane was more work than when they'd brought the aircraft out from its hangar, but they managed the task in record time. David climbed into the cockpit and Jane started the propeller.

After she scrambled into her seat, David revved the engine up until the plane seemed ready to fly into pieces. Then he drove the Fox down the impromptu runway like a scalded ferret. Jane screwed her eyes shut until they were airborne.

"We cleared those boulders at the end of the strip by a good two feet," David said cheerfully as he banked the biplane to return to their previous heading. "Looks like your bubble of calm air is holding despite our airspeed."

"It's the Grail power enhancing my basic abilities," she said.

"Now that I've designed and set my spell, it doesn't take much energy to maintain it. It should last until I get so tired I run out of magic. Which shouldn't happen anytime soon." She hoped.

They leveled off and David opened the throttle to full speed. Though the sky was black and rain slashed through the air all around them, the biplane handled as if this were a windless spring day.

They closed the distance to the firth rapidly. As they started to descend, David said, "Krieger is almost to the water, and we're going to land practically on top of him. Think he knows he's being chased?"

Jane cautiously felt around the dark vortex of the sorcerer's energy. "Probably not yet because of my shielding. He might not know until he actually sees us."

"There's a nice flat area to land on, but it seems to be a bluff, with the sea below."

"There are a lot of cliffs around Moray Firth. Krieger probably has a boat waiting at the foot of a cliff, where it won't be seen." The SS colonel wasn't in sight, so Jane concentrated hard on locating him. "He's either going down a cliff path, or he's on the beach below by the boat."

"The chalice is being carried down the path," David said. "I can feel it as clearly as you feel Krieger. Hang on. As soon as I land, I'm going after him at full speed, before he can get his boat off."

Success or disaster in the next few minutes, and Krieger was surely better armed, and well practiced at violence. "There should be some tools stored in a little compartment on the right side of the cockpit," Jane said, amazed at how calm she sounded. "A screwdriver might make a weapon. Better than nothing."

"Good idea. Hang on now."

The landing on the clifftop was easy compared to their emergency stop, though David had to dodge a pair of frantic sheep that leapt out of hiding. As soon as the Fox rolled to a stop, he vaulted out of the plane, a medium-size screwdriver in hand. "I think I'll keep my helmet on," he said, his voice pitched to cut through the howling wind. "Can you maintain the still air around the plane? Otherwise, it will blow off the cliff."

"The spell will hold as long as I'm alive," Jane said tersely as she jumped out. They'd have an airplane to come back to. If they came back.

"Let's go get the bastard, eh?" He grinned at her, then spun and sprinted toward the cliff, with Jane two steps behind.

As soon as they moved away from the Fox, they plunged into a wall of water, because Jane hadn't figured out how to put separate weather protection around the pair of them. David ran unerringly to the right, dropping into a crouch at the edge of the cliff.

As Jane came down beside him, she saw a small beach below with storm waves crashing hard into the sand. As she watched, Krieger reached the bottom of the cliff path and stepped onto the beach. He was dressed as a tweedy Scottish gentleman and had an olive drab canvas military bag slung across his chest. A good size for holding the Grail.

Krieger pulled an electric torch from the bag and aimed it out to sea. He was signaling his submarine.

The SS colonel was a model of Aryan breeding, blond and whipcord lean, with lines of cruelty cut into his face. Evil pulsed around him so intensely that it made her eyes hurt. She whispered, "He's got a protective weather bubble around himself."

"Thereby keeping his gun dry," David said grimly. "You stay up here where you can see to use your magic. I'm going down."

"I'm coming, too. I might be able to do more if I'm there." When he scowled at her, she said, "I know you want to protect me, but we'll have a better chance of success together. I think I can mask us from being seen until we're almost on top of him."

She could see protectiveness and necessity warring across his face. Necessity won. "Then do the best damned masking job of your life." A moment later, he was over the cliff and on his way down.

She followed as fast as she dared, clutching at bushes to keep from falling while concentrating fiercely on veiling their approach. Luckily, the combination of wind, rain and crashing surf covered up the sounds of their mad scramble to the beach.

By the time David reached the bottom of the cliff path, Krieger's signal was returned with a brief series of flashes from the firth. Satisfied, the colonel signed off and clipped the torch to his belt. He was starting to push the dinghy to the water's edge when he became aware that he wasn't alone.

Krieger whirled and froze for an instant, naked shock on his face. Then his thin lips twisted into a smile. "So, little girl, you survived my assault," he said with a flawless, educated English accent. "You're a stronger sorceress than I thought, so I shan't waste more of my power on you when a mundane method will do."

He reached under his coat and pulled out a pistol. "First this provincial lout. Then it will be your turn, little sorceress."

As David launched himself forward with a roar, Jane attacked Krieger's weather protection spell. Rain immediately drenched him and his weapon. The colonel fired at David at point-blank range—and his pistol misfired.

David tackled him and both men crunched against the side of the boat. They fell to the sand, David on top. He chopped the edge of his hand into Krieger's throat, but the gasping colonel managed to bash David's head with the pistol.

The flying helmet absorbed some of the blow, but David still went down. Krieger hauled himself to his feet. Not wasting more time, he shoved the boat into the water and scrambled inside. The waves had been pounding into the cove, but now they flattened somewhat. The colonel grabbed the oars and began rowing frantically out into the firth.

Wishing she had some kind of thunderbolt to throw at the man, Jane reached David's side as he was lurching to his feet. "Are you all right?" she asked.

"A glancing blow. No harm done." David stripped off his helmet and jacket, then started on his trousers. "A good thing I grew up swimming in the North Atlantic."

Aghast that he intended to hurl himself into the stormy sea, Jane said, "Do you have a chance of catching him?"

"I do." He smiled reassuringly as he kicked off his shoes, then stripped off everything but his shorts. "I'm not suicidal."

"I think I can mask you from being noticed until you reach the boat, and keep you from freezing in the water. Please . . . be careful!" Even as she said the words, she realized how pointless they were.

Better to offer practical help. "If you get into trouble, call on the power of the Grail!"

He thrust the screwdriver into the waistband of his shorts, then tilted Jane's head up and gave her a hard kiss. "I love you, Jane Macrae." He grinned. "It's all right. You don't have to love me back."

Then he turned and dived into the sea.

Chapter 5

The water wasn't as cold as David expected. Blessing Jane for whatever bit of magic she was using to keep him from freezing solid, he followed the dinghy with long, powerful strokes. He'd been a Canadian national swimming champion before joining the RAF. Had the Grail taken that into account when he was drafted into its service?

At first the waves were immense, and possibly worse for Krieger in his small boat than for David in the water. Then the sea calmed a little. More weather magery, he guessed. Probably from the SS colonel but possibly from Jane. The only certainty was the Grail's white light drawing him forward like a moth to flame.

He closed in on the dinghy, which was pitching wildly in the waves as Krieger struggled with the oars. Jane's masking magic worked so well that the colonel didn't see David swimming straight at him.

That was about to change. David glided up to the left rear gun-wale and wrapped his hands around the edge while he caught his breath. He deliberately chose the gunwale rather than the transom because he wanted the small craft to tilt when he boarded. Anything that threw Krieger off balance would help David.

Boarding a boat from the water wasn't easy, and if David didn't manage it the first time, he'd be in serious trouble. After one last deep breath, he heaved himself upward, throwing the full weight of his upper body into the dinghy. He landed on Krieger's lap. The SS colonel squawked with surprise.

David wrapped his right arm around the Nazi's ankles and pulled so that Krieger fell awkwardly back into the bottom of the boat, where water sloshed inches deep. David scrambled onto his knees and swung a punch down at the other man's jaw. Krieger jerked his head to one side, swearing in German, so the blow glanced off his skull.

"You should have stayed on land, boy!" Krieger snarled. He made a motion with his fingers, and suddenly David couldn't breathe. He tried to strike the colonel again, but he had no strength, no coordination.

Jane knew. He felt her horror and her desperate attempt to break Krieger's spell, but she couldn't. David fell awkwardly across Krieger and the dinghy's seats, helpless as a fly bound up in spider silk.

Krieger dragged himself out from under David's body and grabbed the oars, aiming the dinghy into the waves to reduce the rolling. "Ordinarily I would kill you slowly," he spat out. "But I have other matters of greater concern. Shall I leave you there to suffocate, or push you into the water to drown?"

David doubted the method mattered, since he'd die quickly either way. His vision was darkening when he remembered Jane's last words: *If you get into trouble, call on the power of the Grail!*

And the Grail was right here, only a yard away in that canvas bag slung around Krieger's chest. David closed his eyes and reached out mentally to touch the shining light. *Grace,* he thought with amazement as he touched the chalice's energy. *Grace personified.*

When the pastor of his family church gave sermons on grace, David had daydreamed about flying or swimming or girls. Grace was just a word, not anything real.

He knew better now. As the radiance of the chalice rushed through him, he knew that he could die in this moment and be blessed.

But he didn't die. Air began to move into his lungs and his vision cleared. He returned to full awareness when Krieger bent and tried to manhandle him over the side.

David caught the colonel and yanked him down headfirst. A wild struggle ensued as they grappled for advantage. Black magic swirled about like poisonous fumes seeking a way to burn David alive, whole, but the white light of the Grail protected him.

When magic was not part of the equation, David realized that he was stronger and more experienced, and his slippery, wet body gave the Nazi little to grab onto. When Krieger drew back to catch his breath, David threw himself forward in a tackle that slammed the man's head into the gunwale.

Krieger rolled loosely in the pitching boat, temporarily stunned. David sat back on his knees and grabbed the screwdriver, which had stayed tucked in his waistband during the turbulent swim.

Recovering, a wild-eyed Krieger snarled, "The Grail is *mine*! I have spent a lifetime searching for it!" He clasped his arm protectively over the olive drab bag. "I shall become the most powerful man in the Reich, even more powerful than the *Führer*! You shall not have it!"

His last words were accompanied by a magical attack of incredible viciousness. Pure evil slammed David like a club. He gasped, his vision darkening for a moment, but once more the light of the Grail protected him from injury.

Reaching out, he laid a hand on Krieger's bag, feeling the hard shape of the chalice beneath his palm. *Grace.* The antithesis of evil.

Light scoured through him, righteous as a sword. The fog of evil dissolved as the white light ricocheted back into Krieger, illuminating every dark corner of his twisted soul. David caught his breath as he realized that destroying the darkness was also destroying the SS colonel's magic, which was pure evil.

Krieger gave a howl of agony and clamped his hands over his head. "No! *No!*" he screamed as the power and identity that had defined him disintegrated, leaving raw emptiness.

David used the colonel's shock to yank the canvas bag over the man's head, then sling it securely across his own chest. He was shaking with cold and needed to get back to land and safety quickly. But what to do about Krieger?

He glanced down at the screwdriver. It wasn't designed as a weapon, but it would suffice to puncture an enemy's throat or brain.

Seeing the glance, Krieger gasped. "Kill me, damn you! You've stolen the skills and power I've spent a lifetime developing!"

David hesitated. He'd shot down German fighters, then prayed that the pilots would bail out safely. He'd never killed a man with his own hands, but the Nazi's agonized expression made it seem that death would be a mercy.

Thou shalt not kill. At least, not while he carried the Grail. He knew that as surely as he knew his own heartbeat. Or Jane's.

Should he row the dinghy ashore and take Krieger prisoner? No again. His instinct said he must leave. Take the sacred chalice away from the scene of this battle with evil, and leave the SS colonel to determine his own fate.

"No," he said quietly. "Live, and perhaps learn that the Holy Grail is about grace and healing, not power and death." He tucked the screwdriver into his waistband again, then turned and slid into the sea to return to the shore.

Back to land, and to Jane.

⚜

Dizzily Jane realized that she was kneeling on the cold, wet sand and curled into a ball around David's leather flight jacket. She had passed out from pouring every shred of power she possessed into protecting him and saving the Grail.

Now she sensed . . . nothing. Was the confrontation over, or had she permanently burned out her magical abilities?

The rain stopped. She raised her head and saw that the clouds were breaking up and small patches of blue sky were visible. Did that mean Krieger had been killed, or had he been picked up by the U-boat and released the weather magic as no longer needed?

David? David!? She reached out frantically as she sought the pulse of his life. But her mind and spirit were scorched to ashes. Losing her power was like losing sight or hearing.

The despair of that warred with her frantic wish that she had responded to his stunning declaration of love. Though she had no idea *how* she should have responded.

Splashing. Jane's head whipped around, and a hundred yards out she saw the dark head of a man stroking uncertainly toward shore. "David!"

Afraid he was too weak to make the last stretch, she dropped his jacket, leapt to her feet and plunged into the water. She was chin-deep when they met. His arms crushed around her as he gasped for breath, and she almost tumbled backward into the waves.

Regaining her balance, she told him, "The water is standing depth here."

He was aware enough to understand, so he lowered his feet while still hanging on to her. His bare torso was icy from swimming back without her magical protection.

After a dozen ragged breaths, he choked out, "I overestimated how much strength I had left."

"What happened? I burned out my power and couldn't tell if you were alive or dead." She turned and began guiding him toward shore, her arm around his waist. "Much less what happened to Krieger and the Grail. Did he escape?"

"No." David stumbled as he made it to the beach and folded down onto the sand just beyond the range of the waves. She saw that he had Krieger's canvas bag.

"I have the Grail." He pulled the dripping bag over his head. "Krieger tried to strangle me with magic, so I reached for the chalice power, like you said. It saved me, and then . . . it destroyed his dark magic."

She gasped. "Permanently?"

"I'm pretty sure. The chalice seems to put knowledge directly into my mind." After a shuddering breath, David added, "Krieger asked me to kill him, but I couldn't. The Grail does not serve death."

"Good God!" And never had Jane said those words more truly. She extended a hesitant hand. "May I see it?"

"Please do. I want to see the chalice, too, after chasing it halfway across Scotland."

Jane knelt beside him and reverently unfastened the canvas straps that kept the bag closed. The largest interior pocket held a cylindrical object wrapped in a thick towel. Even her scorched mind sensed its radiance.

Hands shaking, she unwound the object. Her first impression was of a brilliant white rose formed of pure light. As she gazed in wonder, she realized that within the phantom rose was a simply shaped chalice of metal. Silver? There was a dent or two.

"I can't quite believe it's real," she said huskily. "But it's impossible to see the chalice without realizing that it's sacred. To me, it looks like a rose formed of white light, and at the same time, a silver goblet."

"I see the chalice inside a blazing white star." David touched the rim with awed fingertips. "I suppose each of us sees it a little differently. I wonder how Krieger saw the Grail? I can't even imagine."

Jane frowned thoughtfully. "If I had to guess, I'd say the Grail veiled itself from him. He would have felt its power, but not seen the brilliance of its light."

"He was unable to use the Grail's energy," David said. "When he attacked me, it was with his own magic."

"If my mother were here, she'd want to know whether the Grail is Christian or Celtic or both, as she's speculated." Jane cupped her palm around the bowl of the chalice, and healing energy flowed through her. The scorched and exhausted fabric of her spirit began to heal into peace and joy.

Something more than joy stirred within her. She looked up into David's gaze, and saw her feelings mirrored in him. She placed her other hand on the chilled flesh of his chest. "You're freezing, and I know just the way to warm you up."

Gently she tucked the chalice back inside the bag. Then she leaned into David with a kiss. His cool lips warmed under her mouth, and he pulled her down to the sand.

He breathed, "I'm warming up fast."

Trousers were good for chasing sacred artifacts, not so good for making love. Every moment that clothing separated them seemed like a moment wasted, so she stripped with frantic hands as he kissed each new bit of her body that was revealed.

They came together with heat and longing and light. In the croft they had made love to increase their power to save the Grail. This mating was joyful celebration. When David slid into her, she laughed with delight and pressed hard against him.

As she'd said in the croft, a relationship needn't be forever to be real and true. Nothing she had ever known was truer than this moment. Passion cascaded through her, burning higher and higher until she shattered into glorious pieces, taking him with her.

They lay locked together as bodies and souls recovered. "I feel more whole than ever in my life," Jane murmured.

"So do I." David's gaze went to the sky. "The storm is gone and the sun is out. The world really is warmer, not just me. But it's still awfully chilly to be lying on a Scottish beach in one's skin."

"I'm not looking forward to putting on wet clothes and getting into a biplane again, but I don't suppose there's much choice." Jane grinned. "I think this little episode answers my mother's question about whether the Christian chalice and the Celtic cauldron have merged their energies. The way fertility and passion were invoked, the answer must be yes."

"An unacademic answer to an academic question," David said with a grin. "Is there any chance we might get tea at a nearby house? I noticed a little farmstead just before we landed."

"Good thought." Warmth and food would both be very welcome. Jane pulled on her wet underwear and other garments. Every stitch was saturated. "What excuse do we have for being fools enough to be out in that storm?"

He thought a moment. "I'm a Canadian RAF pilot on leave. You're the sister of a mate of mine, and you offered to show me some of Scotland. We were forced down because of the storm, and because it's an open plane, we got very, very wet."

"Excellent," she said admiringly. "And more or less true. As long as no one wonders what we were doing between landing and seeking them out."

"Perhaps we took shelter under an inadequate tree." David pulled on his wet trousers as he studied the cliff face. "I can't believe we came down that path without breaking our necks."

"Needs must when the devil drives," Jane said. "And Krieger was a pretty fair approximation of the devil." Her eyes narrowed as she gazed out to sea. "Do you think he's a better man for his time with the Grail?"

"With evil no longer filling his soul, perhaps grace will fill the empty places." David looked at the firth. "Or perhaps not. That's where free will comes in."

"I think the U-boat found him, so he'll have time to change if he wants to." Jane smiled. "I'm giving thanks that my power has been restored. For a brief time that felt like forever, I thought it was gone permanently."

David wrapped the chalice carefully, buckled it into the bag, and handed it to Jane. "You take this. It looks more natural for a woman to be carrying something."

She slung the canvas bag across her back. "Now that we have the chalice, what do we do with it?" she asked. "You're the Grail warden."

"We return it to Rosslyn," he said promptly. "We'll know what to do with it once we're there."

Jane nodded, then started up the cliff with a great deal more care than she'd come down. By the time she reached the top, she was panting and covered with sand. When David joined her, she said, "How fortunate that I was already a complete wreck, because I don't suppose I look any worse now."

He took her arm and gazed down at her eyes, his expression intent. "You look quite entirely beautiful, my Lady Jane. Now, shall we find some tea?"

Chapter 6

The cottage David had seen was about a quarter mile away, prudently set back from the sea winds. Chickens foraged around the yard, and a wisp of smoke rose from the chimney, so with luck, someone was home. David knocked and hoped.

They were almost ready to give up when the door opened and a tired-looking middle-aged woman opened the door. "You're early. . . ." She frowned. "Sorry, I was expecting someone else."

"We're sorry to disturb you," Jane said with disarming warmth. "But David was forced to land his biplane over by the cliff because of the weather. Since we were both drenched, we were hoping we might get a spot of tea before flying home again."

The woman's gaze went over them both, lingering on David's flying jacket. "You're a pilot, then?"

"Yes, ma'am," he replied, laying on his Canadian accent. "My name is David Sinclair, and I fly for the RAF down in Kent."

Her gaze sharpened. "Churchill said, 'Never in the field of human conflict has so much been owed by so many to so few.' You're really one of the Few?"

"Yes, ma'am," he replied, embarrassed. "And so is Miss Macrae's brother."

The woman stepped back. "Then you are both welcome in my home, and God bless you. I'm Mrs. Innes." Her voice lowered. "My son is resting, so I'd be grateful if you keep your voices down."

"Of course," Jane replied as she stepped inside. "Our thanks for your hospitality."

David followed her into the neat parlor. Portraits of King George and Winston Churchill hung above a fireplace where blocks of peat burned fragrantly.

"Would you fancy a plate of eggs and potatoes with your tea?" Mrs. Innes asked. "A lot of things are in short supply, but I have plenty of those."

"That would be lovely." David smiled at their hostess. "I'm on leave for a fortnight, and Jane offered to show me a bit of Scotland. And Scottish weather. I never saw such a storm come out of nowhere. We were lucky to land safely."

"We have braw wild weather here," Mrs. Innes said, not without a certain pride. She studied their saturated garments. "If you have an hour or so, I can lend you some clothes and we can dry those things of yours in front of the fire."

They agreed with alacrity. After Mrs. Innes produced some worn but clean garments belonging to her and her husband, Jane and

David took turns changing in the lady's bedroom. The other bedroom presumably belonged to her son.

Within a few minutes, their wet garments were steaming gently in front of the fire and David and Jane were dry and well on their way to being warm. He thought that she looked like a damp Pre-Raphaelite angel in a vastly oversize blue robe, her wet auburn hair finger-combed straight and drying on her shoulders.

It took Mrs. Innes only a few minutes to serve large platefuls of gloriously crisp fried potatoes with onions, and eggs scrambled with cheese. Grail chasing gave a man an appetite, so David fell on his food like a wolf. When he'd cleaned his plate, he said, "Mrs. Innes, you are my mother's equal when it comes to feeding the hungry."

The older woman chuckled over her cup of tea. "I know how young men eat." Her gaze strayed to the second bedroom door and her levity faded. "It's glad I am that you came here, and no mistake."

"You've certainly fortified us for the flight back to Dunrath," Jane said fervently as she set knife and fork across the plate.

Since she'd eaten only about two-thirds of her meal, David asked, "Are you going to finish that? Or does asking mark me as a hopeless peasant?"

Jane smiled and exchanged their plates. "It's exactly what one of my hungry brothers would do, and a good thing. I hate to see food wasted."

As David tackled her plate with enthusiasm, Mrs. Innes said wistfully, "My boys all ate like that. I wish Bobbie had his old appetite—" She stopped short, glancing at the bedroom again.

"Your son is ill?" Jane asked softly.

The older woman sighed. "He was in the merchant marine, and was injured bad when his ship was torpedoed. Burns. When the doctors gave up, I brought him home. At least he'll be able to . . . to . . ." Her voice broke.

A knock sounded at the door. Mrs. Innes pulled herself together and got to her feet. "That would be my sister-in-law coming for some eggs. She was the one I expected earlier. If you'll excuse me for a few minutes, I'll go out and collect them for her."

"Can I help?" asked David. "I'm well acquainted with chickens."

Mrs. Innes shook her head. "That old rooster of mine will attack anyone but me. You young folks go ahead and finish your tea. I'll be back in a few minutes."

She pulled on a jacket and opened the door. Her sister-in-law made a remark about the eggs, then asked how "wee Bobbie" was doing. Mrs. Innes replied heavily, "It won't be long now," before closing the door and cutting off the conversation.

David sighed. He'd had friends who had suffered horrible burns when their planes crashed. "It's a bad way to die."

As Jane nodded, her face troubled, a thin, agonized voice called from the second bedroom, "Water. Please, Ma. *Water.*"

Jane picked up the bag containing the Grail, which had been sitting by her feet. "I'm going to take him some water, and . . . maybe more can be done."

"I'll go with you." David stood and pumped water into a pitcher that sat by the sink. Then he followed her into the darkened bedroom.

Bobbie Innes was a mass of stained bandages. Though his face was almost entirely covered, David guessed that he was very young, probably under twenty. The youth turned his head when they entered, moving like a man heavily sedated.

Jane said soothingly, "Your mother is gathering some eggs for your aunt, so we thought we'd bring the water." She sat on the chair by the bed and opened the bag, then unwrapped the Grail. "My name is Jane Macrae, and this is my friend David Sinclair, a Canadian fighter pilot in the RAF."

Bobbie's gaze cleared a little. "One of the Few?" he asked in a raw voice. His Scottish accent was so thick David could barely understand him.

"Yes, but I wish people wouldn't say that as if we're special heroes." David poured water into the sacred chalice, wondering if it had the power to heal. "Just about everyone in Britain is serving in one way or another. Like you. Without the merchant marine bringing in vital supplies, we'd have had to surrender by now."

"Aye . . ." It was a whisper. "I done my part. . . ."

Jane held the chalice out to the boy, and David put an arm behind his back to raise him to drink. Bobbie sipped a bit, swallowing with difficulty.

Then he sipped more, and swallowed more easily. In a stronger voice, he said, "That's good water. Pretty cup, too."

Jane offered him more. "Drink as much as you like. This cup is an antique that is said to have ancient healing powers. Just a story, I thought, but who knows?"

"I do feel better," Bobbie said with surprise. He swallowed the rest of the water. David quietly refilled the chalice and the boy drank more.

"May I try something?" Jane asked. "I'd like to moisten a handkerchief and pat some of the water on your face."

Bobbie shrank back against the pillows. "No! Don't take off my bandages!"

"Of course not," Jane said, soothing again. She accepted the folded handkerchief David handed to her and dipped it in the chalice. "I meant to pat over the bandages. It will be cooling."

After wary consideration, Bobbie said, "All right, then."

Infinitely gentle, Jane pressed the wet handkerchief to the boy's face. It took only a minute or so to dampen all the bandages.

"Feels good," Bobbie murmured. Strength exhausted, he settled back onto his pillow and slipped into a doze, his lips curving in a faint smile.

Dipping again, Jane moistened the bandages on the boy's neck and bandaged hands. One of the bandages had loosened on his wrist, so she pulled it up and put the wet handkerchief directly on the ugly burned flesh.

To David's amazement, the burn slowly transformed into healthy skin right before their eyes. Jane gave a nod of satisfaction and got to her feet. "He'll do now. Time to return to being good guests before Mrs. Innes comes back inside."

David glanced over his shoulder at the wounded sailor as he ushered Jane back to the sitting room. "Should all his burns be treated with chalice water?"

"I have a strong sense that drinking the water is all that's necessary, but I thought direct application might speed the process. It certainly wouldn't hurt him." Jane set the pitcher back in its place by the sink.

David shook his head in wonder. "Truly amazing." He checked the drying garments on the rack. "These are just about dry. I'll change first."

"Go ahead. I'll do the washing up." Jane packed the chalice in the canvas bag, then turned her attention to the dishes.

As David changed in Mrs. Innes's bedroom, he heard their hostess come in and say, "There's no need to be doing those dishes, Miss Macrae!"

"It's the least I could do in return for your hospitality," Jane said mildly. "You'd be insulted if we offered money, but what woman will turn down dishwashing?"

Mrs. Innes laughed. "You're right there, lass."

David finished dressing and stepped back into the main room. As he did, their hostess glanced toward her son's bedroom. Jane said, "Bobbie called for some water, so I took a glass in. He's resting now."

Mrs. Innes looked as if she was going to protest. Then she shrugged. "I suppose that seeing a pretty girl will do him no harm."

"And no girl is prettier than Jane Macrae," David said warmly.

"Are you two fixing to marry?" Mrs. Innes asked.

"Heavens, no!" Jane stopped short in the process of removing her clothing from the drying rack. "The wing commander and I have known each other less than a day."

Lord, that was true, David realized. At this time yesterday, he was just arriving at Rosslyn Chapel. "My mother would say I need to know a girl for at least twenty-four hours before proposing." He checked his watch. "So—six hours more before I can."

Jane turned red and escaped into the bedroom to change while Mrs. Innes chuckled. "You seem to be very together for two people who just met. Don't waste time, lad. Not in days like these."

"Excellent advice, Mrs. Innes. Now to persuade Jane." She might think of their relationship as true but brief. David had other ideas.

Jane emerged looking cool and aristocratic despite the wrinkled garments. "Thank you again, Mrs. Innes."

As they left the cottage, a door opened and they heard Mrs. Innes exclaim with amazement, "Bobbie, you're walking, lad!"

"I feel a lot better, Ma," her son said in a strong voice. "And hungry enough to eat stones. Could you fry me up some eggs and chips?"

"It's soup for now, lad!" Mrs. Innes said joyously. "But tomorrow, if you keep improving, I'll make your favorite steak-and-kidney pudding if I have to steal the beef from the butcher!"

Grinning, David closed the door behind them, and they headed back toward the biplane. "We've just seen a miracle, Jane." After a dozen steps, he said, "I don't suppose we could take the Grail to military hospitals to treat other boys like Bobbie."

"A miracle by definition is rare. Today, perhaps the Grail wanted to celebrate its rescue. There are Guardian healers who sometimes perform miracles, but never very often." Jane lifted the military bag from her shoulder and handed it to him. "The Grail must return to its home, and so must we. I think it wants to be with you."

He chuckled as he slung the bag over his shoulder. "Is that your intuition, or just a way to get me to carry it?"

"Intuition." She gestured toward the bag. "I felt the Grail tugging toward you, like a kitten seeking its mother. Because you're the warden, there's a special bond."

"As long as it doesn't require celibacy." Not wanting to think about what the long-term effects of being warden might be, he looped his free arm around her shoulders as they continued walking. "We did it, Lady Jane! We recovered the sacred chalice from one of Hitler's worst thugs."

She smiled. "You did most of the work, David. You're the one who tracked the Grail, flew the airplane, swam through raging waves and won the chalice in hand-to-hand combat. No knight of the Round Table could have done better."

"A knight would sink in all that armor," he said practically. "But we couldn't have succeeded without working together. Your magical talent for putting pieces together, your knowledge of the Grail, and the airplane were all essential."

Jane slid her arm around his waist. "The Grail chose its servants well. I wonder if it does have some kind of awareness? My mother is going to love hearing about this and coming up with new theories."

"Is she at Dunrath now? I'd like to meet her."

"That won't happen," Jane said flatly.

A little stung, David said, "I'm assuming you have reasons beyond feeling that a colonial farm boy doesn't belong in a castle."

"If I didn't need you to fly the Fox, I'd be tempted to knock you on the head with a rock," Jane said without heat. "My mother is a mage as well as a mother. She'll know we've been lovers, and she will be full of avid maternal interest. I . . . I can't face that."

"I can see the disadvantages to having magical parents." He was disappointed, but understood. It had been less than a year since she'd lost her fiancé, so he supposed it wasn't surprising that she needed more time. Introducing a new and obviously besotted man to a parent was a major step.

They reached the plane and he handed Jane up to the observer's seat. He just hoped that time wouldn't run out for them.

The flight to Dunrath was unremarkable, apart from strong headwinds that slowed them down. By the time David landed the biplane, the sun was low in the sky. He taxied the Fox to the hangar, and Jane climbed out to open the doors.

Inside, her note about taking the biplane lay on the floor where she'd left it. After David parked the plane and climbed out, she said, "No one noticed the Fox's absence. I'll restock fuel for the Fox and food for the croft when I'm at Dunrath."

"The Morris Minor is just where we left it, too." He patted the biplane's wing. "A sweet little aircraft. I feel fortunate to have flown her." He removed his helmet and handed it to Jane. His fair hair was deliciously tousled. "It's too late to get back to Rosslyn Chapel tonight. Shall we go to the croft, or is there a better place to stay?"

"The croft is best," she replied. "Peaceful and private. I'll pick up some fish and chips at a shop in the village on the drive back."

He nodded agreement, but she didn't like his intent expression. At some point, they would have to have a discussion. She hoped to put it off until she was less drained.

She'd rather put it off altogether. Easier to smile good-bye and leave without looking back. But even after less than a day's acquaintance, she knew that David would not allow that. Unfortunately.

❦

The fish and chips were excellent. David finished off the last crunchy piece. "Wise of you to get a triple order. It's been a very tiring day."

Jane covered a yawn. In the lamplight, she was achingly beautiful, with her auburn hair loose and her grave eyes. "I'm ready to sleep the clock around."

He stood when she did and asked mildly, "Am I to sleep on the floor?"

"Of course not." She came around the table and flowed into a hug, the whole of her slender body pressed against him. "Why waste the time we have left?"

His body responded with such fierceness that it almost derailed his thinking. But not quite. As he buried his face in the silky strands of her hair, he asked, "Why do you act as if time is limited? We're both on leave and can spend the next ten days or so together. You work in London. I work in Kent, just a short train ride away. Can't we see each other again?" He glanced at his watch. "Better yet, since twenty-four hours have passed—please marry me, Lady Jane Macrae. Then we can book one hotel room without raising any eyebrows."

She froze in his arms. "No! I . . . can't. After Philip's death, I swore not to get involved in another serious relationship until the war is over." She looked up at him with haunted eyes. "You know how swiftly death can strike during wartime. I can't bear to give my heart and have it broken into pieces again."

"Death is always possible, even in peacetime, my darling girl." He stroked her back, trying to knead the tension from her muscles. She was so real, so present, that it was impossible to believe that after tonight he might never hold her again. "And if we're talking about hearts, it's too late for mine. I love you, Jane. That it happened so quickly is another gift of the Grail, maybe, but it's real. It's true. And it's forever."

"Are you sure, David?" she asked quietly. "The connection between us could fade away once we've returned the Grail."

He gave that several seconds of serious thought before shaking his head. "No. That is not going to happen. Not for me. You've ruined me for any other woman, Lady Jane." He caressed her cheek tenderly. "But the reverse may not be true. You must regularly meet men who are a lot more interesting than I am."

"No," she said, her eyes huge. "I don't."

His breathing constricted at her expression. Almost afraid to find out the answer, he asked, "Does your intuition say that what you feel for me is induced by the Grail and will last for only two days?"

He feared that she would say yes. Instead, tears began silently sliding down her face. "I care for you, David. I . . . I probably love you. But I can't bear to continue as lovers now. Go back to your squadron. See other women if you wish. And if we both survive this horrible war, you can propose to me again. If you want to by then."

"You'll probably have recovered from Philip and married someone in a less dangerous occupation," he said, his voice edged. "My timing is all wrong here."

"There won't be anyone else, David. I swear it."

"Since we both think we won't change our minds, why not become engaged?" He kissed her ear. "I'd like to be able to call you my fiancée instead of my girlfriend."

She shivered. "I'm rather superstitious about being engaged. It didn't do me any good before."

He gave her a rueful smile. "You're usually so calm and logical that I find it rather endearing that you're superstitious. I just wish it weren't *this* superstition."

She sighed and rested her cheek against his shoulder. "I'm sorry. I wish I were brave enough to say yes. But . . . I'm not."

"We are what we are, Lady Jane." He wrapped his arms around her, trying to imprint the feel of her body onto his spirit. "As a fighter pilot, my instinct is to grab life now, because there might not be a tomorrow. Which is the opposite of what you feel."

"Enough talk." She raised her face for a kiss. "We have tonight. Let's not waste a minute of it."

They didn't.

Chapter 7

They made love for the last time at dawn. David couldn't bear knowing that he might never again feel such joy and fulfillment. Even with passion temporarily sated, he wanted her within sight and sound and touching distance.

As he dressed, he berated himself for his selfishness. How could he want the woman he loved to suffer agonies by loving him when he might die in flaming pieces, as her first love had? Yet he could not stop the yearning, because she owned his soul, whether she wanted it or not.

They had a light breakfast of tea and some buns that she'd picked up in the village the day before. Since he was awake and rested this time, David drove. After half an hour, Jane remarked, "You're a more conservative driver than I am."

"I have a real airplane to fly, so I don't have to see if I can get a Morris Minor to take off," he retorted.

She laughed. "It's a beautiful morning for a drive, isn't it? You flew over the Highlands yesterday, but this is the first time you've driven through them in daylight."

"Beautiful indeed." He glanced up at a stream that leapt down a hill in exuberant waterfalls. That was called a burn here, he recalled. "I can feel an ancestral tugging, even though it's been two hundred years since my family headed to Canada two steps ahead of the king's troops who wanted to hang them as rebels."

"I'm glad they were quick on their feet. But Scotland does get into one's bones, no matter how far one might travel."

He thought about asking her to be his guide for the rest of his leave, but managed to hold his tongue. Nagging an independent woman like Jane to change her mind would just make her dig in her heels.

The best strategy he could come up with was to leave her alone for six months. Then he would call to see if she was wanting him as much as he wanted her.

Maybe three months.

It was early afternoon when they reached Rosslyn Chapel. David admired its Gothic grandeur as he headed for the unobtrusive parking space where he'd found the Morris two days before. "I've visited a whole lot of churches since I came to England, but this is one of the best. The grandeur of a cathedral on a small, friendly scale."

"My mother loves this chapel because of the combination of Christian and pagan symbols among the carvings." Jane swung out of the car when David opened the door for her. "Angels playing bagpipes, and green men for fertility. We visited a time or two when I was little, but it's been many years."

"I hope I get more time to look around on this visit." He offered his arm. "If I'm a warden of the Grail, am I going to have to stay close to this chapel?"

"I have no idea," she admitted. "Maybe that will be revealed, along with how to return the chalice to its resting place."

They entered through a side door. He gazed at the amazing carvings on the high Gothic ceiling. The chapel made him think of lace frozen into stone and warmed by the light filtering through the stained-glass windows. As on his first visit, the nave was empty, not uncommon for a parish church on a weekday afternoon.

Jane asked in a hushed voice, "Has knowledge flooded into you?"

"Not yet. If I remain ignorant, it will be your turn to come up with some wisdom."

"Which would mean calling my mother, which I'd prefer to avoid." She scanned the massive stone columns. "Where did you find the body of the warden?"

"Over here, in the Lady Chapel." He led her to the location. No traces of blood were left on the floor.

Jane closed her eyes. After a moment or two, she said, "This area burns with energy. Can you feel it?"

He closed his eyes, then said with surprise, "As a matter of fact, yes. I'm not used to paying attention in this way."

"It's not hard to believe this is a portal to another realm of existence, and that the right magic could send the chalice through." Jane's eyes opened. "I don't feel darkness from the old warden's death. Overwhelmed by other energies, I imagine."

A door behind them opened and they turned to see a middle-aged woman enter the chapel from the front entrance. She was tall and her vivid red hair had only a handful of silver strands. Not seeing Jane and David, she walked up the aisle with quick, sure steps.

"That is a woman of power," Jane said quietly. "Like my mother."

"Or you." Now that he was paying attention, he was much more aware of the energy Jane radiated.

"She's not a Guardian," Jane said thoughtfully. "I'd guess Grail power."

The woman stopped in surprise when she saw them. Then she came forward at a near run. "You have it! Oh, blessed day, Father was right!"

"Have what?" David asked warily, his hand resting on the canvas bag.

"The Grail, of course." The woman halted a few steps away. "I'm Màiread Sinclair. I have been raised to be the next Rosslyn warden of the Grail, but when that horrible Nazi came, I wasn't here. I was in York with my daughter, who was having her first baby." Stark guilt showed in her eyes as she continued. "You are the man who was called to save the chalice before it was too late." Her gaze went to Jane. "You're a Guardian, aren't you? I assume that the warden was sent to you for help."

Jane nodded. Though David felt that that Màiread was telling the truth, caution seemed advisable. "How do you know this?"

"My father, William Sinclair, told me what happened." She gestured at the stone floor. "He was struck down here. He said when I returned from York that a Canadian airman was summoned by the Grail to rescue it from being taken out of Britain."

"Your father is alive?" David asked, startled. "I thought he died after telling me that I must retrieve the chalice."

Màiread's expression darkened. "He didn't die, but he was mortally wounded. I believe he has been forcing himself to endure because he desperately wants to see the Grail recovered." She looked at the canvas bag. "Will you bring it to my father?"

"Of course." David held out his hand. "I'm another Sinclair. David, from Halifax. I was just starting a fortnight's leave in Scotland when I felt the urge to visit Rosslyn. My partner is Lady Jane Macrae. As you guessed, the Grail led me to her. I'd have been helpless on my own."

Màiread smiled at Jane and took David's hand. There was an explosion of light that temporarily obliterated the world. David staggered back a pace while Màiread gasped. "The wardenship has shifted to me!"

Jane caught his other hand, steadying him. To Màiread, she said coolly, "Did you know that would happen?"

The older woman shook her head, looking as disoriented as David. "No. I'm sorry, David. I would have warned you if I'd known the power would be transferred. But this situation is unprecedented." She bit her lip. "I wasn't sure that the wardenship would return to me, since I failed to protect it at the crucial moment. I was doing my best to be noble and gracious to the new warden."

Admirably honest. "If you've been raised to it, better you than me," David said, relieved that custody of the chalice had moved to more knowledgeable hands. "The last two days have been . . . educational, but I would rather return to my usual life."

"Then we are both pleased." Màiread beamed. "But let us go to my father. He sent me to visit the chapel, and now I know why. He has very little time left."

David nodded. Jane held his hand as they left the chapel. He was grateful. After having to believe so many impossible things, he needed her as his anchor.

Màiread led them behind the building to one of the ancient workmen's cottages tucked against the wall that surrounded the chapel precinct. Half the front of the stone cottage was covered with magnificent white climbing roses with a hint of scarlet at the heart of each bloom. Heady scent perfumed the air. Jane touched a rose with wonder. "These are magnificent. And early."

"They're Grail roses and bloom through most of the year. A small but lovely miracle of the Grail. If you like, I'll give you a cutting." Màiread's voice lowered. "I made up a bed in his sitting room, since it would be too hard for him to get up the stairs." Stepping inside, she raised her voice. "Father? The Grail has returned!"

A still figure lay on the narrow bed, an old dog curled up on the floor below. Hearing his daughter's voice, William Sinclair snapped open his faded blue eyes, showing awareness. Reaching out a hand, he whispered, "Please, lad . . ."

David opened the bag and removed the Grail. After unwrapping it, he placed it in the old man's frail hands. "Here, sir. The chalice has come home."

William Sinclair kissed the rim of the cup. Raising his eyes, he gazed first at David, then at Jane. "There are no thanks great enough for what you have done." Then he looked at his daughter. "Goodbye, my darling girl. You will serve well."

He rested the chalice on his chest over his heart. Then, face radiant, he closed his eyes and his spirit departed.

Màiread gave an agonized gasp and pressed her hand to her heart while Jane said softly, "There is more than one kind of healing. Rest in peace, faithful warden."

"The warden served long and honorably, and gave his life to the service of the Grail," Màiread said in a choked voice. "But . . . I shall miss my father."

David moved forward and removed the chalice from the old man's clasp, then pulled the blanket over his face. "Is there anyone who should be called?"

The new warden shook her head. "Soon, but not just yet." She took a deep breath and raised her head. "The Grail needs to be returned to its resting place. Do the two of you wish to join me and make your farewells?"

"Yes," David and Jane said almost in unison. As they left, the old dog leapt onto the foot of the bed, turned, then settled down, guarding his master's final rest.

They returned to the chapel at a slower pace, David carrying the chalice for the last time. He could not regret the extraordinary adventure that divine chance had drawn him into. His eyes had been forever opened by a wider view of the world and powers he had never dreamed of. He suspected that he was now a better man for the experience.

Nor could he regret meeting Jane Macrae, even knowing how much it would hurt to lose her. He loved her, and even if he had lost her for now, he had hope for the future.

But he wouldn't miss the responsibility of the Grail. He was good with airplanes and young fliers and things of the world. He would return to his old life better and happier for what had happened to him.

He glanced at Jane, wondering how she felt about their shared adventure. Magic and power were part of her everyday world. Her experience had been hair-raising and exhausting, not to mention emotionally harrowing. For her, the price of love was invoking the pain of a great loss she'd already suffered.

She loved him, he thought, and maybe that love would last and grow and blossom into a lifetime of loving when the war was over. But it seemed equally likely that she wished she'd stayed in London and they'd never met. Of course, that would have meant Krieger removing the Grail to Germany and the war being lost. He suspected that she would be the first to say that it was worth personal pain to prevent such catastrophe.

They followed Màiread to the Lady Chapel. She took the chalice from David, then offered it to Jane. "Do you wish to say your own farewell to the Grail?"

Jane accepted the chalice and stared into it as emotions flickered over her face. First shock, then wonder, finally joy. She took a deep breath and handed it back to the new warden. "It's hard to let it go, isn't it? To me, it looks like a rose of white light. David said it looks like a star. How do you see the chalice, Màiread?"

"As a pulsing heart of white fire." Màiread clasped the bowl of the chalice between her palms. "I am the designated Rosslyn warden and will be for years to come. Yet though the Grail will rule my life until I die, I may never see or touch it again."

"Do you mind?" Jane asked curiously.

"Oh, no. 'Tis a high calling, and a rewarding one." The older woman smiled. "Rather like being a nun, but without the celibacy. I think it was the Grail that directed me to the right husband, and a braw good job it did. One of my children or grandchildren will carry on after me. The wardenship traditionally passes only to those who wish the burden and are worthy of carrying it. You're a rare case of conscription, David. Do you regret being called to its service?"

He glanced at Jane. "Never."

"Now that we've made our peace with power . . ." Màiread raised the chalice above her head, her eyes closed in concentration.

The air began to throb with mystery, like a great beating heart. The chalice flared brighter and brighter until suddenly it was gone, leaving only a memory.

David released his breath. And so it ended. After a long moment, Màiread turned to him. "We're back to worldly things. David Sinclair, you said you were on a fortnight's holiday here in Scotland. Would you like to continue using my father's car until you return to the south? The petrol coupons should be in the glove box."

"That's very kind of you," he replied. "I'd like that. It will give me a chance to drive into the Highlands. I'll return the car here in ten days' time."

"When you're finished with the Morris, just park it 'round back where you found it. Leave the keys in the glove box if I'm not around." She took his hand. This time there was no blaze of power. Just a warm human hand. "Enjoy Scotland, and again, my profound thanks to you both. Now, if you'll excuse me, I'm going to offer prayers of gratitude."

David turned and took Jane's arm and they left the chapel.

Outside, she said, "Do you feel diminished by the loss of power? Or as if there's a hole in your spirit?"

He explored his mind before saying, "No. I can feel the change. The responsibility is gone, and I'm glad. But . . . it's odd. Though I'm no longer connected to the Grail, there is no emptiness. I feel as if some bright power has taken its place."

Jane placed the fingers of her free hand on his forehead. When her hand dropped, she said, "I think you've been granted a goodly dose of Guardian-style magic. The Grail is generous with its gifts. You'll find it interesting to explore them."

Less interested in magic than in Jane, he asked hesitantly, "Do you want me to take you to the train station? Or . . . I could drive you home. I don't have to come in. I can drop you at Dunrath and be on my way."

"The Grail granted me a gift, too. A true vision." She turned to face him, her eyes shining. "When I looked into the chalice, I saw a wedding celebration on the lawn at Dunrath. I knew that the war was over and that Germany was defeated. Not for some time—years. But we won. We won!"

He swallowed hard. "Did you recognize the happy couple?"

She took his hands. "*Us*. And we were surrounded by our families. I saw all my brothers and sisters, David! They survived. Jamie was there, looking so dashing. My sister Margaret had a handsome Frenchman in tow, and there was the most beautiful Asian girl on my brother Andrew's arm."

He began to smile. "Anyone there look Canadian?"

She nodded vigorously. "There were lots of tall people who looked like you. A couple of them were in Canadian uniforms, and no one seems to have been maimed. We all came through, my love. We will survive! And live happily ever after, I think."

Laughing, he swept her up in his arms and swung her around. "Does this mean that you're accepting my proposal?" He set her down with a kiss that left her breathless.

"No," she said, laughing with him when he loosened his hold. "We will have a wicked affair with mad, passionate weekend liaisons that we will never, ever describe to our children. After the war, we will go directly to marriage."

"That works," he said agreeably. "I shall tell my family that I am going to marry the most beautiful girl in Scotland, and I don't even have to spend half a year's pay on an engagement ring." He grinned down at her. "The money can go toward those wicked weekends. Champagne and roses and quiet, romantic country hotels."

"How deliciously decadent." She smiled back, happier than she had imagined possible. "But first, Wing Commander, I'm going to take you home to meet my mother."

The English Rose: Miss Templar and the Holy Grail

BY

KAREN HARBAUGH

Chapter 1

IN WHICH THE FASHIONABLE MISS TEMPLAR ACQUIRES A DIRTY
CASTOFF AND PENS HER IMPRESSIONS.

April 5, 1806

There is nothing more odious than having the Holy Grail thrust into one's hands when one is about to enter Almack's. But what could I do? I already had my foot on the first step of the building's entrance. Mama and cousin Jeanne were before me, already within doors. A crowd gathered behind me, eager to partake of the evening's entertainment.

A touch on my shoulder made me turn, ready to greet a friend, perhaps Clarice, for she is one of my bosom bows and had told me she would attend this week.

Instead, a masked man very boldly took my hand and closed it over the bowl of what looked like a dirty tin cup. He then pulled me too close to him. "You are the Guardian of the Grail. Keep it safe," he said into my ear, and disappeared into the group of people moving toward Almack's.

A masked man. Really. Why could he not have just appeared in normal evening wear, neckcloth neatly tied, presented himself to me in the proper manner, asked me for a dance or two, and then offered a pleasant remembrance of flowers the next day? Oh, no, he could not do that. No, he must appear masked, dare to touch me on my shoulder without any sort of introduction at all, and then converse in a manner that must make any observer assume he was either drunk or an idiot.

I heard titters behind me. It made me quite forget the whereabouts of my fan, so I could not contain my angry blush. I turned and did my best imitation of an offended Countess Lieven, and was gratified when my gaze silenced the two titterers (Gwendolyn Hasborough and Alice Mayfield; I have never laughed at any of their awkward situations, so I do not see why they would at mine).

My eyes caught a movement behind them, and I could see in the lamplight beyond the flash of a cape and two figures that seemed to run after the man who had accosted me. Surely a madman, I thought. I turned back to the assembly rooms.

Mama glanced at me impatiently. "Hurry, Arabella; the air is chill and I am afraid it will rain soon and ruin your gown."

I hastened my steps and almost let the cup slip from my hand. But . . . a strange tingling running from my fingers to my heart made me pause, and I could not discard it. It seemed an oddly familiar sensation, and I thought of the family stories Papa had told me about the Grail and the Grail Council when I was a child . . . and which Mama had pooh-poohed when I questioned her about it.

It is all nonsense, I told myself, but I shoved the cup into the pocket of my cloak nevertheless, and quickened my steps after her.

As I walked into the hall, the cup bumped against my leg; very annoying, for it distracted me from my goal, and that was to have a perfectly pleasant evening at Almack's, full of dancing, conversation and looking at eligible gentlemen.

I am determined that finding a husband shall be my goal this year, for anything else causes nothing but trouble, and after Papa went to his heavenly reward, Mama—

Well, all I will say on that head is that our family has not been quite the same. I wish to make dear Mama happy once again, which means I must be as good as I can be, and to find myself an amiable husband. I have even quit my sword practice and pistol shooting, although I must say I have missed both terribly, as they were things I had enjoyed with Papa. Besides, it is not as if anyone other than Bertie would engage me in sword fighting, and he is not the most accommodating brother in the world.

But, Almack's: I was in a quandary as to what I must do with the cup, and my first thought was to hide it behind a large aspidistra pot. However, some wretched servant or other must have thought large plants should be removed from the halls this week, and there was nothing for it but to leave my cloak on a chair with cousin Jeanne. Some look quizzically at us for taking in a poor relative, and French at that, but it is not her fault that she is French and her family *was* guillotined, after all.

I firmly put the cup out of my mind, however, for I *shall* acquire a husband and make Mama happy again. I succeeded in seeing her smile as she watched me dance with one eligible gentleman after another, until I danced myself into fatigue. I motioned Jeanne to the dance floor with a gentleman to whom Mama had introduced her, for as a de la Fer, she is hardly a nobody, and Mama had procured vouchers for her as well.

I fanned myself lazily, smiling at various gentlemen who passed, mentally willing some of them to fetch me lemonade. None of them did. I have always thought it is a wretched custom that one must have a gentleman in attendance before asking him to fetch lemonade. It would be so much easier to seize one by the sleeve and ask, or even better, pour copious amounts into a very large flagon and gulp it down with relish, especially after dancing four or five dances in a row.

But such things Are Not Done.

I thought Providence had granted my wish at last when Mama's face lit up as Lady Cowper approached with a gentleman in tow. I smiled in return at her ladyship, for any young woman of normal sensibility must be deeply moved when presented with a vision of manly perfection.

"My dear Miss Templar," her ladyship said. "May I present to you Mr. William Marstone? Mr. Marstone, Miss Arabella Templar."

He bowed elegantly, though with a hint of stiffness, over my hand, and I admit to a little flutter of my heart. How could I not be pleased with hair dark like a night's storm, fine sculpted lips, a firm chin, and eyes of a deep green the like of which . . . were oddly familiar. . . .

"It is my pleasure to meet you, Miss Templar," he said.

Our Vicar Bentley once mentioned that God giveth and taketh away, blessed be the name of the Lord, and when I heard this gentleman's voice, I realized this was the taking-away part. Surely I am meant for the fiery realms, for I felt like cursing, and had no remorse at all about it.

"I, too," I lied, thereby consigning myself deeper into Hades' grasp.

Yes, it was he, the masked man, except no longer masked or cloaked. There was no mistaking the voice: low and musical with a pleasing timbre. I have a good ear for sound and voices; my only regret was that our voices would have combined well in a duet. But of course, I do not wish to sing with an idiot—or a madman. I reflected on the two choices and decided on idiot. Madmen generally are not given vouchers to Almack's.

I retained a polite smile despite my wish to have him go away, which must count toward the virtue of fortitude.

"Will you honor me with a dance, Miss Templar?" He said it in a tone that assumed I would agree, but I could also hear a certain urgency within his voice as well.

Irritation warred with curiosity; curiosity won, and I nodded and took his outstretched hand. Besides, Lady Cowper looked on with approval, and it would have caused unpleasantness had I refused. I also remembered that it was best to humor insane persons lest they cause a scene, which simply would not do at Almack's.

Excuse me. Not insane—an idiot.

"We must meet—alone," he said as he drew me close in the dance.

I waved my hand in front of my face as if to cool an embarrassed blush. Indeed, my face was warm enough to show pink, I am sure, but it was from anger.

"La, sir, you are impertinent!" I let out what I hoped was a tinkling laugh. "We have only just met." The figures of the dance parted us, but not before I heard a muttered curse pass his lips.

His frustration gave me satisfaction, and my smile was kinder when we met again in the dance line. It did not dispel the frown from his brow, however, and I noted a slight sheen on his forehead. I felt a stirring of doubt; he was a tall, strong-looking man, and a dance should not cause him fatigue.

Or to become so pale. I looked at him anxiously, and the intensity of his expression caused me to drop my gaze. Something spattered on the hem of my gown, the color at odds with the pale apricot silk.

Blood. It was dripping from his sleeve.

I gasped, and hurriedly pulled him from the dance, ignoring outraged exclamations from the dancers, and hoping the groan from Mr. Marstone was not a sign of a worsening condition.

I also ignored Mama's outraged expression, and went straight to the point: "Mama, we must leave, and must take Mr. Marstone with us. He is bleeding and grievously injured." I turned to him and managed to push him into a chair by Mama's side; in time, I am sure, for he had seemed to become paler and to waver on his feet.

Mama opened her mouth, about to protest, but I had already looked for and found Mr. Marstone's wound. I pointed to a red stain spreading on the left arm of his coat.

"Look, Mama, there is blood."

He began to lean forward, and I hastily pushed him back upright in his chair. Mama gazed at his arm, then at me, and shut her mouth on her protests.

"You are right, my dear." She leaned toward him. "Mr. Marstone, have you a servant here? Can you stand?"

I looked up to see curious glances cast our way. "We must leave soon," I said to Mama. "We are drawing too much attention, and you know how everyone gossips."

"No servant." Mr. Marstone closed his eyes. "No servant. I can walk." He seemed to force his eyes open. "Go. Now." He pushed himself to his feet, wavering only a little. "I was shot, by God." He seemed surprised, and I supposed he must have been in shock not to have realized it.

Jeanne, an alarmed look on her face, had nevertheless gathered our cloaks by the time we entered the assembly rooms' hall. With Mama on one side of him, and I on the other, we managed to keep him upright until we shoved him into our waiting coach—difficult, for he had fainted. I have never been more thankful for Jeanne's presence of mind in calling for the coach, which she must have done while she gathered our cloaks.

"Pull off his coat," Mama said, and I saw a grim expression on her face as we passed close to a streetlamp. "And give me what handkerchiefs you have. We must keep him from bleeding to death."

It was difficult pulling off Mr. Marstone's coat, for he was a tall man and heavy; his unconscious state did not help, nor did the close confines of the coach. But I managed to release him from his sleeve, causing him to moan only a little, and Mama nodded approvingly. "That's enough. Jeanne?"

She turned to my cousin.

"Here, Madame," Jeanne replied, and held out her handkerchief, a pitifully wispy thing. I hastily searched in my reticule for mine, much larger, for what is the use of a tiny handkerchief if one must sneeze?

I found it, and tied Jeanne's handkerchief and Mama's more substantial one to mine, and quickly made a pad and tied it around Mr. Marstone's arm.

"That should do," Mama said, and I could not help thinking she had cut off the words, *I hope*, at the end.

It seemed too long before we finally arrived home, and too long to find a sturdy footman to help Mr. Marstone into the Blue room. I sent out another footman to find Dr. Stedson, and as I climbed the stairs to help Mama and Jeanne, I could feel against my leg the thump, thump of the cup Mr. Marstone had given me.

"Stupid, idiotic man," I muttered. "To come and ruin all my plans to make Mama happy."

But as I helped Dr. Stedson examine the wound while Mama held Mr. Marstone down (he was strong, and inclined to fight even when unconscious), it made me remember a few times when we had done the same for Papa. I glanced at Mama's face, and she had the same fierce look that had once been there when she had attended Papa in the same manner, and for a moment I was glad Mr. Marstone had been injured, if only so I could see Mama look lively once more.

Until he threw up, of course.

I will end my day's journal writing here, and this time hide my little book in a safe place, so that Bertie will not steal it away and laugh at me again. I am weary from dancing and attending to an injured and vomiting man, and very eager for sleep. I will write more tomorrow.

—Arabella

Chapter 2

WHEREIN THE KNIGHT OF THE GRAIL HAS DOUBTS.

April 6, 1806

My wound has not healed as quickly as it should. It must have something to do with the Spear of Destiny that I once had in my possession, or perhaps the Grail. . . .

It is a damnable thing to write in one's journal when one's arm is in a sling, even if it is not one's dominant arm. My leg is an uneven surface upon which to write, and I cannot use my injured arm to secure the book so that it does not slip—

I hope to recover quickly, since the shot I received went cleanly through the muscle and hit no bone. Past injuries I have had healed quickly when I had the Grail in my possession. I shall ask Miss Templar to bring it to me, so that its healing properties may heal me—if I am worthy, of course. At least the Grail is out of the hands of Napoleon Bonaparte's agents and in the hands of the Grail Guardian—for now.

I may be on a fool's errand, however. The chosen Guardian of the Grail, despite her quick action on my behalf, is not much more than a silly little twit, concerned mostly with fashions and dancing and catching a husband. My observations of her before my injury made me certain that the Grail Council is mistaken in thinking she is the Guardian. Though the Templar family is an old and distinguished one, they have been more inclined to die when holy relics are put in their keeping than to stay alive and protect them. They have not stinted in their service, to be sure. But I cannot be certain that this chit of a girl will even try to uphold that family tradition.

Not that I wish her to die. She is a ~~beauti~~ passable-looking thing, and would probably make some man a suitable wife. Not for me, of course, for I am committed to being the Grail Knight, and must remain pure. As she also must—if she is indeed the Grail Guardian.

I did follow her for the last three days to see if she was at all engaged in some sort of charitable or high-minded pursuit worthy of a Guardian, but came to exhaustion instead when I was forced to wander about *every single shop* in New Bond Street in my attempt to observe her character.

Indeed, the council must have chosen her more for her looks than her brain. She ~~is lovely~~ looks well enough, with a slim figure, a head of curling golden hair and a fine bosom, but there is not much more to recommend her except her sharp tongue, which might indicate some kind of intelligence behind it. I acknowledge I might be doing her mind an injustice, as she was quick to come to my aid and did not descend into hysterics. But that is not enough to be a Guardian of the Grail.

Tomorrow, I shall write a letter to the council and request that they reconsider their determination that Miss Templar is the

Guardian. Even if she were, I fear she is not up to the task, and the Templar family would suffer yet another loss. I must make haste, however. It was only through luck that I had been given vouchers to Almack's and thus could escape my pursuers, for without vouchers, even Bonaparte's agents could not pass beyond Lady Jersey's appalled and angry eye. No such dragon guards the Templar household, and thus all within are in danger.

Regardless, I must convince Miss Templar of her duty, or try to bring the Grail myself to Rosslyn Chapel, where it should be safe. I do not anticipate difficulty from Lady Templar, as she must be conscious of her husband's family duty toward the Grail and the Grail Council. The farther away the holy chalice is from Bonaparte, the better. Though I regret dropping the spear into the Thames, at least it is not where any of Bonaparte's spies can get it. Better it be lost forever than any tyrant take it. I have no ambition to rule, but even I had thoughts of forcible conquest when I held the spear.

I hear voices approaching my bedchamber; I cannot write more. . . .

—*W. Marstone*

❧

April 7, 1806

I do not know in whom to confide. Mama, not approving of the supernatural, would not understand. Jeanne . . . Well, Mr. Marstone's feverish mutterings mentioned Napoleon Bonaparte, and though I know she has no connection to that tyrant, I cannot risk any kind of scandal, either real or imagined.

I cannot help taking out the Grail and looking at it. I should not call it so, though there are times . . . It seems to change each time I hold it in my hands. Not suddenly, so I cannot be sure. When I first held it, it seemed nothing but a dirty little tin cup with holes in it. A "holey" so-called Grail.

But the second time I looked at it, there seemed fewer holes, and now as I look at it before me again, there are no holes at all. And oh . . . no, I am mistaken. For one moment as I touched it, it seemed to glint gold. There, I have touched it again, and it is only a tin cup.

With no holes.

It *must* be only an ordinary cup. No doubt there never have been holes, nor gold, but a trick of sunlight and shadows. I am imagining it. It is wholly possible that I am imagining it.

Holy, holey, wholly. Oh, I am writing nonsense. I am a loony bird. I have been to a ball every single evening this week. No doubt fatigue has played tricks with my mind.

I feel foolish for even putting pen to paper. At least I may laugh at my own silliness months from now when I read this journal entry again.

I will tell Mama that I wish for time away from the late nights at balls and routs, and need my sleep. She will agree, I am sure, for I have seen her yawn more than once at a luncheon.

Instead, I will try to persuade Bertram to engage me in a bout of swordplay. Yes, I know, I did say I had quit such activities, but I shall go mad with boredom else, and it is enough that we have one potential madman-idiot under this roof without my becoming another one. I hope I may engage in swordplay—Bertram is becoming harder to persuade, for I am now so good at it that I have beaten him in the last few

rounds. The last time I asked him to show me some advanced tech-
niques, he refused, but I am certain I can wear him down, for he is
truly a dear, kind brother who indulges me terribly. I *must* persuade
Bertram—it will keep my mind off ~~Will~~ the annoying Mr. Marstone.
  Until next time . . .

—*Arabella*

⁂

To: The Senior Grail Councilman, the Hon. James Wrenton
My apologies for not writing sooner. I have been ill with fever, and am
not yet totally recovered. The <u>Object of our Mutual Concern</u> is safe for
now, and Miss Templar improves upon acquaintance, but I nevertheless
think she is not the one. I know time is of the essence, and I would call
upon my sister to aid me with her medical skills, but it is too dangerous
for her to come here. I will find a way to leave with the Object as soon as
it is possible, and take it to Rosslyn Chapel.

Your servant,
William Marstone

⁂

April 10, 1806
I am all out of patience with Mr. Marstone. He is over his fever,
thank goodness, but hardly well enough to be up out of bed, but he

insists he is. Mama has persuaded him, however, that he must stay at least another two weeks, when Dr. Stedson will examine him again.

But that is not all. I am annoyed at Mama as well, for she will find any number of reasons why I must attend Mr. Marstone, and why she must leave us alone together for minutes at a time. I think she schemes to push us together, for no one can deny that the Marstones are a well-to-do, old and respectable family, although some say they are eccentric. My brother says they are known for breeding superior horses, and I suppose that must account for something.

I sound contradictory, I realize. I should wish the annoying Mr. Marstone gone and the Grail with him, but it is an equally annoying notion that he arise from the sickbed while he is still injured.

I do know one thing, however: It is best that Mr. Marstone have the Grail, and not I. As a result, I decided to give it back to him this morning, sickbed or not.

I took it out from under my pillow as soon as I had dressed, unwrapped it from my shawl and then held it to the morning light to look at it one more time before I returned it to him.

There were no holes at all in it, and though it still had a dull tarnish over it, an elusive light seemed to flicker beneath the brown patina. But as I continued to hold to the sunlight that flowed through the curtains of my bedroom, there was no light but that of the sun. It was a puzzle. I was refreshed after a good night's sleep, so I could not blame fatigue for my seeing anything but a tin cup.

It does not matter: I want nothing to do with mysteries.

I wrapped it up in my shawl again, put it aside, rang for my maid and ordered breakfast to be brought to Mr. Marstone's room. When

I knocked at his door, he bade me enter, and I saw that breakfast had indeed arrived, as I had requested—except there was enough for two, not just one. I suspected Mama's hand in this, for I had promised her I would look into Mr. Marstone's condition upon arising. I put my irritation aside, however. It made no difference to me whether I broke my fast in the parlor or at ~~Will's~~ Mr. Marstone's bedside. Besides, I had brought the Grail and would return it to him.

I hesitated before closing the door—I should have properly left it a little open. However, if this was indeed the Grail, and since his manner in giving it to me was quite conspiratorial, I believed it wise to be private.

As a result, his raised brows at my choice annoyed me, for I felt it was hardly his place to say what was proper in my behavior. After all, he behaved improperly himself by accosting me at Almack's. My annoyance increased upon looking at him. He was pale from his fever, and his nightwear was untied at the neck and showed some of his chest, from which I properly looked away before I saw much of its muscled expanse . . . and had trouble not looking at it, for it seemed my attention had become distracted lately, and I had lost the discipline of mind I had cultivated in developing my sword-fighting skills.

If this is what happens when I try to do my duty by Mama, I would rather continue beating Bertie at fencing, for I do not need any complications in my life.

I found myself clenching my teeth. Rumors had gone about town that Mama and I had purposely jumped at the chance of making Mr. Marstone stay at our house, and it was because I was desperate for a husband. You may imagine I was furious hearing this, but there was nothing for it but to laugh it off in public and do my best to see that ~~Will~~ Mr. Marstone leave our house as soon as possible. Refusing the Grail—the tin cup—was a good first step.

But he had no right to look helpless and manly at the same time. It made me want to feel sorry for him, and that would not do if I were to refuse to be the Guardian of the Grail.

"Miss Templar—" he said.

"Mr. Marstone—" I said at the same time. I nearly growled in annoyance, for our speaking all at once nearly cast me out of countenance.

He inclined his head graciously, giving me allowance to speak first, which put me even more out of patience with him for some reason. I gathered my thoughts together before I spoke.

"Mr. Marstone, I have brought the—the Grail to you." My tongue stumbled over the word—there is a part of me that cannot believe it is truly the Grail, despite its change from a hole-filled cup to one of elusive luster.

"Have you? Excellent," he said.

I blinked. This was not the response I was expecting; indeed, I felt oddly disappointed. I thought perhaps he was still feverish and did not know what he was saying. Or, rather, he had come to his senses and thought better of giving me the Grail. Regardless, I unwrapped it from my shawl and handed it to him.

A reverent look came over Mr. Marstone's face—his eyes shone with it, and he drew in a long breath. "You have kept it safe. Thank you," he said, and looked at me with gratitude.

My breath caught, and something in me broke open; he looked

at me as if I had been newly risen on the half shell à la Venus. I looked away from the intensity of his gaze, and could feel my face blush, much to my annoyance. "It is but a cup," I said gruffly. "I am not at all sure it is the Grail." I made myself look at him again.

Fast on my words came regret: His expression of gratitude became one of puzzlement and then disapproval. "How can you doubt it?" he said. "Do you not see how it glows with an inner light? Anyone with eyes must see it."

I saw nothing but a tin cup, no holes, granted, but no light, no glow. I looked at him again, and I felt even more broken inside. I did not like the sensation.

I took a step backward. "No," I said. "No, I do not see anything but a tin cup, and you are fevered, or mad, to think anything else." My words came fast and harsh. "I . . . I will send for Dr. Stedson, and ring for a tisane."

I am a coward: I turned and ran from the room.

"Miss Templar—!" Will called after me, but I did not stop. I could not help glancing back at him, only to see his distressed face and what I thought was a slight glow from his upheld hand. But a second glance showed only a frown, and nothing in his hand but the tin cup.

I will end here—I cannot write more. My mind is filled with astonishment and anger at myself that I could even think to run, acting like a coward before one who is just an eccentric or at worst has lost his mind. Heaven help me for such foolishness!

—Arabella

❦

April 11, 1806

I have done ill by ~~Ara~~ Miss Templar. I should not have been so abrupt in introducing the Grail to her. It is a relic of great power, and it seems she has not been educated as to its qualities or the responsibilities attached to it. Perhaps if she had been told of it before I had given it to her, she would be able to see it for the miracle it truly is.

Even so, I do not know how she can think it looks like a tin cup. I am looking at it now as I write; true, it is said to be made of tin that Joseph of Arimathea himself had worked in his tin shop, and which he had given for use in the Last Supper, but it glows with divine fire, so bright at times that I must avert my eyes.

It has had its effect as well; though it works best through the conduit of the Grail Guardian, my wound has already closed, and the stitches that the good Dr. Stedson had used are beginning to fall out. Such is the power of it that ~~Arabella~~ Miss Templar needed only to hold it for a moment for its healing powers to manifest. I regret my doubts that she is the Grail Guardian. She must be; no other could wield the Grail and effect such a cure.

Yet . . . she does not see the Grail as anything but a tin cup. It is a puzzle. The Grail Guardians of the past had revered the vessel when they had looked upon it. But not Miss Templar.

Perhaps it is a matter of her becoming used to it. I need to remedy her aversion to it when next we meet. It is important that she take on the responsibilities of the Guardian as soon as she is able, for Bonaparte's agents followed me to England. If only they had not shot me outside of Almack's, we would be farther along to Rosslyn Chapel, so that the Grail can be hidden in the most secret and sacred of chambers there. I must make haste. Rumors have spread of my presence here, which can only endanger the Templar family should those agents hear of it.

As a result, I must resume my duties, and must remedy any misunderstanding between me and Miss Templar. I should do better than to present myself as a disheveled inhabitant of a sickbed. Such a sight would put anyone off. I must dress and partake of breakfast, the size of which indicates to me that part of it was meant for Miss Templar as well. . . .

Later:

Closed wound or not, putting on the clothes Lady Templar had brought from my lodgings took a good deal of energy from me: the effects of the fever, no doubt. Nevertheless, I was dressed and in an armchair close to the fire when Miss Templar next came into my chamber, once again without her maid, although she made sure to keep the door open for propriety's sake.

Yet, despite this precaution, she kept her distance and eyed me as if I had suddenly grown a third eye. I pondered this difference in attitude as I gazed at her gingerly sitting on the edge of a chair a good distance from me, and became conscious of a growing irritation. I realized her manner was the same as I had observed in people forced to deal with a rabid dog. My irritation increased.

"Miss Templar, I promise you I will not bite," I said.

Her head tilted to one side, she gazed at me sidelong, as if considering my words against the possible state of my mind. "Of course you will not." Her voice was set in deliberately soothing tones, the like of which would send a less tolerant invalid into spasms.

"You are trying to humor me," I said, discovering a new ability to speak through clenched teeth.

"Not at all. I am merely seeing to the comfort of a guest." She gave a light, artificial laugh.

"You lie poorly." I immediately regretted my words—it was obvious even to me that I had lost my patience. I cleared my throat, unclenched my teeth, drew in a long breath and let it out again.

"My apologies. My injury, and the fever—they have made me rude and an ungrateful guest." There was progress: Her outraged expression disappeared, although her wariness remained. I began again. "My dear Miss Templar, I need your help. My wound is now healed because of the power of the Grail, and I would appreciate it if you would take it back now and take on your responsibility as the Grail Guardian. My illness and my sojourn here do not erase my duty to the Grail to keep it safe from Bonaparte's spies."

She looked skeptical. "Even if I am the Grail Guardian, you can hardly claim to be healed. A bullet wound does not heal in a few days, however healthy a man's constitution might be. Even if it has, you have recently been in a fever, and that can linger for more than a week, at least." A look of frustration crossed her face, and she took her ~~full, plump~~ lower lip between her teeth, looking annoyed. "That is, I am sure you are feeling better and are mending well, and need not stay here more than a day—ah, a week instead of two weeks, as Dr. Stedson has said."

Despite her skepticism, I felt heartened by her medical knowledge; that must point to some kind of healing power appropriate to a Guardian of the Grail.

"I am better, I assure you, and am ready to go back to my lodgings tomorrow," I said. I sighed. "Would you prefer to see for yourself?"

"Yes, I would—ah, I would not—that is, not that you should show anything for me—I mean . . ." To my surprise, a blush suffused her face. She clamped her lips together and looked at once confused and as irritated as I had felt only a moment ago.

I realized then that for her to see that my wound had healed, I would have to remove my coat and shirt. I would not have thought she would have been embarrassed by such a sight, for she had seen me without them and had shown nothing but an efficient air when she attended her mother and the physician whom they had called on my behalf.

I am a wretched buffoon. As I gazed at her, I recalled some snippets of fevered memory, and understood that I had been a difficult patient. No wonder she felt awkward in my presence. I had intended to inform her of her duties as a Guardian of the Grail, had imposed on her mother's household, no doubt keeping them from the pleasures of town life, and all the thanks she had received for it was a tiresome patient who vomited into a bowl she had held, and held unflinchingly.

"My dear Miss Templar, please accept my apologies. I have been abrupt with you and have imposed on you and your mother. Please believe me when I say I am in your debt for your care of me, and your patience in what must be my bewildering—yes, even inappropriate—approach to you. I should not have been surprised at your rejection of me—"

She came forward in a rush, her eyes shining. "Rejection—oh, no, no, you must not feel obliged—it was only unusual—and you were injured and ill. We could not just leave you as you were; think how awkward—it would have caused such a scene at Almack's with you bleeding, and you might have died, and the gossip, it would have been all over town. . . ."

I cannot bear tears in a woman—she had taken in a sobbing breath, her eyes wide and looking as if she would weep. I took her hand and squeezed it. "No, no, my dear—Miss Templar, do not distress yourself. You did well, and I appreciate that you acted quickly and intelligently. I, however, have been wretched in my attempt at doing my duty. I should not have approached you at Almack's, but there is an urgency to the matter, especially since word of my presence here has spread—"

She squeezed my hand tightly. "I know, I know," she said soothingly. "The Grail." She put her other hand on my brow and looked concerned. "Promise me you will stay another few days at the very least. Promise me."

I am certain that Bonaparte's spies will not cease their search for the Grail, and I should have been on my way to Scotland by now, with Miss Templar in tow, for only the Grail Guardian can put the Grail in the sacred place farthest away, and best protected, from Bonaparte. But as I looked into her eyes, a feeling of elation crept into me. At that moment, I felt I could not refuse her anything. I took her hand to my lips and kissed it.

"Of course," I said. "I will stay a few more days, I promise you."

She breathed a sigh of relief, and her smile was so wide and brilliant that all thought of Bonaparte and Grail and duty fled my mind. She held my hand to her cheek, and there was nothing in that moment but Arabella, smiling through her tears, and the wish that time would stop and that I could dwell in the idea that she cared for me.

I am a fool. A cursed damned fool.

—*W. Marstone*

❧

April 11, 1806

I am an idiot child. I am convinced of it. I should have made it clear to William that he was indeed well enough to leave, and with the Grail in hand. Why, he was even up and dressed properly in waistcoat, jacket and trousers, his neckcloth neatly tied. But he must look at me again with gratitude and warmth, and that was the end of my resolution. Indeed, I entreated him to stay longer, and my only excuse was that his forehead did feel quite warm with possible fever, although that could have been from sitting so close to the fire. And then I made so bold as to hold his hand and put it to my cheek. . . .

Although it was after he kissed my hand, so it was under duress. When given warm looks and a hand kiss from a man who has been half-undressed in one's presence, a lady must respond, and I could hardly do so in a repulsive manner to one who had been gravely wounded. Indeed, had I rejected the kissing of my hand, the insult to his sensibilities must send him back into a fever, and it would be my fault if he died from it—

I am lying. I wanted to hold his hand and I wanted the kiss and I wanted to kiss him back. I pulled my hand away carefully, for I did not want to injure his arm again, and I believe I managed to compose myself enough so that we chatted of inconsequential things before I insisted he rest again.

I did not stay long at his side; it was clear he was weary. Instead, I went back to my room and brooded for a few minutes on the injustice of fate forcing me to feel an attraction for a man who was not in full control of his senses. However, I cannot brood for long, for it fills me with ennui. I dressed in my oldest gown, and then went to find Bertie, for there is nothing like swordplay or a round of target shooting to bring me into a better mood.

I let my dear brother win at swords after I beat him roundly the first time, which cheered him so much that he offered me a taste of Blue Ruin. I had never tasted it before, so I brought my toothbrushing cup to him so that he could pour some into it.

It tasted horrible, and I poured it out of the window immediately, rinsing it and my mouth out with water from the ewer at my dressing table. The sunlight glinted on my tooth cup for a moment when I poured out the gin, and I thought of the Grail that Mr. Marstone spoke of so reverently. I sighed, feeling quite low, for except for his claims about that cup, it looked little different from the one I use to brush my teeth.

No matter; he will be gone in a week's time, and that will be the end of the little tin Grail, and this man will trouble me no more.

—Arabella

Chapter 3

WHEREIN MR. MARSTONE DEPARTS, AND
MISS TEMPLAR PONDERS ROCKS.

April 13, 1806

A scream awoke me, jolting me upright in my bed, which caused pain through my wounded arm—much better than yesterday, but still painful. I could hear running outside my door, and frantic conversation.

The cries were too intense to be the result of a servant's mishap. Fearing the worst, I hastily arose from bed and clothed myself as quickly as I could, forgoing any attempt at tying my neckcloth in a decent manner.

As a result, my disheveled appearance did nothing to dispel the suspicious look that Lady Templar bent on me when I opened my chamber door.

"Where," she said in angry tones, "is my daughter?"

Dread became a weight in my stomach as I heard her words. "I do not know," I said.

"But you *suspect*," she replied, eyeing me with chill hauteur, the like of which I had not seen since I had served as a lieutenant on Colonel Wellesley's staff.

I looked directly at her. "It depends on how she disappeared."

"Come," she said. "You shall see for yourself." She turned and led me down the hall to another room and then thrust open the door.

The room was in shambles, and the windows were wide-open. Either Miss Templar fought mightily, or her kidnappers were extraordinarily clumsy and had fallen over the furniture. I hoped there had been a fight; the thought of Arabella as a helpless captive made the dread and guilt I already felt nearly crushing.

I forced back my emotions and made myself look coolly about the room. Perhaps a fight had occurred here; but there were papers scattered upon the floor from a writing table, and . . . a toothbrush near the water pitcher, and no cup.

I looked at Lady Templar squarely. "Yes, I suspect," I replied. "I promise you I shall retrieve her."

"You had better, young man!" she said sternly, as if I had been no more than six years old, rather than twenty-four. "And you had better tell me what you have to do with the disappearance of my child."

I managed not to grit my teeth, and maintained as much as I could an air of concerned politeness. "I shall certainly tell you, but—" I looked pointedly at the servants gathered all agog in the hall.

She cast the same grim look at the servants, who scattered. "Come," she said. "We shall talk in the parlor."

She shut the door firmly after me, and then sat stiffly on a chair near the window. She did not bid me sit; it was just as well, for I had the uncomfortable feeling that I would have fidgeted under her stern and unwavering gaze.

"Well?" she said.

I paused, trying to find soothing words, but none came forward. "I am afraid Bonaparte's spies are after the Holy Grail, and no doubt believe that Miss Templar has it."

Lady Templar gazed at me, aghast. "You brought the Grail in my daughter's vicinity and did not see fit to tell me? Dear heaven!" She stood and paced the floor, agitated. "I have spent years—*years*—keeping my children from all knowledge of the Grail or any other holy relic, for such things have caused nothing but trouble for the Templar family and have even contributed to my husband's death." She stopped and turned an angry look at me. "When, Mr. Marstone, were you going to tell me—if at all?" She held up her hand as I opened my mouth to reply. "Do not speak! Dare I hope you have not brought the Spear of Destiny with you, either?"

I admit I was confounded. I had not thought she would know of the removal of either the Grail or the spear. I could not help grimacing. "No, I have not the spear. I dropped it in the Thames."

"The Thames." She eyed me as if I were a lizard just crawled out from under a stone. "You brought both the Grail and the spear—at the same time—to England."

"So I was ordered by the Grail Council, my lady."

"The Grail Council." Her voice was full of loathing. "As if that group of dusty old men know anything beyond the end of their noses!"

"I think—"

"Oh, they have caused me nothing but trouble! Did they not send my husband into danger, and eventually to his death? Did they not cause me such anxiety that I lost not one, not two, but five children at birth? It was a miracle my sixth child, Bertie, was born alive, and then Arabella not long after!"

"But—"

"And now this, after all my efforts at shielding them from certain death!" She moved her hand, no doubt to forestall me from speaking again, but I barreled in.

"All of which compels me to leave immediately in search of your daughter; I can do little else, especially because of your hospitality to me in my time of need."

She eyed me skeptically. "You! You were wounded and with a fever but a few days ago—" She stopped, her eyes widening with clear horror. "No . . . Too dangerous a combination . . . You did not . . . In my house—"

"I have the Grail in my bedchamber, yes, my lady," I said.

"You *what?*"

"As a result," I said hastily, "it is necessary that I take it away from here as soon as possible, find your daughter and return her safely to you." I gave a short bow, took my leave of Lady Templar and averted my eyes from her decided swoon onto a chaise longue.

Though every sense urged me to depart the Templar household immediately, I had to go over Arabella's chamber thoroughly, in case I could discern something about her kidnappers and develop a plan to defeat them. It was clear she was kidnapped during the wee hours of the morning. Her maid had apparently come upon the villains, but had been knocked out and pushed into the wardrobe, her mouth gagged. Anger burned within me—Arabella's abductors had not the decency to take her maid with them for propriety's sake, and they did not hesitate to brutalize women.

I forced back my fury; I had to keep my mind clear. They had gone down the rope ladder that had been cleverly attached to the window by means of sharp hooks sunk into the windowsill. It was too bad that her room was in the back of the house rather than in the front facing the street. There was a garden in the back, and a sizable fence, ensuring that any activity would have a good chance of being concealed.

I noticed with satisfaction that more than a few strands of black hair were scattered near the window—I could assume from this that Arabella had fought her captors and had done some damage to them. It gave me hope she would do her best to defend herself, and it also meant she might do what she could to delay them. There were also two sets of muddy footsteps on the floor, one large, one smaller. Two men, then. It would be more difficult to escape two men than one.

As to where she might have gone: Bonaparte is not a patient man. I doubt he or his minions would know much about the elements necessary for the proper use of the Grail; the so-called Emperor of France would be interested only in the power the Grail (and the Spear of Destiny) could give him. Therefore, they are traveling south to the coast, heading for France.

I hope. I will question the servants and anyone who might have seen them. As soon as I find Miss Templar, both of us must find our way to Rosslyn Chapel to secure the safety of the Holy Grail.

It is clear I stayed too long in the Templar household. I lost the

Spear of Destiny, and the Grail Guardian has been kidnapped by Bonaparte's spies. As a result, I know I am not worthy to be the Grail Knight. I will therefore offer my resignation to the council.

But I cannot think of that now. I must save Arabella, and do my best to bring the Grail to a safe place and one committed to the forces of good, far away from Bonaparte's ambition. I am impatient to be off, but I cannot afford to be ill-prepared for this mission. Only a minute more, please God, until— Yes, it's a footman delivering the papers I need. At last, I'm off—

—*W. Marstone*

❧

April 13, 1806

I have the most dreadful headache, and the jostling I received in the horribly sprung coach did nothing to remedy it. And *why* am I in a coach when I have a pain that seems fit to split my head? Why, it is only this: I have been kidnapped.

Kidnapped. I am quite annoyed at myself. This is my reward for resolving to put away my pistols and sword and trying to behave in a ladylike way so that I may get myself a husband: I had no weapon at hand in my bedchamber when villains climbed through my bedroom window, and thus could do nothing but bite, kick and hit with my fists. I think I would have been able to knock at least one senseless if I had made a good swing with my reticule, in which I normally carry a sizable rock or two. Unfortunately, I had managed only to loop the reticule's cord around my wrist before one of the men knocked me on my head.

If anyone imagines I am bitter about this, they would be correct. This is what happens when I obey Mama's rules about not carrying such unladylike objects as a pistol (even a lady's pistol!) or a small dagger. However, she said nothing about rocks. As a result, I have a few rocks in my reticule, along with my pencil, a small purse containing a few shillings, a needle and thread, a handkerchief large enough to be practical and a small account book. I felt better for having rocks; I used to carry a pistol in my reticule when Papa was alive, for there had been the danger of being kidnapped for ransom when Papa would go off on one of his missions or other. But after his passing, Mama deemed our situation no longer dangerous, for no one else in our family works for the Home Office or is sent off on missions.

As a result, I cannot fathom why these men wished to kidnap me, for though my dowry is respectable, no one could say either it or my family's funds are anything near a fortune. Unless . . .

I remembered William's insistence that Bonaparte's spies are after the Grail. Yet, I do not have it! How could anyone think that I might—

⁂

I had to put away my account book and pencil—awkwardly, for my wrists were still sore from being tied a few hours ago. The carriage had drawn to a stop, causing the man who sat in the coach with me to give one more oxlike snort before waking.

I was not let out.

One of the villains returned to the carriage with food, a somewhat decent meal of cheese and ham between two thick slices of bread. I confess I was quite hungry, so I ate all of it as well as drank down the large mug of hot tea. There is no use in refusing food, for it does no good to be faint with hunger when the opportunity to escape presents itself. There was not enough room in the coach for me to swing my rock-laden reticule, so I could not do it then. How unfortunate that I did not bring my penknife with me, for at least I would have had the satisfaction of sticking the horrid man who had been sitting next to me with it.

He is a large, dull-looking cad, and would have looked better if he did not have a nose so sharp that he could very likely cut paper with it. He fancies himself, for he attempted a flirtation with a chambermaid at the last inn at which we stopped, but she very intelligently snubbed him. I believe his name is something-or-other Front-de-Boeuf (Beefhead, a well-deserved name, I am sure), which is a French name, but his accent sounds more Irish than French. I have heard that some Irish have rebelled to the point of wishing to ally themselves with Bonaparte. Regardless, either origin bodes ill for me.

The other villain's name is Vaudois, but he goes by the name of Waldo here, as it is an easier name to go by than a French one. He is a slight, lean man, who seems to have a penchant for red-and-white waistcoats. On first sight he seems harmless enough, but he has a way of blending into the background, despite his waistcoat, that makes me feel more uneasy about him than I do about Beefhead.

At least I have a strategy. I have so far pretended to be a senseless, helpless twit of a female, and so they do not suspect I have a plan of escape. I note they have pistols but no swords. I do not know where they are taking me. Screaming does not help—they have convinced almost all we have encountered that I am headed for a madhouse. I did manage to slip a note and a shilling to a maidservant at one inn, asking her to give it to William Marstone, should he come by. A foolish hope, but . . .

After my meal, the carriage took me another few miles to a cottage. I am now in a small bedroom, and from its musty smell, it has not been occupied in a while. Still, the bed has fresh linens on it, my hands remain untied, and I still have my reticule.

I hope that Mama will not worry herself to death and that William will not be so foolish as to try to rescue me, for I fear his injury and illness will hamper him should he confront these villains.

William . . . I wish I had believed him about the Grail. I did, in part. Had I believed him wholly, perhaps the Grail would have been well on its way to its rightful place by now.

However, it serves no one for me to brood over past ills. I must look to the future, and for now put away my account book. Night comes near, and I must be sharp and observe as much as I can. As soon as I find a way, I will escape these villains who have taken me from my home.

If I am indeed the Grail Guardian, I have been a poor one. But I shall make amends, somehow. I hope. . . .

—*Arabella*

April 14, 1806

I am convinced that everything William has said is true.

The villains brought me to another cottage as the sun slipped barely past the horizon, and locked me into a room that was fairly comfortable, though plainly decorated. I decided to rest, for I had little sleep in the ill-sprung coach, and thought it best to be as alert as possible for any means of escape. I left a torn piece of my skirt hanging discreetly on a small bush outside my window. I hope whoever comes after me—if anyone does—will take it as a clue.

It seemed my head rested on the pillow but a few minutes before the door opened and Beefhead entered. It was morning—I must have slept heavily. He eyed me warily, for all the world as if I were a snake about to strike, which lifted my mood considerably. There is something surprisingly jolly about striking fear into one's enemies. Unfortunately, before I could grasp my rock-laden reticule, Mr. Waldo also entered. It was a bit of a letdown that both of them were there, but the wary look also existed in Mr. Waldo's eyes, so I was able to maintain a cheerful frame of mind.

"At the very least, you should have the decency to knock before you enter!" I said, eyeing Beefhead and Mr. Waldo with—I hoped—all the chill hauteur a patroness of Almack's might level on a vulgar mushroom of a person. I had the satisfaction of seeing Beefhead shift uncomfortably on his feet, but Mr. Waldo seemed unmoved.

"And I demand you release me! I cannot see why you have abducted me, for I assure you I am not worth any sort of ransom you might wish to level on my family."

"So you have said before," said Mr. Waldo. "But I assure you that you are worth . . . something." I managed not to swallow, for I did not want to appear as if I knew what he was talking of. I admit to some fear; I have heard of what the abductors of young women have done to them. However, he turned to Beefhead and nodded, and my attention was caught by the two velvet bags—one small and one large—the man held.

"I take it you are familiar with this?" He nodded to his companion in crime, and the other man opened the bags. I noticed that Beefhead had on white gloves, which was not at all complementary with the rest of his attire, but all thoughts fled from my mind when a golden glow peeped from the large bag, and then fully beamed forth from the item that was held carefully in his hand.

It was a spear, but oh, that word is so inadequate to describe it! I managed to see past the pure light emanating from it to the way it was made, and saw that the spear's blade was old, so very old, and the base of it was encased in gold. It had been clumsily attached to a wood handle the size of my hand—*Too short*, was the thought that flashed in my mind. Yet it made me think of the oppressed, the poor, the enslaved, and how it was necessary to free them from evildoers and from those whom power had corrupted. . . .

"And this?"

Waldo's voice pulled me reluctantly from gazing at the glow of the spear, and I looked at the item Beefhead had pulled from the other sack.

It was my tin toothbrush cup. I could not help casting Mr. Waldo a look of disbelief, for what anyone might want with my tooth cup—

I quickly looked away, pressing my lips together. I knew immediately what they had been after, and I was hard put not to laugh. Indeed, I am afraid my shoulders shook with suppressed giggles, and I hoped that the two men would mistake it for suppressed weeping.

"You may refuse to confirm it in words, but your expression tells all, Miss Templar," Waldo said. "You well know what we hold, ordinary though they may seem: the Spear of Destiny, and the Holy Grail."

Ordinary! Well, my tin toothbrushing cup is certainly ordinary, and the actual Grail looks not much more than that (except, I admit, for the slight glow and disappearing holes), but how anyone could look at the spear and think it ordinary is beyond me. The light that comes from it would brighten a room at night as well as any fire.

But I put on a woeful expression, and looked sadly at both Beefhead and Waldo. "I scarce know what all this should mean to me! I am only newly out in London, and have not even been presented to the queen. And if you do indeed have this—this Grail, did you call it?—and that nasty pointy thing, and if they are so important to you, why do you need me? Please let me go home to my mama! I am certain she is ill with worry over me!"

I hated to sound so ineffectual and whiny, but I was counting it as strategy, and if it led them to underestimate me, then it was all to the good.

For one moment Waldo looked uncertain, and Beefhead rolled his eyes. "Mr. Waldo," he said. "The lass doesn't have enough *nous* to do what the Emperor wants done. Why don't we just leave her at the side of the road and be on our way?"

Waldo turned on him in a trice. "Because, you idiot, she is the Guardian of the Grail, and its powers are magnified if she wields it. He who gains the Grail gains abundance. He who gains also the Grail Guardian gains the wealth of the world, even immortality."

Beefhead scratched his nose. "I dunno, sir. It looks like a tin cup to me."

Waldo let out a snort. "That is because only the worthy can see the true value of the Grail and the spear."

For one moment I wondered if Mr. Waldo also saw the spear as I did, but a flicker of uncertainty appeared in his eyes, and I knew that he did not see the bright glow from it that I saw.

An odd feeling—dread and surprise as one—made me glance at the items before me again, and I remembered William describing the Grail to me not long ago, how he had spoken of its glory and light. I pushed away the memory and the thought. I could not think of such things right now, but I knew that I had to choose between escaping and keeping the spear from Bonaparte. Thank God William still had the Grail. If these items have the power that Waldo says they do, then it would not do at all to let either of these things travel to France. I had to find some way to take the spear from these cads.

Well, I could let them take my toothbrush cup. . . . I hid a smile as a plan formed in my mind.

"I must not be worthy, then, sirs, for I cannot see the value of either of these silly things. Indeed, I would not even touch them, for they are no doubt dirty. Especially not that horrid pointy thing." I clutched the cord of my reticule tight in my hand and took a step back.

Waldo seized my arm and shoved me forward, so close that I could touch both the spear and my toothbrushing cup if I wished.

"Enough of your idiocy, girl," he said. "Take up the Grail." A greedy expression lit his eyes. "It would not hurt for me to gain a little from this endeavor, for the devil knows I worked hard enough to retrieve the spear from the Thames."

Beefhead looked affronted. "But, Mr. Waldo, it was me who—"

"Silence, you stupid—"

A loud crash sounded from the front of the cottage, and the two men looked toward it. Quickly, I seized the spear—

I gasped, for a fiery power flowed through me, and I looked at the two men who had turned from me toward the crashing sound. I could see evil like a dark cloud surrounding Mr. Waldo, and a lesser gray around Mr. Front-de-Boeuf.

Evil must be crushed, I thought. *It must be eradicated!* As if it had a will of its own, my hand lifted my reticule, and with a swirl of silk-enclosed rock, I whacked both men on their heads with a swiftness and precision that astonished me. I had not thought I could hit both so quickly.

They fell like cows to the slaughter. Elation filled me. I looked toward the direction of the crashing sound and stepped over the men. I felt powerful. I could defeat *armies*. I raised my reticule and whirled it over my head. "Come, enemy!" I cried. "Come and be defeated! Come and meet your *doom!*"

The door flung open, and Mr. Marstone entered, eyes wild, his neckcloth askew. "Arabella!" he said.

I dropped my reticule, the power flowing out of me. "Oh! Will— ah, Mr. Marstone." I patted my hair awkwardly, suddenly sure that it had become mussed during my exertion. "How—how do you do?" I cringed inwardly. Dear heaven, I sounded like a fool, but now that the power had left, I seemed not to have much energy to gather my thoughts properly.

His gaze shifted beyond me and I turned, noticing the uncon- scious men I had knocked out. He looked at them, and then at me, and his brow furrowed. "What—?"

"They were bad," I said hastily. "Very bad. They also took my toothbrushing cup." These words did not sound any better than my last ones. I took in a deep breath, shook my head and let my breath out again with a whoosh. My head cleared. "They kidnapped me, and they also said I was the Grail Guardian, Will! But I cannot be, for I can see little difference between the Grail and my tooth cup, and oh, they did not see a difference, either, for they took my cup, thinking it was the Grail."

"Dear God." He stepped closer. "Arabella, I thought I'd never find you," he said, and took me in his arms. "I don't know what I would have done—"

For one moment, I thought he might kiss me, but he stopped, took in a deep breath and released me. "I—my apologies. I should not have— It was not proper."

"Oh, no . . . that is, you are no doubt fatigued—the danger, the threat to the Grail. You were naturally upset and did not think. . . ." I admit to disappointment, though he was right that he should not have held me so.

He looked me over anxiously, and I could not help feeling pleased that he was concerned. "Are you well, Arabella?"

"Nothing but a small bump on my head, for they did knock me out, but I suspect they could do nothing less, for I fought them and threatened to scream."

His expression grew stormy as he stared at the two men still unconscious on the floor. "My only regret is that they are not awake so that I may knock them out myself." He came closer, peering at them. "Still, I must say you did good work. I expect they shall have sore heads for quite a long time." He looked at me again and paused, then seemed to go pale. "You . . . the spear. You have it."

I blinked and looked down—indeed, I still held the spear. It fit so easily in my hand that it seemed a natural extension of it. "Yes," I said. "The one called Waldo said he fetched it out of the Thames, although I believe Beefhead—er, that is, Mr. Front-de-Boeuf—was the one who searched for it." I brought it up and looked at it fondly. "Is it not the most beautiful thing? So pure, and so noble of purpose. I cannot think it anything but a relic of true justice and freedom. See how it shines so brightly!"

He shook his head. "It is dangerous, Arabella. Only the Grail Knight can wield it without damage . . . and even I have not been able to contain its power. It is why I threw it in the Thames, once I was pursued and realized I was not a fit Grail Knight."

I shook my head. "Will, I cannot believe you have anything less than pure motives. Did not the Grail shine for you? It did not shine for me." I smiled ruefully. "If you are not a fit Grail Knight, then I am not a fit Grail Guardian."

He touched my cheek briefly. I could not help moving just a little closer to him, and blushed that I did so. I caught sight of Beefhead's foot and sighed.

"I think we should tie them up. I do not want them to follow us home."

"Yes." He hesitated, and then motioned his hand toward the bed. "The bedsheets will have to do, as I do not think we have time to search for rope."

I nodded. "Let's do it, then."

It took less time than I would have thought; though Mr. Waldo had a fairly light frame, Mr. Front-de-Boeuf did not. Yet my energy seemed quite renewed since Will's entrance into the cottage. I helped him drag the two men to the middle of the room and tied them together with a good solid knot of the bedsheets. I looked at our handiwork critically. "I don't think it will hold them that long, Will. The sheets look a bit worn, and Beef—er, Mr. Front-de-Boeuf—is not a weakling."

"I hope they will last long enough for a magistrate to attend to them—if one can be hurried through his breakfast fast enough." He cast me a quick glance. "You called me Will."

I bit my lower lip, then eyed him squarely. "I hope you do not mind. I—I have come to think of you as a friend."

"A friend." For a moment he looked grim; then he smiled at me. "I am glad you think me so."

"You may call me Arabella, if you wish." I felt bold in offering him my given name, but I thought it too late to be so formal after our adventure . . . and he had, I realized, used it already without my permission.

"Arabella." He said it as if he were tasting sweet wine, and this time I was annoyed at myself when I blushed again—I have always had more self-possession than to be blushing all the time. "I thank you," he said. "In private, though, and not in public."

I gathered up my self-possession once more. "Oh, yes, of course. It is only prudent," I said.

"Prudent. Yes."

Silence hung between us for a moment, and then I hastily moved away from the men we had tied up.

"I suppose we should go," I said.

"Yes."

I began to feel annoyed at Will, for he had not been taciturn until now. However, he turned and held open the door for me as we left, and his lips had turned up in a wry smile.

"What is it?" I asked.

"Nothing—or rather, I cannot tell you yet." He cast a glance at the tied-up men behind us. I nodded, understanding. We did not have time to discern whether Misters Waldo and Front-de-Boeuf had gained consciousness and perhaps were only pretending otherwise. It was best to talk away from them.

A fine curricle and pair of bay horses stood before us, and I remembered the Marstone family's reputation as superb breeders and healers of horses. The horses neighed upon Will's approach. A grin spread across his face, but he shook his head. "Sorry, friends, but I'll need you to give me your best speed right now. I'll make sure you'll get your reward as soon as all is safe." The lead horse snorted and shook its head, which made Will laugh. "I promise, Hoof, I promise!" He turned and handed me up into the carriage.

"You talk to your horses," I said, as he put a soft blanket over my shoulders—the gesture warmed me as much as the blanket did. "And . . . 'Hoof'?"

" 'Hoof' is short for 'Hoof-on-the-Wind.' Horses are more apt to do as you wish if you talk to them," he replied. Hoof snorted again. "Very well, if I say 'please'!" He took up the reins. "Please, Hoof."

I reflected that even though Will had been right about the Grail, talking to horses as if they could understand could be counted as an eccentricity. But somehow, I did not mind it.

The horses went forward with hardly a touch of the reins and the carriage rolled smoothly on the road. I was glad to see it was an exceptionally well-sprung one, with well-cushioned seats; it would certainly not cause my head to hurt as Mr. Waldo's coach had.

Although . . . I noticed my head had not hurt since William had come into the cottage. I cast a glance at him; if it was true the Spear of Destiny gave one power and strength—and certainly I had gained enough strength to knock out two large men with my reticule—then it was likely the Grail did just as William had said: It could heal. Therefore . . .

"Will, do you have the Grail with you?"

A definitely uncomfortable look came over his face. "Yes."

Suspicion began to rear itself in my mind. "Was that not dangerous?"

"Yes," he said.

"Did you not suspect those who had taken me might have been after it?"

"Yes."

He was becoming taciturn again, but this time there was nobody to overhear what we were saying. I remembered his words to me about my being the Grail Guardian when he had been ill at home in London. My suspicion grew stronger.

"Would I be correct in thinking you are not taking me home?"

He grimaced. "You are right. And yes, I am well aware that because you still have the spear, you could no doubt knock me out of this carriage in a trice. I ask that you hear me out, if you please."

I crossed my arms and frowned. I admit to a bit of alarm, for once one has been abducted by villains, one cannot feel comfortable about being abducted again. But Will had come to my rescue—very well, I had come to my own rescue, but he would have had I not done it first—and I could not deny that amazing power and swiftness had seized me when I had taken up the spear.

Something more than ordinary was afoot, and I could not help feeling excitement at the thought. I had been abducted, a handsome man had come to my rescue, we had ancient and mysterious relics in our hands and I had defeated my enemies with my rock-laden reticule. Despite my wish to please Mama and marry well, I had always wished for adventure, and now I was having it. My only regret was that I had neither a pistol nor my sword at hand, but I am not one to quibble about small details. My hand sat lightly over the spear underneath a fold of the blanket. I would manage one way or another, I was sure.

Something in my expression must have revealed my thoughts, for his look of discomfort and anxiety lessened. I nodded, but I gave him a stern look nevertheless, for I did not want him to be too comfortable about not telling me immediately.

He sighed. "We are not traveling back to London. Instead, we are going to Scotland."

For one moment elopement to Gretna Green came to mind, but I banished it. Will did not look as if he was in the throes of romance.

"Scotland," I said.

"Um, yes. I would prefer to go to the closer Glastonbury Tor, but I am certain it is where Bonaparte's agents would expect us to go. As a result, we shall travel to Rosslyn Chapel."

"Rosslyn Chapel." Abduction, Scotland and a chapel. If Mama had not informed me of the Marstone family's long and impeccable history of honor and integrity, not to mention wealth, I would suspect the worst. A miserable expression came over Will's face, and I felt sorry for him instead. "Go on," I said, more gently than before.

He cast me a grateful look. "Both Glastonbury and Rosslyn Chapel are places of power. Glastonbury Tor is very old, and legends of it abound with everything from its being the elvenkind's dwelling place to Arthurian tales to stories of the divine." A troubled look entered his eyes, and I could not help putting my hand on his arm. He smiled at me, looking a little comforted. "I was to take you to Glastonbury, to have you, as Grail Guardian, set the Grail in its place of power, but after my injury and your abduction, I must assume that Bonaparte will send his agents after the Grail and anyone who has it in their hands. The spear as well," he amended, after I had lifted my brows and tapped the relic on my lap. "The farther away from France we are, the better, and they will assume we will go to the closest place of power to claim it for the British Isles. And even if they assume otherwise, the Grail Council has more guards available at the chapel than at Glastonbury."

"And how do you know this?"

His expression darkened. "I received word before I left London that the guards at Glastonbury are dead."

A small shock went through me—I did not mind adventure, but it had not occurred to me that Bonaparte's agents would kill. I pondered his words for a moment, then noticed that his expresson had become more uncomfortable than before. "And?" I asked.

"The Spear of Destiny must also be dealt with. I wish it had been lost, as I had intended, for I understand that to have the Grail and the spear together in one person's hands is dangerous beyond imagination. But apparently Bonaparte's agents will go to any lengths to get the spear, and since it seems to have the unlucky tendency to reappear despite my attempts to deny them such a violent artifact, I can only assume that I am indeed fated to deal with it as well."

"You!"

He raised his brows at me. "As the Grail Knight I am allowed to handle it. But I have never liked it, nor felt comfortable touching it for long." He shrugged, and sadness seemed to settle on him.

I squeezed his arm. "I have not had trouble with it, and it has actually helped me against those villains who kidnapped me. Perhaps it is not a matter of being a Grail Knight, but one's affinity for such things, and becoming used to being around it." An odd feeling, like a half-remembered tendril of memory, grew in me, but I could not quite grasp it. I shrugged and pulled the blanket over my shoulders a little closer, for the sun had gone behind a cloud, and the air had chilled.

"No," he replied. "I am sure the Grail Council would have mentioned all of this to me, as it would be an important point in one's training as a Grail Knight. Indeed, they have always said that the female Guardian and the male Knight have in them an ancient lineage that gives them a special gift for handling these holy relics. Both the Templars and the Marstones have that lineage."

The thought crossed my mind that perhaps the Grail Council did not know everything, for I remembered overhearing a few heated discussions between my mother and my father about them, and Mama never did seem to like them. But she had acknowledged that duty was duty, and had given in to Papa's assertions that the council must be obeyed. Will's voice had the same stubborn set as Papa's had.

I began to understand Mama's dissatisfaction with the council.

I shook my head reluctantly, however. "There are practical diffi-
culties, Will. The men who abducted me did not think to bring a
change of clothes for me."

"Well, I did."

I stared at him. "You couldn't have!"

He grimaced. "I did. I convinced your mother to pack some
clothes for you."

"No."

"Yes," he said. "I said that, as it might take days before I could
find you, it might also take days to return you, and therefore it would
be best if you had a supply of clothes." He jerked his head toward the
back of the carriage. "A small trunk is secured to the tiger's seat."

"Well," I said, dumbfounded. "I never would have thought she
would have agreed to it . . . unless . . ." No. She might try to push an
acquaintance between Will and myself at home before she knew of
the Grail Council's involvement in Will's affairs, but she would never
try to arrange anything that was beyond the pale of propriety—

Oh, heavens. I glanced at Will, saw his miserable expression, and
the full realization hit me: Regardless of my unwilling abduction,
regardless of Will's good intentions, I had been away from home long
enough to ruin my reputation. Had he not found me, it would have
been ruined indeed; but it would be just as ruined . . .

If he had not, no doubt, told Mama that he would right that
reputation.

I gritted my teeth. It was clear to me he had no wish to marry me
and he'd been forced to entertain the idea; his grim look alone told
me that. I eyed him with equal grimness.

"I understand the need to secure the Grail and the spear to their proper places. I understand my disappearance from home—in the company of Mr. Front-de-Boeuf and Mr. Waldo, and now you—has endangered my reputation. But if you think these circumstances will force me to marry you, you are mistaken. All we need is to hire a maid when we come to the next inn; she will sit behind us in the tiger's seat, and accompany me from now until our task is done." I crossed my arms. "I am surprised Mama did not offer to accompany you here herself."

A brief grin flashed across his face before he grew solemn again. "She did, but I convinced her—truthfully, as you know now—that it would be too dangerous. By the by, I have already sent ahead for a maid to accompany us, so you need not worry about that. Oh, and speaking of maids, it was clever of you to leave a note with one not far from London. It helped a great deal in locating you."

A blush again warmed my face at his praise, but soon left me, for I did not feel any better when he looked relieved that a maid would solve the problem of my reputation. Nonsensical of me, of course, for I did not wish to marry him, either. If he were indeed the Grail Knight—well, I could not have any doubt about that now—then it seemed he would be in far more danger than Papa ever had been on his missions.

I do not think I could bear that.

It was dark when we came to the inn, and I was too conscious of the curious looks given us when we entered, I without a maid to accompany me. Will has gone to ask about the maid he had hired for me.

We must push forward without delay to where the Grail—and

the spear—will be well guarded against Britain's enemies. Even stopping to take on a maid is more time than we can afford.

I am now having dinner, but feel I must eat in haste and be gone from the inn as soon as possible. I will end my writing here for now—I am tired, and most of all confused. I feel I cannot think of my reputation and the Grail and Bonaparte's spies all at once . . . and of Will and his fate as the Grail Knight.

—Arabella

Chapter 4

IN WHICH THE KNIGHT AND THE GUARDIAN OF THE
GRAIL MAKE DISCOVERIES.

April 15, 1806

The maid for whom I had sent ahead is not at the inn. Dear
God, it needed only this. The situation is bad as it can be,
for now Arabella's reputation is more at stake than ever.
She is the Guardian of the Grail, and it has ever been the legend and
tradition that the responsibility for shielding the reputation of the
Guardian falls to the Knight.

The innkeeper would not release any of his chambermaids, even
when I tried to pay him for one to be Arabella's. The best I have been
able to do is to ensure that a chambermaid stay with Arabella at
night. Even this accommodation makes me uneasy: There is no guarantee this maid cannot be bribed to give information as to our direction after we leave.

I pledged to Lady Templar I would do my best to protect her
daughter. I do not know if her ladyship knows all that the pledge of

a Grail Knight implies, but it is not necessary that she does. I am committed to protecting Arabella body and soul, and to forfeit my life if need be.

It occurred to me that it would be gratifying if Arabella were aware of it, but it seems her education in Grail matters has been sadly neglected.

There is no time to dwell on the lack, however. At first light, we must depart, maid or no maid. It will be faster without one, and speed certainly is of the essence.

⁂

April 15, 1806

I look over the words I wrote last night, and their practicality is no comfort after I saw the dismay that appeared on Arabella's face once I relayed the news regarding the lack of a maid to accompany her on our journey. I do not blame her, and feel my failure acutely. But my admiration for her rose when she lifted her chin and ignored the speculative looks the innkeeper and other guests gave her when we departed from the inn in my curricle.

She said nothing as she sat herself in the carriage, and nothing for the first half mile we traveled. Instead, she gazed out at the country-side, the green and brown hills barely showing the first blooms of spring. I saw her hands twist in her lap, and I was sure she must be feeling the burden of society's eventual speculation and the uncertainty of her future. A look of sorrow flitted across her face, and it made me glance away from her; I felt ill at the thought that I had caused whatever sadness she might feel.

"Miss Templar, I would consider it a deep honor if you would consent to give me your hand in marriage." I blurted out the words awkwardly, and mentally cursed myself for a fool.

She turned, her curls flying about her face as she fixed her startled eyes on me. "I beg your pardon?"

She need not have looked so shocked, I thought. I focused my gaze ahead of me, gaining better control of my thoughts. "Miss Templar, I respectfully ask the honor of your hand in marriage."

She eyed me with disdain. "And I respectfully refuse," she said. "If you think I would accept anyone's marriage proposal under such circumstances as this, you are sadly mistaken."

"It is in such circumstances as this that you should consider it." I glanced at her; her set jaw and angry expression did not encourage me, but I pressed on. "Think, Arabella. You have been gone two days, with no chaperonage. You have defended yourself well, I know. Excellently, in fact. But this means nothing to the world at large. Even if I had returned you to your mother immediately, you would still have spent more time without a maid than is acceptable. Society will judge you harshly, regardless of your innocence. I cannot let that happen to you."

She looked swiftly up at me, her lips parted, her eyes suddenly alight, and once again I was seized with a desire to kiss her. I closed my eyes; I could not. It was not right. I felt it was my duty to protect her, even from myself.

"It is my duty to protect you," I said aloud. "As the Grail Knight, I cannot let your reputation be ruined."

"As the Grail Knight." Her voice sounded flat. I looked at her again, but she had folded her hands in her lap and was looking down at them, as if considering my words.

"It will take at least six to seven days to reach Rosslyn Chapel," I said as gently as I could.

"A week." She looked at me, and again I could see the sorrow in her eyes. I took her hand, ignoring the slowing of the horses as I did so.

"I know you cannot like the circumstances of my proposal. If it is any comfort, your mother has agreed to it if it proved necessary." I fished inside of my greatcoat pocket for the note Lady Templar had given me, and then held it out to Arabella. She stared at it for a moment, then took it from me and read it.

"Oh," she said. "I see." She bit her lower lip for a moment, then sighed. "Well . . ." She took in another breath and looked at me squarely. "Well, may I think about it for a while before I give you my answer?"

I knew from the expression in her eyes that she knew she had little other choice, as did I. But the circumstance in which we found ourselves could not be what a lady would want in a proposal, and the least I could do was let her have the temporary pretense that she had the option of refusal without damage to her reputation.

"Of course," I said.

"It would be more convenient—faster to Scotland—if we were married and did not have to have a maid," she said.

"It would."

"And it is our duty to put the Grail in its rightful place, and to keep the spear from our enemies' hands."

"Yes."

"I do not like duty very much," she said.

"Neither do I," I said.

"Oh, William! We are in a terrible mess." I heard a watery chuckle. I looked at her sitting on the seat beside me, her back straight as an ensign's at military inspection, her lips turned up in a wry smile, her eyes wet with tears.

I was instantly lost. "Ah, Arabella," I said, and then took her in my arms and kissed her.

She did not resist, only let out a sigh and let me bring her closer. Her lips were soft and sweet, sweeter than wine, her breath like honey. A chill breeze blew into the shelter of the curricle's hood, but it did not matter to me; her warmth was enough, her willingness to let me touch her and hold her. I dared deepen the kiss, and still she did not resist. Instead, she put her arms around my neck and pressed herself closer to me. In that moment, I knew she was more precious to me than the Grail.

The Grail.

For the first time in my life, I nearly cursed its existence and my duty toward it. I drew away from her, and the dazed look in her eyes almost made me kiss her again.

"What . . . ?" she said.

I cleared my throat. "We . . . we must be going." Hoof and Thunder had obediently stopped though I had let loose the reins; they knew my mind better than I had myself, it seemed.

"Oh—oh, of course," she said.

Perhaps only a few minutes passed—it seemed like hours—before Arabella suddenly said, "Yes, I will marry you."

She shifted herself closer to me and put the blanket across both our laps. I was glad of the warmth, more glad that she was the source of it. For this short while, I would take comfort in it.

—*W. Marstone*

꧁

April 15, 1806

We were married today, Will and I.

I should have wished for something more than a special license (he had to prove to Mama his intentions before he left London, and nothing but a special license would do), witnessed by strangers in a small country church, but I suppose I must be more eccentric than he, for I could not help thinking it much more romantic to be married while traveling *ventre à terre* from villains bent on destruction and the capture of mystical relics of power.

It was faster not having a maid tagging along, for we needed to leave on a moment's notice, and we were on a dangerous mission—I could not allow someone not dedicated to the Grail or other powerful relic to be put in the danger we had to risk.

Our situation was still, unfortunately, awkward. I went to the rooms reserved for us, and a chambermaid helped me undress and put on my nightgown. But when I answered the knock on the door soon afterward, I discovered that it was not "rooms," but "room," for it was Will, looking decidedly uncomfortable as he entered.

"We are married, so the innkeeper assumed . . ." He stood near the door, his posture stiff and awkward, and looked at something past my left ear. I turned and looked behind me; there was nothing on the wall but a crookedly hung, badly executed still-life painting of over-ripe fruit in a bowl. I looked at him again, and noticed heightened color in his cheeks.

I realized what he had already understood: We would be spending the night together in this bedchamber. I could feel the warmth creeping into my face as well.

I could not bear that he be embarrassed on my part. "Well, and the man assumed correctly. We are indeed married, and I understand it is not at all unusual for married people to share the same bedchamber."

"It is awkward. . . . It is not what either of us had intended—"

"Intended or not, we are where we are," I said stoutly. "I—I do not mind it." I thought of the risk we were taking, how Will had pledged himself to protect me, the Grail Guardian. I knew what kind of risk that could entail. Did not my father also go on missions for the Grail Council? And look at what had happened to him! I felt, suddenly, that I would seize what I could of being with Will, just in case, just in case. . . .

His expression lightened for a moment, but he then shook his head. "You don't understand, Arabella. As the Grail Knight and the Grail Guardian, we must be pure and chaste."

I was conscious of more disappointment than I expected. I admit, I was curious as to exactly what occurred in the marriage bed, for though I had a vague idea—and of its outcome—Mama had not of course told me much about it, other than it could be pleasant, for she had not expected I would be married this soon. "Oh," I said. "Well . . . well, there is not anything to sleep on other than the bed."

"I shall sleep in the common room downstairs," he said. He turned to the door, but I ran to him and took hold of his arm.

"But will not that bring too much attention to us? Especially after we have taken such care to obscure our whereabouts?" We had even

taken on false names: We were registered at the inn under the names
of Mr. Wilfred and Mrs. Rowena Evanhaugh. I never did like the
name Rowena, but it is my middle name, and thus it was more likely
I would answer to it than if the name was totally false.

His expression grew frustrated. "You are unfortunately correct."
He looked toward the hearth. "I will sleep by the fire."

Suddenly I was tired of honor and purity and the Grail and being
the Guardian—all of it.

"Don't be silly. We are married."

His expression grew stormy. "By God, Bella, do you not understand? I should have kept the Spear of Destiny instead of discarding
it, but dropped it into the Thames because I was so unfit a Knight
that I could not properly keep it safe, leaving it to be found by
Bonaparte's agents. I managed to be wounded and disabled in the
course of my duty—which I have not yet accomplished. I did not
keep you from your kidnappers; indeed, I no doubt led them to you.
I have failed at being the Grail Knight. And now, when all I have left
to redeem me is taking the Grail to its proper place with enough
guards to ensure its safety, and the purity to which I have tried to
dedicate myself, as is fit for a Grail Knight, you tempt me beyond
bearing."

"I do?" I felt considerably cheered by his admission. "What a
pretty thing to say. I have never had anyone tell me I am tempting."
I smiled at him, for I do believe it was the first time I had heard him
say something complimentary about my looks. I moved closer to
him and put my cheek against his chest. I could hear his heartbeat—
and it sped up when I put my arms around him.

"Bella, don't—"

"Why not? We are married. Is it not a blessed union? What could be more pure than that? As for chastity—surely you do not intend to be false to me?"

"No, never—"

"Good," I said, and shamelessly pulled him to me and kissed him. He groaned and put his arms around me, deepening the kiss, and it was more glorious than the kiss we had shared in his curricle.

He took me to the bed, and it did not take long before he had discarded his clothes, and I my nightgown, and we were under the bedcovers, kissing lips and cheeks and napes of neck. And, oh, his hands, his hands, featherlight and strong, discovering me like an explorer in a new land.

I laughed and wept with joy as he came into me, and suddenly, suddenly, there was light about us, brighter than the glow of the spear when I had last held it before me. I gasped then, and cried out, for the light that surrounded us pierced me with an intensity beyond anything I had ever experienced. Will's grasp on me tightened as he pressed himself deeply into me, and he must also have felt the light, for he groaned as if from his very soul, and he kissed me again.

We slept. When we awoke, it was not yet dawn, and the inn was silent. Once more Will moved upon me without any persuasion from me at all, and once more there was the light, brighter than the moon that shone through the window.

The next time we awakened it was dawn, and we needed to be on our way. I could not help peeking at Will as he dressed, and found he also was looking at me. I grinned at him, which caused him to come to me and take me in his arms again, kissing me breathless.

But he put me away from him after a while, and shook his head. "We need to leave, Bella." He nodded toward the bed. "And we cannot forget to take the Grail and the spear with us."

I had taken the precaution of stuffing the Grail and the spear inside pillows at the headboard, and carefully took them out. I blinked as I placed the Grail on the bed.

"William . . . does the Grail look different to you?"

He looked at it and shrugged. "It looks as it ever has, beautiful and full of light." He frowned as he looked at the spear in my hand. "However, the spear has changed."

I did not understand it. The spear looked as glowing and as noble as I had first seen it, but the Grail . . . had changed. It looked less like a tin cup and more like a gold—though simple—goblet.

I frowned at him. "How different does the spear look to you?"

"It had been a dull, rusty thing that would not take a polishing no matter how much I tried, but now . . ." He gazed at me. "Did you polish it?"

"No," I said. "There is no need, as it shines bright with silver and gold."

He also frowned. "It does not shine silver and gold to me, but it has lost the rust it once had, and the blade has a mirrorlike shine." He paused. "Did the Grail look different to you before you put it in the pillowcases?"

"No, it did not."

He shook his head. "It is a mystery, and I wish I knew what it meant. Another mystery on top of the fact that you and I see these relics differently and not as we should." He shrugged. "We have no time to ponder it, alas." He picked up his pocket watch and looked at it. "We must leave quickly. I shall order food to be taken with us, and a bottle of ale."

He finished dressing faster than I, and went down to the taproom for our food. I wrapped both the Grail and the spear separately, careful not to let them touch each other, as Will told me to do. I shook my head as I set them into the trunk of clothes that Mama had packed for me. I felt sure the change in our perceptions of the Grail and the spear meant something significant. I only wish I knew what it was.

—Arabella

April 17, 1806

We have been blessed with good weather so far as we have traveled, and I have not seen nor heard any suspicious characters following us. This means nothing, however; a clever enough spy could keep himself unseen and unheard.

We had, by necessity, tied up the villains who abducted Arabella, and not with stout rope, as I could have wished, for we had to make haste, and the bedsheets were all we had. We could not kill them, of course; their blood would have been on our hands, and we could not then put the Grail in its rightful place. As a result, I would not be surprised if the two endeavored to follow us.

Though I have my own horses at regular stops along the road to Scotland, I could not risk that I be tracked by my use of them. As a result, I had to say good-bye to Hoof and Thunder when they clearly grew tired from their exertions (rewarding them well, of course, with pieces of dried apple and good stable provisions), and use horses unknown to me and unfortunately not as fast.

I believe I brought them to their best speed, however, as I know horses well, and these were inclined to do as I willed and with a good nature. Still, the persistent worry nagged at me that it would be much faster for two men on horseback to travel than a man and a woman in a curricle, however well sprung the carriage and however willing the horses.

For all my worries and concerns, however, I found myself greatly relieved upon marrying Arabella. Relieved that the problem of her reputation was no longer a concern, of course, and that we could concentrate our efforts on the mission of the Grail.

I admit it is a comfort as well, and to be frank, giving up the notion that I will ever be a competent Grail Knight is another relief. I had not liked the designation when I was told I had it, but duty was duty. Once we are relieved of the Grail and the spear, both Arabella and I can retire to my family's estate, and can have a good life there. That I feel uncommonly cheerful at the prospect of attending to my horses and at avoiding further inconveniences such as spies and being shot at is further evidence that I am wholly unfit for the job.

Yet I do not feel chastened at all by marrying Arabella, but positively jolly. I had thought I would have to give up hope of a family life, for I have been taught that purity is the tradition for a Grail Knight, but now that I have cast off that designation, a whole new world has opened up for me. I may not adhere to absolute chastity, but I am more than happy to be chaste in our marriage.

And . . . selfishly, there is also the tradition I have heard of (not confirmed, however) that the Grail Knight must at some time give up his life for the Grail Guardian. As much as I am glad I have married Arabella, I am also glad I will probably have a good long life, as long as anyone might expect.

Which no one can expect if we do not ensure that we speed posthaste to Rosslyn Chapel.

I decided to hasten as much as possible, and Arabella, bless her, did not protest. We gathered as many provisions as we could depend upon not to spoil, and for the next eight hours drove on the Great North Road as fast as the horses would take us. We stopped only long enough to change horses and to take brief refreshment, and as a result, probably traveled a good hundred and twenty-five miles in that time.

Had we not felt pursued, I am sure our journey would have been more enjoyable, for the clouds were considerate enough not to drop any rain on us, and even allowed the sun to shine. I found Arabella to have a good sense of the ridiculous, and she is far more intelligent than I had first given her credit for. I am ashamed I misjudged her; I suppose it came from not coming to London much and not knowing whether those mentioned in the society page were as frivolous as they sounded. I should say I did not pay much attention to their activities, as military concerns and my duties as the Grail Knight had occupied my time more than the doings of the ton.

I am tired and will end my writing here; though the Grail has done much to heal me faster than anyone with even a strong constitution might expect, my wound still causes me to tire easily. I am looking forward to my bed, and not least because Arabella will be in it with me.

Speaking of beds—one other thing I must note. There are times when a bright light shines around us when we . . . are together there. I do not know what it means or whether Arabella has been aware of it. I am not sure how to approach her about it; I must be careful of her sensibilities, as she was of course untouched when we married, and mentioning it as something associated with our intimacies might embarrass her.

It's awkward, but I shall try to be as delicate as I can about it. I may not have had much experience with the fair sex, but at least I know that one must approach these things with care and consideration.

—*W. Marstone*

࿇

April 18, 1806

I am not entirely sure whether to be annoyed at the shimmering light that surrounds us or not. I cannot deny it is a great deal of fun when Will and I are in bed together and kissing and touching each other all over. It was even enjoyable when we tried to do it in a chair. But I do not believe I am mistaken in thinking that each time we are in bed—well, even when we are in a chair—the light becomes brighter.

Will has not mentioned it, but surely he must have noticed. While Mama was right in saying the marriage bed could be enjoyable, she never said anything about shining lights. If the glow was the natural result of a man and a woman touching each other, then a certain modesty must require that our activities not be advertised, or at least not much more than a squeaking bed frame might (although the last time we encountered one such, Will took such slow and gentle care to keep it from squeaking, I was hard put not to make noises myself).

If the glow is some extraordinary event, then it is even more important that it not be advertised.

It has become quite distracting. Last night, Will was kissing my breasts, making me feel extremely breathless, and the glow began to brighten the space inside the bed curtains. I had drawn them closed—as well as the window curtains—for fear that the light might be noticed by anyone who could be passing by outside. I closed my eyes, and for a short while it sufficed, and indeed intensified the sensations Will was giving me as he moved his lips between my breasts and down my stomach. I clutched his hair as he descended lower, for what he was doing seemed exceedingly daring as well as excruciatingly intense. But even with my eyes closed, I could tell the glow had grown much brighter, for it was as bright as the sunlight and as annoying as when the morning light strikes one's closed eyes when one would rather be asleep.

Except I did not want to be asleep; I wanted Will to be inside of me again, and not to think about glows and what it all might mean.

"Will—oh, ah!—Will . . ." I tried to speak, but it was difficult, for he had not only kissed all the way down *there*, but was doing something indescribable with his fingers, indescribable because it made me temporarily lose my mind.

The light became even brighter.

"The light—" I gasped.

"Mmm?" He began to kiss his way up my stomach to my breasts again.

"The—oh!" I could not say more. He had risen above me, and I daresay he did not see the light then, for his eyes were tightly shut, and then he entered me and I could not think of anything but him, and him within me, and the touch of his hands and lips. All I could do was hold him tightly, clutching his hips with my legs so that we might be joined as deeply as possible. The light around us flashed, as bright this time as lightning, so that I was glad I had closed my eyes, for I am sure I would have been blinded had I not.

He sank down upon me and I held him close, kissing his neck and shoulder, unwilling to let him go. I dared open my eyes, and the light about us had dimmed, but still glowed as if a full moon had taken up residence inside the confines of our bed.

"Do you see that, Will?" I asked.

He kissed me deeply and said, "I see only the most beautiful woman in the world." We had not parted, and he began to move within me again, but though I wished very much to move along with him, I shook my head.

"Stop, oh . . . Oh, stop, please."

He slowed but instead of moving away from me, he pulled us to our sides, holding me close. "Yes?" he said, and kissed my neck.

"The light—do you see it?"

That made him stop and look at me. "The light?"

"Yes. Every time you service me, a glow appears around us."

He looked pained. "Service."

"Is that not what you do?"

"I am not a horse," he said. "It is called 'making love.'"

I smiled at him. I liked that it was called making love. So much better than *service*. "So, when one makes love is it usual for a glow to appear?"

He parted from me, and I thought I saw an expression of relief pass over his face. But then he grew thoughtful. "You see it, too?"

"Yes, it's very bright and hard to miss, although I was not sure whether you saw it, for your eyes were very tightly closed a few minutes ago."

He smiled and let his finger drift lazily across my breast. I shivered, then realized the glow persisted, for I should not have been able to see his expression at night with the bed curtains closed. I lightly slapped his hand away. "Of course you see it, and right now, too, for I can see your silly grin from here when I shouldn't at all. What does it mean?"

His brow furrowed. "I don't know. Nothing in my training as a Grail Knight mentioned anything like this. I, ah, was supposed to—"

"Remain pure, I know." I thought of when it first happened, and how it appeared each time after that. "I think . . . I think it becomes brighter every time we make love."

"I have not noticed a change," he said.

"Well, it isn't a great deal of brightness each time, just a little." I pondered it—was it progressive, or was the brightness a random thing? "Perhaps we should take note of whether it becomes brighter or not." I reached down to touch his . . .

I do not know the word for it. I shall have to ask him sometime.

Regardless, his response was quick, and the light did indeed seem brighter than the last time. Just to be sure, we made love once more, and yes, it was even brighter.

"What do you think?" I asked, after I caught my breath at last.

"Marvelous," Will said.

"No, I mean the light."

"That, too."

I sat up and eyed him sternly. "Will! This is serious."

He sighed. "Very well. It did change and become brighter. I still do not know what it means." He sat up as well, gathering up the pillows that had scattered across the bed and on the floor, and putting them between us and the headboard (not the pillows with the Grail or the spear in them, of course—*that* would not be right). He looked about the enclosed bed, at the darker corners of the space, at the narrow distance between us, and then took my hand in his and squeezed it. For one moment the light seemed to pulse brighter; then it faded again. He looked at me, his brows raised in surprise. "It is coming from us."

I swallowed nervously. "It's a good sign, isn't it?"

"I hope so," Will said. "It's light, not darkness, and it reminds me of—" He let out a slow breath. "It reminds me of the light that comes from the Grail whenever I look at it."

"Me, too," I said. "That is, I don't see that kind of light from the Grail, but I do see it from the spear." I looked at him hopefully. "Perhaps we were meant to marry, after all? Meant to make love?"

He grinned, then sobered. "That would be a very convenient thing to believe. All I can say is that I hope it is so. Meanwhile . . ."

He took me into his arms again, and settled my head on his shoulder. "Meanwhile, we must sleep, and be on our way as soon as it is light. The sooner we arrive in Rosslyn, the better."

I nodded, and pulled the bedcovers over us again as we settled down on our pillows. For one moment the light pulsed around us again, and I allowed myself to take hope from it.

However, it took me quite a while before I could sleep, for it did not grow dark again within the bed curtains for some time, and I never could go to sleep very well with light shining in my eyes.

We left the next morning at dawn. I could see Will was tired still, and after a few hours on the road, I offered to drive. He was extremely reluctant at first, for I am sure he believed I could not handle a curricle and pair. However, I impressed him enough with my skills so that he permitted himself to take a nap as I drove. I could not help glancing anxiously at him from time to time. He still seemed pale from his injury, and though the Grail had helped him heal quickly, he had lost quite a bit of blood and had suffered greatly from the fever.

Will does not know it, but I have tried and tried to get the Grail to heal him completely. Every morning before I remove the Grail from our room to the curricle, I hold it in my hands and wish and pray that it may rid him of his continuing illness. If he is not a good enough Grail Knight, as he claims, then I cannot be much of a Grail Guardian, for as far as I can see, it has not done much more to speed his recovery.

The Grail does appear more beautiful to me every morning, but it does not glow as bright as the spear. Perhaps the Grail does not like me much. Well, if it is going to be that way about me, a designated Guardian, then I do not feel obliged to like it in return.

I must end my writing for now—we stopped at an inn to secure more provisions, and dared sit for an hour to have our luncheon. Will shall be taking the reins again, and I am certain he shall pick up speed to make up for the time lost in spending an hour here.

—Arabella

Chapter 5

April 19, 1806

It wants only this to make our situation worse. We gained the Scottish border near evening—well past it, in fact, a few miles past Melrose. I had decided to go a shorter, though rougher, route through the middle of Northumberland, and then it began to rain, and rain in earnest. A bolt of lightning, panicked horses and a deep rut in the road was all it took to tip over the curricle.

I seized Arabella as I released the reins and tumbled to the grass— rather, mud—by the side of the road. Pain coursed through my arm, and I hoped I had not opened my wound again. I saw she was well enough, so I released her and went to the horses—a difficult task, as the muddy road made for uncertain footing and the horses were rearing and neighing in fear. But I managed a good hold on the dominant horse's bridle and willed as much calmness as possible to the gelding and spoke in soothing words until both he and the mare at his side settled themselves.

My arm ached, but I could not attend to it then. It was clear the curricle's axle was broken and the body smashed. I worked to release the horses from their traces and glanced back at Arabella. I was glad to see she had assessed the situation correctly: She was already gathering what she could out of her trunk, had tossed a few of her hats to the side of the road, stuffed the Grail into one of her bandboxes and was carefully wrapping the spear into a shawl and putting it into a pillowcase. She tied two ends of the pillowcase with a good, sturdy knot so that it formed a handle.

As a result, by the time I had finished examining the horses for any injury, Arabella was ready to ride on the gelding, the younger and sounder of the two horses. The mare had to trail behind us; the horse had not sustained a severe injury but did have a slight tenderness near her ankle. I did not want to strain it further by burdening her with a rider.

Arabella had found a stump on which she managed a good foothold, and I lifted her up, holding my foot at an angle so that she could step upon it and swing herself up behind me. She smiled reassuringly at me as she took my hand, and I could not help seeing the bruise near her chin as she did so. I hated that she had been hurt, but admired her fortitude.

As we continued to travel, I could feel Arabella shivering behind me, for all that she pressed herself closer to me for warmth. The rain was chill to begin with; as the sky darkened further into evening, the rain became sleet. We had to find shelter soon; I did not want Arabella to become ill. I cursed myself for not changing to a traveling coach along the road, but I had wished to travel swiftly, and my curricle was the fastest carriage I knew of, a compromise between a slow, heavy coach and riding on horseback.

I breathed a sigh of relief when I saw a light in the distance, and the gelding must have sensed my emotion, for he picked up speed. A large building loomed: We were clearly on a gentleman's estate, and if he was inclined to be hospitable, we would soon find respite.

It took three loud knocks on the door to bring a footman to the door. He was about to refuse us, for our bedraggled state could not have recommended us to a respectable household. But a child's voice cried out from behind him and I could see a dark-haired boy who ran up to the door and peered around it. His eyes widened when he saw us. "Are you angels?" he asked.

"Walt, you rascal, come here!" A male, gently accented Scottish voice sounded beyond the two at the door. "It's well, Rob; I'll see to who is there." The footman obediently bowed and moved aside.

"Look, Da, there's angels!"

A large, robust man opened the door wider and peered out at us. "Aye, well, if they are, they're angels unawares. Come in, come in! It's a nasty sight out there, and a shame to keep man or beast out in it."

Little Walt looked at his father gravely. "Da, you said angels can be disguised—or is that just a story?"

Walt's father grinned. "It's true enough, my boy. And if you would go up for your supper, you will see one, I'm sure."

The boy looked puzzled. "But there's only Mama up there."

"And what better angel is there than your own mama? Go now."

The man waved us farther into the hall as the boy skipped up the stairs; then he turned to the footman. "Rob, get some rooms ready for our guests, and tell your mistress to find some clothes for them as well." He eyed me up and down. "Aye, you look about my size, though I'm afraid I have about a stone's weight more than you."

The gentleman did not ask us our names, but ordered warm blankets and tea for us straightaway, for which I was grateful. He went before us—limping a little and favoring his right leg, I noticed—into a small library in which a warm fire blazed in the hearth. Arabella was shivering violently, so I hastened her near it, pulling up a chair for her near the fireplace and pulling off her half boots as quickly as I could so that her feet would be better exposed to the heat. The footman had already taken my greatcoat, but the wetness had soaked through most of it, and I was in not much better state than Arabella.

A maid and footman entered soon after with two trays filled with thick scones, ham and steaming pots of tea. We were ravenous and went at the meal like starving wolves, and the gentleman took to the food with a hearty appetite as well.

Arabella had stopped shivering by the time we were finished, and except for the ache in my arm, I felt quite well. The gentleman sat back in his armchair, his hands folded over his stomach, and gazed at us curiously.

"Well," he said. "What's your story, then?"

I opened my mouth to speak, but Arabella spoke first. "We are Mr. and Mrs. Wilfred and Rowena Evanhaugh, on our way to . . . to visit relatives in Edinburgh. The storm caught us out and our carriage turned over when lightning struck close and frightened our horses." I saw she meant to go on as we had before, giving the false names we had used all along the Great North Road.

The gentleman said nothing, but looked from one to the other of us, his gaze assessing us keenly. I saw his eyes go to Arabella's left hand, where she wore the signet ring I had given her upon our marriage. I could not help feeling insult at his assumption, but acknowledged that he had no doubt heard of more than a few couples who had come up from England to be clandestinely married in Scotland. "I see," he said.

"And your name, sir?" I said.

He hesitated, then said, "Scott. You are at Ashiestiel."

I recalled the name of the man's son. "Are you . . . Mr. Walter Scott, sir? The author of 'The Lay of the Last Minstrel'?"

The man smiled and inclined his head.

Arabella sat up straight in her chair. "Oh, my. Oh, my. I have read it any number of times!" She clasped her hands together and closed her eyes. "'The feast was over in Branksome tower, / And the Ladye had gone to her secret bower; / Her bower that was guarded by word and by spell /—'"

"'Deadly to hear, and deadly to tell— / Jesu Maria, shield us well! / No living wight, save the Ladye alone, / Had dared to cross the threshold stone,'" I finished. I, too, had read the poem. I looked at Arabella and smiled at her look of surprise, and she grinned at me. It was something we had in common.

The clearing of a throat caught my attention, and I looked at Mr. Scott, whose expression was vastly amused. "Newly wed, I see," he said.

"Yes, sir," Arabella said. "How did you know?"

"I have been married myself for more than a few years; I speak from experience."

"But Ashiestiel . . ." I barely kept despair at bay. I had thought to go only a little past Melrose, then north through Galashiels and Stow to Bonnyrigg, and finally to the town of Roslin. I must have heard "Galashiels" in the last hostler's thick Scottish accent instead of "Ashiestiel." No doubt he had assumed I wished to visit the famous poet, instead of heading toward Edinburgh. "We were to head north from Melrose, not west."

Mr. Scott's brows rose. "If you wish, you may give me your relatives' direction, and I shall send a messenger to Edinburgh to tell them your arrival will be delayed." He glanced at Arabella. "You and your lady have been sadly drenched and no doubt shaken by your accident. I doubt you would wish to travel so soon."

"But we must!" Arabella cried. "It is urgent. We are on a danger—an important errand."

He tilted his head to one side. "If it is indeed dangerous—excuse me, important—perhaps I should hear the whole of it. I am, after all, the local sheriff."

I could not feel comfortable about telling a complete stranger of our mission, but Arabella jerked her head a little, clearly indicating that she wished to speak to me privately. I rose and bowed to Mr. Scott. "If you will excuse me, I must confer with my wife, as it concerns her the most."

He rose and gestured to the chair. "Sit, sit," he said. "I am past due to see my children into bed. Speak with Mrs. . . . . Evanhaugh while I am gone." With a twinkle in his eyes that told me he did not believe we had given him our true names, either, he bowed and left the library.

"We should tell him *all* of it," Arabella said, as soon as the door was shut behind Mr. Scott. "He is the author of 'The Lay of the Last Minstrel,' after all, *and* a sheriff."

I did not see what being a poet had to do with how a man might be confided in. Lord Byron, after all, is a poet, but I would not trust the man so far as I could throw him. But that we might confide in Mr. Scott as a sheriff had merit, and in truth, we had little other choice if we were to ask him for aid. "I wonder if he will believe us." If Arabella had difficulty at first believing she was the Grail Guardian, how much more would a stranger?

"He will," Arabella said firmly, which somehow made me think she did not think so at all. "He is a poet, after all, and are not poets used to thinking of the fantastical?"

The door opened again, and both of us gazed at each other for a long moment before nodding in agreement.

We told him our true names, but it was not easy to tell Mr. Scott of our mission, and we did not tell him all of it. He said little as we talked, only asked a few questions for clarification, and then he asked for evidence.

"The Grail and the spear, you mean?" Arabella asked.

He nodded. "After all, it's quite a long tale you're telling me— Bonaparte, spies, holy relics, a Grail Council." He smiled slightly, and the twinkle appeared again in his eyes.

"You might not believe us when you see them. The Grail looked like only a tin cup to me when I first saw it myself." She went to the bandbox and the pillowcase she had dropped by the fireplace and carefully pulled the items out, laying them near the fire.

He rose from his chair and went to the relics, peering at them carefully. "It does indeed look like a tin cup," he said. "With holes." He lifted it up before either Arabella or I could stop him. "However, it is much heavier than a tin cup full of holes should be."

I could not help myself—I took the Grail from his hands, for I felt uneasy seeing it in anyone else's but Arabella's. As I returned it to her, my hands held hers and she gazed at me, smiling. For one moment, I wanted to kiss her.

I heard a slight intake of breath.

"Good heavens." I looked at Mr. Scott, and saw he had taken a step back. "Angels unawares, indeed." He rubbed his eyes and stared at us, then abruptly sat in his chair again. "It's still there."

"What is it, sir?"

"You . . . you glow. The both of you."

Arabella looked at me. "I wondered if other people might be able to see it," she said, and blushed. I knew what she was remembering, and I feared the glow probably brightened even more.

"Well." Mr. Scott gazed at us, his eyes wide. "Well. I do not know what to say."

Arabella went to him and put her hand on his arm. "Say you will help us, sir."

He looked thoughtful for a moment. "You are going to Rosslyn Chapel. The Sinclairs who built it were more likely to betray Templars and whatever treasure they might have than save them, but who knows what a man might do if he is persuaded to repent his wrongdoing. I have doubts, such doubts." He gazed at us again and shook his head. "But then, you glow, and my boy did think you were angels, and he has never said such a thing before."

He stood up. "Go rest. I will have provisions, a coach, and my own coachman ready for you in the morning, although it sits ill with me that you cannot stay for a while." He smiled at us. "Promise me you will call upon me again on your way back from Rosslyn and tell me the whole of your adventures." He nodded at me. "I can promise you good fishing in our streams, and my dear Charlotte will welcome another female to chat with."

Much relieved, we did as Mr. Scott asked, and retired to our room. It was not long before Arabella joined me in bed, carefully closing the curtains around us as she did. She glanced at me, and I could see her still, for the light between us grew brighter, as bright as the Grail and the spear we had secured on the bed with us for safekeeping. I smiled, for I knew what she was thinking. It was more than an hour before either of us fell asleep at last.

—*W. Marstone*

April 21, 1806

I can scarce believe we have been sitting in a famous poet's coach, with Mr. Scott's coachman Mathieson attending us, a large basket of food for our journey, and hot bricks for our feet. I think it was a relief to Will not to drive, for though he does it with skill and precision, he looks ill, and indeed has not looked well since the accident.

As a result, I shall forgive Mr. Scott for giving me a nasty shock after we departed, thus:

We had driven but a few miles from Ashiestiel, and I admit I was still amazed that we had actually met Mr. Scott in person, and was giving voice to my amazement when I noticed that Will was unusually silent upon the matter. I looked at him and noticed he had an irritated look on his face.

"What is it, Will?"

"This." He fished in a pocket of his coat. "It's a letter from Mr. Scott."

"How completely amiable of him," I said.

"Hmm."

I opened the paper and read:

My Dear Mr. and Mrs. "Evanhaugh,"

I hope you will not think this letter an imposition, and I hope you will trust in my discretion. I have given much thought to your situation. It has been a few years since I have been on the council, but I am still conversant with its ways and its missions, and your tale has given me much thought. Though the council generally is right and just in its ways, let us say their interpretation of certain signs and symbols may not be . . . as precise as it could be.

Both of you say you have no affinity for the items you are bound to. Yet you have the signature characteristics that designate that binding. It is not a coincidence my boy Walt thought you were angels; children are more apt to see without prejudice than adults. Nor were my own perceptions wrong. Both of you seem to think you have failed in your roles, and that all you have left is to return said items to a safe and protected place. But the signs are that you are still as the council has designated. In a way.

I abhor being so abstruse, but I am convinced you understand my meaning. Consider other ways you might correctly be designated. Your work is not done, not now, not after you deliver the items.

I remain, your friend,
Walter Scott, Esq.

P.S. A word to the wise: True love's the gift which God has given to man alone beneath the heaven.

I glanced at Will, glad that we were passing a grove of trees whose shadows hid my blushes. Love. I had not allowed myself to think of the word. I thought of how, as the Grail Knight, he was committed to put himself in the way of danger . . . and of the possible outcome of that.

"Well," I said. "Mr. Walter Scott, the famous poet—*and sheriff*—a part of the Grail Council. Did you know?"

"No. But they're everywhere, not that they reveal themselves when you need them most," Will said bitterly. "I should have thought there would be one, or an affiliate, posted near the Scottish border."

"Yet, Mr. Scott—a Grail Councilman," I said.

"Giving us a more obscure letter than a poet has the right to compose," he continued. "Why does he not simply say what he means?"

"I feel betrayed."

"My thoughts exactly."

We brooded companionably together for a while.

"I thought we might be done with it after we bring the Grail and the spear to a safe place," I said.

"I, too."

"But at least he will probably alert the other council members, and they will perhaps come to our aid."

His lip curled for a moment. "Yes. *Perhaps*. Unless the council decides it would be better for us to go through our mission alone, for some tiresome let's-toughen-the-recruits-it'll-be-good-for-them reason. I would not put it past them, frankly. They delight in putting people through the gauntlet." His lip curled again. "'Putting.' Ha. 'Driving one roughshod through, and kicking one's arse—one's backside once they're done' is more like it." He sighed. "Oh, do not mistake me; I am fully committed to my duty. But it is not as if they do anything but *hint*, you know, and it's damnably annoying."

I squeezed Will's hand. "Indeed, and it is my opinion that regardless of Mr. Scott's letter or anything the council might say, we do not have to agree to any more tasks they might think to give us in the future."

Will's expression brightened, and he gave me a kiss. "Sensible wife," he said. "Very true." He kissed me again, which lingered in a lovely way and then deepened as he moved his hand to my breast, and then I had to shutter the coach windows, for the early-morning sky was dim with clouds, and it would not do for passersby to see a coach glowing its way through the hills.

Our journey to the next inn seemed short this time, and I thought of the few miles we had yet to travel before we reached our destination. *One more day*, I thought. *One more day, and we will be done, and Will and I may return home.* A part of me regretted that our adventure would be over, and that we would return to our ordinary lives.

But I wished it for Will. As we entered the inn, I became anxious, for he seemed pale and wan, although when I removed my glove and touched his forehead, he was not warm. He smiled at me and took my hand. "I'm not ill, Arabella. I only hurt my wretched arm again during the accident, and I'm concerned we might encounter those villains who abducted you."

I glanced at the inn's customers, who seemed more sleepy than curious. I did not see any sign of my abductors, but I still did not feel comfortable. I lowered my voice. "Perhaps we should not have been so . . . active as we have been. Perhaps I should have let you sleep more."

Will grinned at me. "One would think so, but I seem to gain strength each morning we are, ah, active."

I shook my head, blushing. "Or perhaps we should have stayed another day at Mr. Scott's house," I said. "Surely it would have made little difference; we must have shaken Waldo and Beefhead from our tracks by now."

He ordered a meal to be brought up to us, and the innkeeper called out to a chambermaid to lead us up the stairs. Will was silent until we entered our room, a small but comfortable place with a lofty bed, and our supper was brought to us.

"We could not risk it," he said at last. "We still cannot."

I knew he was right. When we were finished with our supper and in the bed, I held him close, and when I awoke in the morning, I found I had not moved, and we were as close, skin-to-skin, as a man and woman might ever be. I wish, now, that I knew whether Mr. Scott was right about true love. The word had not crossed my lips, nor had it Will's, and I wonder if I should risk it; we have known each other so short a time, and all reason tells me I know very little about him. But at least I will write it here before we leave this morning:

I love William Marstone.

—Arabella

Chapter 6

April 22, 1806

It was still dark when we arose in the morning. I was pulling on my trousers when Arabella took the Grail from its bandbox and the spear from the pillow in which we kept them for safekeeping. Her gasp made me turn, and I had to shield my eyes at first against the brilliance. Though I had always seen the Grail as a relic of precious gold and amazing glory, it had clearly changed in appearance for Arabella each day since our marriage, and now . . . it changed for me as well. A relief work of roses and thorns had appeared along the edge, which I had never seen before, and it was so full of light within that it seemed brimming with life itself.

"Do you see them, Arabella?" I asked. "The roses along the edge of it? I've never seen that before."

She held it up and peered at it. "I . . . no. But it's beautiful now, without any holes, and it's golden."

"There," I said. "Now you see it as I do. You *are* the Grail Guardian."

Arabella smiled ruefully. "Perhaps. I don't see any roses on it. But . . ." She frowned for a moment, then sniffed the air. "It smells of roses."

She turned to the spear, and as she held it in her hand, a low rumbling filled the air. Light sparked from it and then subsided to a steady glow, as if it were the source of lightning, and as if it were lit from within. I noticed she shielded her eyes, as if against the sun. It was not that bright to me.

It depressed my spirits. As the Grail Knight, I should have seen the spear in glorious lights, and Arabella, the Grail. Nothing had happened as it should. I took a deep breath and shrugged. Very well, then. Mr. Scott's letter or no, we would deposit these "items" we were supposedly bound to, and go about our lives as an ordinary husband and wife, and truth to tell, I was glad of it. I gazed at Arabella; she smiled at me as she put the spear back into the pillowcase, and though I had failed at being the Knight, I knew I would not fail at being her husband, for I love her.

It was a great relief to realize it then. I did not know how she would take it if I were to say it; our marriage was too hasty, my court-ing of her abrupt, even rude. I shall make up for it once our mission is done.

The final stage of our journey to Rosslyn Chapel seemed too short, and our conversation during it stilted and awkward, as it had not been before. We became silent after a while, and I took comfort from Arabella's hand in mine.

The sun had barely peeked past the horizon when we arrived. My wound pained me more than I had revealed to Arabella; this would be over soon, I thought, and I would be able to rest and heal. Perhaps we would receive a little reward for our efforts once it was done. Perhaps by placing the Grail in a place of power and light, I would be fully healed.

I nodded to Mathiason when we left the coach, and then noticed the coachman frowning as he looked at the horses. The animals were restless; something had disturbed them, and I did not think it was the power of the Grail or the spear. I looked about me, but it was difficult to see beyond the shadows in the dim dawn light. I had to stay alert and watch; the horses' uneasiness said "stranger" to me, and they did not mean me, for I had spoken to them and made myself familiar to them, urging them to their best speed upon our journey.

Not for the first time, I wished for a weapon of some sort. But the council had instructed me to avoid violence when placing the Holy Grail into a place of power, especially in a dedicated chapel.

As we moved through the yard, Arabella looked up and gazed at a carved monument. A sculpted angel held a banner that said, LOVE CONQUERS DEATH. She gazed at me and smiled. "That's a good sign, a good sentiment. There is something inside of me that believes it, Will. I don't know why, but I do." She said it with a certain hopeful defiance, and I kissed her hand. I was not sure I believed as she did, but I would not dispel her hope.

Too soon, I spied the area through which we needed to go to enter the sacred chambers. I will not reveal it here in this journal; the danger is too great for both the ancient relics and any who would take them.

"I do believe I like the chapel better than this place," Arabella said, gazing at the knights and ladies in marble repose over their coffins. "This looks distinctly cryptlike."

I think she took comfort in holding my hand as we walked through the gloom of the chambers. Someone had lit the dank rooms with candles set here and there: a member of the council, I believed, for they always had someone in attendance. I took a lantern that sat on a ledge along one of the cavernous halls and held it aloft. The candles and lantern, the sense that we were expected, should have consoled my sense of uneasiness; we were near our goal.

They did not. Something felt wrong. I looked around, and a dark spot on the floor caught my attention.

"Wait here," I said to Arabella, and moved forward. I noticed, much to my irritation, that she did not listen to me, but followed instead. I raised my lantern as I approached the dark spot and saw that it was connected to a hand—a blood-soaked hand. I took a step forward—the man's wig was askew, showing his thinning gray hair, and his spectacles were crushed, but I recognized him. My breath went from me in a rush, as if someone had punched me in the stomach. I put my hand behind me, intending to bar Arabella from the sight, but when I glanced back, she was on tiptoe, looking over my arm, an interested expression on her face.

"Is he dead?" she asked. "He looks dead, perhaps even newly so, although I have seen only one dead person, and that was Papa a few years ago."

"Yes," I said. "It's Mr. Caldwell, one of the Grail Council."

She winced and put her arm around me. "I am so sorry, Will, if he was your friend."

"No, he was not," I said. "And a more harsh and contrary man I have yet to meet, but he was an honest one, and carried out his duties faithfully." I backed away, intending to leave the place, but Arabella stepped forward, peering at the man.

"Will, I do believe he was killed." She pointed to a rock near the body. "See? This rock is matted with his hair."

Once more I lifted the lantern in my hand and came closer. A patch of gray hair and red wetness clung to the rock next to him. She, unfortunately, was right. I swallowed bile, then raised my lantern higher, looking into the dimness around us. Nothing. No indication of an intruder. One could have left before we came here, but the signs also were that Caldwell had not been dead long.

"Come away," I said, for now it was even more imperative that we not tarry. She moved toward me, and I took her hand in mine as I hurried past the body. I frowned at her. "You are not upset or frightened by this?"

Her eyebrows rose. "Of course I am. But it is not as if the poor man will do anything to us, since he is dead, and it cannot be anything but a horrible inconvenience if I were to have the vapors or go into hysterics, so I will not." She took a quick glance about the caverns. "I am more afraid of whoever killed him." She sighed. "I wish I had my pistol."

I stared at her. "You have a pistol?"

"Not with me, of course, for you did tell me that one must not have blood on one's hands before handling the Grail, and there is always that chance with a pistol." She took my arm and smiled up at me.

I shook my head. Why she was designated the Guardian of the

Grail, I do not know. Between whacking villains on their heads with her reticule and wishing for pistols, she must be one of the most violent of Guardians. I thought of poor Caldwell behind us. Perhaps there was reason.

We came at last to the alcove in which we were to put the Grail and the spear . . . but I could not feel safe in doing so. It is said that these holy relics have a spirit of their own, or perhaps were guarded by angelic forces; the legends vary and are not clear. It's said that one should trust that the Grail and the spear would find their way to places where the divine power was strongest. Yet this did not prevent greedy men who wished only for power and glory from stealing and using them for evil.

I took a deep breath. I had to have faith. I looked once more around me, and something flickered at the corner of my eye. I turned and heard a distinct click.

"Oh," Arabella said. "It's Mr. Waldo."

It was the thinner one, the one who fancied red-and-white waistcoats. It seemed always the smaller ones who had tempers, and I supposed our tying him up exacerbated it, if the pistol in his hand was any indication.

"Mr. Waldo it is," he replied. He gestured with the gun. "I suppose you have the spear with you?"

"Don't be silly," Arabella said. "Why would we have a spear? This is a chapel." She looked up at me, and her eyebrow lifted for one moment. I nodded slightly, noticing that she clutched her reticule a little tighter. "We are to be married, are we not, Will?"

Waldo looked around the dim alcove. "It is a crypt, not a church."

"Aye, and 'tis a place to creep the flesh, too," came another voice behind him. "A great lot of dead people—including the gray-headed fellow," the voice said, with a surprising hint of regret. The one Arabella called Beefhead came forward. I remembered she said he was not as intelligent as the other, though obviously much larger. He looked uneasily around him, and then resentfully at Waldo. "Not a place for a weddin', to my mind."

"A crypt?" Arabella's voice rose, and she turned to me. "A crypt! Oh, how dare you!" She stomped her foot. "You are the most horrid man imaginable! You said I would be properly married! You *said* I would have a wedding dress and flowers, and all you have done is bring me to a place with dead people in it!" Her hands flailed about—including her reticule—and I ducked to avoid being hit with it.

Beefhead chuckled as I did so. "Aye, you'd best avoid her little purse—it's a deadly thing." He rubbed his temple, and I could see a large bruise there.

"Silence!" Waldo waved his pistol at us, and Beefhead immediately closed his lips, looking apprehensive.

"My sweet, you must listen to the man," I said consolingly, and moved away from her, stepping between Waldo and Beefhead. I slightly moved my head, indicating the larger man. If she could hit him with her reticule—it would take but a step for her to be close enough—I could seize Waldo and disable him. I prayed that I could get to him before he could pull the trigger.

She stomped her foot again. "I will not! Not, not, *not*! And you!" She whirled toward Beefhead, her reticule flying toward him.

Beefhead cowered and ducked, but it was enough for Waldo to turn his attention toward them and away from me. I struck him across the jaw, his face looking stunned as he fell into unconsciousness.

But not before the report from his pistol sounded in the small alcove, as loud as thunder.

Time slowed. The reticule flew in an arc over our heads, Beefhead continued to cringe and Arabella fell, a surprised look on her face. Red bloomed over her left breast, and I managed, just managed, to catch her before she hit the ground.

I could not speak, only hold her close. She opened her eyes and looked at me. "Oh, Will, it hurts."

"Hush, hush, Bella." Guilt choked off my words. I had brought her to this; I had failed. Never mind that I was a failure as a Grail Knight—I cared not for that any longer. I was a failure as a lover, as a husband. I had not kept her safe even in those roles.

"Don't cry, Will." Her hand lifted to touch my cheek and came away wet. "I will be well; you'll see." But she coughed, and I could see flecks of blood on her lips. "Oh, Will, I never said it—I wrote it, but I never said it, my dear sweet love, my love, my Will." Her voice seemed to bubble in her throat, her eyes closed and her breath left her. A terrible anger and grief clutched me.

"Is she—"

"Shut up," I said. "Just shut up."

Beefhead retreated. "It's that sorry I am," he said. "I'll not want the bloody spear from you, sir, and I'll be sure to return the Grail thing Mr. Waldo took from you." He paused. "The little missus—she's a fierce one. Maybe it won't be so bad. . . ."

The Grail. They thought they still had it, but it was Arabella's tin toothbrush cup, not the real one. *We* had it—Arabella had it, still in her bandbox. Hope and rage filled me. I cared not who should rightfully handle the holy relic; I cared only that there might be a chance the Grail might exert its power on Arabella's behalf, even if I had failed in my mission.

Gently, I set her down, and then ran to the bandbox she had set near the lighted shelf on which we were to put both relics. I seized the box, tore it open, and pulled out the Grail.

Heat and light flowed from it and around me, but I ignored it. I ran back to Arabella and picked her up, holding the golden chalice in my hand. God, she was still, so still. Anger rose in me again, and I stared defiantly at the Grail. "I have tried," I said. "I have tried, and that should count for something. So I have failed as the Grail Knight. But you *will* heal Arabella. You *will* make my wife well. I may not be what you wanted, but don't take my love from me. Don't—" My throat closed. My eyes closed.

My hands grew hot, as hot as the Grail I held, but I only clutched it harder, willing that Arabella be better somehow.

Her body heaved; I held her tighter. "Please," I whispered. "Please." I could hear her breathe, and her breath did not gurgle, but came freely. I felt like weeping, but I held tight to the Grail, willing that she be well, all well, completely well.

"Ouch."

I kept my eyes closed, holding her tighter.

"Ouch. Will, I love you dearly, but you are holding me too tightly." I opened my eyes, and she was looking up at me, love in her own.

"Oh, God. Arabella." I buried my face in her hair, holding her close again. "I thought I had lost you."

"Of course not," she said. "We have been through too much for me to give up on you. My dear love." She touched my cheek again, and then looked at the Grail. "You know . . . I think Mr. Scott was right."

I thought of the poet's letter, of the stories surrounding the role of the Grail Knight and the Guardian, of Arabella's pistol and dangerous reticule, of her sacrifice. "We were indeed dedicated to the holy relics, as he said. Except . . . I believe you are the Grail Knight and I am the Grail Guardian."

"No, silly. I meant what he said about love. I only wish I had been holding the spear when I tried to whack Beefhead with my reticule, because then I would have hit him." She pulled me down and kissed me.

I allowed myself to be persuaded for a while, and then heard Beefhead clear his throat.

"Beggin' yer pardon, sir, ma'am." I looked at him, and he had his hat in his hand, looking ashamed. "It's that sorry I am I listened to Mr. Waldo. It's been hard times, and the money was too good, and I shouldn't have, and the lass didn't deserve being hurt. If all is well, I think I might . . ." He began to shuffle his feet, moving away from us, and I was willing to let him go, more concerned with Arabella. I turned back to her.

"All is not well!" cried a voice. Dear God, it was Waldo again.

However, a hard *thwack*, a thump and a dragging sound told me that Beefhead had redeemed himself and was taking his erstwhile companion away.

Arabella and I rose to our feet at last, and as we did, she gasped. "Oh . . . oh, Will, look at the Grail."

I still held it in my hand, and for one moment had to shield my eyes from its brightness. But I looked at it again, and it seemed three dawn-colored roses sat within it, and silvery streams of light flowed out of it like sunlit water. A sweet scent floated around me, and when Arabella took the Spear of Destiny from its pillowcase, the light grew brighter. The spear had changed entirely: It was also gold, and a piercing light blazed from it. Arabella gazed at it, and for one moment it seemed she grew in stature, becoming stately and stern.

And then she smiled at me, and was my own Arabella again. *Thank you*, I said mentally. *Thank you.*

"Let's be rid—er, dedicate them now, quickly. Then we can be on our way," I said.

She nodded, and we went to the alcove in which the two holy relics were to reside. I gave her the words to say, and she repeated them after me, and together we put the Holy Grail and the Spear of Destiny together in the alcove made for them so long ago. A high humming sounded then, and shortly increased to a dull rumble beneath our feet. I saw cracks form above the alcove, and pieces of rock from which the space had been carved fell to the floor and next to the relics. Arabella shot forward, about to seize them again, but I held her back. "No," I said. "It is better this way."

Instead, I held her to me and pulled her next to a wall, waiting out the increased rumbling and falling rock. Dust rose, and both of us covered our mouth and nose, but we had to move away nevertheless to keep ourselves from being overwhelmed by the debris.

At last the rumbling stopped, and all was silent. The dust settled, and all we could see of the alcove was rubble. The relics were safe. We turned away. Our mission was done.

"I hope they are not ruined by the rocks falling on them," Arabella said when we came out into the spring morning.

I grinned at her. "If they survived two villains, your bandbox, a pillowcase and hundreds of miles of travel, I am sure they are fine. Besides, they may not be there now."

"What? Do you mean Bonaparte might get his hands on them? After all our trouble?"

"No. The Grail and the spear have a way of disappearing and appearing where they will if they are brought to the right places of power and the right rituals are said." I looked at her and smiled. "If one's heart is in the right place. Or so I believe now."

She took my hand in hers as we approached Mr. Scott's coach again. I ignored the coachman's aghast expression as I directed him to the nearest inn.

"Nay, sir, it'll be Mr. Scott's own house in Edinburgh, beggin' yer pardon," Mathieson said. "If you'll forgive me for sayin' it, the wee lass looks a mite alarmin', and you're no' in good shape, either, I'm thinking."

My opinion of Mr. Scott increased greatly upon this news, and I nodded, and then relaxed in the coach next to Arabella. She put her head on my shoulder as the coach went forward, and I noticed my arm hurt no longer. The Grail had healed me as well. I put my arm around her, and she moved closer to me.

All is well with the world for now, and I am a lucky man.

—*W. Marstone*

❧

April 23, 1806

We took our time journeying back to London, stopping at Ashiestiel and enjoying the Scotts' hospitality. Mrs. Scott is a delightful lady, with an interesting mix of a French and Scots accent, and the children are adorable. It made me think that I should like to have children as well, and when I told Will so, he thought it was an excellent idea and said we should begin immediately to bring it about, and we would have to try more than a few times, perhaps every day, for that was what it would take. Though I understand from Mama that the end of the process might not be as pleasant, I thought at least one could enjoy what one could of the process itself as much as possible.

We had our wedding party not long after we returned to London, and I met Will's parents and his siblings, and when they met cousin Jeanne, we found that she was related to them as well, for Will's ancestor was Catherine de la Fer, a sister to Jeanne's own ancestor almost a hundred and fifty years ago. I was glad to see that Jeanne was welcomed with open arms, and indeed was invited to visit the Marstone estate and stay anytime she wished. I certainly would be glad to have her with me.

Meanwhile, I am very happy. As Will promised, we made a great deal of love, especially after the wedding ball, and though the light that had attended our lovemaking was still about us, I was thankful it was not as bright as it had been when we had the Grail and the spear with us. I did try to see if the light differed depending on the length and intensity of our experience, and I must say it did not seem to matter except when we tried something different, such as having me sitting on top of him, or sometimes on a table.

I did notice that Will had gained a distracted air after a few weeks, and I admit I felt a little restless as well. I found I missed traveling across the country, *ventre à terre*, and I suspected he did also. But the Grail and the spear were gone, and that was that.

We were having our breakfast (actually, luncheon, for we had slept quite late) together in the parlor when cousin Jeanne rushed in, looking pale and very upset. She carried a large paper-wrapped package that looked heavy as she held it awkwardly in her arms.

"William . . . Arabella . . ."

I rose from my chair, alarmed. "What is it, Jeanne? Are you ill? What is it you are carrying?"

She looked distractedly about her, spied the open door, and closed it firmly. She turned to us, then laid her package tenderly down on a table. "You must help me," she said, a note of desperation in her voice. "I was just sent this. . . . My relatives, still suffering under Napoleon's rule—persecuted . . ." She swallowed. "You must see it is the only way." She tore open the package and hurriedly unwrapped the padding.

A magnificent sword lay within the cotton-wool that had surrounded it. I came closer to look at it; it was long-handled, and the blade had curious marks along it—crosses, I thought, or perhaps a row of fleurs-de-lis. A glow began to come from it, and I looked at Will, whose eyes had widened, and then at Jeanne.

"It is the sword Fierbois," she said. "The sword carried by the blessed Jeanne d'Arc—Joan of Arc—into battle." Her voice lowered. "It must be kept safe. I thought, since you are the Knight and the

Guardian . . ." We had told her all, since she was family on both sides. She looked at both of us pleadingly. "The council could help—"

Will and I looked at the sword, now faintly pulsing with light, then looked at each other.

"Dear heaven," he and I said at once.

And then Will smiled at me, and I took up the sword.

Eternal Rose

BY

Barbara Samuel

Chapter 1

"It's haunted, you know."

Alice Magill peered into the pearl gray fog that swirled around the garden of her freshly rented flat in an English village. Over the ancient wall bounding the property was an old woman, stout and bespectacled. She wore a dark blue sweater and a rain hat.

"The house?" Alice asked.

"Well, yes, that, too, but the garden is what I meant. All manner of things come and go through there. I reckon you'll want to be careful at dusk, miss."

"Ah." Alice carefully tucked her skepticism beneath a polite smile. "What kind of things?"

"Cats, for one thing." The woman caught sight of something behind Alice. With a wave of her hand, she said, "Shoo!"

Alice turned to see a big black-and-white cat, very well tended, sitting on a stone bench, his long, fluffy tail curling and uncurling in typical cat boredom. He did not seem to mind the old woman's dislike. As if he were raising a brow in silent complicity with Alice, his left whiskers twitched ever so slightly.

"He looks harmless enough."

"You'd think that, wouldn't you?" She tossed a twig toward the cat, and he dashed into the bushes. "They're not harmless, miss, and I'd watch them if I were you."

Wrinkling her brow quizzically, Alice said, "Thanks."

"American, then, are you?" The woman leaned in more curiously. "What brings you here? Are you studying at the foundation? That's who usually rents those flats, students and teachers."

"Guilty." Alice tugged off her thin gloves and walked over to the wall. The old woman was probably lonely, looking for a little conversation. Nothing wrong with that. "My name is Alice Magill. I'm here to do some graduate work in literature."

"Oh, all of that nonsense is over my head, but welcome anyway."

"Thank you . . . er . . . ?"

The woman gave a lighthearted, almost girlish laugh. "Silly me. I'm Mrs. Leigh."

"Would you like a cup of tea, Mrs. Leigh?"

"Oh, no, my dear. I have to get my garden to bed before the freeze."

"All right. Thanks for the warning. About ghosts and cats. And things." Alice turned back toward the old manor house where she had rented a flat only two days before. The fourteenth-century building came complete with mullioned windows, a pelt of thick green ivy and climbing roses, and a moat. A moat with actual *water* in it, which alone would have cinched her selection.

Under the current light conditions, the possibility of a haunting seemed not only possible, but likely. Fog drifted in clouds of mysteriousness, showing a clump of white asters near a stone bench, then parting to illuminate a single yellow rose on the vine climbing around her bedroom window. So beautiful!

Gratitude rushed into her chest. As long as she could remember, Alice had dreamed of traveling to England. Born to a sprawling Irish-American family in Chicago with more love than money, she had put herself through college, then graduate school, and now had saved enough to come to this little village and its Foundation for the Study of English and Scottish Ballads. From the moment she'd spied the rolling green land beneath the plane, her heart had been singing. England! She was here, she was here, she was here. Even better, now she was wandering around the garden of an ancient manor house with a moat. A moat!

As if that were not enough, she was studying and teaching her favorite legends, all rooted right in these green lands. Life, she thought with a happy sigh, didn't get any better than this. Some— her extremely superstitious Irish grandmother among them—might say she ought to be watching for the other shoe to fall out of the sky and give her a black eye, but Alice subscribed to a cheerier superstition: If you listened to your heart, it would lead you where you were meant to go.

Some said that made her naive. But *they* were stuck back in the sharp winds of the Midwest, while here she was collecting flowers from a centuries-old garden for her kitchen table. With a pair of heavy-handled scissors she'd found in the kitchen drawer, Alice clipped a fistful of blue asters and pale chrysanthemums, and then headed toward the back door. Up the back of the house climbed the rosebush, glossy dark green against the soft gray day. The roses were nearly spent, but a few still bloomed bright yellow. She reached for one, a little bit over her head—

Movement at the edge of her peripheral vision caught her attention. Alice turned in time to see . . . *something* . . . distinctly skitter through the trees. She caught a flash of scarlet, the impression of long black hair, and then the fog closed around her so completely that she felt as if it were a blanket, smothering and too close.

She might as well have been blind. Panic clutched her throat as she spun around in a circle, seeking a marker of any kind with which to orient herself. Nothing. She made a stab at heading toward the back door.

Or at least, she thought it was the back door. Instead, she stumbled over a round clump of aromatic lavender and fell, face-first, in the wet grass. Flowers went flying from her basket, her teeth clicked together painfully and she jarred her right elbow. The wind was knocked out of her, adding to her panic, and she felt as though she might pass out, right there in the garden.

Maybe, she thought, struggling to take a breath, her grandmother was right.

"Breathe!" said a voice.

Alice struggled to obey, but it felt as if two fists were squeezing her lungs tight. The edges of her vision began to blacken, which sent her spiraling into absolute terror, even though some distant part of her brain knew that passing out would be the end of the whole drama, because she'd relax. Her body would take over and do what was required.

"Breathe!" said a man's voice, and a blow struck her between the shoulder blades, startling enough that Alice sucked in a giant breath. Air filled her lungs, then flowed out, and she coughed.

She sat up, turning to thank her rescuer, but the fog was so thick she still could see nothing. "Thank you," she said.

No one answered. The cloud shifted ever so slightly, and she thought she saw a foot in a soft leather shoe, but then it was swallowed again.

Uneasy, Alice went to all fours and gathered the flowers that had scattered when she fell. The basket could wait, since she couldn't see it anyway, and the scissors would likely rust, but she wasn't going to risk another tumble. Getting to her feet, she stepped carefully. Eventually she would come to the wall, the moat or the back of the house. All sound was muffled, but she could distantly hear the water in the moat chuckling along its way. It was at least a point of orientation.

Moving cautiously, she peered into the dense air, and finally spied a single gleam of yellow, like a torch in the gloom. It was the rose against her kitchen window, dewy and bright. It led her the last few steps to the door safely.

Only then, with her palm flat against clammy bricks, did she look back into the fog-shrouded garden. Who had helped her?

Maybe the garden *was* haunted. A cold shiver crossed her shoulders, rushed down her spine.

After her class tomorrow, she would poke around the library for some research on the house. Who knew what dramas and lost loves she might uncover?

❧

Her flat had been modernized with a gas fire in the sitting room and a kitchen the size of a teacup. The bathtub was a bonus, vividly pink, long and deep, but the bedroom, along with the moat, had been a major deciding factor in settling on this flat over another that had been available.

She had to climb a circular staircase to reach it, a hand on the stone wall. As she climbed, it was easy to imagine knights with swords swinging in scabbards at their sides, and ladies in flowing gowns, and the whisper of conversations held for centuries in the walls. At the top of the stairs, an arched wooden door opened into a purely medieval room, with heavy timbers overhead and a vast hearth—where of course she could not afford to light a fire—and a deep window seat with mullioned windows on three sides. Piles of pillows in purple and red and gold littered the bench. A small table stood nearby, ready to hold a cup of hot chocolate or buttered toast. Alice had brought an afghan from home, woven with her grandmother's trademark rose stitch.

After her fall in the garden, she carried a cup of chocolate and an apple upstairs and sat on the wide window seat with the afghan around her shoulders. The fog was so thick that the only thing she could see was the branches of the climbing rose, winding around a drainpipe just outside the mullioned windows. One yellow bud, a perfect flame, was framed in a wavy square of ancient glass.

To ground herself, Alice settled in to read the materials she hoped to shape into some sort of cogent narrative. The history of the Grail was long and deep in this area. A handful of scholars thought it might be buried nearby, deep in the bowels of a church crypt, perhaps, or tucked behind a false wall in a castle ruin. Alice theorized that the lyric poem "Roman de la Rose" held clues to that location, and she'd written a thesis about it. While doing her research on that, she'd stumbled on a little-known ballad from the Cavalier period that seemed to connect the dots. It had been written here, in Hartford.

Lulled by the quiet and the dark day, Alice dozed off over her books and fell into a dream. In it, she was still in her bedroom, but everything was different. Instead of the fluffy floral duvet, the big bed was covered with velvets and hung all around with heavy curtains. A fire blazed in the hearth. Arranged around the leaping, friendly flames were two chairs and a love seat, the fabric embroidered with hunt scenes and stags all in shades of green.

Before her, the window opened, and a man came in. The moon rose over his shoulder and shone over his pale long hair. He smiled as he knelt by Alice, and touched her cheek with the tips of his graceful fingers. "Wake up, my fair Alice," he said in a deep, melodious voice. "I've brought mead and bread and a little cheese."

Cradled by the enchantment of the dream, Alice was not in the least afraid. Instead, her heart caught as she looked up into the young man's face. He was as beautiful as a prince, with aristocratic cheekbones and red lips. His eyes were a deep, velvety blue. His form, too, was beautiful—lean and elegant, with wide shoulders beneath a poet's shirt with flowing sleeves and cuffs, left open at the neck so that she could glimpse his throat and a scattering of hair on his chest. Her blood quickened.

"Come," he said. "Let's sup by the fire."

"Who are you?" she asked, taking the hand he offered, allowing herself to be led to the hearth. She noticed that her clothing was no different. She still wore a simple plaid skirt and blouse, with the afghan around her shoulders as a shawl.

"I am William of Knotfield," he said. "We met in the garden."

"That was you?"

He gave her a chivalrous nod. "It was, my lady."

"Thank you. I don't know what happened. I was very disoriented." She frowned. Confessed the whole truth. "Scared out of my wits."

"It is not . . . the simplest place to navigate." Settling his things on a low table, he said, "I am here to help you learn the rules of this place." They sat on a thick fur rug on the floor before the hearth, where it was warm enough that Alice set the afghan on the floor beside her. He settled a pottery jug next to a loaf of bread on a wooden board with a slab of white cheese. From his belt, he took a dagger and sliced the cheese and handed it to her.

"So what are the rules?"

"There are a few. Do not wander in the garden at dawn or sunset, and when you are walking toward the village, stay well away from the tree at the center of Farmer Potts's field."

Ruddy light from the fire limned his straight, elegant nose, caressed the angle of his jaw. Along his chin and upper lip, tiny glints of gold showed that it had been a long day since he had shaved. She wanted to brush her hands over the hair—would it be prickly or soft? Aware suddenly of her thoughts, she turned her attention to the bread and cheese in a most un-Alice-like acceptance of the odd situation.

And yet . . . "Might I ask why?" she said, and took a bite.

"I am not at liberty to grant you that information."

Alice smiled, thinking how cleverly her dream was supplying details. His speech was so mannerly, his gestures as courtly as anything in a Shakespearean play. "All right."

He caught her smile and inclined his head. "Do you find me amusing?"

"No," she said. "Not at all."

"I'm glad." From someplace she did not quite comprehend, he produced a goblet. "We will have to share this. I am afraid there is only one."

"I don't mind."

The cup was gold, carved with roses that seemed almost to move and grow as he held it within the cradle of his long-fingered hand. From the pottery jug, he poured a thick amber liquid and offered it to her.

His eyes glittered, and for a moment, Alice was afraid. Was this some test? If she drank first, would she be enthralled by him? He was certainly beautiful enough to be a member of the fey. Perhaps she was already falling under his spell!

Seeing her hesitation, William sobered. "I give you my word that I mean you no harm, my lady."

"You drink first."

"Very well." His lips curled up on one side, giving his face an impish cast. He lifted the cup and took a deep draft, then grinned and gave it back to her. "It is mead from my own father's bees."

Firelight moved on the goblet, making the vines seem to creep around the cup. It almost seemed as if the roses were gaining color. Intrigued, Alice curled her palms around the cup and, with a sudden ripple of excitement, wondered whether it could possibly be the Grail. It seemed alive, warm—

Don't be silly, she told herself. The metal was warm from his hands, but no more than that; no living vines crawled over her palms. She smiled at her fancifulness and drank.

The mead warmed her tongue and throat, gliding like summer into her belly. "It's wonderful!"

"Aye," said William. "There are two more things—"

A sudden screech cut through the air. It was a terrible noise—half scream, half roar, a sound of mingled pain and fury.

Alice was torn from her dream, finding herself curled up against the windows, shivering in the cold. Darkness had fallen beyond the window, and she straightened so abruptly that her book fell hard to the floor. Her heart was pounding.

Thinking of the horrific screech, she stayed poised, listening, but the air was as still as a grave.

After a moment, she relaxed, feeling the spirit of the dream return to her, that beautiful young man, the mead and the roaring fire, and that goblet they shared!

"Rich," she said, realizing how she'd woven all the elements of history and legend together. Very nice dream, at least until the end.

But now she was ready for a little supper. All that bread and cheese in her dream had made her hungry for the real thing.

Chapter 2

Morning dawned in gauzy gold, the fog lingering only in the lowest spots. Alice dressed for class in a skirt and boots, donned a light coat and headed for the old castle on the hill that housed the foundation. Her elbow was a little bruised from her fall in the garden, but otherwise all was well. After she tugged her door closed firmly, she spied the yellow rose. Thinking to tuck it into her hair, she stood on a nearby wall and tried to reach it. Instead, as if in protection, a thorn scratched her inner wrist and another pierced her index finger.

"Ow!" she said to no one, and sucked at the bead of bright red blood that appeared on her finger. "All right, all right," she said to the rose. "I get the message. You don't want to be plucked."

Smiling at her own silliness, she crossed over a little stone bridge that took her over the moat to the back gate. One of the best things about the manor house was the fact that it sat a little apart from the village and the walled campus of the foundation. Alice could either drive three minutes on heart-stoppingly narrow lanes bound by hedgerows and blind corners, or she could take the footpath that ran through a meadow, beneath a tunnel of rhododendrons and walnut trees and around the edge of a wide, green pasture. Through the hedges, she could glimpse modern houses built of brick with sturdy glass conservatories attached to the back, but if she looked the other way, across the open pasture to a single tree, she saw only ancient rooftops and the spire of the church. It made her feel she had been transported to another time. As she walked, her feet getting wet from dew-heavy grass, she imagined the centuries of people who had walked this path before her—poets in wigs and flowing sleeves, peasants carrying their goods to the village, maybe even Romans! It thrilled her.

Only the tree was slightly bothersome. It stood there in the center of everything, boughs reaching elegantly in all directions. Perhaps it was for shelter. But wouldn't it be annoying to plow around it?

Suddenly she remembered that her dream had warned her away from the tree. Obviously it had bothered her even more than she realized. She'd have to look up references to such trees.

The walk into the village was a brisk mile. Fields emptied onto narrow lanes lined with modest and very tidy homes built of dark brick. Everyone who could afford to do so had built a sunroom on the southern exposure, and nearly every garden boasted a bumper crop of autumn flowers—mums and late roses and asters.

The lanes led to the High Street, an ancient throughway that had been laid by the Romans and later served as a carriage road to London to the north and the sea to the south. It now wore a hodgepodge of time on its shoulders—a pharmacy with crisp medicinal packages in its windows sat next to a pub housed in a building so old that it hunched like a dowager over the street; a proper little supermarket next to the old church that had been turned into a movie theater. Alice stopped to buy a cup of tea in a paper cup from a coffee shop tucked into a corner of an ancient hotel called the Crown and Thorn. It looked like a painting in a child's book of fairy tales, half-timbered walls and the shape of what must have once been a thatched roof. The window glass was thick and distorted. Inside, people clustered at small tables and lined up at the counter.

Alice joined the queue, breathing in the heady scent of coffee. So misleading, she always thought, because nothing could ever taste that heavenly. She'd never been much of a coffee drinker, not even with the funguslike proliferation of coffee shops across the States. She preferred tea, strong, sweet and milky, something the English did very, very well. Now, *that* was heavenly.

The crowd was the usual mix of commuters on their way to London wearing somber suits and overcoats, students in uniform from the grammar school ordering complicated mixes, and musicians and lecturers from the foundation. There was a gray-haired man, stooped, with funny glasses; a busy woman with sensible shoes. Most intriguing was a cluster of youths who were astonishingly beautiful. One of the girls, in particular, was so lovely that it was impossible not to stare for a moment or two. As willowy and graceful as a dancer, she wore a red cape over which her long, long black hair fell in ribbons. But her face was the lure, long green eyes dominating a face as delicately balanced as a cat's. She seemed the ringleader of the group—the others, varying degrees of stunning themselves, gave her their attention.

This morning, as Alice waited her turn, the girl looked over and cast a disdainful glance down Alice's form. A tiny mean smile turned up her pink lips as she turned her attention back to the group.

Dismissed.

And yet, even as Alice puzzled over her response—was she meant to be embarrassed? angry?—the girl looked back once more, blinking in a way that would have felt malevolent in an animal. Alice thought of a mountain lion eyeing its prey, aloof and predatory.

Then it was her turn and she stepped up to the counter. By the time she ordered her tea and waited for it, the girl was engrossed and did not look back to Alice again.

Odd, she thought, carrying her tea with her into the street. But it was no concern of hers. Today she would lead a lecture on the ballad that had drawn her here, and afterward she could dig into the vast library of folklore and music that was housed in the castle's former great hall.

She was more than a little nervous as she made her way to the classroom she had been assigned. It was a dark and drafty room with enormous windows facing the cold north and a wood populated with birches and oaks with trunks as wide as cars. The green shadows below the shedding branches looked faintly threatening—and Alice had to laugh at herself. That odd fog yesterday had obviously spooked her a bit.

Never mind. She put down her things on the desk at the front of the room and looked for a light switch, but even when she found it, the lights did little to chase away the gloom. She wished for a shawl.

She had been awarded a grant to lead six weeks of study grouped around the ballads of roses and the grail and "The Romance of the Rose," and there were only a dozen students who would join her. The class met once a week, giving each student—and the graduate assistants teaching—plenty of time to pursue their individual courses of study.

As the students milled in, this one smiling, that one ignoring Alice entirely, her nerves settled. She was no more than a few years older than anyone here, of course—twenty-four to their twenty or twenty-one. It somehow made it easier to relax.

Until a knot of the coffee-shop group came in, led by the beautiful girl in her red cloak. She sauntered in wearing tall leather boots and low-slung jeans on her slim hips, a slight smile turning up the corners of her mouth as she met Alice's eyes. Again there was that unreadable glitter. Challenge? Anger?

"Ah, what have we here, boys?" she said over her shoulder to her entourage. Her voice was as low and throaty as one would expect from a face and body like that—everything about her was meant to enchant. Ensnare, Alice thought with sudden ferocity. Like a spider. "The little American appears to be our teacher. Isn't that quaint."

"Hello," Alice said, deliberately looking away from the woman to the youth just behind her. "I'm Alice Magill, and your friend is right: I'm here from America. Anyone else?"

A lithe, athletic-looking girl with long blond hair raised her hand. "I'm Crystal," she said, "from Seattle."

The woman in her red cloak made a derisive noise. "Not Barbie?" she said.

"Very funny. Like I've never heard that before."

"If everyone will get settled, we can introduce ourselves and get started. We have a lot to cover in a short time."

They went around the room and told who they were and what they were studying. The red-cloaked woman was last, of course, after her three minions—all lean and long-legged and somehow from some other era—introduced themselves as John, Laithe and Nicholas. "I'm Acacia," the woman said in her throaty voice. "I'm a singer."

"Thank you." Alice pulled out her notes. "The piece we're going to study next is a folk song that was born of a lyric poem written during the War of the Roses, 'The Ballad of William of Hartford,' which some think might hold a link to the Holy Grail, which most of you know is the cup that Jesus used at the Last Supper, offering his blood to his disciples."

"Ew," someone said.

Alice lifted a shoulder slightly. "The Grail is said to have great powers. And some indications point to its being carried to this very county." She paused to flip open a text, aware of an almost subvocal rustling through the room. She glanced up, but aside from one student rifling through a rucksack, everyone seemed to be patiently listening. Even Acacia sat straight in her chair, her elegant hands crossed quietly in front of her. "Has everyone read the poem?"

"It's pretty obscure," a plump girl said. "Even in the library, there wasn't much on it."

"We've all read it," said Laithe, gesturing to include the knot of students clustered around Acacia.

"Would you like to talk about it?"

"No," he said.

Disconcerted, Alice said, "Anyone?"

Crystal raised her hand. Relieved, Alice nodded at her. "Please."

"It's a chivalrous poem about a young man who catches the eye of the fairy queen, but remains immune to her because he is protecting the Guardian of the Grail. The queen curses him and he's doomed to live in fairyland until a mortal woman frees him."

"Right. As with all chivalrous poems, there is a series of tests before he'll be free. Who can tell us what they are?"

"She has to fall in love with him of her own free will," said another girl with a blurry north-country accent. "And she has to find the Grail on her own to bring it to him."

A snort from the elegant group. Alice thought of them as the Lords and Ladies. "Only one little problem," one of them said.

"Which is?" Alice asked.

"She has to be the seventh daughter. Not many of those left in the world." At a scowl from Acacia, the boy ducked his head, but Alice seized the comment.

"True, there are not many families of that size these days, though I will confess I am the youngest of nine." She smiled. "Anyone else?"

Two others raised their hands. "I'm one of six," said a rough-looking youth with buckteeth. And a girl with long red hair spoke up with a smoky voice. "I'm the seventh daughter. I'll free him. He sounds hot."

The class laughed.

"Why do you say that? What makes him appealing?"

"He protects the woman and the Grail, and he even resists the fairy queen, who is the most beautiful creature in the world." She lifted a shoulder. "It's appealing to think of honor and fidelity. Men don't seem to value those things nowadays."

"They never did," said one of the ladies. "Men have ever been as duplicitous as their cocks lead them to be."

Again, laughter.

"There are some who say," Alice interjected, "that the author was in love with the young man who was spirited away."

"How can they know the writer was in love with the guy if they don't even know for sure who wrote the poem?" Crystal asked.

"It's all speculation," Alice agreed. "The most likely author is Edmund Hightower, who was a young nobleman sent to court in 1465. He was a diarist who wrote a lot about the War of the Roses, and also a young woman by the name of Elizabeth, and it is known that Hightower was devastated by the death of a friend. The poem is said to be a tribute to that friend."

"He made up a fantasy to make himself feel better," said Acacia. "He's a sop."

At least it was something to get the discussion going. "Is fairyland a metaphor for heaven?"

"We call it Summerland around here," one of the boys said, roundly rolling his Rs. "'Tis better than heaven."

"Beautiful. Thank you." She met his eyes. "Would you like to begin reading for us, please?"

He glanced over his shoulder at Crystal, who studiously ignored him. "Aye," he said, and straightened. "I'd be glad to."

After class, Alice headed for the library, where she made notes until her stomach reminded her she had skipped lunch. Looking up, she saw that a light rain had begun to fall, and she shrugged into her raincoat and headed back to the High Street to the pub, where she ducked into the dark room and ordered a ploughman's lunch of cheese and pickled onions and bread, and a pot of tea from the bartender, a baldheaded man with a white apron wrapped around his substantial middle. "Sure thing, miss. You want egg?"

"No, thank you."

"I'll bring it right out. There's a nice spot by the window over there, if you're looking to study."

Alice lifted a hand in acknowledgment and carried her books over to the spot he'd pointed out. Through the leaded window fell pale silvery rain-light, and on the other side was the comfort of the fire, crackling and smelling of resinous pine.

It wasn't until she sat down that she noticed the blond woman from class this morning, head over a thick text. Heavy rectangular glasses gave her an intellectual air. As Alice sat down, the woman looked up. "Hi," she said. "Remember me? Crystal from Seattle."

"Of course. Don't let me disturb you."

"I'd welcome the disturbance, honestly, unless there's work you're focused on. Would you like to join me? I'm about to have a beer."

"I've been studying all day." Alice pointed to the bench seat next to her. "This is a better seat. Join me."

Crystal picked up her book. "It's nice to talk to another American," she said. "At first, I tried to speak only with the locals, but—well, as much as it seems like things are kind of the same, the culture here is different."

"I've hardly been here for a week," Alice said, "but that's something I've noticed."

The barkeep, who had brought over Alice's tea, overheard. "You Americans always want to hug and talk," he said with a wink. "We've done just fine for two thousand years keeping everything to ourselves."

Alice chuckled. "I see."

"What can I get you, dear?"

"Ale, as always, please," Crystal said.

"Half pint, luv?"

She rolled her eyes. "No, sir. You know I like a pint."

He laughed and tapped his hairy fingers on the table, then headed off to fetch the ale.

"His name is Phillip," Crystal said, "and he's one of the nicest people in town."

"Where are you staying?" Alice asked. She pulled the stainless-steel pot over to her.

"Right around the corner, above the pharmacy," Crystal said. "There are three of us sharing a flat with the tiniest kitchen you ever saw, and one bedroom with twin beds and a foldout couch."

"Great tub, though, I bet," Alice said, laughing. "I have the biggest, most beautiful tub I've ever seen in my life!"

"It's true. But we have to turn on a little dial to heat the water. It's totally amazing. I forget half the time and then just have to wash up fast at the sink. There isn't even a shower."

Phillip brought Crystal's pint. On his way back, he put coins in a jukebox, and quiet Celtic music came into the room. Crystal sipped her golden pint. "How about you? Where are you staying?"

"I found a flat in the manor house."

"I'm sure it's beautiful," Crystal said, "but it's a long way to walk, isn't it? Do you drive?"

"No, not yet. I'm sure I'll give it a try."

Phillip delivered the platter of cheeses and onions, and Alice dove in with the grace of a famished dog, inhaling good white cheddar and brown pickles spread on hearty white bread, and the sharpness of pickled onion. "This," she said between bites, "is fantastic. I was absolutely starved."

"There's a cafeteria at the foundation, you know."

"I get wrapped up," Alice said with a shrug. "Lost in my research, and I sometimes don't remember to eat until I'm half-starved."

Crystal inclined her head. "I can't say I ever forget to eat, sadly. If I did, I wouldn't have to run every day."

"Shouldn't be running so much anyway," the bartender said, wiping a nearby table. "A smart man likes his women with a little meat on them. Americans are all too skinny or way too fat; that's the truth."

"Don't you need to keep to yourself or something?" Crystal asked.

He chuckled. "Can't blame a bloke for chattin' up a pretty girl." He picked up a tray of glassware and headed into the back, whistling.

Crystal watched him. "Don't you love the accent? I think that's the whole reason I came."

Her immediate starvation sated, Alice sat back and took a sip of tea. "Tell me about Acacia," she said.

Crystal's gaze skittered away. "What do you want to know?"

"Whatever. She's obviously very bright."

"Mmmm. I don't know very much. She's never very nice to me. One of her little boyfriends talked to me the first couple of weeks and she hasn't let any of them near me since. She really needs to be the center of everything."

"Does she always dress like that? So dramatically?"

"It's sometimes even more so."

People began to drift into the pub, taking seats around the bar and a nearby cleared space where a stool and a mike sat. "What kind of music do they play?"

"Ballads, of course. They're all studying at the foundation."

Alice glanced at the window. Maybe only an hour or so of light left. She wouldn't have time to stay. "So tell me what brought you to England."

"The usual study-abroad thing. I'm an English major, and at least this got me out of Seattle for a while. I'm enjoying the travel. Not so much the studying." She gave a wicked little grin. "Maybe I'll save money and go backpacking around, like the Australians."

"I'm sure it would be fun."

"How about you, Miss Magill? You must be a good student or you wouldn't be in grad school."

"Oh, please call me Alice! I do like to study," she admitted. "I like getting swallowed in the pursuit of some idea, or the romance of a poem. But I've been wanting to come to England since I was a very young girl. My grandmother loved English literature, and she used to read poetry to me."

The bell over the door rang and a flurry of students came in, all swirling hair and colorful coats and long limbs. Two of the boys had been in the coffee shop this morning, and the three girls she had seen here and there. All of them were lovely in a way that was startling and strange. They had red hair and black, sable and gold and wheat, all of it glossy and long. Not a single one had buckteeth or a bad complexion or bitten fingernails.

It was the same group from this morning. "If they're here," Alice said, "Acacia can't be far behind."

"No doubt."

Tugging out a sheaf of bills, she waved them toward Phillip. "Are they all boarding school kids or something? They're awfully well tended."

"I get the impression that they've known one another since they were toddlers, and they do seem to have a lot of money. Very nice cars and clothes and that kind of thing."

"The children of dukes and marquesses and princes, no doubt."

Crystal scowled, particularly at one youth with black hair spilling over his shoulders and wearing a green coat embroidered in a Finnish style around the cuffs and collar. He glanced at Crystal, caught her scowl and his cheeks went red. He turned, as if to come over, but the door opened once more and Acacia swirled in, seemingly accompanied by a gust of green-scented wind. She wore a gauzy blouse that displayed her graceful collarbones and the upper swell of obviously perfect breasts, and her tiny waist was cinched with a thick belt, as if from the Middle Ages.

Behind her came two women and three men, the lot of them laughing, except one.

His head was bent, so Alice could not quite see his face, but her heart squeezed painfully. In the angle of his neck, the fall of his hair and a certain stillness in his movements, he made her think of the man in her dream.

Could it be? She stared, willing him to raise his head. Two of the others passed in front and the man stepped back, shrugging out of a leather jacket he hung on a hook near the door; then he moved forward into the light.

High cheekbones, dark blue eyes, the wide brow and beautiful mouth. Unmistakable, down to the last detail. It was the man from her dream. As this strange recognition settled into her bones, he raised his eyes, caught her gaze and his eyes widened as if in fear.

He recognized her from her own dream? In what world did that even make sense?

Chapter 3

Riveted, holding her breath, Alice gave a startled cry when Phillip spoke at her side. "All set?"

Crystal turned to look at her, and Alice ducked her head to hide her expression.

"Steady there," Phillip said. "I'll just bring back your change, luv."

"No, no, that's fine."

He shook his head. "Too much, even for an American. I'll be right back."

Feeling the heat in her ears, Alice busied herself with a last swallow of tea. She was being ridiculous. A dream didn't come to life!

"What's with you?" Crystal asked.

Alice glanced up to see that the man had disappeared. A wash of emotions, agitation and relief and disappointment, rolled through her, and she blotted her damp mouth with a paper napkin she'd somehow shredded. "What do you mean?"

"You're all flustered."

"I'm fine."

Acacia's group settled at a big round table near the stage and ordered drinks, laughing and chatting only among themselves. The other patrons gave them a wide berth, as the students in class had done, and just as in class, there was an outer circle—hangers-on. The term, mean as it was, came to Alice with particular emphasis.

One of the young men carried a drum to the stage, and a waifish girl with long red hair and an outfit reminiscent of Robin Hood took a seat. "Must be Celtic," Crystal said. "My brother has a drum like that."

"And who else would wear those poet's clothes?"

"Everyone around here. Haven't you noticed?"

And now that she pointed it out, Alice saw that most of the young people in the room did wear the same kind of flowing sleeves and the like. She shook her head.

"Not a fan of Celtic stuff?" Crystal asked.

"It's not that." She looked around herself, at the heavy beams overhead and the fire leaping so merrily in the hearth, and even the heavy wooden platter on which the barkeep had brought her food. The room lacked only torches on the wall to be a completely authentic replication of a pub from centuries before. "It's just that things feel slightly off, don't they?"

"I'm not sure what you mean."

"I don't know, either."

A few more people wandered in, and Alice reluctantly picked up her change from the table. "I suppose I need to get moving."

"Oh, stay for a bit. One or two songs. Just to see what they're like. We'll split a pint."

If she went home, there would only be more studying, maybe yet another depressing letter from her ex-boyfriend, whose decision to climb mountains in Nepal had given life to her desire to finally come to England. He didn't communicate by computer at all, even when he could, considering it a cold method, and letters sometimes took a very long time.

Wasn't the whole point of coming here to see what kind of life she really wanted?

"All right. Not long, though. I don't want to walk home in the dark." She blotted her lips. "I need to powder my nose. Where is the loo?"

Crystal pointed toward a narrow hallway, and Alice made her way to the low-ceilinged passageway and found the ladies' room. A sense of excitement danced in her throat, and her cheeks in the mirror were flushed. It was daunting to glimpse her ordinary face, the ordinary features, when inside she felt so alight, but it was true: There was nothing at all remarkable about her.

But it was difficult to be in the company of the glorious, perfect beauty clustered in the Lords and Ladies.

Lords and Ladies. She frowned, drying her hands beneath a blower, as a waft of an idea sailed through her mind. The fey were uncommonly beautiful to mortal eyes. What if . . . ?

Ridiculous, even for her wild imagination. Fairies!

Really, her imagination had been going wild all day. There must be something in the water.

She headed back toward the pub, but after a moment she realized she must have turned the wrong direction in the gloomy hallway, for she came to a dead end, a cold brick wall behind which she could hear kitchen voices. It was so dark she had to put her hand out to guide herself back in the right direction. The bricks were cold, faintly damp against her fingers.

Within the space of a breath, she realized she wasn't alone any longer. She felt the presence only an instant before a large male hand covered her mouth, stifling her urge to cry out.

"I mean you no harm."

It was the voice from her dream, that unusual accent, the velvety timber, so unusual and fine. She closed her eyes and nodded, feeling his body pressed into hers from behind. His chest, his thighs. He let go of her mouth and allowed his fingers to trail down her arm.

"My heart died three times over in fear when I came in and saw you sitting there." He twined his fingers around hers lightly. "You must not dance." His breath, moist and hot, whispered over the bare skin of her nape, and Alice shivered. His fingertips trailed over the bones of her wrist, her knuckles. "Swear it!"

"I swear I will not dance," Alice whispered.

"'Tis nearly dusk, and you must return home before darkness falls. When I sing 'The Elfin Knight,' make your departure."

"All right."

In the darkness, he edged infinitesimally closer, and his thumb moved in the cradle of her palm, circling upward to her inner wrist. Alice felt every centimeter of her body where it touched him at shoulder blade and buttock and the back of her knee, and felt every centimeter that did not touch him—the weight of her breasts and naked throat and quivering heart.

He bent in, and she felt his lips barely brush the side of her neck. "Do not dance," he said again, and then he was gone.

Alice put a hand to her mouth. Every hair on her body stood on end, and even her scalp seemed as if it had been electrified. Shaking, she took several long breaths to compose herself, then headed back down the hall. This time, she managed to find the right room. It was crowded and jovial, and Alice paused for a moment, feeling curiously as if she had been gone for a very long time.

As she began to cross the room, there came a soft rustling of excitement, as if a dozen hands were smoothing a dozen skirts and sleeves, a dozen feet slid across the dusty wooden floor in soft boots. The excitement was not directed at her, Alice saw, but toward the stage. She turned.

And there he was, the man from her dream. A shaft of light cast a high gloss over the crown of his head, edged the sharp cheekbones, threw into relief the bones on the back of his long white hands. Her lungs were airless, as if she were suspended in some other dimension. He picked up a stringed instrument that was unfamiliar to her. A girl gathered her bells, and a piper clambered onstage, burly and short, with the musculature of a discus thrower. The man from her dream— William, she remembered; his name had been William—gave a nod to the other two and they began to play.

Alice helplessly sank down to the booth. It wasn't as if he just looked like the man in her dream. It *was* the man in her dream. He wore the same green doublet, the same flowing sleeves that made his shoulders so impressive. And that face, so elegantly, brilliantly carved. She thought of him offering her cheese and mead, the air so charged around him, thought of his voice in her ear a few moments ago, his thumb pressed into the hollow of her palm. As if even her thoughts of him carried enchantment, she felt her skin grow hot.

"Who is he?" Crystal asked. "I have never seen him before tonight."

Alice shook her head, transfixed. The drummer hauled up his drum and began to patter out a rhythm. The girl raised her bells, and the piper began to blow. William inclined his head at them, then began to pluck his strings with long fingers. His hair caught the light.

She found she was barely breathing as he leaned forward to the mike.

Even his voice was the same, with a timber and richness that were rare in any case, and his accent so very different from those of the others around him. His voice wove through the pipes and the bells and the strings and the drum in a bawdy, cheerful song that awakened the room.

And yet, he seemed oddly joyless. The others in the band were lively and smiling, even laughing and shouting out at certain points, but William did not. He gave the song a resonance and he even injected the right rhythms, but he lacked their involvement.

William.

As if you could learn a name from a dream! Shaking her head, she took a long draft of ale, hoping to cool her hot throat.

"God, he's beautiful." Crystal sighed beside her.

Alice could only nod. With everyone else in the room, she fell under the spell of the music. She recognized many of them, old songs from the Child ballad collections, which she had studied along with the literature surrounding "The Romance of the Rose." Songs of warning to young women to beware of charming young men; songs of warning to young men to beware of the lure of a sparkling eye; warnings above all to beware of bewitchments and falling in love across classes.

When they began to dance, Alice watched hungrily. The drums pounded right into her ankles, making her tap her toes and fingers. The dancers laughed and swung one another around, and it was utterly magical. She resisted.

A boy, maybe twelve or thirteen, rushed into the pub and made straight for the table of elegants. He bent and whispered in Acacia's ear. She waved a hand, then stood and followed him out. Alice and Crystal exchanged a shrug, and returned their attention to the music.

William had been singing desultorily, but suddenly he stood straighter, and although she had been sitting there all evening, it seemed that he was looking straight at Alice now. For one long moment, their eyes locked, and Alice swore he had some electrical field around him, one that knocked open every cell in her body to his charge. She felt aglow, as if she would lift a hand and find it shining.

And then he looked beyond her at the windows and his expression changed to one of alarm.

It all happened so quickly, within the span of a stanza of a song, which they finished. William leaned into the microphone and looked toward the bar, as if directing his words toward a pretty girl sipping a glass of wine. "Beware the fey and the fall of night," he said, his voice silky and dark. "We've one more song to sing before we take a little break."

"Come, pretty Nelly, and sit thee down by me
Every rose grows merry wi' thyme
And I will ask thee questions three
And then thou wilt be a true lover of mine."

As he sang, his attention was wholly fixed on Alice, and she felt as if her brain were fizzy, lost in some wave of enchantment.

It was Crystal who pulled her out of it, nudging her hard in the ribs. "He's staring right at you! And so are all of Acacia's minions. You're in trouble."

Alice fell to earth. Leaping to her feet, she grabbed her purse and her books. "I have to go!" she cried. Without even looking over her shoulder she dashed into the street.

The gloaming had fallen, not full dark, only the purple light that obscured details and made the world seem as if she could step between times, dimensions, lives. Along the western horizon still burned a line of bright rose sunlight. If she hurried, she could make it home before dark.

The street was bustling. Everyone was in high spirits, strolling together in groups of two and three, with the odd lone woman carrying groceries home from the market in a string bag. As Alice entered the flow of traffic, their utter normality eased the panic that had overtaken her in the pub, and she tucked her hands deep in her pockets, shaking her head. What had gotten into her?

It was the village itself, she decided. The fog and the manor house . . . The very ancientness and atmosphere lent themselves to all the old stories. Not to mention the fact that she'd spent the entire afternoon immersed in tales of an enchanted rose and a lost chalice and all manner of bewitched creatures. Her imagination was running away with her!

Still, once she left the main road to walk across the meadow, she shivered. Shadows crept out from the hedgerows, and cold, damp air swirled around her feet. Somewhere out of sight, a cow mooed. A white cat sat on a fence, bigger than he should be, his gold eyes slanted and focused on her.

Alice walked briskly, keeping her eyes on the bright ribbon of light that edged the horizon. On one side of the path grew a dense bank of trees, walnuts and oaks tangled with rhododendrons. On the other was the fallow field and that lonely tree, sharply outlined against the horizon. In her heightened state, it seemed there were shadows moving around its base, and—so quickly she couldn't be quite sure she'd truly seen it—a thin spill of soft green light.

Despite her nervousness, Alice halted. Peering into the gloom, squinting as if it would clear away some detail obscuring the truth, she tried to separate the gloaming from the shifting velvet darkness.

A noise in the trees startled her, and Alice spun around. An animal slipped out of sight. She started walking again. Time enough to figure out the mysteries of this field, if indeed there was anything but her imagination at work.

And it was hard at work, making it seem as if there were someone following her. Resolutely she kept walking, trying to step quietly and hold her breath. Was that the jangle of a dog's collar? A primeval shiver shook her spine.

The last band of daylight suddenly disappeared and the gloaming fell dark around her in a living grasp. Panic, pure and unreasoning, swelled through her chest, and Alice started to run, a sense of danger tugging the hairs on the back of her neck, clawing at her spine.

In her haste, she stumbled over a root and fell, slamming the heels of her hands and one knee into the earth. The snuffling breath of some creature wuffed across her ear, and Alice cried out, leaping to her feet. Claws captured her upper arm. She turned and slammed a fist toward whatever it was, connecting to a furred nose or neck. It made a furious noise and let her go.

Stay away, said something or someone or her wildly out-of-control imagination.

Alice ran, stumbling, careening, and then—

There was nothing. Only the quiet of nightfall in the air and the chuckling of a stream—the moat!—and a lone insect singing mournfully over the change of the season.

She slowed, her ragged breath coming more easily, and carefully picked her way down the path another hundred feet to the gate and the bridge and her own garden, where a rose burned yellow like a torch against the night.

Safe, she thought, opening her back door. Her hands were shaking.

Chapter 4

In her tiny kitchen, Alice washed her hands and examined the damage. One skinned knee, two muddy palms and a long, undeniably ugly scratch that beaded with blood. "That," she said to the empty room, "was not my imagination."

After making a pot of restorative tea, Alice sat down with her notes. What a day! Something was going on here; that much was true. Not only what had happened tonight, but from the encounter in the garden last night, to the hostile group in the classroom, to the strange—and thrilling—encounter in the pub, it felt as if something were in opposition to her, that she had somehow upset the balance of things by her arrival.

In the back of her mind, her younger sister, Kate, snorted. *Ego, much?*

As if her sister were really there, Alice flushed. It was crazy to imagine that she could have any influence on the inhabitants of such an ancient village.

And yet, she had not imagined the creature in the field. Perhaps it was just a wild animal of some kind—though she had no idea what kind of wild creatures still lived in southern England. Dogs did not have claws like that, and it had been much too large for a cat. Crazy. As crazy as dreaming of a man and then seeing him in real life.

A sense of panicky nerves rose in her chest again.

Oh, come on now, don't be a ninny, the sensible part of her brain said. *Assemble the facts.*

Taking a sip of tea, she took out a pen and piece of paper. Facts. There had been a big fog in the garden. She tripped and fell. Someone had helped her, but then she didn't see him after that. That evening she fell asleep and dreamed of a beautiful troubadour who came in through her window—

No. Facts were not what she needed here. The facts would not give her any answers. Instead she wrote, *What do I think is happening here?*

I think, she wrote with her black pen, *that there are fairies in this town.*

As soon as she wrote it, she felt like a fool and crumpled the paper into a tight little ball. All the reading about the Grail had gone to her head. What she needed was a nice hot bath, a hot toddy and a round of ordinary television.

It would all make more sense in the morning.

⁂

In her dream, Alice saw herself asleep in a pale blue rectangle of moonlight falling through the mullioned window. Wavery lines cast by the panes crisscrossed her cheek and shoulder, her hands clasped neatly by her face. Odd, but she thought she looked lovely with her dark hair spilling over the white linens, in the simple cotton nightgown. Virginal and unawakened.

The window opened quietly and William came inside, again carrying mead and bread and a bag he settled upon the wooden desk. Darkness hid his movements for a few moments; then light flared up from the hearth from the fire he'd built into leaping, friendly light. Still she slept, oblivious.

He lit candles, on the table and by the window. As her observational self, Alice noticed his long legs, his hair caught back in a leather thong like some medieval prince, his tenderness when he bent over her sleeping form. Gently, he touched her hair—a gesture Alice both felt and observed. When her sleeping self turned, however, she was only in her body, looking up at him, feeling the sleepiness. "Hello," she said, again unafraid. "What are you doing here?"

"There may be trouble, sweet Alice. I've come to offer words of wisdom, and to bring you some protection."

It was terribly intimate, Alice lying there warm in the bed, flushed and malleable from sleep, William sitting so close that she could smell the cloves on his breath, oranges on his palms. She looked at his mouth, wide and sensual, and wondered how it would be to kiss him. It hardly seemed dangerous, only heady, the possibilities he presented her.

He took her hand. "Wake up, my sweet. You think you are dreaming, but you are not. Come sit by the fire and listen to my story, and then you may return to your cozy bed."

Alice allowed herself to be tugged upright, pleased when he

seemed to be the one who was trembling, she who was more in control. She smiled at him. "If this is not a dream, how could you even come into my room?"

"It is complicated to explain." From the back of a chair, he grabbed the rose-patterned afghan her grandmother had sent with her and flung it around her shoulders. Safely covering her, she thought. Standing, she took his proffered hand and they settled before the fire. He poured wine into a goblet and gave it to her, then took some for himself.

"This"—he gestured with his hands to the room around them—"was once my home. Long ago."

"Are you a ghost?"

His expression was almost unbearably sad. "No. I am not mortal nor ghost nor fey. None of them, between all."

"But how—"

"That is not important now," he said, and took her hand. "I do not mean to be abrupt, but my time is short. You need know only that my sister was the seventh sister, a protector of the Grail, which was highly desired by one who will not be named. We call her only the Lady. My sister ran afoul of her, and I stepped in. The Lady made a bargain—I was cursed but the Grail was safe."

Even in her dream, Alice felt the creeping cold of her fear begin to return. "I don't see what my part is in all of this."

He bowed his head for a moment, looked into his cup, then back to her. "It is written that a woman may arrive every score of years to try to find the Grail and break the spell. She must be a seventh daughter. She must be of the old line. She must have a quest of her own, and she must come from a land far away." He lifted his eyes. "There are other requirements, but that is where it begins. Shall I go on?"

"Yes." Alice said the word as if answering a vow.

"If the Grail is found and carried to the other side, I can drink from it and be free."

He seemed so desperately weary that Alice moved closer and put a hand on his cheek. "Every twenty-eight years someone comes?"

"More or less."

"For how long?"

"Centuries," he said without inflection. Then again, "Centuries."

"And in all that time, no one has carried out the quest?"

"None." He clasped her hand to his cheek, turned a little and kissed her wrist. "Most cannot even hold their own for a day against enchantment. You have done better than anyone in two hundred years or more."

Alice narrowed her eyes, sliding her hand from his grasp. From her work with legends and ballads, she could guess where this was going. "And you must seduce me, is that it? Make me fall in love with you?"

"Yes."

"Do you love in return?"

"I have not," he said. "But I am not unwilling."

"You don't have to love me, then, for the spell to be broken? I only have to love you?"

"No one has asked that before." He met her eyes without flinching. "But for all I ask, what I can offer is honesty."

Alice lifted her eyebrows in question.

He bowed his head. "I do not have to love you in return. Only seduce you."

"Well, I suppose the fey are not exactly known for their commitment."

That surprised a laugh from William, a deep and throaty sound that was as alluring as everything else about him. "Truer words were never spoken."

As their eyes met, a frisson of desire sparked between them, as if an electric blue arc were hanging in the air. "That was not just me," Alice said.

"No," he said, and leaned closer. "I admit I have been admiring your beautiful mouth since I first spied you in the garden." His gaze touched her lips, and his hand, braced on the back of the love seat, trailed down to brush over her shoulder.

"If the goal is to find someone to fall in love with you, why didn't the Lady curse you with the looks of a troll or something?"

His face hardened. "She wishes for me to be as I am." In the words were shame and fury and something Alice couldn't quite pinpoint.

"You are her—"

"Plaything," he said harshly.

"I'm sorry." Again she felt drawn to put her hand on his jaw, her fingertips near his ear.

He bent his head closer, and she felt his moist breath on her lips, and she swayed closer, feeling him move excruciatingly slowly, his lower lip brushing hers ever so lightly—

A high-pitched whistle sounded beyond the windows, and William leapt up. "I must go very soon. There are things you must know to stay safe. Do not eat or drink from their hands. If you meet them on your own, turn your coat inside out. And wear this to help you see them, and know when you are in danger." From his pocket he took a bracelet, carved of wood, and put it on the table. "Now I must flee, and you must sleep, beautiful Alice. I would that I could stay."

And he was gone.

When she awakened on Saturday morning, Alice did not immediately remember her dream. Sunlight, bright and golden, streamed through the multipaned windows, spilling over the wide wooden planks of the floor, touching the bed where she lay. She felt extraordinarily rested, and gazed up at the window, where the reliable yellow rose added splendor to the morning.

As she rolled over, memory flooded back in: William's long pale hair, his beautiful hands, his confession that he—

She scrambled out of bed, remembering the bracelet he'd left. But of course it wasn't there; nor was there any sign of wine and bread or a fire burning in the hearth. All was just as she'd left it last night, the stacks of research materials, her notes and pens and reading glasses.

Frowning, she rubbed her face. Clearly she needed to get out and get some fresh air. She washed and dressed, then collected her notebooks and a thick-nubbed pen she had purchased for a hideous twelve pounds at the local stationer's. She put on her glasses, to make sure she saw everything plainly, and told herself she would go to the library and do some factual research on the location of the Grail throughout history. It would ground her in the purpose she had in coming to England in the first place, and give her some material for class the following week. And she would stop drifting in this silly infatuation with all things fey.

In the kitchen, she paused for only a moment to have a glass of water. She would buy a tea on the High Street. Elderberry tea, if she wished, just to show she wasn't afraid of enchantment.

Taking her coat off the hook by the door, she turned to put her arms in the sleeves, and for the first time saw the table.

On it sat a carved wooden bracelet, and a bowl of some kind of dark fruit, and a big juicy apple. In a very spidery, old-fashioned handwriting was a note:

Things are not always what they appear to be.

Yrs, W.

It—he—was real.

For a long moment, Alice stood there staring down at the offerings with a sense of breathlessness. What was she to do with them? How could they protect her?

If she was going to have to battle the fey, she ought to at least be prepared. She picked up the bracelet and slid her hand through the opening, put the apple and the dark fruits in her pockets.

William had told her that she would have to find the Grail and bring it to the fairyland, but he had not told her where to find it, or how to battle the fey when she got there, or any number of other things she really must find out.

Tugging a sensible hat on her head, she headed for the library. One could always find answers in a library, no matter what the conundrum.

Chapter 5

Williiam awakened in the pasture, curled beneath the foot of the tree, and knew immediately that he was in the mortal realm again. How long had it been this time? He sat up and looked about, but the fields, fallow with autumn, were much the same as ever. Against the horizon, he could see the church tower and a row of trees. In the faint gilded haze of morning, a white horse grazed near a house he remembered.

His stomach growled, a mortal belly hungry for mortal food, and he knew from experience that he had no money to exchange for it. He would have to scrounge for something, or beg some bread. Or steal. He hated this last, but he had done it more than once.

This landscape had belonged to him since birth, and he knew it intimately. Even over the long years of enchantment, there were things that tended to remain the same—he knew where to find berries and corn and the lushness of an orchard, according to the season. His own manor garden offered hidden splendors that time had forgotten: walnuts and apples, fresh water running clean from a deep well.

In the gauzy morning, he wandered toward the manor house, taking pleasure in the imperfections of the day. The haze, smelling faintly of leaves burning; the sharpness of the air, rather too cold for purest comfort, but gloriously welcomed by a man who knew only the perfection of Summerland.

From the opposite direction came a woman with long dark hair, wearing a sensible garment of dark wool. When she caught sight of William, she plainly started, pausing midstep as if she didn't know whether to come forward or stay where she was. In the end, she set her foot down and kept walking. He liked the firmness in that step, in the undaunted tilt of her chin. As she came closer, he saw that her face was oval and smooth, with large dark eyes behind spectacles. A woman who was much more beautiful than she knew, he thought, and half smiled. "Good morning, my lady," he said.

"It is you," she said, frowning. "Where is your girlfriend?"

"Girlfriend?"

"Acacia."

Darkly, he said, "She is not my anything, but along with the rest of them she is no doubt abed this morning, sleeping off her drunken revels."

"And you are not?"

"Plainly. Do I stand before you?"

"You drank with them last night."

So she knew him in his other guise, when the monster let him out on his leash, fiercely under her control. A wave of anger licked at his lungs, and he bowed his head to hide it. After a moment, he managed, "I am a moderate man."

Studying him with level gaze, she said, "You look different."

"Do I? How so?"

"Modern clothes," she said. "And you look . . . I'm sorry. You look tired."

"You are not from England," he said, and a little buoyancy crept into his heart.

"No. From Chicago." At his blank look she added, "In America?"

"Ah!" He nodded, though he had no idea what that meant. "Yes, of course."

Again she frowned up at him. "Is there something wrong?"

"I'm hungry," he said. "And forgive me, but I do not know you."

She narrowed her eyes. "Don't know me." She held up her wrist. "Don't know this bracelet?" She took out the apple, vivid and beautiful. "Don't remember this?"

His stomach growled. "I would that I did. I am very hungry."

The apple was nearly too big for her hand, and for a moment she only looked at it, then glanced back to him. "I don't know why you can't have it. Maybe that's what it's for."

"I would be very grateful."

"Have it, then. And I suppose we should get you some breakfast. I was going to go to town, but maybe not." She turned and gestured to him. "Come with me."

"Thank you, my lady," he said, biting into the apple. It was crisp and sweet, and he had to stop for one moment to simply revel in the joy of eating something so fine. Mortal food. He devoured it with a singular lack of grace.

She stood looking at him, her head tilted sideways, her beautiful hair falling down her arm.

"It's Alice," she said.

"Pardon?"

"My name is Alice. You don't have to call me 'my lady.'"

He laughed softly. "Alice, then." Apple in one hand, he gestured with the other. "Please show me the way."

When she reached the bridge he knew so well, made of ancient stones covered with tiny daisies growing in the cracks, he halted. "Where are we going?"

"To my apartment. Er, flat. Just in that building there."

She was pointing at the manor house, his own garden. "You live here?"

"In part of it."

"I once lived here. A long time ago. It was my family's house."

"I'm sure it has changed a great deal. Would you rather not go inside?"

He bit from the apple. "On the contrary, I'd love it."

She gestured him before her, suddenly looking over her shoulder with narrowed eyes. "Go on that way," she said, frowning.

"What is it?"

"I'm not sure. I thought I saw—" She shook her head. "Never mind."

William moved through the garden, but as he neared the door, his heart suddenly felt hollow. In memory, he saw his sister's long blond hair and the embroidered vest she wore, heard her warm laugh. He supposed it had been hundreds of years now, but in his time line it felt like only a few years. He missed her. And his friends who lay now in their crypts, nothing left of them but bones. He had been stolen away from them all, from the natural arc of his own years.

He stopped. In the quiet, there was the twittering of a bird, far distant. "Perhaps you were correct. I do not think I will go inside."

She turned, put her hand on his arm. "Are you all right?"

William looked at the windows with a vast sorrow. "What is the year?"

"Two thousand ten."

An involuntary sigh came from him. So long! "I don't think I've been out since . . ." He frowned. "There was a war. A lot of explosions. Bombs?"

"Yes. That would have been World War Two. More than sixty years ago now."

Breathless, he sank down to the bench.

"I think," she said, "that you need to eat something more solid. If you don't want to come in, I'll bring it out."

He nodded; then a thought popped into his mind. "You wouldn't have any cake, by chance?"

The request startled a merry laugh from her. "I'll see. If I don't, I'm sure we can find some for you."

"That would be very nice." In the meantime, he took a big bite of apple, keeping an eye on the edge of the garden for no reason he could particularly name.

Alice hung by the door, watching him. In the gilded light, she was as lovely as a song.

"I'm glad to meet you, Alice," he said. "Will you have a picnic with me? I know some secret places 'round these parts. Or I did."

"Yes, my lord," she said with a wink. "I'll be right back."

In the kitchen, Alice searched for things for William to eat. There was a pair of boiled eggs, a few slices of ham, sliced thick, and bread and butter, which was how the English seemed to eat their sandwiches. She stowed it all in her rucksack, added grapes and a green bottle of Italian sparkling water, and a clear one of hard cider. As for cake, it wasn't something she particularly liked, but there was no lack of them at the market.

As she put the things into her pack, her body felt airy, as if she were not a being of blood and bone, but constructed from a skeleton of light. Through the kitchen window she could see William, his hair tied back in the same leather thong, his legs clad in ordinary jeans. He wore a white shirt that was more flowing than usual, and it showed the tanned column of his throat and a glimpse of his chest. Looking at him made her giddy.

How had she fallen into this strange tale? She had no idea, but today she didn't care. Hoisting the bag onto her shoulder, she went back out to the garden.

And for the first time, she realized the roses were spent. Not a single bloom remained on the vine climbing her wall. There had been a freeze overnight, obviously. Too bad.

Tugging her hat down more closely over her ears, she waved to Mrs. Leigh on the other side of the wall.

"Hello, Alice!" she called. "Where are you off to this bright morning?"

"We're going to have a picnic."

"We?" the old woman said, and peered around a tree. She grinned. "Oh, ho, I see!"

"This is William, Mrs. Leigh."

He gave a courtly bow. "How do you do?"

"I'm well, lad, very well indeed."

Alice had a little brainstorm. "Mrs. Leigh, you wouldn't by any chance have any cake? William most particularly wanted cake, and I haven't got any."

"Well, of course I do! Made a jam sponge just last night. Stay right where you are and I'll fetch it."

"Oh, you needn't trouble yourself, madam. I won't fade away for lack of cake."

"Nonsense. I'll be back in a trice."

Alice grinned up at William. "I had a feeling she might be the kind of woman who keeps cake around."

"And you were right." He moved closer. "In gratitude, I suppose I shall have to show you something secret."

"I should beware—what if you are a murderer who leaves my head in the woods?"

"I suppose you have no guarantees."

Mrs. Leigh bustled out, carrying a box tied with string. "There you are! Plenty for both of you!"

"I'll bring you another later," Alice said. "Thanks for not minding my cheekiness."

"Go on now, have your picnic."

"Shall we?" William clasped her hand and the pair of them dashed across the moat and across a field to a barely discernible path that led away from the open pasture and into a stand of slim white birch trees. Their feet crunched through piles of deep leaves, releasing a fragrance of childhood into the air, and sun dappled down on their shoulders. When they came to the river, William turned smartly to the west and led her up a hill. Faintly came the sound of traffic, and in the distance was a row of back gardens, each house neatly fitted with a conservatory made of white iron. William looked at them silently, but only kept moving with purpose until they reached a tumble of boulders. "The others don't like it here," he said. "I've never known the reason, but it is as safe as we can be in this county."

Ducking beneath the arms of a willow tree, they came to rest next to a waterfall. The air seemed utterly calm, and though the day was cold, they spread their blanket in thick grass by the water, and it immediately seemed warmer.

"Now, sir, your breakfast," Alice said, smiling.

"Cake first."

She obliged him, opening the box to reveal a white cake spread with thick layers of red filling. William looked as if he would swoon. "Oh, here's a glory." He took a fork and dug in, closing his eyes in bliss. "You must taste it."

"What if you're a fairy trying to trick me into eating?"

He regarded her soberly. "I am not, but 'tis wise of you to wonder."

"You are beautiful enough to be one of them."

His cheeks darkened. "I am not one of them, no matter how they desire it." Fiercely, he stabbed a bite of cake. "Nor will I ever be, no matter how many centuries they keep me."

"What is it like there, William? In the land of the fey?" She picked up the other fork Mrs. Leigh had thoughtfully included, and dug into the cake with him. The white crumb was as light as clouds, the jam a perfectly preserved day in June. "Oh, my," she said. "That's terrific."

"Terrific?"

"Very good."

He shook his head with a quizzical smile. "The language is the thing. Each time I emerge into the mortal world the language has changed, shifting like the light, still the same but always different."

"It must be so very lonely for you."

"Yes." He let go of a sigh. "It is very beautiful there. Just as the fey are the most beautiful of us all, so their land is perfection itself. Gardens and forests and great castles, and nary a flaw, ever." He put down the fork. "But let's not talk of that land. Tell me of yours. This America, this Chicago."

So Alice began to tell him, and as she talked, he looked over the other foods and began to sample them. She found herself drinking in every detail of his person—the flat angle of his wrist and the aggressive bridge of his nose; the soft leather boots he wore, the way his throat moved when he swallowed. It was hard to pinpoint his age—twenty-five? Thirty?

When he'd finally eaten his fill, he stretched out in the grass and looked at the sky. "I dare not sleep," he said, "but that is the thing one wishes after so fine a repast."

Alice chuckled and fell backward herself. Long grass swayed in a soft breeze, tickling her ear, and prickles of growth poked her shoulder blades. Water rushing over the waterfall was the only sound. The buzzing of facts and theories and remedies in her mind slowed, and she took the first deep breath she'd known since the encounter in the garden. "Will you remember this?" she asked.

He propped himself up on one elbow to look down at her face. "Not when I am there. Only when I return to this realm again." He took her hand and lifted her fingers to his mouth, the vivid blue of his eyes locked on hers. Alice opened her hand and touched her fingertips to the edge of his lips. His eyes darkened and he leaned in to kiss her.

And this time there was no interruption, only his lips pressed into her own, then the velvet sweep of his tongue against her lips. Alice opened to him and he moved closer, his hip against her side, his hand sliding across her shoulder, the bare flesh of her neck. They played, the kiss a dance of greeting, lips pressing, plucking and teasing, now tongues meeting, darting apart, twining, slipping. A sensation of gilded heat centered in her throat where his fingers stroked her gently, and his fingers began to radiate in ever-widening circles, rippling down her body in a rush, awakening every pore and cell and tiny branching nerve in the bend of her elbow and the dip of her belly button and the flesh along the front of her thighs. She made a soft noise and raised her hand to his hair, pulling loose the leather tie. The weight of hair tumbled down across their faces, falling cool and heavy on her shoulder, and even that delicate sensation made her cry out softly.

William raised his head and looked down at her, fingers tracing her cheekbones and nose, her eyelids, and slowly, slowly, running across her lips. "You have a face like no other I have ever seen," he said, "as lovely as a field of bluebells."

"No, I am plain," she whispered, feeling the flush in her skin as his fingers moved across her jaw, down her throat, crept along the edge of her neckline.

There he paused and met her eyes. "May I?"

"Yes," she whispered, and his long-fingered, beautiful hands slid down over the top of her blouse, beginning to trace the curve of her breast. He looked down into her eyes, and Alice felt overwhelmed, overheated, too hungry.

This was too much: too much to want, too much to lose. "Wait," she said, catching his wrist.

He halted immediately, but his head lowered and there was the enveloping nectar of his mouth, his exquisite kiss, the slow, long sweep of tongue. Against her hip was the unmistakable thrust of his member, nudging her flesh. His hand, still and heavy, curved around her breast, and without meaning to do it, Alice arched upward, pressing herself into the cup of his palm.

"Sure?" he whispered, and she said, "Yes, please," and he found the pointed tip and rubbed back and forth over it.

Alice drifted in sensations, light and heat and pleasure, the sweetness of tongue, the feeling of his long hair sliding through her fingers. Kissing and kissing and kissing, until she felt thoroughly drunk on it. When he slowly drew up her shirt and trailed his fingers on her bare skin, she shivered and pulled up his shirt in return, and then somehow they were both bare chested in the cool day, naked torsos sliding together as they kissed, their legs tangling, their lips still dancing.

All at once a fog swept into the clearing, and as if doused with it, William leapt away from her. For one instant Alice saw him in all his splendor, the long pale hair falling over his strong shoulders and chest, his slim waist and sturdy thighs in jeans, and she felt no shame at her own half nakedness. It felt as if this were what she had come around the world to find—William and his kiss.

"Be quick, my lady," he said now, looking around in alarm. "There is danger here."

"What danger?" she said, and he took her by the hand, yanking her to her feet. With a swift gesture, he gathered her blouse in one hand and pressed it into her arms. "Go, my lady! You must go."

"I don't know my way!" she protested.

He pulled her close to him, kissed her hair, her shoulder. "Forgive me," he said, "but it matters not where you run, only that you go now." He shoved her, not ungently, and Alice stumbled, dumbly holding her clothes in her hands, ashamed and frightened.

"Put it on inside out," he said. "Now! You must do as I say, Alice. 'Twill be dire if you do not."

The fog rose upward from their feet, thicker and thicker, until it was as it had been that evening in her garden, until she could see nothing at all. Shaking in terror, she managed to put on her blouse, inside out, and cried, "William!"

"Run!" he said, sounding distant. "Run back the way we came."

She could see nothing, but run she did, following the thin bit of trail as best she could, banging once into a tree and scraping her arm. Behind her was no sound at all.

At the pasture, the fog suddenly thinned, enough that Alice could see a trio of Lords coming in her direction. They seemed not to see her and walked right by, as if she were invisible.

She looked down at the inside-out shirt. That was all it required?

A movement in the obscured middle distance caught her eye, the flash of a long red cloak near the tree at the center of the field. Acacia! The woman did not seem to see Alice, either, and it made her bold. Alice dashed toward the tree, not sure what she meant to do, but needing to somehow force a confrontation. *Why me?* she wanted to ask the beauty. *Why are you targeting* me?

But directly in front of her loomed a great dark shape that suddenly coalesced into the body of Mrs. Leigh. "Ah, there you are, lass!" She carried two net bags full of groceries, and shoved one into Alice's hands. "Be a love and help an old woman home, will you?"

Alice looked over her shoulder, but the red cloak was gone, along with any sign of the Lords, or even William. Deflated, she took the bag and accompanied the old woman home.

Chapter 6

Three days later, Alice found herself restless, sorting through her notes. She had heard nothing from William—the mortal William in modern clothing, or the William of her dreamland, who arrived in velvet doublet. In class on Monday, not all of the Lords and Ladies had been there, nor had Crystal, but those who did show up seemed only students. Wealthy and eccentric students, but no more enchanted than she was herself.

The world again seemed utterly mundane. And yet, there was that bracelet on her wrist. There was that rose, fading each night, and blooming anew every morning outside her bedroom window. There was the hodgepodge of items she found each morning on her doorstep: a pot of forget-me-nots, a beautiful walking stick, carved with symbols and polished to a deep shine. One of her neighbors, a middle-aged man, said it was rowan wood.

On Tuesday afternoon, the skies grew pregnant with snow, the depth of softness lowering until the treetops were engulfed. Despite the threat of snow, Alice made her way to the library. There were not many students about, and she had a whole table to herself. In a room somewhere down the hall, a study group drilled one another on some subject she couldn't quite catch.

She reread the poem about William of Hartford, a highborn son of the county who had defended his sister from the fey and had been spirited away to their land, never to be heard from again, and made note of anything that seemed it might be significant if she was required to battle the fey.

Again, she felt the sliding sense of reality: dreams that came to life, and fairies, and ancient curses and the Grail, buried somewhere in this county. If she told anyone what she was thinking, they'd lock her up.

But wasn't the reason she had come to Hartford in the first place to trace the link between the ballad and "The Roman de la Rose" and the Grail myths?

Yes, but she was a twenty-first-century woman. She had not believed the myths.

A good scholar did not try to fit facts to the reality, but made use of facts to assemble the truth. By that measure, she had no choice but to admit there was something strange afoot here. Her arm still bore the angry mark from being attacked by that creature in the field, and the bracelet on her wrist had come from a dream man who then appeared and disappeared.

However strange it seemed, the laws and rules she understood no longer served. If she were to find the Grail and take it to Summerland, as her student had called it, what would she need to keep herself safe?

The rules, as she discovered in the literature, were much the same as William had already instructed her: no dancing, no eating or drinking. She should fill her pockets with fronds of thyme to help her see the fey more clearly, and the bracelet of yew would enhance her abilities to navigate in that odd world, and perhaps lend some abilities to defend herself.

Would she need a weapon? The carved staff could make a sturdy weapon, but only if she were a strong man, which she was not. Could one even wound a fairy? Rubbing her forehead, she let go of a long sigh. She wished for someone to talk to, someone to help her understand all this material. William had obviously been tugged back to the other side. The only friend she'd made here was Crystal.

Maybe Crystal knew more than she'd let on. She had admitted to drawing Acacia's ire. And one of the Lords seemed to want Crystal's attention.

Closing her books and tugging a cap back down over her ears, Alice set out to find the girl's flat.

It wasn't difficult, in the end, to find the flat. Alice headed down a narrow lane with snow starting to float out of the dark sky, and knocked at an upstairs door. Another young woman with a short haircut and skinny shoulders opened it. "Hello," Alice said. "Is Crystal here?"

"No, she's not back."

"Back?"

"She went to the pub last Saturday and I haven't seen her since."

Icy fingers shoved themselves down Alice's spine. *She is no doubt abed this morning, sleeping off her drunken revels,* William had said of the fairies. "And you weren't worried?"

"She's stayed out this way before, with that guy. I forget his name. It's something kind of odd. The Scottish one. Laird?"

"Laithe," she said. "Thank you."

Back on the lane, she paused, slightly airless. What if Crystal had, like William so long ago, been lured over into enchantment? Brushing snow from her arms, she headed to the pub, where to her relief, Phillip was wiping down the old wooden bar with a white towel. Spying her, he said, "Well, hello, lass. What can I get for you today?"

"A half pint," she said, sitting at the bar. There were only a few other customers, a couple of elderly men sitting near the fire, and a single businessman eating a late lunch. Alice piled her notebook and rucksack on the bar next to her. "Have you seen my friend Crystal, the one who was here the other night with me?"

"Ah, she was dancing her heart out that night." He skimmed a head of foam from the top of her glass and set it down. "Danced her feet right off, I reckon."

"Did she leave with that group? The musicians?"

"Ah, you mean the lot from London? She did. One of the lads has a yen for her, you know. A Scot with black hair. Nicer than most."

Alice said, "I see." She sipped her ale, wondering what Phillip might know. He'd been serving in a pub where fairies had enchanted the customers for quite some time, after all. Maybe he knew more than he let on.

Or he was one of them. She watched him covertly, eyed his jiggly belly and his gnarled hands. No, not fey.

"Are you familiar with the legend of the Holy Grail?"

"Not so much, luv. I'm a simple man." He polished a glass

carefully, setting it neatly in a row of other spotless friends. "Ain't it the thing Merlin wanted?"

"Yes, that's right. It's the cup that Jesus drank out of with his disciples at the Last Supper."

He nodded, chewing gum vigorously. "Thought it was magical?"

"Some think so. I've always thought just the existence of it was magical enough. The pleasure would be in being able to see something so very sacred and very old."

"Indeed."

"There's a folk song that seems to say the Grail is somewhere around here. 'The Ballad of William of Hartford.' You know it?"

"Sure. They sing it here all the time." He launched into a verse, rousingly and badly, then laughed when the businessman at the counter groaned. "Can I get you another before you head back to the missus?"

The man said, "All right."

Alice opened her notebook and found the words to the ballad, examining each verse to see if anything new leapt out at her. Roses, the seventh sister, the queen's tree, the Star of Hope. On a fresh sheet of paper, she wrote the phrases and drew a bubble around each one.

The queen's tree? She thought of the elm standing in solitary splendor at the center of the field. And the Star of Hope—would that be the Star of David? Venus? Or was it a shape to follow to the location of the Grail?

She tried to visualize a map of the area. Where were the manor house and the village in connection to the tree? Would that make a star?

Now that it appeared Crystal, too, had been taken, Alice was committed to crossing into that realm to help them both, but she must be prepared.

"Let's say you had to go into the fairy realm. What do you use to protect yourself against enchantment?" she asked Phillip idly.

"Rue," he said without a moment of hesitation.

"Ah, of course!" Her grandmother had kept rue by the doors of her house for that very reason. Because of that habit, Alice had noticed the rue by the back door of her flat.

Growing at the foot of the climbing yellow rose.

Roses pointed to the Grail.

"I have to go," she said, and scrambled for a five-pound note, slapped it on the counter and rushed out. The snow was falling more heavily now, making the light resemble twilight, and the idea of getting caught in that field in darkness was more than she could bear. She ran all the way to the pasture, then halted at the edge. Snow covered the field and the tree with a deceptively beautiful glitter, like a Christmas card, making the tree appear entirely benevolent.

All the same, she took off her coat, turned it inside out, and then ran as fast as she could all the way across the pasture, not resting until she made it to the small stone bridge over the moat. Panting, pressing her hand to a stitch in her side, she turned around and looked back at the tree. Around it was a lavender haze, glowing in the low light, and did she hear music? She took a step forward, and then stopped.

No. Not tonight. Not like this. When she entered their realm, she would be well prepared.

Ducking her head, she went through the gate to the garden, and bent to brush snow from the rue and lavender growing around the back door. The cold had not injured them, and she went inside to the kitchen, found a pair of shears and knelt to clip several long fronds of both. She put them in water to keep them fresh, and only then did she think to check the roses. She stepped back outside into a snow that seemed much heavier than only a moment before. Shivering, she put her arms around her chest.

Nearly all of the roses on the vine had been dead for many days, but the one that bloomed afresh every morning outside her bedroom window had continued to seem newborn. Now for the first time it was wilted, its head hanging low.

Urgently, she ran upstairs and flung the window open. "You'll be all right," she said, as if it were some being that could hear her, and brushed the snow from the petals. The edges were marked, as if something had hit them, leaving behind thin brown stripes.

If it continued to snow, the rose would be dead by morning, and Alice couldn't bear it. For a moment she considered finally clipping it, but that would certainly end the magic.

Instead, from her desk, she took a sheet of paper and some string, and constructed a makeshift shelter for it, securing it to the vine.

That should keep it safe. For one more night, anyway.

❧

When the clock—the clock that had narrated his own childhood and still rang out the hours in the manor hall—struck midnight, William found himself at the window of the bedroom once more. Within, a lamp burned, and he could see the top of Alice's dark head, bent over her books. She had fallen asleep, her cheek against the page. Vast tenderness filled him. He opened the window quietly and entered, bringing with him a trail of snow.

Tonight her hair was loose, falling in thick tumbles over her arm and back. In contrast, her skin was as thin and white as milk. Her black lashes and brows and the scarlet of her rose-shaped mouth gave the only color.

He felt he knew her. Only a taste of her mouth and she had roused a vivid hunger in him, a hunger to hold her in his arms and listen to her laughter. And yet he was reluctant to disturb her.

Over her shoulder he saw the diagrams and notes she made to herself, a plan to steal into the fairy realm and rescue him. With approval, he noted the protective measures she had written down, and next to the list, there sat the rue and the bracelet of yew he'd given her, and a bowl of untouched berries. But where was the apple? He would procure another.

In dark letters she'd written, *Grail?*

He was not allowed to tell her directly, but she had given him the means to assist her. Moving quietly, he stepped closer and picked up her pen. A wave of scent rose from her, and William longed to bend and press a kiss to the smooth white flesh of her nape. He steeled himself against temptation and drew her a map of sorts.

Then he backed away in the silence. Perhaps this would be the last time he would see her. Perhaps she would fail, or lose heart, or be unable to find the Grail. Another chance lost to him, and a sentence of another two score years in the realm of fairy.

Dear God, he could not bear it.

And perhaps for that reason, he could not seem to depart. He sank to his knees beside her and took her fingers in his own and kissed the very tips, feeling her stir slightly, then jolt upright. "William!" she said. "I have been worried about you! Where did you go?"

Her warm human fingers, small and kind, touched a bruise on his cheekbone that he had acquired on his last foray into the mortal realm, and his heart ached with the tenderness. "There is some enchantment on me when I walk in the world," he said. "I must drink from the Grail, or I will die on this side of the world." In sudden emotion he bent his head to her lap, wordless and hungry.

"I will not fail, William," she whispered, putting her hands on his hair, and for the first time in more centuries than he cared to recall, he wanted to weep. Instead he straightened and, with a fierceness that burned him, took her face in his hands and kissed her with all the hunger of his desire to escape, the longing for the mortal realm, the endless loneliness of the world he could escape, only rarely, like this.

"Do not," he said fiercely, feeling her arms around his waist. "Dear Alice, do not fail, and I vow I will never fail you." And then he gave himself up to her, tasting her mortal lips and mortal breasts, and feeling her human skin sliding against his, hearing her very human cries as they joined, feeling the very human spilling of his own seed into her waiting womb.

Grateful, he departed before dawn, leaving her fast asleep. "Do not fail," he whispered against her forehead, and pressed a kiss to her brow.

Chapter 7

Alice stirred as morning crept, pale and bluish with snow, into her bedroom. Beneath her heavy duvet and the crocheted afghan of roses she moved her limbs and felt—

Naked!

She sat upright, memory flooding in—William's grace and elegance, his fierceness when he kissed her, his hunger as he took her, the force of his loneliness and longing a thing she burned to assuage.

He was gone, but on the pillow next to her own was a single yellow rose. Horrified, Alice was afraid she had cut the rose by her window, but when she gathered the afghan around herself and dashed into the cold to see, it was still there in its temporary housing of paper and string, blooming anew. Unable to resist, she opened the casement and removed the shelter, then bent her head into its petals, drinking in the bright lemon fragrance. The petals had lost their battered look overnight and even seemed to be edged with a line of vivid pink she had never noticed before.

Beyond the window was a vast winter landscape painted in shades of white and gray and diamond frost, smoke steaming up from roofs and chimneys. She could see the tree in the center of the field, and it merely looked like a tree. Absently, she bent to smell the rose one more time, thinking—

The rose! William and the rose.

Lightly she touched the petals with the tip of one finger, her memory tumbling with images of him last night—his ripe mouth and tender hands, his heart-wrenching sigh of completion, the way he collapsed against her.

Do not fail.

The words came back to her, and with firmness she closed the window and went back to the table where she had left her notes. She must find the Grail!

And there, on her notes, was an arrow, pointing from the circle she had drawn around the word *Grail* to the window.

The window.

The rose.

The rue, planted at the doorway in a long line beneath the window, to protect the Grail from the fey.

She scrambled through her ablutions, donning a heavy sweater, and thick socks beneath her jeans. Further protected with coat and gloves, she headed out to the garden to examine the earth beneath her window.

The snow was only a few powdery inches deep, nothing like what she was used to back in Chicago, but she was smart enough to know that the ground would be too hard to dig. If the Grail was in the earth, how would she ever get it out?

Frowning, she folded her arms. That didn't even make sense. If it were buried, someone would have found it by now, and England being the land of gardeners, anyone who hid it would not have risked discovery in such a fashion. Stepping back as far as the wall, she looked at the outside of the manor house for possible clues.

Made of gray stone, the house rose three stories. Her portion was entered through a door that had obviously once been a side door into an anteroom of some sort, perhaps a cloakroom. That had been transformed into her kitchen, and then were the stairs into the main portion, where her beautiful bedroom/sitting room overlooked the garden from the window seat.

Alice narrowed her eyes, thinking of the pillows and the bench there. Surely after all these years, someone would have found it if it were beneath the window seat. . . .

But not if no one had ever been looking.

She went back inside and dashed up the stairs and pulled all the pillows from the bench seat. It appeared to be solid, with no hinges or betraying hardware, the top carved of a single thick plank of oak. She ran her hands over it end to end, feeling for an irregularity or indentation that might be a clue to a secret panel, but found nothing. Undaunted, she carefully examined the grain of the wood, looking for variation in color or whorl or anything at all.

That was how she found the star. It was a natural occurrence in the grain of the wood, but very clearly a four-pointed star. When she glanced up at the window, she saw that the rose bloomed directly over it.

With a cry of glee, she took the lamp from the desk and brought it over to the bench to see if there were some answer to how to open it. She pressed and poked at anything that seemed as if it might hold a lever, but nothing happened.

There had to be an answer. She looked around the room for clues, and examined the rowan walking stick for carvings, and thought back over everything in the ballad. Nothing.

Which left William's arrow. Had it been pointing to the window seat? Or—

She reached over and unlatched the window, feeling along the wall where the rose was growing—fully open now in the freezing cold—and found a latch. Stiff with disuse, it wouldn't move, but when Alice found a wrench and pulled, there was a distinct click. Stepping away, she gently felt along the window seat. The section beneath the star creaked when she pulled it upward, and finally opened to reveal a very dusty hole.

And there was an object wrapped in fragile silk that seemed untouched by time. Brushing away the cobwebs, she reached inside with shaking hands. Her fingers curled around the body of the object, a stem and a bowl, a goblet.

Could it really be the Grail?

With a pounding heart, she untwined the silk covering it, and revealed a simple gold cup, the only detail a carving of roses around the lip. It seemed extraordinarily warm, and she knew that it was what she had hoped to find.

Do not fail.

"I will not fail," she said aloud. "I will not."

A woman who was going to do battle with the fey would need a good breakfast, and Alice took the time to boil a pair of eggs and prepare a nice thick slice of toast with butter, along with a hefty pot of tea. One didn't want to go into Summerland with an empty stomach, after all; that much seemed plain. As she ate, she reviewed her plan and the things she would need to carry with her. The only thing she lacked was an apple. She had fed it to William when he was so hungry.

So again she called on Mrs. Leigh. Knocking on the door next to her own in the hallway, she hoped the old woman was warm enough. The hall was drafty.

"Good morning, dear!" Mrs. Leigh said, opening the door. Although it was not yet eight, her hair was neatly pinned back in a bun, and she wore a uniform of gray skirt and white blouse and dark blue cardigan. "Would you like some tea?"

"I'm so sorry to bother you again, but I have a rather pressing errand and I need an apple. I remembered that you had some the other day when we met in the field. Any chance you have one left?"

"I do. Come in, girl." As she headed for the kitchen, she called over her shoulder, "Come have a cup of tea."

"No, thank you," Alice said, but found herself drawn more deeply into the room. It smelled of cinnamon and something more exotic, sweet and sultry. "I really should be going."

"You'll need tea," she said firmly.

Alice acquiesced. "All right," she said, sitting primly at the chrome-

and-Formica table stuck into a corner of the rather large kitchen. "Thank you, that's very nice."

Mrs. Leigh brought over a cup that smelled of thyme. "It won't be the most pleasing tea, but it will fortify you for . . . the cold."

"Oh." Alice narrowed her eyes, thinking of all the ways the old woman had protected and helped her since she had arrived. Like a guardian angel, or a magic protector.

"And here is the apple you will need." Mrs. Leigh put down a giant red apple, as big as the one Alice had before.

"Is it you who has been leaving things for me?" Alice said, finally understanding.

"Some of it. Not all. Only little things to keep you safe. It's a dangerous game you're playing."

"Is there a way to defend myself physically? Can a fairy be wounded? Or killed?"

"Not exactly, and not at your level of understanding, lass." From a closet she brought out a cloak of green wool. "But I've made this for you to help keep you safe and accomplish your desire."

"Who are—"

Mrs. Leigh tapped her index finger against her lips. "Shh-shh. None of that now." Bustling around the kitchen, she produced a tidy cake wrapped in waxed paper and tied with string. "You'll need this, as well."

"Cake?"

"I am very good with cake, you know."

Alice laughed. "So you are."

"Drink up now," the old woman said. "Be on your way."

❧

In the cold, still morning, Alice set out with her rucksack. She wore the green cloak that was remarkably warm and boasted pockets into which she could slip the sloan fruits William had left for her in case of hunger, and the apple as an offering if she should need it. She carried the walking stick of rowan to protect her, and wore a rose in her hair and forget-me-nots in a posy tied around her neck. The bracelet of yew would help her see the fey.

Everything according to legend.

As she walked across the snowy field, its sparkly crispness unbroken beneath a gray sky, she had to admit to a slight feeling of ridiculousness. She was dressed for a play, billowing along with her heavy pockets and walking stick. The snow soaked her feet and ankles, and her breath hung in clouds. In the distance, the church bell rang the hour.

And for a moment, Alice felt transported not to another land, but another time. William's time, a less complicated, less hurried era. The horse in the distance wore a blanket over his shoulders today, and the birds twittered everywhere but in the queen's tree.

She didn't know what to do. Now that she was so close to it, it looked like any other elm tree in the world. She walked around it, noticing that the snow had melted beneath it, but there was no door to the other side that she could see, no marking.

And then, startling her, she saw a young man, beautiful and glossy, like a young lion. "Good morrow," he said with a slight ironic tip of his head. "Do you have a gift for me?"

"I do." She reached into her pocket and pulled out the apple, offering it from the center of her palm as one would make an offering to a horse. Was she afraid of teeth?

He plucked it from her hand. "Very pretty," he said, biting into it even as he looked Alice over. Then he bowed. "You may pass."

And in front of her was another world. Right next to the elm tree glowed the exact landscape she stood in on this side, but it was summer there. The horse in the distance flicked his tail lazily, and on the horizon gleamed . . .

She stepped through the portal, drawn by the promise of a beautiful town in the distance.

Immediately everything shifted. The smell of flowers and honey scented the air, and a blaze of summer sunlight cascaded through the full bloom of the trees, so thickly yellow it almost seemed a liquid. In the distance were the same rooftops and spires that she saw from the same vantage point on the other side, but the roofs were thatched, the spires glittery, as if made of crystal. Trees hung heavy with fruit: apples and peaches and cherries in such abundance they fell in ripe splendor to the earth. From somewhere came a piercingly sweet song.

Alice found herself falling into the sound of those notes, her feet setting out all on their own to find the source, in a direction that led to a deep green wood. She imagined pausing to gather peaches, and taking a long drink of the chuckling water and stretching out in the grass for a wee nap—

From the corner of her eye, she spied a flock of birds, feathers flashing turquoise and emerald, and when she turned, just fast enough, they morphed into bats that flew away with nasty sharp noises.

Gripping her stick, she swallowed and tapped it against the

ground to remind herself that it was all illusory, the perfection and the seduction. The fey—or perhaps only the queen—wanted the Grail she carried, wanted William for their own nefarious ends.

The thought of William steadied her. His piercing loneliness, his deep hunger for all things human, made her want to help. She had fallen under his spell, it was true, and perhaps he did not love her in return. The thought gave her a twisting sensation in her belly, but even that would not distract her just now.

Later. There was time enough for that later.

Where would she find him?

Turning in a little circle, she realized this seemed to be simply a replication of the other world, a more beautiful, more sensual version, one that showed no wear and tear, but the same world nonetheless. If she were to find William, where would he be?

At the manor house, of course.

She set out walking, taking from her pocket a couple of the sloan fruits to nibble, just in case. The peaches, lying in rosy temptation in the long green grass, were still difficult to resist, and it seemed her throat was parched to the deepest level a person could be thirsty.

And yet, she had only just had her tea, hadn't she? Illusion. All illusion to tempt her. The bracelet of yew helped her see the truth.

There was no one about, and the lack of confrontation began to make Alice nervous. Was she simply to walk in, pour wine into the Grail cup for William to drink, then walk away again?

An elegant Siamese cat slid from the hedgerow as she approached the bridge over the moat. He had a long nose and a black tail and jeweled sapphire eyes. "Hello, mortal," he said in a surprisingly attractive voice. "Where are you bound?"

As if it were perfectly normal for cats to speak, Alice said, "Only to the manor house. What is your name?"

"I have no name to tell a mortal," he said, and nimbly leapt to the stone railing, ran ahead of her and turned into a lithe and elegantly dark-skinned fairy with stunning blue eyes. "Would you like to come have a meal with me?" From his pockets or the air or some magical envelope in the summery day, he produced a golden bottle of mead.

A dizziness overtook her, longing and thirst, and she imagined the mead that William had brought, honey wine flavored with the long afternoons of a good season. And the fairy with his silky hair and long blue eyes and smooth skin was a temptation, too, the way he cocked his head, and the promise on his lips.

She closed her eyes, gripped her rowan stick, thought of William. From her pocket she took Mrs. Leigh's cake. "Thank you, kind sir," she said respectfully, "but I am on an errand. Might I trade this cake for your fine bottle?"

"I might be persuaded."

She held out her hand, and then the fairy grabbed the cake, turned back into a cat with a long tail and dashed away. The wine was perched on the stone bridge, and Alice reached for it. Then she hesitated. What if even this was enchanted?

No. This she required to pour into the chalice. She tucked the bottle into the voluminous pockets, gripping her walking stick for reassurance as she crossed the moat and paused before the door cut into the garden wall. From somewhere came the sound of a stringed instrument, and a woman's sinuous voice sliding around a song in a language Alice did not understand.

It might be Acacia, playing the lute she'd brought with her into the pub. Perhaps Alice should wait for a little while.

But even standing still, she could feel the lure of the place on her senses, an offering of such deliciousness it sang through her mind like the heavy buzz of nectar-laden bees, making her limbs weighty, her eyelids—

She jerked herself awake. Disaster if she fell asleep here!

Which left no choice. Making not a sound, she circled the wall around the garden, visualizing where things were in the mortal world. Near the front of the manor house was a tree, with branches reaching long arms out nearly to the stream that fed the moat.

Moving as quietly as possible, she climbed into the gnarled branches and peered over the wall. There was the queen wearing a long green gown, her black hair cascading in ribbons over her back and arms. She bent over the lute, playing and singing sweetly, the song a narcotic to stun her swain, lying across a bench in a patchwork of sun and shade, his eyes closed.

William!

A sudden vision of that mouth devouring hers, his hands moving urgently over her breasts . . . his lean belly, his sorrowful cry, the low groan of him as he—

As if her thoughts nudged him, he opened his eyes and stared right at her. The queen noticed nothing amiss, but William was riveted, slowly coming to a sitting position, and then he stretched, reaching for a cup near him on a table. Lifting it slightly in her direction, he drank, and Alice understood the question.

She patted her pocket.

He bowed his head, acknowledging her, then turned his attention to Acacia. He stood and pulled the leather tie from around his hair, and bent to kiss the fairy queen along the nape of her neck. She leaned backward, and he whispered something in her ear. She laughed, and Alice died a thousand times as William stroked the other woman's throat, touched her breasts, tugged her to her feet, and gave her a tiny push. She heard clearly, "I'll be along in a moment."

Acacia ducked inside, and practically before the fairy queen had begun to move, Alice was scrambling down the branches, dropping lightly into thick grass. From the other side of the wall William opened the gate, and they flew into each other's arms, arms tangling, mouths devouring.

William halted, taking her arms. "You brought it?"

"I did." She swept the cloak from her and took the chalice from her pocket. It had taken on a slight rosy cast. "And I bought mead from a Siamese cat."

That startled a chuckle from him. "Ah, that must have been Curran."

He took the cup in his long-fingered hands as Alice tugged at the stopper in the bottle. As she poured golden mead into the golden cup, she noticed that he was breathing too fast, and his hand shook the slightest bit.

Their eyes met, and Alice knew three things at once—that she had fallen deeply in love, that he was desperately grateful to her and that he wanted to love her in return, but did not. The knowledge struck her heart like a hammer, stopping it cold for a moment, sending hot tears to her eyes.

"Drink," she said.

"Do you love me?" he asked soberly, holding the cup.

"Yes," she whispered, and blinked fiercely. *Fool that I am.*

A harridan's shrill cry rent the air, and William looked over his shoulder. From the window on the second floor, which would be Alice's bedroom in the other world, Acacia leaned out and screamed, as if summoning all the demons of the netherworld.

"You fool!" she cried. "It will not save you! Not as you wish."

William lifted the cup and drank. "I welcome death if I escape thee, Lady," he cried, and grabbed Alice's hand.

"Run," he said. "As fast as you can. If I do not make it to the borderland by the time her unseelie hordes find me, I will wither to dust and all will be for naught."

Alice gathered her cloak to her tightly. "You didn't tell me that part!"

They ran back across the bridge, into the open field. In the distance was a sound like the baying of wolves, a sound that sent horror through her, and she thought, suddenly, of Crystal. "I have to find Crystal," she cried. "I can't leave her here!"

He paused. "If we do not exit, I will die."

"But I won't." She pulled her hand from his. "Run, and I will find her myself."

"No," he said fiercely. "Together we will leave this place. I will not leave you behind."

There was about his face a slight difference she had not perceived before, a thinning, a loss of glossiness in his hair, and her heart clutched. "Go without me! I can't leave her. She was enchanted, just as you were."

"Then we will both find her."

They turned at the renewed sound of baying, closer and closer. "Is that what came after you the day in the meadow?" Alice asked.

"In the meadow?"

She looked at him, remembering. "That's right. You don't remember that person, the visits as the mortal you to the mortal world, where you eat cake."

He looked wan and gray. "Would that I did."

He was growing older right before her eyes. In sudden decision, she asked, "Is there another portal to this place?"

"In the pub, of course."

"Go, then," she said, "through this one, and meet me in the pub on the other side. Can you do that much?"

"No, I—" The wolves came closer, closer. He hesitated, and with a piercing sorrow Alice saw the fretfulness of an old man, one who had lost the lustiness of youth.

"You will be dead before the wolves get here," she said, and hauled him bodily through the portal, gasping at the sudden cold and the snow around their feet, and with all her might she shoved him hard so that he fell into the guardian. They tumbled, and Alice bolted back into Summerland.

Turning her cloak inside out, she ran as hard as she could, her breath coming in ragged, tearing gasps by the time she reached the High Street. It was crowded, a market day, every table spilling over with rosy peaches and ripe tomatoes and piles of braided herbs sending their scents to mingle with the fragrance of baking bread in the air. Throngs of beautiful Lords and Ladies milled down the rows, chattering brightly, laughing, the sounds like a symphony, each fairy more dizzyingly beautiful than the last, in every possible arrangement of color and size and style of beauty one could imagine. No one paid her the slightest bit of attention.

For a moment Alice swayed dangerously and put a hand to the wall to steady herself. Her throat was parched and her stomach grumbled and she had to make her way to the pub to see if Crystal was there.

Through the fog of seduction, she suddenly remembered the sloan fruits she carried in her cloak, and scrambled through the voluminous fabric to find the pockets. In her haste, she dropped the cloak; then she put it back on, forgetting to reverse it inside out, and suddenly the placid scene changed.

"Mortal! You, there!" cried a willowy brunette cloaked in sapphires.

Heads turned in her direction. Alice backed away, trying to think. She shoved the fruits into her mouth, slipped sideways into the alley and flipped the cloak back around.

She tucked herself into a doorway and waited. It seemed to take a very long time before the crowd all went back to their shopping and gossip. The sun threw long shadows across the cobblestones and edged across a doorway across the way. Carefully, she slipped back into the street, keeping the inside-out cloak on her shoulders. She should have done this when she first arrived!

"Not everyone is fooled," said a black-and-white cat on windowsill. She glared at him, but he only twitched his tail and blinked as she passed.

At last she made it to the pub and pushed the door open into a dazzling scene of dancing and music and fairies engaged in all manner of celebration and debauchery. Alice slipped around the room, slinking like a cat between and betwixt, under and around.

She rounded the edge of the dancing crowd, and there by the fire was Crystal, tapping her foot in time to the music, looking flushed but otherwise exactly the same. Next to her was the dark fairy, Laithe, who sat protectively near his prize, kissing her and feeding her fruits, and sometimes touching her face in a way that made Alice feel sorry for him. Did the fey love?

That was not hers to decide. For now, she was here to retrieve Crystal, and then find the way out of this place. Biding her time in a corner where no one would inadvertently stumble on her—and reveal her presence!—she looked for something that might be a portal. Thinking of the night she'd been here drinking, she wondered if it might be down that dark hallway that had confused her so.

A new dance began, and the the crowd swirled into a circle dance. Crystal's consort dived in, tugging her hand, but she held back, touching her head.

Come on, come on, Alice thought. *Leave her; go dance.*

When he did exactly that, Alice made her way to the table and sat down. "Hey!" Crystal said. "I thought you were going home."

She took Crystal's hand. "I need you to pretend I'm not talking to you. Ignore me. Can you do that?"

"Is this a game?"

"Yes. Just listen. Look at Laithe and wave."

She did. He left the dance and started to come over.

Alice squeezed Crystal's fingers urgently. "This is all going to sound completely strange, but will you come with me to the loo? So I can tell you something that's weird?"

"I need to go to the loo," Crystal said as Laithe sat down.

"Very well." He bowed. "I'll be dancing."

Alice walked close behind Crystal into the hallway and pressed a sloan fruit into her hand. "Eat this," she said, and when the gloom grew deep, she flung the inside-out cape around them together. "I'm not trying to make any moves on you, Crystal, but I need you to trust me."

"This is weird. I don't even really know you."

"And you know him? Them? Who do you know out there?"

By the silence, Alice knew she was on the right track. "You can always come back in here, but will you help me find the door? I really need to get out of here."

"Will you give me an A?"

"Absolutely."

"All right."

"Good." Alice spied a door in the wall, a door she had not seen from the mortal side the night she met William here. She tugged Crystal behind her. "Keep the cloak around you and hold on to my hand."

"How will we get by that big guy in front of the wall?"

"He won't see us." She started to slide by, but the man was enormous, both tall and wide, and he felt them. Reaching out blindly, he caught a fistful of Alice's hair. "Who passes without leaving me a gift?"

The only gifts Alice had left were the Grail and a last slice of Mrs. Leigh's cake. Remembering how William had loved it, she took out the latter and put her hand through the opening of the cloak. "Here is your gift. Trust me."

"That will do," he said, and stepped aside.

And just like that, they were through, standing not in the pub, as Alice had imagined, but in the street outside, in a swirling snowstorm that had them both shivering.

Crystal blinked. "How did that happen?"

"I'll explain everything later," she said. "Run home and I will find you tomorrow. Don't ever eat anything the Lords and Ladies give you, do you understand?"

She nodded. "God, I'm tired!" she said, and stumbled toward the lane.

For an uncountable number of times that day, Alice ran. Ran as hard as she could, heart pounding, breath ragged. As she reached the edge of the field, a powerful stitch stabbed her side and she doubled over involuntarily. A whip of wind blew icy snow into her eyes and she could not see at all.

After long moments, she straightened and peered across the field to the tree. No light leaked out around the portal, but there was a dark bundle lying beneath it, utterly still.

Cold pushed through her.

Wading through ankle-deep snow, Alice moved as fast as she was able, thick dread in her gut at what she feared she would find. As she came closer, she saw the half-snow-covered lump was a man, and as she knelt beside him, she saw it was William, a very, very old man.

Who had died in his sleep.

And had not loved her.

Chapter 8

William awakened with a start to feel something cold and wet on his face. Bolting upright, he found himself in the garden of the manor house. No one was about, only the winter-still garden, covered in snow.

Snow!

In wonder, he tilted his face back to it, letting flakes cover his forehead and cheeks and eyes and lips. How many centuries since he'd felt the cold kiss of it on his eyelids, tasted the bite of it in the air? It was so cold he had to wrap his arms around himself. As he sat there, snow beginning to collect in his hair and on his arms, he became aware of his hunger, as ever, and something more—a sense of lightness that he could not, at first, recognize.

The gate clicked and a woman in a green cloak came through, her dark hair loose on shoulders that drooped in dejection.

Alice!

Everything about her rushed through him: Seeing her in the garden the first time, cutting late-autumn flowers; opening the window to her bedroom to come and sit by her fire. He saw the night at the pub and the day he had arrived in the mortal world to court her, and his heart swelled at the memory. He thought of her ripe red mouth and the ease of her laughter and, above all, her brave, strong spirit, for she had ventured into Summerland to save him. She had found the Grail and broken the spell, and he thought he had never seen a woman so lovely. Emotion crowded his throat so that he did not think he would be able to speak.

He remembered her shoving him through the portal by the tree, remembered lying down in the cold snow, and the enchantment that had kept him finally breaking.

But the Grail had saved him, giving him back the life the unholy fey had stolen. Because Alice had been brave enough to enter Summerland and bring him the Grail, he could now have his life back.

With her.

She had not seen him, and he turned and saw the last rose of his enchantment waiting on the vine. He stood on the wall and reached for it, a dewy new bud, yellow at its base, with the deepest, most passionate red bleeding through it.

As she came closer, he saw that she was weeping, and at last he stepped forward. "Alice," he said quietly.

Her head shot up, and for a long moment he could not read her expression. It wavered, washing from joy to sorrow to bewilderment. "William! But you—"

"The being who lived in the land of the fey could not come back to this world after so long a time. By bringing me the Grail, you restored my life. You see I stand before you, whole and young." He offered her the rose. "If you will have me."

"Which William are you?" she asked, and he could see the blue circles beneath her eyes. "The one who was enchanted over there, or the one who came to the mortal realm and made love to me by the river?"

"Both, my lady, in that I have memory of all that transpired."

"And are you here out of obligation? Because I saved you from eternal enchantment?"

Ah! Suddenly he understood. "I am grateful," he said, moving toward her. "But as I sat here in the garden, what I thought of was your kiss, sweet Alice." He touched her cheek with the rose, drew it down her throat. "Your lion's heart." When it seemed she would not resist, he bent to kiss her, lightly at first, and then he could not bear it—he hauled her into his arms and held her tightly, and at last she gave in. "I am yours for all of time, Alice. I love you—not for saving me, but because it seems now that my enchantment was a gift to give me leave across all of time to find my one true love."

She kissed him fervently, her cold fingers on his cheek. Suddenly she pulled back. "Do you smell that?"

He took in a breath of sugar-laden air. "Cake!" His stomach growled.

"I am so hungry!" Alice cried, taking his hand. "Let's go see Mrs. Leigh, shall we?"

He held her hand tightly. "Wait."

She halted, perplexed. "What is it?"

"Do you love me, Alice? Love me now, the way I am? Mortal?"

Alice laughed. She stepped forward and stood on her toes. "Yes, William, I do. I love you just as you are."

Mrs. Leigh, angel or guardian, magical cake maker, poked her head out of her back door. "Yoo-hoo! I've got strawberry sponge if anyone is hungry after all that hard work."

Joining hands, William and Alice dashed through the snow to her snug, warm kitchen.

"Did you bring me a cup?" she asked.

Alice withdrew the Grail. "What will we do with it?"

Mrs. Leigh tucked the chalice into a pocket of her skirt. "We'll return it to Glastonbury, where it belongs," she said, and for one long moment Alice could see the shimmering of her benevolent and protective spirit beneath the glamour meant to fool the world into thinking she were mortal, when in fact she was what many would name a fairy godmother, although the term had terrible connotations right now because of the drama they'd just undergone.

William stuck his finger in the cream. "Oh." He sighed and closed his eyes. "Cream and cake and snow and Alice, all in the same day."

Alice laughed and kissed him.

And they all lived happily ever after. Or at least Alice and William did, and that is what matters.

She was the keynote speaker at the 2000 National Romance Writers of America Conference. Ms. Putney lives in Baltimore, Maryland. Visit her Web site at www.maryjoputney.com.

Karen Harbaugh is an award-winning author and RITA finalist who has published eleven fantasy/romance novels and three novellas, with more forthcoming. She graduated from the University of Washington with a BA in English, and has also had various other occupations such as quality assurance analyst, technical writer, legal word processor, and whatever other job might add to her store of miscellaneous knowledge and get her out of the house from time to time. She is happily married to a software engineer and has a college-aged son. When she is not writing stories, she does volunteer work, knits, cooks, spins yarn, gardens, watches reruns of *Buffy the Vampire Slayer*, and occasionally finds time to annoy her cat, Newman. Visit her Web site at www.sff.net/people/KarenH.

A passionate hiker and traveler, **Barbara Samuel** likes nothing better than setting off at dawn for a trip—anywhere! Her favorite places so far include the Tasman Sea off the coast of New Zealand, the pungent streets of New York City, and the top of her beloved Pikes Peak. Between books, she's currently planning trips to India and China, and a long rest in the damp and misty United Kingdom. Barbara has won five RITA Awards from the Romance Writers of America. You can explore her columns on rambling around France and Scotland, working the Pikes Peak Marathon at twelve thousand feet, and many topics about the writing life at www.barbarasamuel.com. She loves to hear from readers at awriterafoot@gmail.com.

About the Authors

Jo Beverley is widely regarded as one of the most talented romance writers today. She is a five-time winner of Romance Writers of America's cherished RITA Award and one of only a handful of members of the RWA Hall of Fame. She has also twice received the *Romantic Times* Career Achievement Award. Born in England, she has two grown sons and lives with her husband in Victoria, British Columbia, just a ferry ride away from Seattle. You can visit her Web site at www.jobev.com.

Mary Jo Putney graduated from Syracuse University with degrees in eighteenth-century literature and industrial design. A *New York Times* bestselling author, she has won numerous awards for her writing, including two Romance Writers of America RITA Awards, four consecutive Golden Leaf awards for Best Historical Romance, and the *Romantic Times* Career Achievement Award for Historical Romance.